AROON

M. B. Gibson

M. B. Gibson Books

Blackville, South Carolina

M. B. Gibson Books
2728 Reynolds Road
Blackville, South Carolina 29817
www.mbgibsonbooks.com

Publisher's Note: This is a work of fiction. Names, characters, places, and incidents are a product of the author's imagination. Locales and public names are sometimes used for atmospheric purposes. Any resemblance to actual people, living or dead, or to businesses, companies, events, institutions, or locales is completely coincidental.

Book Layout ©2015 BookDesignTemplates.com

Ordering Information:
Quantity sales. Special discounts are available on quantity purchases by corporations, associations, and others. For details, contact the "Special Sales Department" at the address above.

Aroon/M. B. Gibson. -- 1st ed.
ISBN 978-0-9972234-0-8

Dedicated to
Evelyn Connor Kelly

Merry Christmas 1969!

I wish, I wish, I wish in vain,
I wish I had my heart again

—FROM "SHULE AROON"

A TRADITIONAL IRISH FOLK SONG

CHAPTER ONE

Kilmacthomas, County Waterford, Ireland

1750

Will Bridge was jolted awake when his wagon wheel crashed into a dip in the road. He squinted, then wiped sand from eyes that widened at the sight of the Scully homestead ahead.

"By God," he mumbled. He hadn't seen the place since the old man's funeral twenty-three years before.

Back then, he'd found a small, thriving farm with a neatly-kept two room house. Cows and sheep grazed alongside a flourishing field of potatoes. On this day, no livestock dotted the farmland, which had shrunken to the size of a small garden. The house, crumbling in disrepair, sat amongst four or five mud cabins.

At the pleading of his old friend, Paddy Scully, Will had come to fetch his daughter who was to be a maid at Duncullen Manor in County Tipperary.

When he pulled up to the hovel, Mrs. Scully, whom Will had never met, hobbled out to greet him. Her eyes were sunken, her skin grey. Three children, who looked to be from five to ten years old, surrounded her. They resembled scrawny potatoes with twigs stuck in them for arms and legs.

"Paddy wasn't expecting no one today," she said. "Down the road, he is, sharing a swallow of poteen with his mates." She turned to a boy of about nine or ten years. "Run, Nolan. Tell yer da of his visitor and to come straightaway."

The boy took off without a word.

"Mrs. Scully ..."

"Mary, please."

"Mary, I'm Paddy's friend, overseer at the Duncullen Estate of Sir Edward Lynche. When last I saw yer husband at the market, he asked that I seek a position for yer girl, Eveleen, and I believe we can use her."

Mary Scully sucked in her breath. Her eyes misted and she paled even more. "Ah, forgive me. 'Tis a blessing and a curse." She exhaled, staring at her bare feet. "A blessing and a curse."

Will's heart went out to her. "That it is."

"Eveleen, come out here, lass."

An older version of the children slid around the door opening. Will couldn't tell if her head hung from shyness or fear. Clearly, she'd been listening inside the house.

Her dark hair appeared to have a reddish hue, but of course, it was dirty and matted so Will couldn't be sure. Her dress was tattered and stained. He and his wife had expected that, so Noreen had placed more appropriate clothes in a sack "only to be brought out if needed." They didn't want to disgrace the Scullys, but the clothing was needed.

After a moment or two, the girl raised her head, revealing the fairest green eyes Will had ever seen. "Good day to ye, sir," she muttered.

A loud, boisterous voice interrupted them. "Who ye calling sir? Are ye daft, girl? 'Tis only Willie Bridge from the old days. He ain't no sir!"

Will turned toward his friend scuttling up the road, an older, hunched version of the lad who'd been his salvation when, side by side, they'd toiled on the Burke farm. His first time away from family, Will had been wretchedly homesick, unable to keep down an ounce of food. Paddy had lifted his spirits during those dark times, and Will was now grateful to repay his friend during his own tough spell.

The two met, grasped forearms, and patted each other's backs. While Paddy's breath reeked of the crude whiskey, he didn't stagger or slur his words.

"I see yer age hasn't caught up with ye," Will cracked. "Ye can still hold yer grog with the best of 'em."

"I'm a bloody sponge, Will. Always was and always will be." He turned to Mary. "'Tis me old friend, Ma. The one I told ye about." He took a deep breath and peered at Will. "Have ye brung us good news?"

"I have, Paddy. The mistress can use yer Eveleen. She's to be a lower housemaid to start." He turned to Mary and the girl. "That means lighting fires, cleaning rooms, polishing brass, and carrying water when needed. 'Tis hard labor, lass. Are ye up for that?"

Paddy answered for his daughter. "Of course she's up for it. And anything else ye can throw at her." He shook Will's hand all over again. "Yer a true friend. Ye'll never be forgotten by the Scully family for what yer doing."

Will smiled and nodded. He looked over to find Mary's lips quivering and her hands shaking. Eveleen looked as though he had sentenced her to the gallows.

"What's wrong with the two of ye? I'll not be shamed by yer ingratitude." Paddy took a menacing step toward Mary. "This man has stuck his neck out with the boss for us."

Mary cowered. "Forgive me, sir. I'm just a wee bit startled by the suddenness of it all. Ye know we're beholden to ye for giving Eveleen this chance." The girl slid into the house and her mother turned to follow.

Paddy laughed too loudly. "There we go with the 'sir' again."

Will called out to Mary before she disappeared. "There's no need for a mother to apologize when a fella comes to take her own child. I've a wife and a boy meself."

Mary turned back, wearing a relieved smile. "Your boy—is he still with ye, then?"

"His boy will always be with him, Mary," Paddy said. "He's simple, I told ye. Ye never listen."

Will's jaw clenched. While his son, Jack, was twenty years old, his mind was that of a child. The previous winter, Will had taken Jack to Clonmel to buy cattle for Sir Edward where they ran into Paddy Scully. He'd not seen his chum in years.

As he introduced his son, Jack nodded slowly. "Good day, Pad-dy." He thrust his hand forward, still nodding.

Paddy gaped at Will with eyes that questioned, then pitied. He made a quick grab, then released Jack's hand, mumbling, "G'day."

Will had seen those looks many times, yet they never failed to stab him in the gut. As usual, he sighed and swallowed his anger, anxious to return to Duncullen. "One more thing," he said.

4

"And I mean no harm. None at all. But the lord and lady require a certain dress, ye understand."

Paddy drew his head back and cocked it to the right. Mary gasped, folded her hands, and looked down.

Will pasted a smile on his face and spoke quickly. "Now, we didn't expect ye to have the necessary clothing, so me wife packed some things Eveleen could use." He reached for the satchel he'd brought and chuckled loudly. "She's a wee bird, so these clothes may hang on the girl a bit, but me wife's magical with a needle." He looked from Scully to Scully.

Paddy stiffened, apparently deciding if he was insulted. Mary snatched the bag and bustled into the house. She turned at the door. "A little time, please."

Will nodded. "Take what ye need."

In a huff, Paddy emptied his lungs. "I never thought I'd have sunk to this." He belched. "'Tis a sad day, Willie. A sad day indeed when Paddy Scully has to grovel before those bloody bastards." He hammered his fist on the fencepost and bellowed, "The blasted left-leggers are starving the Irish out of existence!"

Will nodded in sympathy.

In a hushed tone, Paddy spoke through gritted teeth. "Ye know as the eldest son, I was to have all me da's property." He waved his hand over the now-dilapidated land. "But they said if I was to inherit, I had to turn me back on the church, Will." His voice rose. "I had to rebuke the Catholic Church and become one of them—a Protestant, a left-legger. I wouldn't do it! I stood me ground and chose me own soul over their dirty, lowlife tricks." His voice started to quaver. "So they split the land between me and me brothers—all five of us. None with enough to make a living, mind ye. All of us scraping by, just as they planned it. Just as the heartless, scheming devils plotted all along."

"The homes around the place, they belong to yer brothers, then?" Barely fit for livestock. Will was well aware of the laws that prohibited the eldest son to be the sole heir—if he remained Catholic, that is. And, with it against the law for a Catholic to buy property, the land must remain split up or turned over to Protestant officials. He just let Paddy talk, though.

"They do. All but Jamie, who set out for Cork years ago." Paddy cackled and jabbed his finger at Will's chest. "Remember our plans? All them half-witted ideas we come up with?"

"I'll never forget 'em."

To endure the dreary farm work, they'd weaved cunning schemes that would get them to Dublin or Cork. From there, they'd hop a ship and see the world. "I'll be a man, Will," Paddy had said. "Not some oafish clodhopper up to me brow in mud, but a real man."

"Well, Ol' Jamie," Paddy was saying, "he went out and done it, he did. He done it for all of us, God bless him. We've not heard from him for—oh, fifteen, twenty years."

"Ah," Will said, then the conversation died. As the silence became uncomfortable, Will wondered how there could be so little to say with twenty-three years of life gone by.

Paddy was digging his toe into the dirt beneath his foot. He hacked a couple of times, then spat. "I feel the need to explain things to ye. About sending Eveleen off, I mean."

"Times is hard for us all. We do what we must."

Paddy lifted his hand. "Hear me out. 'Twas nine years ago, during the Great Frost. Ye know how bad things was then."

"The Year of the Slaughter."

"We had Eveleen, of course, and Nolan was but a babe. We also had Ned between them in age, named for me da." Paddy looked off to the distant hills. "All of us was starving, like everyone else. Some from the Church of Ireland was giving out soup to the poor." He snorted. "Well, I'd have none of it. 'No Scully will ever take the soup' I told the entire village. Other fellas thought like meself."

He looked back at Will. "Then I found out Mary was sneaking up to the church—the king's own church, mind ye—and getting food for the young ones. When I learned of it, I went off me head. I gave her what for to remind her of her place."

Paddy teared up, then breathed deeply to collect himself. "The memory of this will haunt me 'til I breathe me last. Mary, laying on the floor in a heap, her nose and lip bleeding, and she looks me straight in the eye. No fear at all. She says, 'I don't care what ye do to me, I'd cross ye again.'" He swallowed, and lowered his voice. "Then she starts bawling, ye see, and says, 'But I waited too long. Too late, it is, for our poor, poor Ned.'"

Will's chest tightened. He could not imagine the heartache Mary must suffer every day.

"Me own son starved to death. And I wouldn't take the soup." Paddy stared at his wringing hands as though they belonged to someone else. Then he studied Will. "Now I send me little girl off to work for those whoresons. It hurts me arse to do it, but I don't dare lose another one. I don't dare. I have to give her a chance." He stood straighter and swiped each eye with a dirty sleeve. "I put me Eveleen in yer hands now, old friend. I have none but you to keep her safe."

An anchor chained itself to Will's soul. This had become far more than carrying a new maid to the manor. "Ye can count on me, Paddy. I'll treat her as me own. Ye have me word."

CHAPTER TWO

Duncullen Manor, County Tipperary, Ireland

Eveleen Scully stumbled into a world she neither understood nor, at a gut level, could believe was real. This she did know—keep your head down and your mouth shut. Work hard and stay out of the way of the gentry. Be invisible.

For that, she'd had practice. When Da came home in one of his moods, she and Ma each had their parts. She'd take the children to the dark corner of the cottage where their pallets lay. There, they'd curl up in tight little balls, feigning sleep. When Katie and Grace were wee lasses, Eveleen would sing a whispering lullaby into their little ears to calm them.

Ma would pet Da's head and say things like, "Hush now, Paddy. The children are asleep" or "Let me fix ye a bowl of stew, still warm from supper."

Sometimes Ma could coax him to eat a few spoonfuls, then crawl into their straw bed. More often, though, something would remind him how bitter and wretched he was and he would thunder and rail. "Ye expect me to eat this slop! There's not an onion in it. Me ol' Ma wouldn't serve this shite to man nor beast."

Once, he hurled the bowl at Ma who shrieked from the blistering of her skin. The girls shook with fear as little whimpering sounds escaped their lips. "Oh, there ye go! Now ye got the whole brood wailing like banshees against me! Shut yer gobs—the lot of ye!"

On rare occasions, he buried his head in Ma's breast and sobbed like a child. "I'm sorry, Mary. Ye know I'd never hurt ye." Lies, thought Eveleen. He'll do it again as sure as I'm breathing. And he did.

Eveleen knew quite well the need to be invisible.

✤

Eveleen glanced at Mrs. Noreen Bridge, wife of Will and no-nonsense housekeeper of Duncullen. She supervised the young maids from the head of the breakfast table. Eveleen was the newest, having arrived two weeks before. She sat beside Biddy, who had been serving the longest—five years now. Biddy was the personal maid to Lady Nancy and Mrs. Bridge's right hand. All the girls knew not to cross her.

Elly and Fiona, a few years older than Eveleen, were best friends. An odd pair, Eveleen thought, since Elly was shy and Fiona flirted recklessly with every groom on the place. Both were friendly enough, but not at all interested in adding anyone else into their confidences.

To her left sat Maeve and Brea, both nearer her own age of fifteen. They should have been her friends, but Maeve took an instant dislike to Eveleen. Poor, dull-witted Brea thought whatever Maeve told her to think.

When Eveleen first arrived, Maeve jeered at her loose-hanging dress and sunken cheeks. All the girls wore plain brown home-spun frocks covered by white aprons. Mrs. Bridge worked the magical needle Mr. Bridge had promised, but the girl still looked gaunt and sickly.

When she ignored the taunts, Maeve said, "Are ye too dumb to talk, ye lumbering cat-eyed oaf?"

Never in front of Biddy or Mrs. Bridge, though, and certainly not around the proper butler, Mr. Hogan. Lost in her thoughts, Eveleen ate her pinhead oatmeal splashed with milk and drizzled with sweet treacle. This was far better than the breakfasts she'd had at home. Ma'd had to thin the oatmeal 'til it was soupy so all had a share. Milk and treacle were unheard of luxuries.

"Eveleen." Mrs. Bridge's commanding voice crashed into her thoughts.

She set down her spoon and licked her lips. "Yes, Mrs. Bridge?"

"I've noticed yer starting to get a little meat on yer bones and some color to yer cheeks, isn't she, Biddy?"

"That she is," Biddy said. "Yer settling in nicely, I'd say, Eveleen."

The girl's hands fluttered to her face, her hair, back to her lap. "I am."

"Always keep yer hands still when spoken to. All of ye remember to fold yer hands before ye when Lady Nancy speaks. No flitting or flapping, girls."

"To be sure, Mrs. Bridge," they all answered.

"Beg pardon," Eveleen said.

"Ye can beg all ye want," Maeve whispered. "But there's no pardoning trash like you."

✢

Within the hour, Eveleen found herself in the parlor dusting a pair of porcelain doves—a male and a female. She was in awe of them, wondering how the artist shaped such delicate feathers, formed one by one as they were. The yellow shades of the female were striking against the soft browns of her nest.

Eveleen cradled the ornament in her hands. So intently was she studying the bird that her surroundings faded away.

"A beauty, eh?" Maeve's voice squawked into Eveleen's ear.

The little bird soared into the air, then smashed to bits on the floor. Eveleen stared at the pieces in horror.

Maeve sneered. "Ye'll have to pay for that. Straight from yer wages, it'll come."

Maeve's cheerful lilt rankled Eveleen. Her stomach churned as she dropped to the floor. "Jesus, Mary, Joseph, and all the saints," she said, gathering the shards into her apron.

"'Tis all ye deserve, ye little dolt," Maeve said in a hissing whisper. "Ye think ye can sweep into Duncullen and take whatever post ye want whilst me sister, Tara, toils like an animal in the kitchen. I could scratch yer beady eyes out!"

Eveleen's heartbeat thumped in her head. Ma and the young ones would get nothing. She'd have no wages to send them at all.

Maeve's prattle only added to her distress. A curse escaped Eveleen's lips before she even thought it. "Maeve," she blurted, "what are ye gibbering about? Ye've no cause to be in this room. Get on with ye. Out!"

Maeve snatched a handful of Eveleen's hair. "Now ye think ye can order others about, ye scrawny cow."

A stern voice cut through the clamor. "What is going on here?" It was Mr. Richard, the tall son of the master.

Maeve released her and stepped away. A flush rose from Eveleen's toes to the crown of her head. She scrambled to her feet as the broken glass clinked to the floor and bowed her head. "Beg pardon, sir," she mumbled. Maeve did the same.

"Have you both been ordered to clean this room?" he asked.

"No, sir," Maeve said. "I came to help Eveleen, being new."

"Leave," he snapped. Maeve hastily followed his order.

Eveleen inspected the grain of the floor's wooden planks and willed herself not to collapse under Mr. Richard's scrutiny. The drawn-out silence weakened her knees.

She yearned to spit out her explanation, anything to end the stillness, but it was forbidden to speak first. For any of the family to hear the raised voices of servants was prohibited. Weren't these rules drilled into her head as soon as she set foot on Duncullen?

"How long have you been here? I've not seen you before today." The young master's tone was softer now.

Having been spoken to, she peeked at Mr. Richard when she answered. "A fortnight, sir."

"That makes you alarmingly quick to create bitter enemies."

"I look for no troub—" Eveleen spotted the laughter in the young man's gray eyes and stopped. She let out her breath and risked a small grin.

"I have a confession." Mr. Richard lowered his chin as though contrite, yet his eyes twinkled. "I was eavesdropping and I heard the whole thing from behind that door." He pointed.

Eveleen spun to see another entrance at the far end of the parlor. The house was so large, she was baffled by the rambling maze of rooms, let alone extra entries for some. She turned back to Mr. Richard. She wanted to laugh at the mock pitiful expression he wore, but she didn't dare. One word from him, she'd be dragging her feet back to Kilmacthomas in shame. At the thought, her heart beat faster.

"'Tis yer home," she answered. "Ye may listen where and when ye please." She looked to the shards at her feet. "The bird. I'm sorry. I'll be paying for it, to be sure."

"I'm not entirely certain it was your fault," he said. He picked up the male figure. "Actually, my mother has so many of these

12

trinkets, she likely won't miss one. Gather up the pieces and I will dispose of them." He flashed a smile. "This mishap will be our secret."

Eveleen lowered herself to the floor and began collecting the broken bits of bird. Had she been alone, she might have mourned the porcelain piece, but her heart was racing and her head was a jumble of thoughts. The young master seemed too kind to be real. When her father's warnings about the gentry clanged in her head, however, she frowned. It could be a cruel trick.

When all the pieces were gathered into her apron, Eveleen found Mr. Richard before her with an empty tea caddy. She hadn't realized he'd left the room. Carefully, she spilled all the shards into the container. Such gentle eyes, she noticed.

Mr. Richard replaced the lid and grinned. "I will handle this from here." Then he left.

Eveleen sighed. Was Da wrong about the gentry?

✦

Neither Maeve nor Eveleen spoke or even glanced at each other for the rest of the day. All the maids slept on pallets in the kitchen, yet no words passed between them. While the other girls babbled and cackled, the two lay in silence. They'd both broken far too many of the housekeeper's rules and Mrs. Bridge insisted on "a tight household." Woe to the girl who caused a disruption.

Eveleen saw that Maeve looked pale the next morning. The girl hadn't a clue of Mr. Richard's courtesy after she left, so she had slim hope that nothing would come of it. Eveleen took her seat at the breakfast table and smirked. She'd be cursed if she'd tell her.

Truth be told, Eveleen couldn't be sure what Mr. Richard might do. While he said it was their secret, he was within his rights to show the little bird's remains not only to Mrs. Bridge, but to his mother, Lady Nancy.

✠

Mrs. Noreen Bridge watched Eveleen set down her spoon, lick her lips, and wipe her hands across her apron. Had she and Maeve passed a look? The girl had been nervous and jumpy ever since Will drove her into the yard. Her da was tough on her and all his family, Will had said. "A hard man. But he loves them the best he can."

Humph. Paddy Scully sounded a lot like her old man, so wrapped up in his own misery he couldn't see the fire and brimstone he wreaked upon everyone else. Mrs. Bridge was blessed to have married a man who'd never laid a finger on her and rarely spoke a harsh word.

After assigning each girl her duties for the morning, Mrs. Bridge climbed the stairs for Lady Nancy's instructions. She found her mistress awake and eating breakfast in her brocade wingback chair beside the fireplace. Mrs. Bridge noted with satisfaction the fire flickering in the hearth, toasting the room to Lady Nancy's liking. This was Biddy's domain for a reason; she had never let Mrs. Bridge nor her mistress down.

Yet, the large curtained four-poster bed was unmade and the lady was still in her bedclothes. She'd slept late again, the housekeeper realized. This new habit was becoming more and more frequent.

After listing the chores she wanted done on this day, Lady Nancy sat up straighter. "Mrs. Bridge, I have a most unpleasant topic we must discuss. While reading in the parlor last evening,

I noted one of my precious birds is missing. Who was assigned to that room yesterday?"

"I believe the new girl, milady, Eveleen."

Her face darkened. "Retrieve that bird, then dismiss the wretch. I abhor thievery."

"I'm sure she's no thief, milady."

Lady Nancy glared at Mrs. Bridge. "Discover what happened to my bird. I want a report in one hour."

"One hour it is."

Mrs. Bridge frowned as she curtsied and left the bedchamber. Surely Eveleen would not pocket the piece. Was she even crafty enough to pawn it? Or thick-headed enough to think she could? Will had rarely seen his friend over the years. Who knew what the Scullys had resorted to in their desperation. If only she could speak to Will before reporting to Lady Nancy, but he was somewhere on the grounds, seeing to his duties.

Mrs. Bridge remembered the last servant, a mere boy, who snitched goods from Lady Nancy. A woolen shawl for his ma, it was. Lady Nancy had several and that one was so old. Yet, the poor fellow was flogged before the entire staff. His wounds became diseased and he died within the week.

Mrs. Bridge's head ached as though crushed by a vice. She made her way downstairs and back to the kitchen, becoming more nauseous with each step.

"Are ye ill?" called out Orla, the cook. "Is it one of yer spells again?"

Her voice pounded against the insides of Mrs. Bridge's skull. "It is, Orla." She darted out the door and vomited beside the house.

"Ah, there ye go." Orla slapped a cool, wet cloth over Mrs. Bridge's forehead. "Ye'll need to lie down, ye know. Biddy can keep the Big House running. How about a drop or two of laudanum?"

Mrs. Bridge used the rag to wipe her mouth, then returned it to Orla. "There's trouble," she whispered, still panting. "The mistress says her glass bird is missing."

"Who?"

"Eveleen—the new one."

"I don't believe it. That little snip, Maeve, maybe." Orla supported Mrs. Bridge by the arm as they headed back inside.

"Hush, Orla. A slur even in jest can take on a life of its own." She plopped into the chair at the big table and placed her head in her hands. "I was remembering little Denny."

"Don't think on that, Mrs. Bridge," Orla said softly. "Here, I'll look through the girls' things." She headed to the corner where the maids kept their pallets and scant belongings. "And pray I don't find nothing."

Mrs. Bridge laid her head on the cool table, closed her eyes, and breathed deeply. What would she do without Orla? The only one in the house she dared share her burdens with.

A rolling rumble jolted her. She snapped up to find the scullery maid, Tara, and a small mountain of turnips before her.

Tara had turned toward Orla. "Why ye going through our things? That's me sister's box yer holding."

Orla's chest heaved as she spewed a great waft of air. "Yer a bold one, Tara. 'Twas the lady herself who ordered Mrs. Bridge and me to go through yer things. Have ye any complaints about that now? Or shall I tell Lady Nancy that Tara demands an explanation?"

"No."

"Good." Orla studied the pile of turnips. "We'll be needing about three more, then. Off with ye."

With a sour look that reflected her sister, Maeve's, Tara trudged back to the garden.

"The girl is thick as a ditch," Orla said. "And a bloody bitch to boot." The two women giggled like lasses though it pained Mrs. Bridge to laugh.

After a few more minutes, Orla stood and stretched her old back. "Saint Peter be praised, there's no bird to be found."

Biddy appeared at the kitchen door. "Lady Nancy will see ye in five minutes, Mrs. Bridge." Her brow wrinkled. "Another one of yer spells, is it?"

"Tell the mistress I'll be there."

"Certainly, Mrs. Bridge."

"And Biddy," the housekeeper added, "speak to Eveleen about the lady's bird, would ye, lass?"

"Of course."

Every muscle ached as Mrs. Bridge wended her way up the staircase. While her head still pounded, at least the nausea had eased. When she tapped on the mistress' chamber door, Biddy opened it to reveal Lady Nancy in her grey linsey-woolsey gown, looking every bit the lady of the manor. Except for a sadness in her eyes, there was nothing to reveal her growing changes.

After Mrs. Bridge entered, Biddy slid from the room. The housekeeper crept across the floor and stood before Lady Nancy.

"This entire matter causes me great distress," the lady began. "I agreed to your request to hire this new girl because you assured me of all her finest qualities, including her honesty. Did you not?"

Mrs. Bridge's head pounded, making it difficult to hear or even to concentrate. "That I did, milady."

"And yet—oh, Richard. There you are." Lady Nancy's face lit up.

"Am I interrupting?" Mr. Richard asked, standing in the doorway.

"Of course not," Lady Nancy cooed. "Join me. This unpleasantness will not take long."

Mr. Richard crossed the room and sat in the chair next to his mother. He held a black leather-bound volume in his hand. "Carry on," he mumbled and opened the book.

"Now," Lady Nancy scolded, "that fine porcelain bird I spoke of is very dear to me. This girl who cleaned the parlor yesterday. Have you retrieved it?"

"Eveleen is a good worker, milady," said Mrs. Bridge, "and I believe her to be honest. I have searched all the girls' belongings and found nothing amiss. Each has none but her own goods."

From the corner of her eye, Mrs. Bridge thought she saw Mr. Richard's head tilt, but likely not. The men of the manor rarely took note of household affairs.

Lady Nancy's fists lay in her lap in white-knuckled balls. "Don't be a dolt. What does that prove, after all? Surely this little filcher would stash her booty in a less incriminating location. On your word, I opened my home to the vile little ingrate! Where is that bird? If it is not found, the consequences will be dreadful—for both you and the girl!"

Mrs. Bridge's nausea returned. "Yes, milady. I'll see to it."

"Uh, Mother," Mr. Richard said.

"Son, one moment, please." Lady Nancy's eyes held the fires of hell.

"No, Mother," Mr. Richard pressed on. "I have something to contribute."

Her nostrils flared as she turned to her son. "Speak."

Mr. Richard closed his book and twitched in his chair. "As it happens, I was in the parlor yesterday."

"For what reason?"

"No particular reason." Mr. Richard chewed his bottom lip. "I was there and I picked up the little bird."

"Yes?"

"Well, I was lost in thought when some crow or other screeched outside the window. It startled me. I dropped it and I'm afraid it smashed. I'm sorry, Mother."

Lady Nancy's cheek twitched. "And you chose not to tell me?" She turned to Mrs. Bridge. "Go."

The housekeeper bowed and withdrew from the room.

"My father gave me those birds when I was a girl, Richard," she heard Lady Nancy say. "How could you be so reckless?"

In the hallway, Mrs. Bridge flinched at the unexpected appearance of Sir Edward, forcing her to scuttle to the wall and face it as was proper to do.

The master strode into the chamber without knocking and bellowed, "So I find my daughter here by his mother's side. Isn't that sweet? And why am I not surprised?"

Mrs. Bridge cringed. Poor, miserable Mr. Richard. The old bastard was once again in a foul humor.

Chapter Three

After his father's clamorous entrance, Richard's heart began its familiar pounding. Sweat seeped onto the palms of his hands and brow.

At times like this in his youth, he would struggle to draw enough air into his lungs. His stomach and bowels often cramped. Once, accosted by Sir Edward, he had even fouled himself. His father rarely hit him, but on that unfortunate occasion, he had knocked Richard to the floor and kicked him in disgust.

He was no longer a child at sixteen years old. Richard drew himself to his full height, three inches taller than his parent. A sneer crept onto the boy's face as he looked down on the little orangutan.

Sir Edward was not impressed. He snickered as he pulled a handkerchief from his pocket and swept the beads of sweat from Richard's forehead. "Oh bloody hell! Is there no end to your weakness? It takes nothing more than a loud voice to bring you to your knees? Please, please son. Don't piss or shite yourself. By the grace of God, spare us that."

"Leave the boy be," Lady Nancy said. "A man who can torture a child as you do is of the lowest character. But that should not surprise us, considering from whence you've risen."

Keep silent, Richard told himself, not wanting to be an actor in this worn-out drama between his parents. True to form, they rehashed the history of their disastrous relationship.

"A crypto-Catholic, nothing more." She glared at her husband. "William Lynche not only betrayed his religious beliefs for material gain, his flagrant lies pauperized his own brothers."

This was true. Richard's grandfather, upon his father's death, had undercut his brothers by converting to the Established Church. He made profitable use of the Penal Laws designed to eradicate Catholicism, which required all five sons to share the estate. Unless one was a Protestant.

"Your uncles may have been ignorant, superstitious Irishmen," his mother went on, "but at least they had the spine to stand up for their beliefs, such as they were."

Richard's mother was not the only one to accuse William and his son, Edward, of being Protestant in name only. Catholics at heart, people said. Richard laughed at the idea. That would require they had hearts.

"Rather we should all be like the FitzAdens," Sir Edward retorted.

Richard cringed at his father's sinister gleam. He was going straight for the kill.

"We can pretend we're too good to wipe our own arses, then sell our daughter to the highest bidder—even if it's some oaf whose family boasts Gaelic blood."

His mother's shoulders sagged.

Sir Edward's arrow had hit the mark and he gleefully wriggled it. "Let's see, your oldest sister, Marianne, the beauty of the family, is married to the Earl of Farnmont. Lillian, the charming wit, to the Viscount Kilmullah. And what of Amelia, the gifted musician?" He paused as though thinking. "Oh yes. How could I forget? She captured the heart of the dashing Earl of Clanford."

Lady Nancy's eyes glowed like burning coals, but her bottom lip quivered ever so slightly.

"Then we have poor Nancy. The plain one," Sir Edward went on. "No earls or viscounts for her. She was shuffled off to the Gaelic savage, far from decent civilization. Lynche, wasn't it? Vulgar, of course, but he is landed."

His mother stood and lifted her chin. "You got what you bargained for—a son with FitzAden blood."

Richard winced. He had hoped to remain unnoticed.

"Ah, yes. The famous FitzAden blood. My ill-fated attempt to bring quality and respectability to my house." He flung his arm toward Richard. "And look where it got me. What should have been a stallion is no more than a gelding, sitting at his mama's feet, whimpering and whining."

"You are base!" Lady Nancy said with a hiss. "Base and beneath contempt!"

"Mother," Richard said, his disgust overriding his better judgment. "Do not rile yourself over him. He is not like us, being without the intelligence or breeding to even comprehend."

"You mealy little bastard!" Sir Edward strode toward his son, stopping only inches from his face. "I believe we'll allow your high and mighty FitzAden kin to send you to Trinity College, eh? Let's see how quickly you get there."

Sir Edward's proximity and putrid breath caused Richard to lean back. His jaw clenched while his father spun, and stomped from the chamber. With knotted stomach, Richard looked to his mother. "He doesn't mean that."

It sounded like a statement, but was actually a question.

"I don't know, Richard. Get my medicine." Lady Nancy collapsed into her chair. Patches shadowing her eyes darkened against her pale skin. "It's in my armoire. Top drawer, to the left."

Richard's heart thumped. "I must go to Trinity. I need to further my studies."

"Don't prove your father right by whining now. Bring me the bottle."

Richard lifted the amber vial from the drawer and noticed it seemed very light. "Mother, how much have you been taking? This is nearly empty."

"I'll not tolerate scolding from my own son. These have been trying days."

Richard brought the laudanum to her. She withdrew the eye-dropper and sucked down one, then drew up a second dose of the liquid. Richard frowned. "That seems a large measure."

With a cracked voice, Lady Nancy blurted, "What do you expect of me? Your father does nothing but torment me. He undermines my every attempt to find happiness. I am a prisoner here, Richard."

Her voice grew small as she stared at her lap. "He wants me gone. He has someone he'd like in my place. I can feel it."

"Mother, that's foolish."

"Foolish!" Her panic-stricken eyes reddened. "Did I not hear him talking to someone about sending me to Mr. Chesser's Asylum?" She bit her lip. "He claims I am mad. Just like my addlepated mother, were his exact words."

Richard sat in the chair beside her and softened his voice. "Who was this stranger and where did you hear the conversation?"

"I confess. I was eavesdropping outside his study." She picked at the folds in her skirt. "I can only assume the man was a doctor—or Mr. Chesser himself, for all I know."

"Mother, are you sure it wasn't a dream? An effect of the medicine, perhaps?"

She tried to glower at him, but her eyes were already growing heavy. "I am not daft! I know what I heard." She blinked her eyes, then whined, "I cannot go to a madhouse. My mother was tortured in that very place."

"It's one of his idle threats. One of his many idle threats." Richard had tried to make his voice soothing, but he wondered if that was also the case with Trinity College.

"I fear you'll let him take me," she said.

"Of course not."

Her eyes closed. "I can't go there. I'd rather be dead." She sighed and looked at Richard. "It's no use. He's defeated us already."

Richard summoned Biddy and commended his mother to her care. He snatched his copy of Pindar's poetry and set about finding some desperately needed solitude. His father would spend the remainder of the morning hearing the complaints of his tenants and resolving disputes. Richard prayed the ogre was besieged by issues on which to decree.

Oh, how he loves to reign over the lives of these people, Richard thought. His own little kingdom where he fancies himself a god.

Making his way to the third floor, Richard moved his lips, reciting an excerpt of the ancient Greek's lyrical verse. "Now for me/Is it needful that I shun the fierce and biting tooth of slanderous words./For from old have I seen sharp-tongued words of hate./The best that fate can bring is wealth/joined by the happy gift of wisdom."

Replace Archilochus with Edward Lynche and they were one and the same—growing fat from their words of hate.

Richard reached the hallway of unused guest rooms. He could barely remember the last time they'd entertained. Richard was a child when his mother played the gracious hostess of grand balls and fox hunts. These now-gloomy corridors were once filled with the dazzling laughter of neighbors and friends. How and when had all that changed?

As he strode the hall, he noticed a soft glow on the floor before the Blue Room. Stepping inside the opened door, he saw the draperies pulled back as though the room were waiting for him.

A rustle sounded in the far corner. Richard spotted a maid facing the wall, with bowed head and hunched shoulders. On second glance, he noticed her fiery hair, kindled by the sunlight from the window.

"Oh, Eveleen, right? I did not expect to find anyone in this part of the house." Richard knew she could not speak until he had.

"Beg pardon, sir," she answered, scuttling toward the door. "I was assigned these rooms for the day. I'll take me leave, then."

There, the girl hesitated. "If I may speak, sir." Her pale skin held the hint of a blush.

"Yes, certainly." Richard was pleased, actually, to talk to anyone who wasn't his parent.

"Ye did me a great service with yer ma—I mean mother. I don't know why ye done it, but I'll be forever grateful." With an awkward curtsey, she turned to leave.

"Well," Richard said, stopping her, "it was the right thing to do. I know what happens around here to servants suspected of theft."

With pursed lips, the maid waited to be dismissed.

Was it her warm, green eyes or his staggering loneliness that compelled him to continue talking? Whatever the reason, he didn't want her to leave. "When I was young, five or six years old, I used to play with our hall boy."

Eveleen's eyebrows questioned him.

"We don't use one now, but Denny did errands for the staff. There were no other children nearby, so they allowed him time to keep me entertained. During one particularly cold spell, the boy seemed upset. I ordered him to tell me what was wrong. He was worried about his ma, he said. She was ill."

He gripped his book tighter. "So, I went into Mother's room, found her oldest shawl, and presented it to him. She had so many." Why was he telling her this? "Denny's face lit up so, I knew I had done a good thing. Foolish me. I was quite proud of myself."

Eveleen cocked her head to one side. Richard noticed her eyes had softened and her mouth held the hint of a smile.

Almost against his will, he kept babbling, "After a day or maybe two, the house was in turmoil. Mother's maid at the time— thank God she's no longer with us—noted the shawl was missing. Maybe she feared being accused herself, but she reported it to Mother. Lady Nancy will not tolerate theft, you know."

Infidelity, verbal assault, abject cruelty—yes. But to pilfer a faded shawl? There she drew her line. "The house was turned upside down until Denny's mother was spotted wearing it."

A branch scratched the window with the breeze. Richard studied it, then went on. "I was so disturbed by all the anger and commotion, I stayed hidden and silent." His heart beat faster. "All were ordered to the courtyard except me. No one knew, though, that I watched from my nursery window."

His words became little more than a whisper. "I saw it all. My only friend took twelve lashes with the whip. When they untied him from the post, he was unconscious. He caught the fever, it seems, and died within a week." The recollection haunted him still.

"Ye were but a wee lad," Eveleen said. "'Twas not yer fault."

Her voice tugged him back to the present where her green eyes gazed at him. What he'd believed was understanding now smacked of pity. He spoke tersely as he lifted his chin. "I don't know if it was or it wasn't. But I hope this morning I made up for it, a little. Maybe it is Denny who deserves your gratitude." He swallowed. "Um, you may go."

In his head, images swirled of the girl gossiping with the other maids in the kitchen, mocking his cowardice. Alarmed, he realized Eveleen still stood at the door.

"Ye needn't fear, Mr. Richard." Her voice was gentle, comforting. "I'll not betray ye. I've carried burdens of me own and know the relief ye might be feeling now, getting it off yer chest like that. Yer secret is safe with me."

As the girl vanished down the corridor, Richard spotted the churlish maid, Maeve, gawking at him from across the hall.

In a blink, she, too, was gone.

✠

As soon as Mr. Richard caught her eye, Maeve slipped away to the second floor where she was supposed to be. She dared not get caught shirking her duties after yesterday's episode in the parlor. On her way to the east wing, however, she couldn't resist ducking into the barrack room where Brea was polishing windows.

"What are ye doing here?" Brea hissed. "If Mrs. Bridge catches ye away from yer station, ye'll be back in the scullery with Tara."

"Oh, hush, Lily Liver. The old hag has taken to her cabin with one of her never-ending ailments. 'Tis only Biddy to deal with today and she's off counting linens or some-such."

Brea was not convinced. "'Tis not only you, Maeve. If yer caught in here, there'll be hell to pay for me as well."

"Fine. I'll not tell ye what I seen upstairs." She turned to go.

"No. Come back. Tell me quick is all." Brea kept one eye on the doorway, rocking from foot to foot.

Brea was so easy. She could resist neither listening to nor repeating gossip that came her way. Maeve closed in and the two spoke in guarded whispers. "When I seen neither Mrs. Bridge nor Biddy was about, I took the chance to run upstairs to talk to Eveleen."

"Why would ye talk to that shrew? Yer not friends now, are ye?"

Maeve laughed. "Hardly that. Ye see, I ran into Biddy earlier. She was looking for the heifer, saying the mistress called for ol' Bridge and 'twas something about Eveleen. I was merely befriending her to find out what she did." And to make certain the wench didn't sing Maeve's praises to Lady Nancy over the cursed porcelain bird.

Brea nodded.

Maeve widened her eyes. "But instead of that, I found her and the young master, Mr. Richard, in the Blue Room. They were talking real low and rather friendly, I'd say."

Brea's mouth popped open. "No! I—I can hardly believe that. She doesn't seem that sort at all."

"And how does that sort seem?"

"I don't know. She's too timid. Those girls are saucy, brazen even. Did they see ye?"

"I think not." She paused, then said, "Should we speak up, do ye think? Someone should tell Bridge. Or Biddy, at least." Maeve looked toward the door. "Well, I'd best get back to me polishing."

Brea wasn't listening. She stared ahead with furrowed brow, twisting her hair with her finger.

Maeve smiled. The seed had been sown.

✚

Maeve quickly, but carefully, dusted the little trinkets in a guest room. There would be nothing missing or broken by her. Yet, she was behind schedule due to her mischief and needed to catch up. It would soon be time to bring the hot water for washing to Sir Edward and Mr. Richard's chambers as well as outside the lady's room for Biddy to tend. Of course, Maeve'd have to lug the gray, dirty water back down while they ate their midday meal. And don't dare spill a drop onto their precious wooden floors. Wouldn't the feathers fly then.

A smirk crossed Maeve's lips. She especially couldn't be late for her daily cleaning of Sir Edward's study, one hour past their luncheon. The master spent mornings in there, listening to the gripes and woes of his tenants and making his rulings. Maeve had seen a few of the wretched bastards today, waiting in the entryway, looking so small and meek it made her sick.

"Saucy, brazen even," she mumbled. "If that's what ye think, 'tis fine by me." She'd lived in enough filth and starvation, with bad-breathed boys sticking their tongues down her throat only to laugh and call her names 'round the water trough. She'd watched her mother grow old before her time, waiting hand and foot on her crude, stinking father, only to die birthing one of his brats. That was not for her. Not Maeve O'Geary.

She reached for the broom. It was such a waste of all their time to keep up these guest rooms. There had never been any guests to fill them, not since she'd worked here. She would shut the door and not even bother, but Biddy checked behind each of the girls every day.

Stretching the broom under the bed, she wondered if Sir Edward would want her today. If he did, he'd quietly return to his study while she cleaned and that bald prig, Mr. Hogan, would be dismissed. Sir Edward would lock the door and the fun would begin—for him, anyway. Maeve took pride in her skills and worked hard to satisfy the old coot. She'd make him cry out for her in his sleep.

He would give her anything she wanted as long as she asked before and not after. Before, he had that hungry dog look, practically panting as she teased him. But there was no denying, his dismissal of her afterward was as cruel as the mangy boys back home. Once, while pulling up his breeches, he'd even said, "My chamber pot needs emptying. Do so at once."

Maeve had big dreams and big plans, but right now she wanted young Richard Lynche. Not for romance. That was a silly girl's fairy tale. No, she wanted to keep the gravy pouring even after the old man had wheezed his last. She would become irreplaceable to both father and son.

Sir Edward had recently remarked that it was time his son had some manly experiences.

"Let me be his first," Maeve had cooed. "I could teach the boy a thing or two."

He leered at her. "I believe you could."

Maeve smiled and greatly rewarded the man she believed was her partner in his son's seduction. She'd overwhelm the boy; he'd never find better. And, in return, Mr. Richard would be her guarantee of a better life, the life she deserved.

The room was clean. Now, to haul the buckets of warm water up two flights of stairs from the basement. The mere thought of it made her back ache. Eveleen was new. Why couldn't she do the hauling?

Maeve hated that hussy from the first day. No, not the first day. Maeve had cackled at the bedraggled slattern Old Will Bridge drove into the courtyard. She looked like any other half-starved beggar found in the Irish countryside.

After Mrs. Bridge cleaned her up, though, Eveleen's hair came to life and her green eyes glowed with nervous excitement.

When Maeve witnessed Sir Edward's first lustful look, with his hooded eyes and mouth agape, dread swallowed her.

But fear soon shifted to fury. She'd not sweep in and take Maeve's place—a place she'd worked so hard to get.

Let her try, Maeve fumed. I'll tear those cat eyes right out of her pretty little head. My fingernails'll rip bloody gashes into those pasty, white cheeks of hers.

Now Eveleen was far too cozy with Mr. Richard. Improper was what it was. Despite Maeve's fantasies of violence, she would not risk all to quench her thirst for revenge. She had hoped the broken bird would be enough to send the girl home in disgrace. But Eveleen might be tying her own noose with this morning's encounter. If the dim-witted, unsuspecting Brea did her part, Maeve's little problem would be solved.

Chapter Four

As the days went by, Eveleen began to relax. Her confidence grew as she became familiar with the routines of the manor house. While at times she caught Mrs. Bridge watching her closely, the housekeeper treated her with the same kindness and concern she had before the porcelain bird incident.

Maeve was no longer as hangdog as she had been after the scene in the parlor. Instead, she belittled Eveleen with abandon. Brea's behavior was beastly, sneering at her at every turn.

Once, she came upon the two whispering behind a door. "Have ye said naught of it to Bridge nor Biddy?" she heard Maeve ask.

"Not yet," Brea answered. "Ye know how Mrs. Bridge feels about loose tongues. I'm waiting for the right time."

Maeve growled, but Eveleen slipped off. She would hear no more. Those two were trouble and, after the fright of her near dismissal, Eveleen decided it best to keep out of their way. Her mother often told her, "Be as good a person as ye can be, but remember, even the Christ Jesus Himself had enemies."

She had no further contact with the master or his family, keeping properly mute and discreet whenever they were nearby. Yet, when the next day came to clean the guest chambers, Eveleen was startled to find the Blue Room opened and the draperies pulled back.

In a large rocking chair by the window, Mr. Richard sat, leafing through a small red book. He looked up as she entered. "Oh. It's you, Eveleen. Could you light this fire for me? The room has a bit of a chill."

"I will, sir."

She picked up the brass scuttle and took it downstairs for some burning coals. When she returned to the chamber, Mr. Richard seemed lost in the book. She knelt before the fireplace and set up sods of turf across the back of the grate, all the while sensing the young master's eyes boring into her back. With the tongs beside the hearth, she placed hot embers against the peat.

"Where are you from, Eveleen?"

She froze at the question. "The village of Kilmacthomas, sir," she answered. This sudden familiarity made her uneasy. Despite their last encounter, gentry rarely had friendly conversations with servants.

"Have you any family?"

"I do, sir." She turned to look at him. His sparkly gray eyes and lopsided smile caused her heart to pound faster. "I've both me parents, a brother, and two sisters." She wrenched her face toward the fire and set broken pieces of turf over the coals.

"This is awkward," she heard him say.

Eveleen scrambled from the hearth and clasped her hands before her. "Beg pardon, sir."

"Oh no. Not you." He was flipping his book over in his hands. "I mean myself. I, uh, wanted to speak to you again." He looked at his fumbling hands and chewed his lip. "You were so kind last time we talked, and I, um, want to thank you."

Saints above, she thought, he's shy. Eveleen was dumbfounded that a lad of his station would be so rattled. She studied him more carefully. He'd already touched her heart with his compassion toward the servant boy, Denny. She now saw his eyes matched his tender heart—honest eyes, she would say.

And yet, whispers about the manor spoke of Sir Edward's harsh treatment of his son. She, too, knew the agony of a cruel parent. A real person, she decided, not so different from herself.

"Yer always welcome, sir." Boldly, she added, "I, too, enjoyed our chat."

Mr. Richard's head snapped up. His face flushed and he smiled broadly. There was no help for it. She smiled back.

After that, she happened upon him every few days, when they shared a few moments away from the prying eyes of others. Mr. Richard rightfully did most of the talking, but it seemed they could discuss anything. Eveleen listened intently when he spoke of his father's shameless refusal to pay for his schooling. His frustrations brought forward feelings toward her own father.

Oddly, the longer she was away from Da, the more bitter she became. She'd listened to him rail against the privileged all her life, and here Mr. Richard was the most decent person she'd ever met—aside from Ma, of course.

Lying on her pallet at night, she wrestled with what it all meant. Mr. Richard was fast becoming her only friend at Duncullen. She almost giggled aloud at the madness of it. What would Da think of her fondness for the lad, one who reaps, he'd say, his good life from their misery?

She didn't give a care what he'd think. As the idea sank in, she was uplifted, freed.

Da's not here, she decided. I am. I'll be making me own choices from now on.

But a shroud of dread smothered her joy. Da was not the only one placing manacles on her behavior. She and Mr. Richard were both lonely and they found in each other someone they could trust. There was nothing wicked or dirty about it. Yet, who would believe that? The lowbrow, nasty minds of gentry and common folk alike would twist their friendship—and a friendship it was—into some kind of scandal.

Still, she eagerly awaited their next meeting. Mr. Richard flattered her with these little visits; his attention stirred her blood. To be honest, the danger itself caused a tickling in her belly. What could she do? She never sought him out; he found her. She couldn't refuse to answer when addressed by her master, could she?

✟

Will Bridge savored the end of his workday, relaxing in his own cabin, immersed in the aroma of a bubbling lamb stew prepared by his beautiful wife. I'm a lucky man, he thought.

Noreen Bridge stood beside their rough-hewn wooden table. "'Tis trouble we'll have from the new girl." She pinched her husband's cheek and shook it. "The one yer so sweet on."

"Aaach," growled Will, wresting his face from his wife's grip. "I've no idea what yer talking about."

"Eveleen from Kilmacthomas. The one that causes ye to stand up straighter when she speaks."

Will stared ahead with furrowed brows.

Noreen Bridge laughed and shoved his shoulder. "Did ye think I'd not notice me own husband a-gushing when a lovely maid walks by?"

Will snatched his wife around the waist and planted her on his lap. "Ye'll not rattle me this time, woman. I know better than to let yer foolishness worry me." He kissed her well.

She tousled his hair, then slid onto the bench beside him. Her expression grew serious. "More than a month, it's been, and she's settling in nicely. The girl's a hard worker, Will. And I know her father's yer old friend, but the way Mr. Richard looks at her." She cradled his chin in her hand. "'Tis a tight household I run. We don't need backstairs roguery upsetting me staff, or worse, Lady Nancy."

"Yes, Madame Housekeeper. I'll have a talk with the lad, if the opportunity arises."

She spoke directly into his ear. "Make sure it arises. Ye may be merely the overseer, but the boy listens to ye. Mr. Richard's lucky to have a good man like yerself to guide him, with the worthless, half-headed nob of a father he's got."

Like his wife, Will kept his voice low. There was no privacy here; the very wind could carry tales to the manor house. "But at sixteen, how much longer will he listen to the advice of a servant?"

"And a fine-looking young man, he is, with his great height and broad shoulders. 'Tis hard enough for a lass to keep her head in a grand house like Duncullen, but when the master's son, future lord of the manor, whispers in her ear ..."

"He may be grown and look like a man, yet he sees the world as a boy. I'll speak to him. I told ye I would."

Noreen grabbed the sides of Will's head and kissed him on the mouth. "Where's Jack? It gets dark early now."

"He's seeing to the livestock as he does every evening."

Noreen shuffled to the hearth. "I don't like him alone after dark, Will. Ye know how the ruffians torment the poor lad. They're no more than brutes." The cast iron pot clanked as she lifted the lid and peered inside. Grabbing a wooden spoon, she stirred the remnants of yesterday's stew, then turned to her husband. "Go see about him. I worry."

"We can't have that." Will left the small cabin his master provided, inhaled the crisp evening air, and headed to the pasture.

At twenty, Jack was as strong as any grown man. Yet even small boys who chucked a few stones or called out childish cracks could set Jack to wailing and covering his ears. Will had talked to his son time and again with all the patience he could muster, but Jack reacted the same way every time—to the great delight of the village gadflies.

"Why do some gain so much pleasure from taunting the weak?" No matter how many times he asked himself that question, Will found no answer.

As dusk cast shadows over the meadow, Will was surprised to find Mr. Richard helping Jack fill the feed troughs. Actually, Mr. Richard was filling the troughs while Jack coaxed a newly-weaned calf to eat the grain mixture.

"He won't eat, Da," Jack called out. When the calf groaned, he knelt beside it and wrapped his arm around the creature's neck.

"Ye'll teach him, son. No one can talk to the animals like you." As Will tramped toward the troughs, his boots stirred the familiar odor of manure and mud. "Well, Mr. Richard, what brings ye out to do a laborer's chores?"

Mr. Richard raised his eyebrows and smiled. "I will be in charge one day. Wouldn't it be wise to know what's to be done around here? Besides, Jack could use the company."

Will sighed. "Was there trouble?"

Jack tensed, but said nothing. He stroked the calf and spoke in soothing whispers.

"Oh no," Mr. Richard said. "Some neighbors considered dropping by, but they decided against it."

Will nodded. "Give me the bucket, sir," he said. "Shouldn't ye be dressing for yer supper?"

The young heir bit his lip. "Will, you know why I'm here."

"Do I?"

"My father." Mr. Richard leaned against the trough and peered wistfully through the rustling trees. "Another lecture this afternoon on my multitudinous failures. It's no surprise I continue to disappoint him."

Will took the bucket, poured feed into the pans, and spread it with his hands.

"It's the Irish in him," Mr. Richard said, oblivious to Will's Gaelic roots. "He has no appreciation for a classical education or any sort of refinement. Even you can see how boorish he is."

"He's a mighty fine horseman, sir." Will loved Mr. Richard as much as Jack, but Sir Edward deserved some defense.

"True. If only he would restrict himself to that, but at a cock-fight, he is as coarse as any peasant. And bear baiting! A vulgar endeavor, to be sure."

"To be sure." He'd not deny the master could mix it up with the peasants, yet he commanded their respect. While the man had many faults, Will considered this one of his gifts.

The young gentleman studied some dirt beneath his finger-nails. "He insists I grow up, as he calls it. You know. Do manly things." He aped his father. "By your age, I had carnal knowl-edge of every maid on the estate and in most of the villages."

The rich lie as much about their conquests as the poor, Will thought.

Richard resumed his normal voice. "I should come to the mar-riage bed with command, he said, not as some simpering babe."

Will took a deep breath. "Well, I'm just a working man, but I believe God gives each of us the tools to do what must be done. Love covers the rest. If ye love yer wife and she you, ye'll be right."

The boy shrugged. "I think the girls are pretty. There's one in particular who's fine to talk to—not as empty-headed as some. I've pondered stealing a kiss, but ..." Mr. Richard dropped his head and studied the toe of his boot.

Will's heart leapt. Not Paddy Scully's girl, Eveleen. "If yer speaking of a housemaid or such, she may not be of yer high quality. Yet, she has a da and a ma who love her and want her treated right. That's something to think on." This speaking in riddles was addling his brain. He was a straightforward man who liked to call a thing by its name.

"Yes, yes, of course." Mr. Richard had stopped listening. His brows hooded his eyes and his lips were taut. He glared darkly at the manor house, hearing other voices.

✛

As Eveleen finished her evening meal, she was told to report to Mrs. Bridge's cabin. The other girls raised their eyebrows, but said nothing. It was growing dark as she stole across the courtyard, then tapped on the door.

"Come in, Eveleen. Come in." Mrs. Bridge waved her hand, indicating where she should sit. "Me husband and son are off tending cattle. We've a few minutes to ourselves." She sat across the table and folded her hands like a tent.

Eveleen's uneasy curiosity was turning to fear at the creases between the housekeeper's eyebrows. "Is all as it should be, Mrs. Bridge?"

"Eveleen, your work is fine. Ye do as yer told with no sauce and yer chores are well done. As a housemaid, I'm quite pleased. 'Tis another matter I've brought ye here to discuss."

Her alarm grew. "What is it?"

Mrs. Bridge took a breath, then spoke. "A thorny subject, to be sure, but one I must broach." She leaned a little closer to Eveleen. "The young master is a kindhearted lad, but a man he is. Ye may not know much of the breed, but the truth of it is, they don't think as we women do."

"I don't understand."

"Ah, we lasses love the romance. True love wins the day and the like." She smiled and her eyes crinkled. "How can we resist?"

Eveleen tried to smile, too. "I can't say."

"Yet the young fellas' brains fasten on the lust and 'tis there they freeze. They can think of nothing else." Mrs. Bridge leaned in further. "They get a fix on their prey and will do and say anything to land it. Ah, the lies they tell would make yer eyes spin in their sockets and yer ears flap. Even the kindhearted ones, Eveleen."

"Mrs. Bridge, why are ye telling me this?" Her knees were shaking beneath the table.

"Lass, I've seen the looks the young master's been casting yer way. He's just becoming a man and 'tis only natural he'll want to sow some oats, as they say." She reached out and grabbed Eveleen's hands. "'Tis a heady thing to come to a grand estate like this when ye've known only the mud huts."

Eveleen sucked in her breath as her cheeks warmed. She lowered her head and wondered with which shades Will Bridge had painted her pitiful home and struggling family.

"I've come from a humble start meself," Mrs. Bridge went on. "How well I remember me shock and wonder at a place like Duncullen. But there's a wise saying I'd tell me own daughter if I was to have one. 'At all costs, avoid the eldest son of the house. Ye'll get nothing from him but the big belly or the clap and probably both together.'"

Eveleen felt the bottom drop out of her stomach as she pulled away from the housekeeper's grasp. "Mrs. Bridge, there's nothing of that sort going on, I swear it." She felt exposed before the older woman. Her mind raced and she stumbled over her words. "'Tis true, he speaks to me, but nothing coarse. Nothing foul or indecent in any way. I dare not ignore him when he speaks. What would ye have me do?" Eveleen's heart pounded in her ears.

"Hush now." Smiling warmly, Mrs. Bridge took hold of her hands once again. "Yer not accused of nothing and, of course, ye mustn't shun the young master of the house. 'Tis a warning, nothing more. From one who has seen more of the world than yerself."

Mrs. Bridge opened her mouth to continue when low-toned voices interrupted them. "Ah, 'tis me husband and son."

Another rich, now familiar, voice was heard. "Mr. Richard is with them," Mrs. Bridge mumbled. "He'll not likely join us. Be still 'til he passes."

Eveleen heard Will Bridge. "'Twas kind of ye, Mr. Richard, to lend me a hand. Especially with some of the rough sorts 'round here."

"Of course," Mr. Richard answered. "Jack, I expect to take a mid-morning ride tomorrow. Could you have Black Bess ready for me?"

"She'll be set, sir," Jack said.

"Good night, then."

The wooden door creaked and the two Bridge men entered, then stopped in surprise.

"Ah, Eveleen, I didn't expect to see ye there," whispered Will. He and his wife locked eyes as though they shared a secret. "Is all well, then?"

"'Tis," said Mrs. Bridge, making her tone light. "We're just a couple of hens clucking and cackling." She turned to Eveleen. "Well, off to bed with ye. Another long day starts too soon." She squeezed her hand as Eveleen rose from her seat. "I thank ye for keeping me company."

Mrs. Bridge bustled to the doorway and leaned out as she waved Eveleen back. She watched, then turned to the girl. "He's inside now."

Eveleen nodded and took her leave. Slipping across the court-yard, she wondered how she would answer the girls' nosy questions. Had everyone been prattling about her and Mr. Richard behind her back? She would expect nothing more of their dirty little minds, but surely Mrs. Bridge should know better. Mr. Richard was the most well-bred person Eveleen had ever met.

Yet, that glance between Mrs. Bridge and her man. What did they know that she did not?

Chapter Five

Eveleen brightened when Mrs. Bridge announced Sunday's trip to the village of Duncullen. At last, a chance to escape that dreary house and its tiresome people, if only for a bit. Yet, riding in a wagon to town with Maeve and Brea would only be more of the same.

"Would it be possible to stay behind, Mrs. Bridge?" Eveleen asked. "And fish, perhaps?"

All the maids, including Tara and Orla, turned to gape. She might as well have been an Indian from America.

Eveleen shrugged. "I used to fish with me da, is all." Met with silent scowls, she added, "I'm homesick for it, I guess."

Mrs. Bridge mercifully filled the dead air. "Of course, Eveleen, yer welcome to fish. Get me son, Jack, to show ye where. He'll be a fine help to ye, enjoying as he does to put in a line himself now and then."

The girls looked from one to the other with raised eyebrows and snickers. Eveleen knew they would have plenty to say when Mrs. Bridge and Biddy weren't about.

Taunt all ye want, she thought. I'll be rid of the lot of ye for a few hours, at least.

✦

When the day arrived, Richard watched Old Will and Mrs. Bridge drive the wagonload of giggling maids from the courtyard. He turned to his mother. "Is it the servants' afternoon off again?"

"Do you need something, dear?" his mother asked listlessly from her chaise longue. "Fiona will fetch it."

"No, Mother. I merely hadn't realized a fortnight has passed so quickly." He studied the passengers of the wagon. She was not among the chittering girls bouncing through muddy ruts, anxious for a visit to the village.

Weeks ago, he'd stood on this very spot and watched Old Will drive the tattered, pale waif who was to become Eveleen onto the estate. He smirked remembering Mother's comment as she stood beside him.

"Oh, heavens, where does Mrs. Bridge find the bestial strays she drags into our household? That one is too much. She looks diseased."

He swallowed a grin as he contemplated the beauty that stray possessed, inside and out.

"... so we are trapped."

He snapped back to the present. "What was that, Mother?"

She twisted in her chair to face him. "I was saying it is somewhat peaceful here on the odd Sunday with most of the lowborn away. It would be so much nicer to have servants of English descent, but we are trapped."

"Trapped?"

"Yes, Richard. Where is your mind today? Trapped by our demand for service. My father often said we would have wiped the race from the island but for the resulting shortage of servants and laborers." She studied her nails. "They do satisfy a need, I suppose."

He sighed. "Of course."

When he looked out the window once again, his chin snapped up. Heading down a footpath were two figures. He squinted for a clearer look. It was Eveleen and Jack. What was Jack carrying?

He went to his mother's side, knelt, and took her hand. "You seem in good spirits today. Perhaps you won't mind if I go out for a bit."

"You should, son. The air will do you good."

He stood and kissed her forehead. "Why don't you come? The air will do you good as well. We'll ride, racing through the woods as though mounted on the hippoi athanatoi."

Mother chuckled. "The horses of the gods. You silly boy. You know I'm not well. The only way I'll take that ride is through my imagination."

I know, Richard thought. I was counting on that.

He bounded down the stairs with an unfamiliar tingle of— what? Energy? Spirit? Passion? Oh no, too strong a word by far. He vaulted off the last three steps, nearly crashing into their butler, Hogan.

The old fellow took a dignified step back and dipped his head. "Beg pardon, sir."

Richard strode a few paces, then turned. "You're always here, Hogan. Have you never taken a few hours for yourself?"

For an instant, the butler's eyes widened in surprise. "My duties are with the family, Mr. Richard."

"Of course," he answered and mentally shook his head. He wondered what that sour old prig would think if he knew where Richard was headed. He imagined Hogan huffing that despite his FitzAden pedigree, Richard harbored his father's sordid vice of debauchery.

That would never happen. He would not allow himself to become the boorish oaf his father was. Never.

He mumbled to himself as he strode toward the stable. "This is not the same. Not at all." He swatted a fly from his face. "Eveleen is merely a good sounding board. A friend of sorts. Like a faithful dog or a steady horse."

✠

Let them laugh, Eveleen thought, watching her cork bob in the water. It was worth their scorn to be alone in this clearing where birds flirted, the river babbled and gurgled its way to strange and exciting places, and the brisk breeze finger-combed her hair. She'd been anxious to loosen it; she so loved the wind's tickle.

Well, Da was good for something, Eveleen said to herself.

Her father had taken her fishing from time to time, and she was grateful for it now. He dragged her along to carry gear, bait hooks, and string their catch. But for all his harshness and cruelty around the house, he was a different fellow at the river. He talked to Eveleen rather than barking orders and finding fault. Instead, he revealed story after story of his boyhood. They'd even shared a laugh once or twice.

Once they returned to the house, however, it was as though those easy moments had never happened. He fell into his usual blustering and browbeating, and for that, Eveleen hated him all the more. He could have shown them some kindness, she reasoned, if he'd wanted. He simply chose to be cruel.

Eveleen cast her line and turned to more pleasant thoughts. It was fine weather, rare for a winter day. Here at the river, it was like she'd been unburdened from a heavy sack of grain she'd been lugging for weeks. She felt lighter, taller even.

Who did Da take fishing these days? she wondered. This was not the best season, but pike could be caught anytime. Grace, likely. She was a year older than Katie and followed directions well. Poor Katie would get so confused, Da'd constantly scold her as a numbskull. She prayed it was Grace, for Katie's sake.

If only the two sat on each side of her now, life would be perfect. On many an evening, the three would cuddle together while

Eveleen spun a story. Nolan was invited, but scoffed at faeries, monsters, and merrows of the sea.

Eveleen smiled at the memory. "I believe Nolan is a changeling," she told the girls, "switched at birth by his faerie mother to torment us."

"No," Grace teased. "He's too ugly to be a changeling. He must be a grogoch."

Nolan grunted and scowled, but his eyes glowed.

"Yes," Eveleen went on, "a grogoch. A hairy, half-human who never, ever washes. I believe I see some twigs in his hair right now."

"Ugh! Phew! The smell!" the girls called out, laughing.

Eveleen was rattled. The solitude was a blessing, but her memories caused a dull ache in her chest.

Me belly is full, she lamented, but what a foul trade. I'm alone in this world without a trace of loving care to be had.

✚

Richard proceeded into the stable as a ruse he was looking for Jack, but stopped short at a rustling in the back stall. The quick pop of a white linen cap caught Richard's eye. Hopefully, his mother had no immediate need for Fiona. Within seconds, Samuel, the disheveled stable hand, stumbled into the alley. "I'm sorry, Mr. Richard," he said. "I didn't know ye were here, sir."

"That's fine. I was looking for Jack, actually. I have some concerns about the mare, Bess."

"Right, Mr. Richard, sir."

Samuel's behavior should have exasperated Richard, but he found the stable hand's shuffling and ear-pulling somewhat humorous. Rather than chastise the groom as he should, he went along with the pretense.

"Well," Samuel said, "as it happens, Jack went off for a bit, sir."

"Where can I find him?"

"That I cannot rightly say, but he did go off with some fishing gear."

"Thank you, Samuel. You may go back to your—nap."

Upon exiting the stable, Richard was surprised to see Jack ambling toward him, empty-handed. "There you are. Uh, we need to discuss something." He quickly led him away from the barn.

"What is it, Mr. Richard?" Jack looked at the stable doors in confusion while Richard steered him back toward the brush.

Once several yards off, Richard spoke in hushed tones. "I saw you from the window earlier, walking toward the thicket with one of the maids."

"Eveleen?"

"Yes, Jack. Eveleen." Richard struggled to keep the impatience from his voice.

"We weren't doing nothing wrong. She likes to go fishing, is all."

"Fishing? At the Multeen?"

"We ain't done nothing wrong."

Richard put his hand on Jack's shoulder. "Of course not. I merely thought I would walk to the river myself. Just to talk."

"I took her to the pool where there's a bit of a clearing."

"I know the spot. Jack, I need this to be one of our secrets. You'll not tell anyone I've visited a maid, will you?"

"No." He wagged his head back and forth. "Yer me master and me only friend. I wouldn't tell this secret no more than I'd tell yer others."

Richard looked into the only eyes he'd ever fully trusted. "I know that, Jack. Thank you."

He made his way down the footpath as quietly as he was able. Fishing? Although he knew some women fished, it intrigued him somehow. What other mysteries did Eveleen hold? He suddenly needed to know all there was about her—as a friend, of course.

Was it the anticipation or the forbidden nature of this rendezvous that caused his body to pulse with electricity? He no longer cared. As he neared the spot Jack had described, he crept soundlessly to the clearing's opening. He paused a moment to plan his approach.

Then he saw her. His breath caught in his throat and his heart hammered. His entire being was awash with warmth. There was no other word to describe it; he was captivated.

She sat with her legs tucked beneath her, staring at—nothing, seemingly lost in her own thoughts. Gone was the cautious maid scuttling about the manor. Her thick, coppery hair was loose, toppling down her back, but there was something more.

She had a bearing, a demeanor no dullard dragged from the bogs could ever effect. So serene. So beautiful. Almost ... noble. He was ashamed of his earlier thoughts. There sat no faithful, steady companion.

There sat a goddess.

⚜

Eveleen heard the grass crunch. She twisted toward the sound to find Mr. Richard several yards away.

"Oh!" Abandoning her pole, she leapt to her feet and, while smoothing her dress, spun to face him. "Beg pardon, sir."

Mr. Richard's face lit up as he bounded toward her. Shocked, Eveleen stepped away only to watch him dive to the ground at her side.

He snatched the fishing pole and gave it a tug. Eyes twinkling, he handed her the rod. "I believe you've caught one."

"Mercy!" She took the pole with both hands. The two of them tugged and pulled on the line until a black-banded perch sporting red-tipped fins flipped onto the bank.

Eveleen deftly removed it from the hook, dropped the pole to the ground, and placed the fish in her basket. "A nice size to flavor a stew," she said, wiping her hands on her skirt.

She looked at Mr. Richard and saw his fancy clothes smeared with mud and grass stains. He swiped at his face, painting it with dirt before replacing the strands of thick, dark hair that escaped his ponytail.

"Ah, yer nice clothes, sir," she said, remembering herself. "Please forgive me."

Sweet baby Jesus, her hair! Her cheeks burned as she recognized her loose appearance before the young master. She reached for her bonnet on the ground with one hand while snatching up her locks with the other.

Mr. Richard brushed her arm. "No," he murmured, "leave it."

Her breath caught at his touch. A tingle ran from head to toe as she dropped her hair and cap. While lovely, this unfamiliar tenderness unsettled her and left her confused. She opened her mouth to respond, but no words came.

He smiled crookedly and said, "Sit with me. I don't care about these old clothes. I merely wanted a chance to speak with you— without all the rules and trappings of the house."

"As you wish, sir." They lowered themselves to the grass. Eveleen folded her hands in her lap and studied them. She pressed her lips together to keep from screaming, "What do I do?"

Mr. Richard took one of her hands in his. "You look like an angel. A goddess, actually."

Eveleen's heart pounded. This was crazy! One of her silly daydreams come to life! "I'm no goddess, sir. Just a plain girl."

"You're no plain girl," he insisted. "You're of noble blood—you must be. No one of your beauty and bearing could come from common stock."

She searched his eyes to see if he mocked her. They were soft, yet firm. How could that be? He was sincere. Somehow he meant what he said.

He grinned. "Perhaps the old fairy tales are true. You were born to royalty only to be hidden with common folk to save you from some sort of evil."

"I look just like me ma. Everyone says so," Eveleen answered. "And Da was never one to take on more mouths to feed without them being his very own."

He whooped with laughter. "You are delightful. Just delightful." Then his face grew serious as he looked her in the eye. "I don't know where you came from and I don't care. You can speak all day in your silly Irish brogue, but underneath, I know there's more. Much more. I want to learn all I can about you. Even if it takes the rest of my life."

Eveleen's eyes widened and she struggled to breathe. "What are ye saying?"

He grabbed both her hands and flipped them over. His face was alive, glowing. "Look at your hands, roughened by work you should never have had to do. You are highborn, Eveleen. I see it in your face, your posture, your eyes, your lips. Your sensitivity and intelligence could never have come from such low beginnings."

"But—"

"Hush. I don't know how, but I am going to restore you to your rightful place in the world." With that, he leaned in and brushed his lips so slightly, so gently across hers that she wasn't sure it even counted as a kiss. But it left her full and empty at the same time.

Mr. Richard's eyes were as tender as his voice. "We'll meet like this again, my princess. But not at the house. We'll meet here whenever we can. Do you agree?"

"I do," said Eveleen, with her heart full and her head spinning.

Chapter Six

Just back from their jaunt into town, Maeve let Brea run her fingers over the bolt of Buckram linen she had bought.

"I can't believe I finally have it," Maeve said. "I've been saving for months."

Brea smiled. "I'll help with the stitching if ye like."

Their heads bounced up at the sound of Tara sniping from the scullery. "Ye'll clean up behind yerself if ye know what's good for ye. I'll not be cursed for yer mess, that's for certain."

Maeve, Brea, and Elly bustled through the kitchen to find Tara, arms akimbo, glaring at Eveleen, who was removing a fish's scales. The dead, glassy eye stared at Maeve.

When Maeve realized the others watched for her reaction, she moved in closer and snickered. "One paltry perch, eh? That's all ye have for a whole day of fishing?"

Eveleen continued scraping the fish with short, firm strokes. The rest looked at each other with rolled eyes.

She refused to be ignored. "So poor ye are," Maeve continued, "ye pretend to fish rather than go to town. Better to confess yer shame than to waste yer time on this foolery." She set her hands on the table and leaned in. "Yer clearly not good at it."

Eveleen's eyes flashed in a way Maeve had never seen. She grabbed the tail of the fish and scratched the knife across the entire carcass with such force that scales peppered Maeve in the face.

Heat surged through Maeve like a rampaging river, pumping her muscles with might. She dove across the table and grabbed for Eveleen's bodice, but missed.

Eveleen drew back, clutching the boning knife in a white-knuckled grasp. "Ye'll want to be stepping back, then," she said, in a firm, even voice. "If ye know what's good for ye."

From the servants' hall, Fiona said too loudly, "Biddy, what did ye buy in town today?"

Brea and Elly scampered from the scullery. Tara latched onto her sister's arm and tugged repeatedly, but Maeve would not budge. Instead, she threw an evil eye at Eveleen that should have withered the girl, yet Eveleen never blinked.

"Get out of here," Tara whispered through clenched teeth. "I'll not have ye sent home for the likes of her. And me along with ye."

Maeve glanced at her sister, whose eyes were wide with panic, then back at Eveleen. "No. I'll not be going home. But you will, heifer. You will."

Eveleen lowered her knife when they turned to leave.

Tara was tugging Maeve along by the wrist when they nearly crashed into Biddy.

Biddy frowned. "Is something amiss?"

"No," said Tara, pasting on the cheery, simpleton face she used to avoid trouble. "We were just admiring Eveleen's catch. There's just the one, but she's a beauty."

They bustled out of the kitchen and into the courtyard. It was nearing dusk and a drizzly mist chilled them. "Ye can stand to cool off a bit," Tara told her sister.

Brea followed them outside. Seeking privacy, the three huddled near an ancient yew a short distance from the house.

"Never have I seen Eveleen with the hard look," said Brea. "I didn't know she had it in her."

"And it can be slapped out of the hussy just as quick." Maeve didn't feel as sure as she sounded, however. Something had stiffened the chicken-heart's spine.

Brea said, "She has some bite to her, is all."

Maeve's ire rose once again. "She's a fine one with a knife in her hand, ain't she now. Let's see how she does when I catch her alone where none can hear her screams for help."

Brea drew her shawl tight around her shoulders. "Watch yerself, Maeve. 'Twas not just me who saw ye threaten the lass. Elly was there, too. If Eveleen gets a drubbing, yer the one they'll send packing."

"No one's getting a drubbing, Brea," said Tara. She gave Maeve their signal, a quiet tap on the foot. "Maeve's hot-tempered, but ye know she's all talk."

Maeve jammed her ragged fingernails into the palms of her hands. "Did ye tell Biddy or Bridge what I told ye—about her and Mr. Richard?"

"I did." said Brea, "Mrs. Bridge thanked me and said no more. Maeve, be careful with that bad humor of yers. I couldn't stand this place without ye. Or you either, Tara." She shivered as she looked from one to the other. "I'm going in to stand by the fire. We'll be back to work before long."

When Brea was out of earshot, Tara asked, "What are ye planning? I know ye'll not let her by with that. Waving a knife, for the love of God!"

"I nearly lost it for sure, Tara. I thank ye for steadying me." She took a deep breath. "I'll not pummel her, though I sorely want to."

Tara laughed, probably relieved, then followed Maeve's gaze toward the window of Sir Edward's study.

Maeve turned to her sister. "I've much more devious ways to get rid of unwanted rubbish."

Tara smiled. "And she'll not even know it was you."

✦

How could Eveleen's life change so drastically in just one day?
After her encounter with Mr. Richard at the river and the skir-
mish with Maeve the very same evening, danger skulked around
every corner of the manor house.

She had stunned even herself with the spine to stand up to
Maeve—with a blade, no less. Yet, she felt like a real person,
someone who mattered and could handle her own life. A rare
sense of pride washed over her.

People often said that standing up to browbeaters would
force them to back down. At first, it seemed to prove true. Tara
had pulled her sister away and no one spoke of it for the next
day or so.

But, in short order, Maeve regained her brass. When none of
the others was near, Maeve leaned in close to Eveleen's ear. "Me
and me spies, we're watching ye. Every day. Every minute."

Between Brea's sly sidelong scrutinies and Tara's open sneering at every move and remark, Eveleen did not doubt it. She had
not forgotten the porcelain bird episode that Maeve had plotted.
Only the kindness of Mr. Richard had kept her from great hard-
ship, with loss of pay being the best possible outcome.

Nearly a week later, Eveleen was carrying a bucket of gray
water down the backstairs when Maeve appeared at the bottom
step.

Eveleen halted midway down the flight since there was barely
room for two to pass, especially with the water. Instead of making way for her, Maeve closed the door, and mounted the staircase in a calm, unhurried approach. Her unblinking eyes bored
into Eveleen's as she climbed, step by step.

Eveleen's own heartbeat thumped in her ears. She knew she had humiliated Maeve in front of the others and could not be sure what she'd do. She knew only one thing; she must lock eyes with Maeve. To turn or look down would show weakness.

Once they were face-to-face, Maeve elbowed the bucket, causing water to souse the stairs, flowing over each step in a series of little waterfalls. "Well. Glory be," she said, her glare unchanged. "Yer quite the clumsy one today."

She nudged past Eveleen, gave the bucket a kick, and continued on her way.

Eveleen seethed, biting her lip until she tasted blood. She clenched her fist to keep from grabbing the wench's ankle and dragging her bump, bump, bump over the stream of dingy water she'd created.

Yet, with her whole life on the line, she dared not take revenge. Not now that she had a secret love, her aroon. Mopping the nasty water Sir Edward had likely used to wash his bollocks, Eveleen managed a smile. She could not believe it.

Me, she realized. I've me own aroon.

This new bond with Mr. Richard eased her distress. She had no doubt he would rush to her defense if Maeve or her lackeys hurled false charges her way. He was Lady Nancy's pet, her darling. His mother would certainly listen to his pleas on her behalf.

Unless, of course, she knew of their friendship. More conversation with Mr. Richard than receiving commands was improper; some would say even vulgar. For the two to meet at the river alone—and to kiss—Lady Nancy would never understand. Never. Eveleen would be ousted from her post in disgrace, with little chance of ever securing another.

That was why the two agreed to avoid each other at the manor house, for the very suspicion of their familiarity was risky. Their first chance encounter reminded Eveleen of the wisdom of this.

Alone in the parlor, she stood atop a ladder polishing the chandelier when Mr. Richard poked his head in. Seeing her, he quickly withdrew, but Eveleen felt the heat creep up her neck to her face. How many times had her brother mocked the rosy red blush on her cheeks and ears whenever she felt exposed? Her lips were sealed, but her complexion revealed all. Hard work seemed the only safe path.

"Ye've become a little blue butterfly, Eveleen," Mrs. Bridge once said, "flitting from task to task. No one can keep up with ye."

At night, she moved her pallet closer to Biddy. While she slept, she couldn't trust the Three Banshees, as she called the other girls now. That is, if she slept.

Night after night, every close encounter swirled through her mind in a frenzy. The "almosts" and "what ifs" turned her fingers to ice. Just before drifting to sleep, however, she could not resist reliving each precious moment with Mr. Richard. Or Richard, as he said to call him at the river. But that felt too strange, too daring, even in her own head. Who might be eavesdropping on her very thoughts?

Their second meeting had taken place two long, dreary weeks from the first. They talked and giggled awkwardly while both fished.

"A salmon would be nice," Mr.—er, Richard announced. After Eveleen caught another perch and a nice brown trout, the young master hauled in a sizable salmon.

"Even the fish in the streams obey your commands," Eveleen said. "How fine it must be to rule yer world in that way."

Richard faced her. "If I ruled my world, we would not be sneaking off like naughty children to be together."

Her stomach knotted. She pursed her lips and helped him add the fish to her basket.

He proceeded to take up the gear and set it aside. "Three fine specimens should be enough to prove where you've been," he said. He lay on his side, propped up by his elbow.

"You've bewitched me," he told her. His dancing eyes spurred her heart to flip. "I think of you morning, noon, and most especially, at night."

Eveleen revisited a craving to lunge into his soft lips for a lingering kiss. Instead, she smiled nervously and said, "I think of you, too."

He brushed back a strand of her hair and chuckled. "Your ears are blushing."

His teasing relaxed her and she shoved his shoulder. "Ah, yer no better than me brother, with yer mocking ways."

He grabbed her wrist. "I don't want to be like your brother," and leaned in for that sweet kiss she'd dreamed of.

Although she summoned this memory often, she never failed to go weak and warm from head to foot.

That day, and again during their third tender visit, he spoke of his future plans with deep passion. He would go to Dublin and attend Trinity College to study with the greatest minds of the country. From there, he would travel the continent, teach, and write of wondrous things.

She became caught up in the excitement of such marvelous ambitions. The only plans her people made were where to get their next meal or how to hold onto what meager land they still had. That one could choose from such opportunities made her head swim. Speak the truth, she chided herself. Just listening to Mr. Richard makes ye giddy.

Every now and then, a tiny part of her asked how she fit into these plans. Where was this going? How could it end? But those were sulky, joyless questions and she refused to entertain them. She stuffed them into a crate in her brain and chained it shut.

Chapter Seven

"My darling Richard, has something happened I should know about?" asked his mother. "You seem lighter, happier somehow."

"The spring air, I suppose," he answered. "I can think of nothing else." He struggled to adopt as casual a stance as possible.

"Stand up straight, son. Don't slouch."

Richard bit his bottom lip. "I beg your pardon, Mother." Suddenly, he was desperate to leave her chamber. "Please excuse me. I must check on Black Bess ... in the stable."

Lady Nancy tilted her head. "Oh dear. It's back to the brooding Richard, I see. Well, go then." She huffed. "Why do you look at me with that peculiar expression? Go!"

He turned on his heel and left without another word. She was driving him insane. He could not take another moment of being treated like a bumbling child.

He stomped down the staircase and out the door. There he turned toward the stable, away from it, then back again. There was nowhere to go, it seemed, where he could be himself—a man now, not an infant. He was tired of being his mother's little boy, his father's shame, his tutor's prodigy. Even Old Will saw him more as a lad than a man.

Where could he just be Richard?

He knew where. At the river. With her. But it was only Friday—two more days until they could slip off to the Multeen. He grit his teeth, unable to bear it until then.

He strode into the stable, calling, "Jack! Saddle Bess."

Samuel stepped out of a stall with a forkful of hay. "Jack's in the pasture, Mr. Richard. I'll outfit her for ye."

He nodded to the groom, then paced about, hands on his hips.

"I see yer in a hurry," Samuel said, adjusting the saddle blanket. "Ye haven't missed Sir Edward by much. He rode off just minutes ago."

Blast! "Which way?"

"To the east, I believe."

"Ugh." Richard felt he could burst into a thousand small pieces. He needed to talk to Eveleen, but that was impossible. If his father learned of their love, he would slap Richard on the back, wink, and treat his enchanting Eveleen like a trollop. Mother would be aghast, devastated even, and hastily dismiss her.

"Trapped," his mother had said weeks ago. He finally knew what she meant.

"I need a friend," he mumbled.

Samuel looked up. "Beg pardon, sir?"

Damn, he'd said that aloud. He waved his hand. "Nothing. Is Bess ready?"

"That she is," said the lanky groom. "Have a fine ride, sir."

Richard grunted, straddled his charcoal mount, and prodded Bess onward—to the west.

Through pale green fields of newly-sprouted wheat, he spurred the horse toward the woodlands, delighting in the crisp, clean breeze that swept his face and cleared his head. He slowed once he reached the forest, where his mind wandered to his younger days.

Until the age of fourteen, he'd attended a boarding school, Clonmel Grammar. There, Richard immediately felt at home with languages and books. He devoured Latin until, as his schoolmaster loved to boast, he could have rivaled Cicero in his oratory. While he pored over the great histories and writings of ancient Rome, his classmates preferred to snicker and mock their gangly, pallid tutor. Better yet, they'd perfect their fencing skills, or sneak into cockfights and bare-knuckled boxing matches.

Richard had no interest in such spectacles, and his skills in the manly arts were mediocre at best.

Since his return to Duncullen, he met with Father Healy on Monday afternoons where he adopted the Anglican priest's passion for ancient Greece. Together they soaked up the plays of Euripides and Aristophanes, the epics of Homer, and the philosophies of Socrates, Plato, and Aristotle.

"Ah, how you will love the scholarly atmosphere of Trinity," Reverend Healy often remarked. "You were born for it."

"I have to go to Trinity," he now whimpered to the wind. "I'm dying here."

His chest tightened at the thought of his father's threat to withhold university funds. Sir Edward had been angry, to be sure, but that was weeks ago and he still showed no signs of relenting. Surely, he wouldn't make Richard grovel before Grandfather FitzAden when Duncullen had ample resources for his education.

Sir Edward would readily pay for a year or even longer on the Grand Tour of Europe, a rite of passage for young men of his class. Richard ached to see firsthand the excavations of Herculaneum and the new site of Pompeii, but too many who returned whispered enthusiastically of whoring and drunkenness and said little of Italian architecture.

Richard feared he would no more fit in with his fellow travelers than he had with his classmates at Clonmel Grammar. Reverend Healy painted such a picture of scholarship and devotion to knowledge at Trinity that Richard knew he could be happy nowhere else.

As long as Eveleen were there.

The thought slammed into his head like a sledgehammer, rattling his brain. Its very truth shook him. He had no chance for happiness, he realized, without Eveleen.

Bess slowed to a walk over the mossy forest floor. The thickness of the woods closed in on Richard, and he shivered with the cold. Beyond was a small clearing beside a pool of water where he could let Bess graze while he pondered this new reality.

Shafts of light broke through the leafy trees. A soft giggle. A deep moan. Someone was ahead. It was ludicrous. On this entire estate, was there nowhere to be alone? Richard inched Bess to the edge of the trees.

There in the clearing, before his eyes, two fleshy lumps of humanity rolled, grunted, and rutted like a boar and its sow. He was aghast at the spectacle.

A closer look caused a cannonball to plunge into his stomach. The red-faced, sweaty boar was none other than his father and the sow was the Widow Dunne, a tenant with five young children whose husband had dropped dead in the field two years past.

Richard backed Bess from the scene as soundlessly as he could manage. While he agonized over the hideous image, a confrontation with his father in his present state of arousal was more than he could bear.

Away from the clearing, his disgust, if possible, grew. It was one thing to know in theory of such goings-on. To come face-to-face, as it were, jarred Richard to the core. Shock ripened into rage.

He was making a complete fool of Richard's mother, cheapening her, dragging her esteemed name through the slime he so callously wallowed in. He was the lowest of the low, the most putrid scum of the earth!

With every nerve in his body ablaze, Richard yanked on the reins and leapt from his horse. He paced through the foliage, snapping small branches that dared block his way. With a curse, he heaved a fallen log like a javelin. Finding no relief, he scrambled onto his mount and tore over the open fields. He hurdled hedgerows and vaulted stone walls with a fury he'd not known before.

Richard despised his father more than he knew was possible. And the old man would pay.

✚

Eveleen grew nervous. "Have I done something to vex ye, then?"

Richard had been restless and aloof since they first plopped their lines into the Multeen. His mood matched the low, sooty clouds blanketing the Galtee Mountains.

"Hmm?" His brows drew together. "Of course not."

He caressed her cheek with the back of one hand, holding the pole with the other. Then, biting his lip, he stared across the river. "I've got to get away from Duncullen—from my barbaric father, naturally, but also my mother. She means well, but she's smothering me."

He turned toward her and squeezed her hand until she winced. "I'm withering away here like a parched sapling, Eveleen. Trapped in an existence that has no meaning for me. I've got to escape. I will escape!"

Her stomach twisted. "What are ye wanting from me, Richard? I don't know what to say."

His chest heaved. "I want—" He looked down for several seconds, then into her eyes. "I want to go to Dublin. I want to go to Trinity College. And I want you to come with me."

Eveleen snatched back her hand. She grew faint from all the emotions whirling inside—joy, confusion, disbelief, dread. "How? Has yer da given in?"

He scowled. "My father will see things my way, of that I am sure. Without a doubt, he'll provide the money."

"But I cannot go along, Richard. That's foolishness, ye know that." How she wished it were not.

"No. You see, I'll set aside some of my money for you. You can leave my mother's employ and I'll lease you a room, an apartment in Dublin."

"To do what?"

"Be my companion, of course." He leaned in for a kiss.

Eveleen cringed and leaned away. Mrs. Bridge's warning flashed in and out of her head. "That I will not do. Me da don't have much, but he raised me to be a good and proper girl."

Richard's eyes widened. "I didn't mean that at all." He reached for her, but she flinched from his touch. "I love you," he pleaded. "Don't you know that? I want you with me, that's all." He sighed. "I don't know what to do."

"Nor I. But I can give meself to no man unless he be me husband. Nor can I be yer companion, as ye call it."

His eyes softened. "I would never hurt you. Never."

Eveleen's anger seeped away. "I believe ye, I do. But I don't know what kind of future we could have. Ye know we can never marry."

Richard leapt to his feet and paced as he ranted. "Why are we trapped by so many rules? Who is to say our love is bad or wrong? Love is a beautiful thing, is it not? Or is everyone so old and miserable, they cannot recognize a gift from God when they see it?" He pulled Eveleen up and bundled her into his arms, holding her as though he feared she'd vanish. "That's what we have. A gift from God. A love so pure and wondrous, it could only come from heaven."

Eveleen drank in his scent as her head lay on his chest. "I cannot imagine a love more true than ours."

Richard took a step back to look into her eyes. "A divine honor, bestowed upon us two. What else can it be? Who are we to reject it? Romans Chapter Eight, Verse Thirty-one: 'What shall we then say to these things? If God be for us, who can be against us?'" His voice took on new life. "Who? My mother? Your father? The king? Even the church dare not go against God Almighty."

"What are ye saying?"

"I say we marry, Eveleen. I want to marry you with every cell in my body. We can have our own ceremony right here on the land He created, taking our vows before the only one who counts: the Lord God Himself."

She laughed, caught up in his spirit. "That's lunacy, Richard."

"Is it? Is it? The Almighty brought us together and He will bless us. He will!" He dropped to one knee and clasped her hand in both of his. "Marry me, Eveleen. Right here before God. Marry me."

Her head was spinning, yet anything seemed possible. "I'll marry ye, Richard Lynche."

He grabbed her by the waist and swung her around in a frenzy until they dropped to the ground, giddy.

Once the laughter dwindled, Richard rolled toward Eveleen, who lay on her back in the grass. He peered into her eyes with such tenderness, all seemed right and true. Leaning in, he kissed her with more depth and passion than she knew either of them contained.

And it was good.

☩

Richard was more hopeful than he'd been for many months. He would go to Trinity. Once confronted with the disgusting spectacle Richard had witnessed, his father dared not deny him. Even better, he would be with Eveleen, as husband and wife. All in secret, of course.

He ran his fingers through her luxurious, coppery hair and basked in her emerald eyes. Kissing her sweet lips, he knew they were meant to be one.

Finally, he rose to his feet. "Are you ready?"

"I am." She stood and locked her arm within his.

"I've been to a few weddings. I don't know the exact wording, but God will help us through the important parts."

"Are ye sure?"

"I've never been so sure."

They looked across the river, facing the hills. The mountains were nature's altar, it seemed to Richard, a testament to God's power. The clouds had thinned, allowing rays of sunshine through. The river glistened and a songbird trilled.

"Listen," said Eveleen. "Music for our wedding." She giggled, which he found more melodious than the bird.

They straightened and grew solemn.

"Dear God," Richard began, "we are before You here, on this day, to be joined together as man and wife. We come reverently, discreetly, advisedly, soberly, and in the fear of God—uh, You—duly considering the causes for which matrimony was ordained."

He looked at Eveleen, who nodded, and they turned to face each other. "I, Richard Jonathan Lynche, take thee, Eveleen ... uh ..."

"Scully."

"Eveleen Scully to be my wedded wife, to have and to hold from this day forward, for better for worse, for richer for poorer, in sickness and in health, to love and to cherish, till death do us part, according to God's holy ordinance; and thereto I plight thee my troth." Heart pounding, he bowed to Eveleen. "Now you."

She took in a deep breath, then spoke as lyrically as the songbird. "I, Eveleen Scully, take thee, Richard Lynche, to be me wedded husband, to have and to hold from this day forward, for better for worse, for ..." She looked to Richard and blushed, causing his heart to flip.

"For richer for poorer," he prompted.

"For richer for poorer, to love and to cherish, till death do us part, according to God's holy ordinance; and thereto I plight thee my troth."

"You forgot in sickness and in health."

"Oh. In sickness and in health." She blew out a puff of air.

Richard gasped. "I've no ring. I forgot about a ring."

"I'd not be able to wear it, if ye had one, now would I?" Her green eyes twinkled like the North Star.

He smiled, then lifted her left hand. "With this kiss, which stands in good stead for a ring, I thee wed, with my body, I thee worship, and with all my worldly goods, I thee endow: In the Name of the Father, and of the Son, and of the Holy Ghost. Amen."

He kissed her lightly on her finger, and then on her lips. "For we whom God hath joined together, let no man put asunder."

They both made the Sign of the Cross.

"We've done it!" Richard sighed. "Do you feel any different?" With a jolt, he noticed Eveleen was frowning. "Are you sorry already?"

"I didn't know that part was in there." Eveleen's lips were smiling, but her eyes were not.

"Which part?"

"Where ye endow me with all yer worldly goods. Ye should've left that out."

Richard chuckled. "Well, I have no worldly goods of my own at this point. But when I inherit from my father, our secret will be out, and ..."

"I have nothing, don't ye understand? Nothing to give in return." Then, her eyes lit up. "Except me maidenhood. 'Tis me greatest treasure, the dearest thing I own." She placed her hands on either side of his face. "Stolen or seduced, it has no value at all, but I give it to ye, freely, with all that's in me heart. That's what I have."

Richard bit his lip to stave off the tears that threatened. He kissed Eveleen deeply and hungrily, experiencing an ecstasy he had not known was possible. Then, he reached for her hand and led her to the soft grass beneath a small stand of trees.

⚜

Eveleen lay beside Richard covered in a thin sheen of sweat, in awe of all that occurred. She felt a bond with him unlike anything she'd ever imagined. Something sacred had happened to her—to them.

She looked at her new husband and was startled by tears rolling down his face. "Richard?"

"I'm sorry." He brushed his cheeks. "I'm ... overwhelmed, Eveleen. Overwhelmed by you, by your love, and by your most precious gift." He sniffed and faced her. "That was the most beautiful, the most—no words exist for what you've given me. I will never forget this day and how lovely you look at this moment."

Eveleen's own eyes filled as they kissed, not with the passion of earlier, but with great tenderness. Once they broke apart, they held hands and studied the sky. When reality could be pushed aside no longer, they sat up.

"It's late, my love," Richard said. "We risk too much if we don't get back soon."

"I know." Suddenly conscious of her nakedness, exposed to anyone who should stumble upon them, she snatched up her garments.

"I don't know how I'll wait the fortnight before we can meet again," Richard said, slipping on his shirt. "But I am more determined than ever to get us to Dublin where we can be together."

Eveleen was tying the string of her bodice when she heard a rustling. "Hush! Do ye hear someone?"

They both listened.

"A rabbit, I'd say," mumbled Richard. "Or a fox."

As though slapped, she awoke to a new awareness. Like crossing a field of briars hidden beneath a blanket of wildflowers, this peculiar, hallowed love would make her life so much more treacherous.

Chapter Eight

E veleen stayed behind again?" asked Fiona.

Four months after the fish scales incident, the servants huddled in the back of the wagon on their fortnightly trip to the village. Mrs. Bridge rode in the front with her husband, so the servants gossiped freely, though in a whisper.

"You'd think she'd be wanting a break from the place," Fiona went on.

Brea leaned in. "Maeve says she's too ashamed to come to town, poor as she is."

"I've no money meself, but I can still look around," said Elly.

Maeve raised her eyebrows and smirked. "Unless she's got something better going on at home."

"Like fishing?" said Brea, and they all giggled.

Mrs. Bridge turned in her seat, silencing the group. When she faced frontward once more, Maeve said, "Maybe 'tis a person, not a thing. You were there last time," she said to Fiona. "What'd ye see?"

"I saw Jack take the girl to the Multeen, and I saw her come back hours later with her catch," she answered. "That's all there was to see."

Maeve looked around before speaking, and they all leaned in, anticipating something juicy. "Maybe she's got her hellcat eyes on Jack, then."

There was an intake of breath as Brea and Elly covered their mouths. Tara and Fiona carefully raised their heads to be sure the Bridges hadn't heard.

"Watch yerself," Fiona cautioned.

Tara gave her a warning look, but Maeve ignored her. "Ol' Jack may be more of a man than ye think." Maeve made an exaggerated kissing sound that caused them all to crumble into laughter.

"Nearing town, we are, and I'll expect proper deportment from the lot of ye." Mrs. Bridge's tone froze each servant to the spot. Maeve looked up and saw with relief that the housekeeper had no clue what had set off their cackling.

"Ye'll have it, Mrs. Bridge," she said, as they all laughed soundlessly.

Maeve had kept a careful eye on Eveleen, especially when Mr. Richard was around, but he'd shown no interest in anything but whatever book or other he carried.

A late bloomer, she'd decided. Most fellows his age couldn't keep their eyes off her. Or their hands. Yet she might as well be a table or chair where the young master was concerned. Not even when she bent completely over, practically tumbling out of her bodice, did he give her more than a distracted glance.

Once in town, the wagon passed a small mob of lads who winked and whistled as they rode by. The other girls dipped their chins and peeked at the boys from under their lashes, careful to keep everything save the hint of a smile from their faces. Maeve, on the other hand, sneered and turned away with her head held high.

Old Will pulled the cart before the public house where he'd drain a few pints and soak up the town's latest gossip while his wife and the lasses shopped. The maids scrambled from the bed of the wagon, leaving Maeve the last to step out. She saw Fiona drooling before the milliner's window while Tara and Brea bustled off to ogle the newest fashions. Which neither of them could afford.

"No use for them lads, has ye?"

Maeve turned toward the raspy voice and found a foul be-draggled hag crouching in a heap against the pub. Her steely gray hair was frizzled and wild. In the middle of her bloated face were sunken eyes and cracked, purple lips. Yet her pale blue irises held a light, as though Maeve had somehow amused her.

The woman took a slug from a small flask. "Ye got something better, do ye? Is that what ye think?"

"What I got don't concern the likes of you," Maeve snapped. "Yer drunk."

The woman chuckled. "That I am, but I know you."

Maeve felt a tingling, an uneasiness inside her. She took a step back, but could not turn away. "Keep yer distance, with yer filth and disease. Ye've no better stench than the arse of a goat."

"Harsh words ye speak for all ye're looking at yerself in twenty years." With the back of her hand, she wiped the drool from her chin before taking another slurp from the bottle.

"To hell with ye!" An anxious nausea overcame Maeve as she spun on her heel.

"Yer young and sassy, as I was. Pretty too. But Lynche, the ol' one, not the one's there now, booted me outa his bed and onto the roads without so much as a 'thank ye for the ride.' Just like this one'll boot you."

The hag's screeching cackle sent a shiver from Maeve's neck to the soles of her feet. "Damn ye!" she called, glancing back.

"Damned? That I am," mumbled the hag, her eyes glassy now.

"Maeve, come look at the new combs at Walsh's," Brea jab-bered, racing toward her. "Ivory, they are. Fit for a queen."

Tara passed Brea, grabbed Maeve's arm, and hustled her down the street. "What are ye doing talking to the likes of that?"

With her head tilted, she peered at her sister. "In the name of God, what's going on? Ye look like death." She called back to the woman, "Go on with ye. Leave the young lasses be."

The woman lifted her bottle to Tara in a toast, and sucked the last drop of her elixir.

"Mother of God!" gasped Brea, who'd just noticed the wretched creature. "What did the old bat say to ye?"

Maeve squared her shoulders and lifted her chin. "Her? Why, nothing. She asked for a penny, is all. 'A penny?' I told her. 'I'd give ye a swift kick before I'd give ye a farthing, ye old fool.'" She shrugged. "She called me vulgar. Can ye believe the cheek on her? I'm vulgar?"

Well aware of Tara's sober stare, Maeve laughed along with Brea.

The woman was no more than a broken-down sot. Likely mad as well. Why, then, was she so flustered? She felt fidgety, as though a swarm of flies had invaded her body. "I know you," echoed through her brain without end.

"Are ye ill?" asked Brea, shaking her arm. "Did that witch back yonder spell ye?"

"Ha!" Maeve pulled herself up. "I'd like to see the witch who could spell me."

Tara glanced back at the woman and yanked her sister's arm. "Ye fool! No need to vex them what might be cozy with faeries and such."

Despite her tough words, Maeve felt a flutter up her spine. She held a healthy respect for the spirit world. Had she seen a witch's mark on the hag's withered left hand? She couldn't be sure. The houseflies buzzed within her as though crazed.

☦

Over the next weeks, Maeve shivered in cold spots around the house. Unexplained aches and pains pierced her thighs, her neck, and sides. She often woke in the darkest of night in a cold sweat, with the hideous face of the hag bedeviling her dreams. At these moments, Maeve would have sworn on the grave of Saint Patrick that the woman was indeed a witch. But in the light of day, among the chatter and giggles of the other girls, she chided herself for her fears.

☩

Standing in Sir Edward's study at the designated hour, Maeve sighed. Alone. Again. While their trysts had never been a daily or even a regular thing, it had been too many weeks since her master had joined her, his face leering and hungry.

She was uneasy. Although he was long in the tooth, his gluttonous appetites were without limit. Even when he became red-faced and unable to perform, he still required her to dance or carry out her duties unclothed.

Maeve prided herself on her mastery of men's cravings. She never believed she was his only source of amusement, but she did fancy herself the best. The crone's refrain continued to torture Maeve. "Just like this one'll boot you ..."

Then there was Mr. Richard, whom she'd so haughtily planned to seduce with his father's blessing. How long would he remain an innocent? Could he be one of them mollies? Maeve had heard of men who liked other men, but thought it a crude joke boys liked to tell. Another uncomfortable thought. She preferred to believe him slow to grow up, as some boys were.

Whatever the reason, she felt control over her world dissolving. If all her skills failed with father and son, she was doomed.

"... yer looking at yerself in twenty years."

What wouldn't she do to prevent that? Nothing. Her blood percolated with fury. There was nothing she wouldn't do.

Maeve had no doubt this was all Eveleen's doing. Things had been going her way until that cow showed up. Whenever the girl came to mind, Maeve relived the stings of fish scales pelting her face. Her heart thundered with pent-up rage. The disdain she held for her mealy-mouthed mother, her drunken sot of a father, and all the lewd, stinking ruffians who'd groped her so clumsily paled against her loathing of Eveleen.

She'd hoped to use her wiles to convince Sir Edward to discharge the little wench. What did he care who emptied the chamber pots? Any bogtrotter would do. But she'd not seen the raffish blackguard in two months and dared not make demands now if she did.

Something to take to Bridge herself was what she needed.

Then it came to her. She'd only been joking about the lass wooing Jack, but without a doubt, something was going on. A little nosing around would pull back the cover.

✟

On the next Sunday off, Maeve climbed onto the wagon with the other lasses. As the wheels plunged in and out of the ruts in the road, those familiar houseflies ran amok throughout her body. At each turn, Maeve grew more agitated, with images from her nightmares harrying her to the marrow of her bones.

She stared at the landscape, avoiding the others. She could not bear to behold that hag's face again, she realized. Or hear that voice—that harsh, rasping claptrap. She'd avoided the witch over the past weeks, but, each time, feared a new confrontation. She breathed deeply to ward off the tears that threatened to spill. No more than an old sot, she reassured herself. But when Brea touched her shoulder, she flinched as though struck.

Brea's brow wrinkled with worry. "Are ye well, then?"

Not far from the courtyard, Maeve thought she would pop. "I'm not well. Not at all." She called to Old Will. "Stop the wagon! I'm getting off."

As Will pulled on the reins, Tara leaned forward. "By God, what are ye doing?"

Maeve scrambled over the side before the horses came to a complete stop.

"Whoa, whoa—what's this?" Will called.

"I'm ailing," Maeve answered from the side of the road. "I'll spend the afternoon on me pallet, resting while I've got the chance."

Tara frowned. "Ye'll not come to town?"

"Go on yerself," Maeve answered. "I need rest."

As the wagon lumbered off, Maeve patted her belly, signaling to Tara that her monthlies had come. Her sister nodded.

Maeve took a deep breath, slowing her heartbeat. The houseflies came to rest. Meandering back to the manor house, she smiled. She'd not be curled up on her pallet today.

Avoiding the open courtyard, Maeve wended her way toward the path to the Multeen, making sure she wasn't seen by Jack or Timothy in the barn nor by Elly in the house. Every nerve in her body was on full alert. Not with the terror she'd felt earlier, but with eagerness and high hopes that her greatest desire would be granted.

We'll see what yer about now, Eveleen, she thought. Lady Nancy had a strict "no followers" rule. Just meeting some bloke from the countryside was cause for dismissal. The more Maeve had thought about it, the surer she was that Eveleen indeed had a fellow she was meeting at the river.

She moved slowly with her slippers in hand to avoid rustling branches or leaves. She could not risk scaring the lovers away. Feeling a light brush on her forearm, she looked down to find a butterfly with blood red wings and blue spot that nearly glowed. She breathed softly so it would not fly off. After a moment, the beautiful creature flitted into the trees.

Maeve tilted her head. She heard whispers. She almost giggled aloud as she crept closer to the clearing. Noticing movement, she dropped to a crouch in the brush. It wasn't by the river, either. Eveleen's poles and basket lay unattended beside the rushing water.

She nearly clapped with glee at the sight of two figures slinking in the grass beneath some trees. A large bush gave Maeve only a partial view.

She could wait all afternoon. The butterfly—it was an omen. Her luck was finally turning.

The pair was rising. Maeve held her breath, anxious to identify the hussy and the clodhopper with her.

Finally, a figure emerged, tucking his shirt into his breeches. He turned, and before her stunned, disbelieving eyes, stood Mr. Richard, her ticket to the life she craved. Sidling up to him, tying her bodice, was the harlot she loathed more than any person on the face of the earth.

Chapter Nine

Biddy placed the protective toile around Lady Nancy's shoulders, then lifted her favorite rosewood brush.

Her mistress picked up a teacake. "Take your time this morning, Biddy. Your brushing so relaxes me."

"That I will, milady." Gently untangling the long locks, Biddy studied the graying strands. The gentlewoman was aging before her eyes. Her heart ached for her mistress.

The chamber doors struck the wall with a crash, announcing another unwelcome visit from Sir Edward. He strode across the floor, proclaiming, "I have good news for you, madam. And for you as well, Biddy."

Biddy curtsied, alarmed at the cruel smirk the master wore. He seemed to relish torturing his poor wife, and her reliance on elixirs and tonics grew with his malice. Lady Nancy steeled her back, but the fear in her eyes belied her bold manner.

Sir Edward went on. "I have just received word from your illustrious father that he is happy to accept your request for a fortnight's visit." He paused. "Well, he didn't use the word 'happy.' He said you could come."

His cutting tone infuriated Biddy.

Lady Nancy's eyebrows rose. "I made no such request."

"No?" Sir Edward asked. "Oh. That's right. It was I who requested he welcome home his beloved daughter."

"Edward, I have no desire to make such a journey. In case you've not noticed, I am unwell and not up to such a trip. Richard has three more weeks under the tutelage of Father Healy and he will be unable to accompany—"

"Richard will not be accompanying you. I need him here with me. Biddy will escort you."

Lady Nancy grew crimson. "That is out of the—"

Sir Edward snorted and his voice became oily. "Nothing, my dear, is out of the question. You have no say in this. Do you forget, Lady, that I am your husband and lord and you will do as I command?"

With wide eyes and a shrill voice, Lady Nancy cried, "How dare you!"

His hard, determined glare caused her to quickly change tack. "Edward, don't do this. I am your wife. You cannot send me off like some recalcitrant servant."

"Actually, I can." He tilted his head. "My, my. All this fuss because you must visit your magnificent family. I thought you'd be pleased. Maybe you and your father can share memories of your dear, demented mother."

With this, Lady Nancy lost all semblance of decorum. Leaping from her seat, she jostled the teapot, dumping its contents to the floor. In a rush toward her husband, she skidded on the spilled tea and crumpled in a heap before Biddy. As the maid bent to help her up, Lady Nancy scrambled across the room on her hands and knees and latched onto Sir Edward's arm with both hands.

"You can't send me there. I'll do anything. Anything, Edward. Please!"

Biddy shrank back in horror. Never had she seen her mistress in such a debased and wretched state.

"What do you want from me?" she pleaded as though mad. "More children? I thought Richard was enough, but maybe I was wrong. I'll have another child, Edward. I'll do that for you. I will."

Sir Edward peeled her hands from his arms and shoved her to the floor. His face grew dark and threatening, causing a shiver down Biddy's spine.

A demon, he was. A savage brute. Her heart pounded in fear. Then she saw a flash of something in his eyes. Pain? Sorrow? Maybe not.

He spoke in quiet, measured tones. "Now you offer yourself to me? After all this time? Once I would have ridden to China and back for the pleasure of your hand upon my cheek, but you scoffed. You turned me out, as though my attentions were more vile than you could stomach."

With nothing but venom in his eyes, he shook his head back and forth. "It's far, far too late, Lady Nancy. Now you disgust me equally as much."

He turned on his heel and left.

The lady remained in a heap on the floor, sobbing from somewhere deep in her gut. "I want to die," she cried over and over. "Please let me die."

✠

Mrs. Bridge was surprised to find herself summoned to Sir Edward's study. There, her master informed her that Sir Nathaniel Moore and his son, Alistair, of County Waterford would be spending a week at Duncullen.

"I have taken it upon myself to speak to Biddy," he said. "She and Lady Nancy will visit the FitzAden Estate while the gentlemen are here."

Her pompous employer disgusted Mrs. Bridge with his missing teeth and frizzled gray hair. His once-elegant nose now wore a jungle of red and purple veins brought on by the drink, his unquenchable thirst for the rum-shrub.

If I was the lady, I'd run home to me folks, too, with the goat of a husband she's got, she thought. Yet, her face reflected nothing.

"Lady Moore, of course, will not be accompanying her husband and son, so all arrangements should go through me."

"All to yer liking, sir." *With his wife away, he could carry on with his free and easy ways.* Wearing her well-rehearsed wooden expression, she asked, "And will young Mr. Richard be joining her?"

Sir Edward lifted his eyes and sneered. "Of course not, you clodpate. He's the entire point of the visit." He returned to his papers and mumbled, "Without his simpering mother hovering about, perhaps we can make a man of him."

Though rich and powerful, Mrs. Bridge had never seen a more ignorant person. Oh, he could run a manor and keep accounts. He spoke fine words, they said, in the Parliament meetings. But he knew naught of manliness, and even less of what it meant to be a proper husband and father.

He was a fine one for the corruption of young girls, though. She knew that all too well. *Poor, stupid Maeve.* She thought herself so clever. What else would be going on behind a locked door with a lecher like Sir Edward? And her with the cocksure attitude. She had no idea how quickly she'd become yesterday's scrapings.

Back in the kitchen, Mrs. Bridge and Orla were preparing a menu for the upcoming visit, one the housekeeper would present to Sir Edward, ignoring the rightful role of Lady Nancy.

"'Tisn't decent." Orla shook her head as they worked. "I don't like the feel of it at all. Never in all me days have I seen a household where the lady is so scorned."

"Nor I," said Mrs. Bridge, her voice low. "I feel like Judas himself when I speak to him, creeping into the den of the Pharisees for me thirty pieces. The man is the devil."

Orla's usually kind eyes darkened. "No good can come of this. Mark me words. No good will come of this."

As though conjured by Orla's words, Biddy burst through the kitchen door. "Another vial of laudanum, Orla. Lady Nancy will be needing it."

"Get Biddy a dipper of water, Orla," Mrs. Bridge said, though she was unsure the girl's trembling hands could hold it.

After Orla brought Biddy the cup of water, the three huddled around the table while Biddy recounted the tragic scene she'd witnessed.

"I would not have guessed the gentry could feel so very keenly," said Biddy, dark circles surrounding her watery eyes. "'Twas a pitiful sight. I gave her the last of her laudanum and put her to bed."

"What happened?" prodded Orla.

"Sir Edward barged into the room like he does and proclaimed good news," Biddy said. "But I saw the look of him. 'Tis little wonder the lady is needing more and more of the elixir the way he tortures her." Biddy pulled a handkerchief from her pocket and dabbed her tear-filled eyes.

Mrs. Bridge's voice shook with anger. "I just come from the old pismire. He wants rid of her, is what, whilst he has fun with his cronies."

Biddy went on. "When she told the old man Mr. Richard couldn't make the trip, he told her Mr. Richard's not to go. 'He is needed here with me,' were his very words."

"To learn a bit of manhood, he says," Mrs. Bridge added. "And who is here to teach him that?"

Orla sniffed and nodded.

Mrs. Bridge rolled her head back and saw Tara, standing still as a stone wall by the door. "What are ye doing, girl, listening where ye don't belong?"

Orla reached behind her for the broom, ran around the table, and swung wildly at the scullery maid. "Get yer rump back to work. Ye've no better sense than to sneak around yer betters? Off with ye, 'fore I have ye flogged!"

After Tara flew from the kitchen, Orla returned to the others. "She's like a weasel, creeping here and there, up to no good."

Biddy's eyes glazed with tears that spilled into rivulets down her cheeks. She wound her handkerchief through her fingers. "Lady Nancy begged that man—begged, I tell ye—like a pauper for a scrap of food. It broke me heart to see it, and 'twas all I could do to stand by without pulling her away, saving herself from this shame."

Mrs. Bridge's eyes, too, welled with tears. Her head began to pound.

"But he left her there," Biddy said, "like she was no more than a useless cur."

With closed eyes, Orla shook her head. "Jesus give me patience; Mary restrain me tongue."

"I gave her the rest of the laudanum and put her to bed, then stayed with her 'til she slept."

Orla sighed, pushed her heavy body from the table, and waddled to the small glazed crock near the fire. "The poppies are about ready. The opium's near sweated out."

"I doubt things will be much better when she wakes," Biddy said. "Can ye have some ready by then?"

"I can," Orla answered. "Mrs. Bridge, would ye tell Mr. Hogan 'tis a bottle of wine we'll be needing to blend it?"

Mrs. Bridge nodded. "So much pain. So much suffering. Where can it lead but to more of our own private hell?"

84

✠

Richard was rattled. His mother's wretched pleas were heartbreaking, but what was he to do?

"He's sending me off." His mother's eyes were weak and watery. "I'm to leave in five days, never to return."

"Of course, you're returning." He tried to sound comforting, but her constant harping on the topic was wearing thin.

She sat up straighter and glared at him, her voice shrill. "I've tried to spare you the ugly details, son, of what became of Grandmother. You were a mere child when she was stashed away in that horrific place."

Her words set his teeth on edge. "I remember her."

She leaned forward in her chair with bulging eyes. "Day in and day out, she was fed only water and bread. Excuse my crudity, but she was then forced to disgorge every morsel." Her lower lip trembled. "'Flushing the illness out' was the doctor's excuse and Grandfather, being ignorant of such things, believed him."

In his studies, Richard had learned the importance of balance in the animal spirits. He suspected the doctor was trying to drain his grandmother's nervous fluids.

"And the bleeding! She withered away in that place, pleading with me all the while to get her out." She focused on her hands, each massaging the other. "And I did nothing. I knew not what to do, so I did nothing."

She began to weep, her shoulders bobbing up and down. "She perished there, lonely and forsaken." Then she cracked her knuckles, making Richard's skin crawl.

"Please stop that, Mother." In as soothing a voice as he could muster, he told her once again, "Father is not sending you to an asylum. You are visiting Grandfather and your sisters. If you were to go to a madhouse, Father would not hide the information. He'd gleefully torture you with it—and me, as well."

He sat on the end of her longue and took her hand. "On the bright side, this may be an opportune time to ask Grandfather about supporting my education—in case Father reneges."

Snatching her hand back, Lady Nancy leaned forward and slapped Richard's face with startling strength. Falling back into her chair, she clenched her fists as though hoping to rip her palms open with her fingernails.

"Get out! Get out!"

Shaken, Richard leapt from the chair and backed away from his mother, mumbling, "What did I do?" His hands shook as he rang the bell.

Biddy bustled in and made straight for her mistress. Lady Nancy latched onto her maid and blubbered into her shoulder. "He hates me, too. They all despise me."

Richard tried to speak, but Biddy shook her head. "There's nothing to say, Mr. Richard. I've got her now."

For the first time, Richard pondered his mother's sanity. Could what he'd always attributed to her miserable marriage be an affliction of the spleen? Educated gentlemen commonly believed disorders of the spleen created a pronounced melancholy in those of aristocratic birth.

How could a barbarian like Father understand the sensitivities of his betters? he thought.

The arrogant simpleton was driving his mother to delusion, no longer capable of reason. Richard's blood simmered. He had to go to Trinity before he met the same fate. Only his clandestine meetings with Eveleen, more frequent now, kept him sane.

⚘

He and his mother spoke little until her departure. With sallow skin and sunken eyes, she seemed to have aged over these last days.

"Enjoy yourself, Mother," he said, helping her into her carriage. "Away from Father, with your own kind, you can rest and become more yourself."

"More reasonable, you mean? More sane?"

"Yes. Wouldn't that be nice?"

Her eyes frosted. He had said the wrong thing.

"There's no reason to concern yourself with me, Richard." She settled into her seat across from Biddy and stared ahead.

Richard sighed, closed the carriage door, and stepped away. She needed him. He should be with her, he realized, rather than humoring his father and his boorish cronies, Sir Nathaniel Moore and his beast of a son. He remembered Alistair from his days at Clonmel Grammar. Always the instigator, Alistair had found Richard an easy pawn. If he noticed him at all.

His heart ached at the sight of his mother's carriage lumbering down the road from Duncullen. While he was certain he'd see her in a fortnight, he couldn't shake the feeling that he'd lost something very dear.

⊕

Two days later, Hogan knocked on his chamber door, then entered. "Your guests are arriving, sir," he said, dressed in his finery. "Sir Edward has requested your company on the portico to welcome Sir Nathaniel and his son."

Richard nodded to the butler, excusing the most scrupulous, most loyal servant Duncullen had ever had. Loyal to his father, at least.

He moaned. This was another of Sir Edward's vulgar attempts to fix him, to mold him into the son he'd always wanted, a beastly chip off the old block. If it were a just world, Richard could join the scholars at Trinity College to pore over ancient texts, explore modern thought, and discuss the writings of Dr. Jonathan Swift with the great man's contemporaries.

Dean Swift had died five short years past, "a raving lunatic," his father claimed. "It was all that reading and thinking that brought on the madness," he derided. "I'd say with your mother's demented blood coursing your veins, you dare not risk it. You've all the education needed to take on the titles and rule the lands I've claimed in our name. But you've a damn long way to go before you can fill my boots."

Richard burned at the memory of his father's rant. He'd have loved to ask him what it took to pronounce which thick-skulled tenant owned the disputed chickens or to determine the penalty for pummeling a neighbor during a drunken brawl. What skills were required to guzzle rum-shrub and shout obscenities while watching animals mutilate each other? Or to hump every whore in the countryside?

And now this visit from Moore, the Elder and Younger, designed to force Richard to accompany Alistair on the Grand Tour of Europe, a trip supposedly designed to educate, but more often an excuse for drunkenness and debauchery. No wonder his father was anxious to send him.

Shortly before the midday meal, the Moore coachman pulled their elegant carriage up to the front steps while Richard stood dutifully beside his parent. His father reached out to grab Richard's shoulder for, he assumed, one last sarcastic bit of instruction.

With no noticeable change in his bearing, he slid to the left, just out of his father's reach. He fixed his gaze on the emerging guests, but could feel the rage radiating from the old man's frame. With the Moores climbing the steps, there was no recourse but to maintain decorum. Richard smiled inwardly and stood a little taller.

How did that feel, you old bastard?

Moore the Elder was the same height as Sir Edward, about five and a half feet, with a distinguished, yet fleshy face. He was somewhat portly but cut a fine figure in his well-tailored clothing.

His son, the Younger, towered over him. While Richard had only exceeded his father's height by a few inches, this fellow was nearly six feet. Richard remained thin and gangly, yet his counterpart had already filled out to a more muscular frame.

The older men grasped one another's hands. "Sir Nathaniel," Sir Edward said, "welcome."

"Sir Edward, your servant," he responded, dipping his head. "May I present my son, Mr. Alistair Moore, the Defender of Mankind."

The Younger bowed to Sir Edward, then clasped Richard's right hand with a grip designed to strangle more than greet.

"I jest, but Alistair, in fact, does mean Defender of Mankind," Sir Nathaniel said. "Which is precisely why I chose it."

Smiling, Sir Edward said, "And rightly so. Look at the lad. A Greek hero in the flesh." His look soured. "And this is Mr. Richard Lynche, named for the Lionheart, but we refer to him as Richard the Li-brarian."

His father howled at his cruel joke which brought a crooked smile to Alistair's face, but Sir Nathaniel merely nodded.

Instead of the usual shame he felt at his father's remarks, Richard's blood boiled. Who did these dullards think they were to judge him? His father's ignorance spoke for itself, but Richard remembered with spiteful satisfaction Alistair's fumbling to read the simplest words and his total inability to grasp basic Latin. Now, the dunce's entire arm trembled with the effort to pulverize the bones in Richard's hand. And he was succeeding. At last, the brute released him with a sickening, self-satisfied smile.

Richard refused to stand silently before a nincompoop like Alistair Moore. "Well done, then. To you goes the first laurel wreath."

All laughing and talking stopped. Alistair's eyes narrowed.

Richard smiled under the glare of the others' grim faces. "You win the first event," he explained. "The Handgrip Competition. That's the purpose of this visit, isn't it? A Greek Olympics of sorts to see who's the better man?"

Sir Edward's face was scarlet. His balled fists turned his knuckles white.

"May we be shown to our rooms?" Sir Moore's icy tone further chilled the reception.

Hogan stepped forward. "Follow me, sirs," he said and the two Moores immediately did so.

Sir Edward turned on his son. "In my study," were his only words. His raspy voice chafed Richard's tightly drawn nerves.

Once there, Hogan brought a mug of rum-shrub that had been prepared for the visit. "Your guests have been given like refreshment, milord," he said. Nothing was brought for Richard.

"Well done," his father said. He guzzled the punch and thrust his empty mug toward Hogan, who took it, bowed, and closed the door as he left.

"You little son of a bitch." Sir Edward's teeth bared like a wolf poised for attack. "Your life has been one mortification to me after another. If not for your high brow and Lynche nose, I'd wager my life your mother had screwed a troll."

"I'm sorry my attempt at humor offended you." Richard's voice was breathy as he struggled to draw in air, but part of him remembered the power he felt when he spoke to Alistair. Maybe, despite his father's wrath, it was worth it.

His answer, however, ignited his father's rage even further, turning the rest of his face as purple as his nose. It looked like his head might burst.

Out of nowhere, Richard pictured Sir Edward's head splitting like an overripe tomato. An urge to laugh seized him. This could not be happening. A snort escaped his nose.

"You flaccid little bastard!" Sir Edward drew his right arm as far over his chest as he could reach, and whipped it with all his might across Richard's face. The crack knocked the boy to the floor where his head swam and his vision blurred.

"Get up. Get up and hit me, you woman!"

Richard mustered his senses and became aware of a sharp, stinging pain on his cheek. He lifted his hand to inspect the area. It came away red and sticky.

Sir Edward had his fists raised, repeating his taunts when Richard saw the crimson-stained ring that had gashed his face. The ornate gold ring had many sharp edges and featured a cut ruby at its center. His father told all it was passed down to him from an illustrious grandfather, but Richard knew the truth. Sir Edward had bought it himself at a London antiques shop.

"You're not man enough, are you? Your only weapon is your moronic tongue. I've a mind to cut it out with a gelding knife." Sir Edward kicked Richard's side, prompting him to fight.

"Milord! Sir Edward, please. Allow me to see to your son." Hogan appeared before Richard with a handkerchief and pressed it to his cheek. "This wound is quite deep. With your permission, we'll take him immediately to Will Bridge." Without waiting for a response, he went to the door and called for the footman, Samuel.

Richard lifted his eyes to his father whose face still burned red, but whose fists had dropped to his sides. In a strange, dreamlike moment, an image flashed of his father's dead, bloated body dangling from a rope, his skin ashen, his mouth agape. He was not hanging from the gallows like criminals he'd seen executed in Clonmel, but from the rafters of their own stable. Then it faded.

"What are you staring at, you bloody idiot?" Sir Edward growled.

Richard didn't answer. He was stunned by—what was that? A vision, a hallucination, a premonition? Or was it a sign of the lunacy Sir Edward insisted was flowing through his veins?

Chapter Ten

Will ran his finger over the blade of a scythe, testing the fine edge he'd honed. With the roar of his name, the tool sliced his finger. "Blast!" he yelled, shaking off the blood as he ran toward the barn's door.

Samuel worked mostly as a groom, but was called to the Big House whenever a tall, fine-figured footman was needed. Usually a calm, mellow sort, the urgency in his voice alarmed Will.

"I can walk on my own, Samuel," Mr. Richard was saying, but the groom-turned-footman would not release the young master's arm.

"A mishap, Old Will, in need of yer attention." Samuel's voice shook as he steered the lad through the door.

Will took over for Samuel and sat Mr. Richard on a bale of hay. "Well, what's all this?"

The boy was as pale as newly-washed fleece, a bloody handkerchief pressed to his cheek. To Will, he looked like a wretched puppy who'd just been whipped and wondered why.

Will peeled the cloth from the wound and gasped. A deep tear, still dripping blood, had opened the boy's cheek practically ear to mouth. A large bruise had begun to cover the right side of his face.

"By the Holy Baby Jesus in his cradle, what went on here?" He looked to Samuel.

The lad's eyes were wild, glancing from Will to Mr. Richard and back again, but he said nothing.

Will sighed. "Man, fetch me Jack. He's a good one to help. Then get yerself back to the Big House. Mr. Hogan'll be missing ye."

After Samuel fled the barn, Will turned to Mr. Richard. "What happened, son?" He pulled his own handkerchief from his pocket and dabbed the wound.

The boy flinched. "I made a joke, Old Will. A stupid joke." A solitary tear escaped each eye. "My own father hates me. Hates the very air I dare to breathe." He stuttered as he inhaled. "What's the use? Why go on?"

"Hush, Mr. Richard," Will muttered. "That's foolish, sinful talk. Where would yer ma be without ye? Or Jack? Yer his one true friend."

"My own father bashed me with the back of his hand, slicing me with that blasted ring."

"'Tis a bad one, I'm afraid. Ah, Jack, there ye be. We've some doctoring to do on Mr. Richard here. First, I'll be needing a bucket of clean water."

Jack stood in the doorway, agog. "Mr. Richard, what's wrong? Did ye fall off Black Bess? Please don't beat her."

"Jack!" Will's tone was sharper than he meant it to be. "Enough jabbering. We need water now."

"I'll get it." He lumbered off, returning within minutes with a pail of clear, cool water.

Will swished his handkerchief in it. "Go to the Big House, Jack. Tell Orla ye need to see yer ma without delay. Tell her we've an emergency, son, but say nothing to no one else. Do ye understand?"

"I do," he answered. His eyebrows and mouth drooped as he stared at Mr. Richard.

Will wrung the cloth. "Tell yer ma to make haste. We need her here."

Jack nodded and bolted from the stable. Will winced along with Richard as he gently cleansed the injury. Shaking his head, he said, "This jagged gash won't heal well. I'll stitch it up, but it'll scar, to be sure."

Mr. Richard's pallor betrayed his pain. Yet, the corners of his lips rose when he said, "If only my father had sliced me cleanly."

Will's shoulders fell. He wanted to say something, but would not belittle his master. Sir Edward was still the boy's father, after all. Though he'd be damned if he acted like one.

Mrs. Bridge ran up behind him, followed closely by Jack. "Will—ah, Jesus, Mary, Joseph, and the wee donkey!"

"Guard yer tongue, Noreen." At times like these, Will knew she couldn't hide the disgust in her voice. "Mr. Richard is going to need a few stitches for this gash. Go to Hogan and tell him 'tis wine I'll be needing to wash it out. Then round up some silk threads."

"The whiskey, too," she said. "Ye'll be wanting a healthy swig of that, Mr. Richard." She waved Will to the side, out of earshot of the others. "What am I to tell Hogan of this?"

"He knows."

"Just as I feared. 'Twas the old scoundrel, then."

Old Will placed his hand on his wife's shoulder and looked her in the eye. "Take Hogan aside, away from the guests as soon as ye can."

They looked up to find Jack had pulled a stool beside Mr. Richard and sat with his arm around the young master's shoulders. Even though it was forbidden, Jack peered into Mr. Richard's eyes and whispered to him as he would a frightened calf. Mr. Richard looked at his hands, but occasionally glanced at Jack and nodded.

"Will ye look at that?" Noreen had tears in her eyes. She put her lips to Will's ears. "And him with a blackguard for a father the likes I've never seen. I can stand no more of this, Will. The old fool's wife is hastened away in a stupor and now this. He's about ripped the lad's face off." Her voice was becoming shrill.

Will pulled his wife into a tight hug and hushed her. Please, darlin', none of yer headaches now, he mentally pleaded. "Ye must be calm," he said. "Me heart is broken, too, for we can do so little, but even Jack can bring comfort." They turned to watch their son. "He's a fine lad."

Noreen Bridge brushed Will's cheek. "A heart of gold, he has, like you." And off she went to do her part in the Big House.

Returning to tend Mr. Richard, Will stopped dead. The lad was gazing, trance-like, at the rafters, wearing a look of horror.

✦

Richard lay on a small cot in Old Will's cabin.

He had guzzled a couple shots of his father's whiskey while the overseer cleaned his wound and sewed it together. It stung, to be sure, as the needle wove its way in and out of his cheek, but the spirits dulled his senses enough to make it bearable.

When Will had finished, he encouraged Richard to rest in his cabin as long as he was permitted. It was anyone's guess what Sir Edward would demand.

Richard was grateful to have been left alone the entire afternoon. Mostly, he slept. When awake, he realized, at least for today, he was glad his mother was away. Her frenzy over this incident would have become high drama from which the family reputation would never recover.

Hogan came to the cabin to check on him, ordered to make a proper report to the old man, most likely. Richard's mind was muddled and, while Hogan and Will whispered near the door, he kept his eyes closed. He couldn't bring himself to care what his father thought or wanted. Then, oddly, he sensed someone approach the cot, stop, and pet his head. As the person walked away, Richard opened his eyes to slits. He was stunned to see it was Hogan.

In the late afternoon, Samuel appeared with a clean set of clothing. "Mr. Richard," he said, "begging yer pardon, but yer father requires yer presence at the evening meal."

"Thank you, Samuel," he answered, his speech slurred.

The footman bowed and left the cabin.

Old Will helped him up. "Yer well enough, Mr. Richard. We'll set ye right."

Seated on the edge of the cot, Richard's head pounded. The entire right side of his face ached and the sewn-up gash burned. He felt as though he'd been beaten with a stick.

Old Will smiled. "Yer face is swelled up some. I'm afraid yer not going to be the dapper fella ye used to be."

Richard tried to smile back, but his face wouldn't cooperate. "I'll not be able to eat."

"Soup it'll be for a day or two."

Once ready, Samuel reappeared to escort him to the Manor House.

Though his head was still swimming, Richard stopped the footman from taking his arm. "I'll not appear before my father held like a cripple."

Looking sheepish, Samuel backed off.

His father and the guests were assembled at the table when Richard arrived. Samuel held his chair as he sat, then left.

Sir Nathaniel and Alistair could not hide their shock at his condition. "For the love of God, you've made a proper mess of yourself, lad," said Sir Nathaniel.

Richard nodded, wondering what to say. The servants brought various foods and set them on the table. A tureen of soup took the center surrounded by stewed trout, roasted wild duck, fried rabbit, and plum pudding, none of which Richard could eat.

Hogan and Samuel began serving, offering Sir Edward and the Moores each of the dishes. Richard was grateful Samuel filled his bowl with soup and left it at that.

"My son is not only a clumsy oaf when he speaks," Sir Edward said. "He cannot even walk across the room without stumbling." He turned to Richard. "Isn't that right?"

Richard was briefly confused, but recovered. "Yes, sir," he said, as clearly as he was able.

"We were conversing in my study when the clod tripped over the carpet and sprawled into the corner of my desk," Sir Edward went on, lying shamelessly. Then he snorted at the sheer imbecility of his son.

He's fooling no one, Richard thought. Well, maybe Alistair. Sir Nathaniel would not even look at Sir Edward, focusing on his own plate instead.

Alistair glanced at Richard and smirked. "You've got some blood on your face." He pointed to the stitched wound.

Richard blotted the spot with the tablecloth. The pain was overpowering. "Samuel, a glass of whiskey." If he had to sit there, he would take his relief where he could get it.

All, including Samuel, looked at him in surprise. This was not routine for an evening of this nature. Sir Edward snarled, then opened his mouth to speak.

"Say, old man," Sir Nathaniel said, "surely you don't object to the lad having a nip or two after the day he's had. He's in the company of gentlemen, after all."

Sir Edward grunted.

It's genius, Richard thought. If his father was so fired to make a man of him, could he now, in front of his friends, chide him as a child when he asked for whiskey? Sir Nathaniel shot Richard a glance with a twinkle in his eye.

Alistair, on the other hand, may have had the physique of a Greek god, but he had the intellect of a goat herder. "I'll have a glass as well," he said. He seemed to think this was the next event in the Virility Olympics.

Normally, Hogan stood at his station near the sideboard and blended into the wallpaper. Richard was startled, therefore, to find the butler glaring at him without his usual mask. Hogan was shaking his head in a way only Richard could see.

The impudence! was Richard's first reaction, but that was replaced with confusion. He remembered the petting of his head in Old Will's cabin. Hogan risked the most severe reprimand if caught by Sir Edward or if Richard called him out. He didn't know what to think.

Samuel deposited a glass of the amber liquid before him. "Your drink, Mr. Richard." Then he set one before Alistair. "And for you, Mr. Alistair."

Richard caught a look between the servants that seemed to relax Hogan. Lifting his glass, Richard sipped the whiskey. It was harsh, yet soothing.

Alistair glared at Richard. Then, with drink in hand, he toasted the gathering and guzzled it down. Satisfied, he plopped the glass onto the table. "Aahhh. The water of life."

Sir Nathaniel frowned. "Careful, son," he said. "It's best to sip it as Richard is doing."

"Come now, Moore," said Sir Edward. "A whopping young lad like that can handle his liquor. Samuel, fix us all one. Another for Alistair." He looked at Richard's glass. "Drink it down. You want to be a man. Drink like one."

Richard gulped the rest of his whiskey, then held his glass up for Samuel. Within minutes, he felt a wash of relaxation. His facial pain didn't disappear, but eased to where he could think of other things. Amidst the talking and laughing, Samuel and Hogan served the next round.

When Hogan leaned over with Richard's glass, he whispered, "Beware. Hair of the dog, sir."

"What in God's name are you doing?" roared Sir Edward, rising to his feet. "What did you say to the boy?"

Hogan's face stiffened into his usual mask. "Beg pardon, sir. I reminded the young master of the whiskeys he drank before his surgery earlier today. 'Hair of the dog,' I told him." He bowed and stepped back from the table.

"I've never seen such brazen behavior," his father railed. "You forget yourself."

"You're quite correct, Hogan," Sir Nathaniel interrupted. "Those drinks will bring the booziness right back."

Richard took a long swig of his drink. He was in a dreamlike state; he could not see or hear clearly.

"Aaahhhh," Alistair said loud enough that all would notice he'd drained another glass of spirits. Samuel rushed to refill it.

"Good ol' Alstilair," Richard mumbled. "Winner of the drinking compe—, uh, matchup." He looked up to see all were staring at him. "Did I say that aloud?"

"Get him out of here," he heard his father bellow. "He's a disgrace."

Chapter Eleven

The dream was frightful. In it, his da had ordered Jack into the paddock to calm the raging roan as it leapt and reared. Sir Edward stood by, cross-armed, waiting to ride. But once Jack climbed the fence, the creature's eyes lit up with fire and charged him at full speed. Frozen with fear, he curled into a ball and waited to be trampled.

With a grasp on his shoulder, Jack awakened with a whoop. His da, Old Will, chuckled. "Ye were having a beauty of a dream, lad."

Jack stumbled from his pallet and rubbed his eyes. A mere hint of the sun touched the horizon.

His ma stoked the fire for breakfast. "Will, go up and check on Mr. Richard's stitches now, before the family and guests are up. Hogan says he had a ghastly night."

After Will nodded and left, she kneaded the dough for their soda farls. Noreen Bridge usually served the fried bread circles with butter and jam, but Jack liked his with honey.

"Son, I need ye at the Big House today, for a while at least. Mr. Richard has been puking all night. Samuel and Mr. Hogan took turns nursing him, but now they must see to their duties." His ma petted his cheek. "Ye'll nurse Mr. Richard for me, won't ye? I can't very well send a young maid to do it, now can I?"

"I will," he promised. "Mr. Richard is me friend."

Noreen Bridge smiled. "That he is."

Jack had been worried about Mr. Richard since Da'd stitched him up yesterday. A nasty gash, that one. It had hurt his heart to see it. "Why did the master hit him like that?"

His mother's head snapped up. "Keep yer gob shut about that, Jack. 'Tis family business and none of ours. If ye speak of it, there's trouble in it for ye. Do ye hear me?"

"I hear ye."

Her voice softened. "Besides, it might embarrass Mr. Richard. Hurt his feelings. Ye wouldn't want to do that, would ye?"

"I wouldn't. Mr. Richard is me friend."

He could never upset Mr. Richard, who talked to him, even shared some of his secrets. Like fishing with that pretty girl, Eveleen. Most people told Jack to do things and expected him to obey—and he did, but Mr. Richard asked him questions and listened to the answers. Jack smiled. Mr. Richard knew he wasn't as dumb as people thought, that sometimes he had real smart things to say.

✠

Samuel leapt to his feet when Jack entered the young master's bedchambers. "He's been asleep a couple of hours. The worst may be behind him, poor fella."

They both looked at Mr. Richard's pale, haggard form. Samuel shook his head. "He sure can't hold his liquor," he whispered, then poked Jack in the chest. "Now don't let no one in except me or Mr. Hogan. We'll be by to see how he's doing."

After the footman slid out the door, Jack took his post beside Mr. Richard's bed. He stared into his sleeping friend's face. A deep purple bruise covered the right side from his high cheekbone to his jaw. The tear was gruesome, but the stitches had held. The shadowy skin around his eyes probably came from the puking.

Before long, Jack's breathing matched his best friend's, relaxing his entire body. His eyelids grew heavy.

"Is that you, Jack?"

He lurched in his seat. "Oh. That it is, Mr. Richard." Shamefully, he'd fallen asleep and neglected his duty. "Are ye in need, sir?"

"The chamber pot."

When Mr. Richard finished, Jack slid it under the bed to be emptied later. "How are ye feeling, then?"

"Better. The sleep did me some good. I need water, though."

Jack poured a glassful from the pitcher on the table. Mr. Richard gulped it down, then flopped back onto his pillow. Once Jack retrieved the empty cup, the two sat in silence.

"Yesterday was a bad day," Mr. Richard pronounced at last.

"I'm sorry for it, sir, that I am."

"I know you are, Jack. You have a pure heart. A rare thing, it seems." Mr. Richard's eyes grew cloudy as he leaned in closer. "I had a strange vision. I don't know what else to call it."

Jack waited while Mr. Richard's nostrils flared and his lips pursed. He wanted to think of the right words, a struggle Jack understood.

"I saw my father hanging by a rope in the stable. Dead."

Jack gasped. "Is that what ye saw yesterday, looking up as ye were?"

"Yes." His eyes narrowed and darkened. "What kind of person sees his father in such a way? I'm the devil's own disciple."

Jack jumped up. "Don't say such! Yer the only one besides me own ma and da that treats me like a true person. Yer good, do ye hear me? 'Twas a dream and no more. It don't mean a thing."

Mr. Richard's eyes softened. "Sit down, Jack. So be it, then. I'm a good person. I didn't mean to upset you."

Jack was breathing hard, but did as he was told.

"This is our secret, right?" Mr. Richard said. "As always."

He nodded wholeheartedly. "As always."

Samuel came within minutes. "Ah, Mr. Richard, yer awake then? Would ye like to try a little tea? Maybe some bread soaked in buttermilk?"

"I had better put something in my stomach. Jack, get me more pillows. I'd like to prop up."

Samuel moved toward the door, then stopped. He returned to the bed and leaned over. "Mr. Richard, please excuse me presumption, but I thought ye'd like to know."

"Go on."

"Mr. Alistair is feeling a mite feeble. He's kecking and retching right forcefully, sir."

Mr. Richard's eyes widened. "Is that so?"

Samuel's eyes twinkled. "I'm afraid somehow his drinks were twice as strong as yers."

The young master's mouth curled into a lop-sided smile.

Jack cocked his head. How was it funny that their guest was puking?

⧟

Maeve ground her teeth. In the name of all that was holy, if those ninnies didn't stop their twaddle, her head would blow to bits.

Reciting the old saw, Orla announced, "When pies chatter upon the house, 'tis a sign of evil tidings." She aimed her wooden spoon at the bevy of maids twittering in the kitchen. "All ye gossiping magpies are inviting the curse upon our home. Hush yerselves. We've trouble enough."

Jesus be praised! Maeve had never in her life been so grateful for one of Orla's rebukes.

The girls shut down their gossip. It was true. A foreboding had chilled the manor.

How could things have gone so wrong? Maeve hadn't any opportunity to unleash her damning secret concerning Mr. Richard and that hussy.

First had been the fuss caused by the arrival of the guests. It'd been so long since their routine had differed that all the servants welcomed this flurry of activity. Upon the Moores's arrival, the maids giggled and jabbered about the handsome Mr. Alistair.

Maeve had secretly hoped Sir Edward might offer her to the tall, dashing, young man. What a riotous romp that would've been.

Yet, less than an hour later, the staff was murmuring rumors of strife between Sir Edward and his son. This morning, they could speak of nothing else.

Maeve kept her distance from the other girls. She could not shake her distress. The day before, her routine duties had kept her close to Sir Edward's study. She'd heard the master's roars, then that horrible thud when Mr. Richard must have hit the floor. The curses and threats coming from the room did not come from a gentleman's mouth, not one speaking to his own flesh and blood.

When Hogan darted up the stairs, she'd hidden in a vacant room down the hall. Her entire body quivered like grease on a hot griddle. She'd known vicious violence and abuse all her life, but that had been home, back in their squalid mud hut. Here it was supposed to be different, wasn't it? Better.

Against her will, Maeve's mind replayed the events until she thought she'd go mad. She remembered the door to the study creaking open. She'd heard the shuffling of feet and mumbled voices of Mr. Hogan and Samuel. With utmost care, she peered into the hallway through a crack in the door. There they were, with Mr. Richard between them. The young master's head and shoulders sagged as he held a blood-soaked cloth to his face.

That gruesome image in particular was one she couldn't shake. How could this be happening? She and Tara could not have fled their woeful lives any faster. To come here? It was supposed to be genteel. It was supposed to be safe. Worst of all, she had placed her fortunes—her whole life, really—in the hands of a man no more worthy than her own dung pile of a father.

If Sir Edward could do such to his own son, future lord of the manor, what might he do to her? A shiver sizzled up her spine and she was tortured once again by the drunken hag's warning. "Yer looking at yerself in twenty years." She could not let that happen.

Maeve had kept her maw shut about all she'd seen. That old crone, Orla, was right. The danger in the air was suffocating Maeve. She had to find relief, to feel safe once again.

ϕ

Commanded by his father to "get his arse down to the garden," Richard prayed he would catch sight of Eveleen, and discreetly sought her out. He was torn between his desire for her loving gaze and the fear she'd be repulsed by the sight of him. He stunned himself by a quick glimpse in the looking glass. His face was blotched and puffy; the wound looked threatening.

Two teak benches had been set up in the garden with a round table between them. Richard sat on one and asked Samuel for a footrest. Carrying two upholstered stools, the footman soon returned directly behind the ashen Alistair.

The young gentlemen exchanged nods as Alistair plopped onto the second bench and stretched his long legs onto his stool. Hogan followed with a tea tray containing a steaming pot, two cups, and a plateful of muffins and crumpets.

After Hogan completed the pouring, Samuel returned once more with a chamber pot, which he placed beside Alistair. Richard inwardly smiled. Still vomiting, apparently. Though he couldn't afford to be too boastful about it.

The two sat in silence, each staring ahead lost in his own thoughts. Richard fumed over his father's callousness. Why was he even there? He was in agony, he was nauseous, his brain felt like sawdust, and he had to sit beside that peacock. His humiliation knew no end. He folded his arms, threw back his head, and committed to speak no more than decency required.

Far too soon, Sir Edward and Sir Nathaniel approached in full riding gear. Richard pulled himself up, mustering all the dignity he was able. He'd not give them the satisfaction.

Sir Edward wore his usual sarcastic sneer. "Well, will you look at this piteous picture? These milksops have some growing up to do before they can outshine their old ones."

Sir Nathaniel laughed and slapped his friend on the back. "What say you, Lynche? These dainty moppets might need a bit more of their mother's milk, eh? Leave the spirits to the grown men."

"Why don't you ladies sit here and stitch something pretty whilst we spar over the fine quality of my thoroughbreds? I've a lively filly you should try out, Moore."

The two lords lumbered off toward the stables, gesturing and laughing, undoubtedly mocking their sons. Richard fumed in silence as they got farther and farther away. They could barely have been out of earshot when Alistair grabbed his chamber pot and surrendered what little he had in his stomach.

After wiping his mouth on his sleeve, he nodded in the direction of their fathers. "There go two of the most beetle-headed louts ever to walk through Erin's green valleys."

Richard twisted his head in shock and burst into laughter. His jaw ached and his wound burned like Hades, yet it felt so good, as though he was finally exhaling after years of holding his breath.

The "Did I say that aloud?" mimicked by Alistair spawned another round of howling and snorting.

"Stop!" pleaded Richard. "My face can stand no more."

The roaring eased to a whimper until the two looked at each other, then exploded into another bout of laughter. Tears rolled down Richard's face, whether from the cackles or the pain, he knew not.

Alistair performed a near-perfect caricature of his father. "Meet my son, the Defender of Mankind."

Richard grew serious. "You should be glad your father is proud of you."

"Proud? You were taken in by that bluster?"

"You heard how my father speaks of me. He has no appreciation of learning, of academia." He stopped, remembering Alistair's similar contempt.

Alistair pursed his lips. "Nor I, is what you're thinking. Well, what I do understand all too well is your father's jealousy of your intellect."

"Jealousy?"

"Of course. He knows he can never match you, so he belittles you and all you love." A small, guilty smile crept onto Alistair's lips.

Comprehension came slowly to Richard. "You?"

Alistair's eyes closed as he laid his head against the bench. "Ah, yes, the hellish days of Clonmel Grammar. I was as big and dumb as any village peasant." He shook his head. "It just didn't come to me. You all figured out the code, but the mystical key escaped me."

"I ... I never thought."

Alistair lifted his head and snorted. "You weren't supposed to. Now I'm Alistair, Greek god, as your father says." He sat up and looked Richard in the eye. "And the biggest joke of all is that I'm here to convince you to become more like me. A ridiculous situation."

"All would be well if I were the athlete you are. You could outride any of us. Have you ever lost a race to this day?"

He raised an eyebrow. "I have not. You know, with your brain and my brawn—and handsome face—we'd together make the perfect son."

When Richard scowled with his jaw clenched, Alistair reached his long arm across the table and ran the back of his hand along Richard's good cheek. "Come on. Laugh. Don't look so sad."

Richard flinched with an odd sense of unease. "Well, my face is gashed in and will leave a beastly scar, my stomach is unruly—that heaving of yours isn't helping—and my father thinks I'm a woman. But no, I'm not sad."

They chuckled, easing this new tension. Alistair settled back onto his bench. "Go on the Grand Tour, Richard. You and I both deserve to get away from our wart-necked fathers, just so we can breathe. And those Parisian girls. They'll take you all the way to heaven, they say." He wiggled his eyebrows.

"That's not the kind of education I want. Besides, I have heaven right here at Duncullen."

Alistair leaned forward. "Oh ho ho! What's this about? Old Richard's been holding back. A few of the maids? Or tenants' daughters?" He lifted one side of his mouth in a self-satisfied smirk. "I've had my way with a few comely wenches myself."

"Not a few comely wenches. Aphrodite come down to earth disguised as a lovely colleen."

"You old devil, you've still got a way with words. Do you actually use such language with these charming coquettes?"

"To this one girl, yes."

"I see you're taking good care of the horn. But you've got to watch these country lassies. Once they're in an interesting situation, you can't rid yourself of them. At least that's what my cousin says."

Richard frowned. This buffoon knew nothing of the elegance of Eveleen.

"What you'll want, see," Alistair went on, "is some pennyroyal, dried or fresh, made into a tea. The lass drinks it for four or five days and the situation is no longer, um, interesting." He laughed while Richard stared in disbelief. "I've never been in such a position myself, but it's good to know what to do if it happens."

A lead weight threatened to crush Richard's chest. He'd been so sure he had everything under control. He would confront his father with his vulgar indiscretions and insist he be allowed to go to Trinity. He wouldn't threaten to blackmail him right away, but exposing him to Grandfather FitzAden, an earl in the House of Lords, was not out of the question. He and Eveleen would live in Dublin as man and wife, secretly, until he was well-established and could introduce her to his family and society. Surely, they'd acknowledge the charm and refinement he'd so clearly seen.

Twenty-four hours had turned his plans on their head. Confronting his father on any score seemed risky, at best. And what if Eveleen bore his child? Could he then present her in the dignified manner she deserved? A few short weeks ago, things had seemed so straightforward. Now his life reminded him of the juggler he'd seen on Market Day in Clonmel. With five balls in the air, one got away and the flustered fellow let all tumble to the street.

"Think about the Grand Tour in September. If you can bear to leave Aphrodite, that is." Alistair smiled, but for once, was not mocking.

Our Father in heaven, Richard pleaded, bring Mother home with good news. May Grandfather see the wisdom of my Trinity education.

✟

"We've got to get away from here," Maeve repeated. She realized she'd become as shrill as an off-key piper. "'Tis no longer safe."

But Tara wouldn't listen. "'Keep yer nose clean and we'll be right,' ye always said. And me nose is clean."

Maeve wanted to slap her sister, but knew it would only harden her already-thick skull. "Things are not as they were."

She gritted her teeth, determined to tell Tara or anyone else as little as possible. Her only hope now seemed to be her secrets. She kept silent about what she'd seen at the river clearing and concerning Sir Edward—well, the very words felt dangerous on her tongue.

Tara smirked. "What happened? The old man turned ye down?"

"Yer a little fool, Tara, and ye always were. Ye must keep yer mouth shut tight about what I tell ye. Can ye do that?"

She pouted. "I can."

"Sir Edward done that to Mr. Richard. The lad no more tripped over himself than you did."

"Of course, there's been talk. There always is."

Maeve thought she would explode. "Ye bloody numbskull, I was there," she hissed. "Just down the hall and I heard it all. The

111

screaming, the slap, the crash to the floor, the whole damned thing. I heard it!"

"Holy God. Fiona asked Samuel about it, but he said nothing."

"And we'll do the same, do ye hear? Say nothing. The man's no gentleman, no matter his titles. He's a brute, no better than our own da." Maeve glared at her sister. "You do what ye want, but I'll not stay. He's done that to his own son. He'll treat us no better."

Tara hugged herself tightly and chewed her lip. "Where would we go?"

"To Dublin. To Cork. A city is where we'll go. But we need money, Tara. No more trips to town," Maeve said. "We'll save every farthing."

Tara sighed and nodded. "Ye know, a messenger stopped by this morning. Lady Nancy's coming home early. She's ailing."

When Maeve scowled, Tara explained, "I heard Bridge tell Orla about it."

"Yer spying will get ye whipped one day."

Tara laughed. "Orla scolds and swings the broom, but they don't fret over a witless dolt like Tara."

✛

The following morning, Maeve was filling buckets of water to take upstairs when she felt a tap on her shoulder.

She spun to find a pale, puffy-eyed version of Eveleen. She almost laughed in the poor lovesick moppet's face. It took a grand effort to avoid blurting the sarcastic remarks that flooded her mind. "What is it?" she asked instead.

"Uh." Eveleen looked everywhere except at Maeve, who greatly enjoyed her discomfort. "I come to offer me help ... with the water, I mean." She reached for a bucket. "I'll carry this one for ye."

Maeve grabbed the handle, splashing water on her own feet. "Do yer own work and I'll do mine." Then, thinking better of it, she softened her tone. "'Tis kind of ye, but ye don't really want to do that. Things are bad upstairs, especially for poor Mr. Richard."

When the girl gasped, Maeve inwardly smiled. "Have ye seen him?"

"No." Eveleen's eyes filled with tears. "How bad is it?"

This was too easy. Maeve savored being in control again. "The poor lad's flesh is hacked open from his temple to his chin, and his once-lovely face is marred with a bloody, purple gash. Ye'd hardly know him for the swelling." She couldn't resist adding, "God bless him, his right eyeball's bulging near out its socket."

What color Eveleen had drained 'til she looked like Maeve's drowned cousin, Nessa, laid out in her coffin. Little did the idiot know Maeve hadn't been close enough to Mr. Richard to know how he looked. Halfwit Jack wouldn't open the door a crack at her knock.

"His lips," she went on, "them soft, gentle lips he has, are so swelled they've ripped asunder from the strain."

Eveleen could no longer prevent the tears from spilling. "Poor fella," she murmured before scuttling off.

Maeve barely contained her laughter until Eveleen was out of earshot. I was just beginning, she thought, striding toward the Big House.

Chapter Twelve

As the carriage approached Duncullen, the lady of the manor craned her neck to see the assembly of servants awaiting her arrival. "Is my Richard there?" she asked. Somewhat timidly, Biddy thought.

If she could, Biddy would have folded Lady Nancy into her arms and rocked her back and forth like her ol' ma used to do. The visit with the FitzAdens had been disastrous, a great embarrassment for the family and a humiliation for her poor, poor mistress.

"He is, milady," Biddy said, herself relieved. "Right beside Sir Edward."

As they neared the entourage, however, Biddy was flabbergasted at the sight of the battered young master. Lady Nancy squealed in distress. Only through comforting her mistress did Biddy herself avoid bursting into tears.

When the carriage jolted to a halt, Lady Nancy fumbled with the door, unwilling to wait for the footman to open it. With more vigor than Biddy'd seen in a year, she scrambled from the carriage, trampled her gown, and tumbled toward the dirt. By the grace of God, the footman's quick reflexes saved the lady from plopping face down into the mud.

⊕

Richard's mother drew back her shoulders and strode past the servants. Ignoring Sir Edward, she gingerly touched Richard's wound as she choked back a sob.

"Get a bloody hold of yourself," Sir Edward grumbled through gritted teeth.

While Richard would never have been so coarse with his mother, he, too, was dismayed by this uncharacteristic display of emotion in front of the attending servants.

"It's fine, Mother," he whispered into her ear. "Take a deep breath now."

She pulled herself up and, stuttering, inhaled. "Escort me to my chamber, my dear."

She latched onto Richard's arm as though grasping a lifeline. With chin out and head high, she made her way into the house. Sir Edward snorted and escaped to who knew where.

✤

Once Biddy settled Lady Nancy into her bed, she stepped into the hallway to give mother and son privacy while catching her own breath. Within a few moments, Mrs. Bridge joined her.

Biddy nodded toward the chamber door. "Never did I think me heart could ache as it does for the two of them," she whispered to the housekeeper. "The young master looks like he's been mauled by a mob of ruffians."

Mrs. Bridge remained stone-faced when Biddy added, "And to think it all came from crashing into the hearth tools." She frowned at the housekeeper's lack of response. "Old Will did the surgery, did he?"

"He did. The lad's in for a nasty scar."

"There's more troubles than that for our mistress, and I'll tell none but you. Not even Orla, Mrs. Bridge."

The older woman's brow creased. "Go on."

"The visit to her childhood home was a calamity. The closer we got, the more melancholy she grew. By the time we arrived,

Lady Nancy was so agitated, I feared she might crack." The memory laid a weight on her heart.

"I accompanied her once years ago," Mrs. Bridge said. "The family was cold as a school of trout. What ye might expect from the high and mighty, was how I saw it."

"Ha! Heartless, to be sure. The way the sisters sat in her chamber, criticizing and mocking. All the while pretending how happy they were to see her. Her frock was out of fashion, why didn't she do something with her hair, how horrid for her to be stashed away in a godforsaken place like Duncullen—and with such a husband."

"That part is certain."

"At least they gave her some attention. Her father, who she praises to the high heavens, barely spoke to her. Upon her arrival, he said, 'Why are ye here? Are yer husband and son weary of ye?'"

"The bastard."

"She sobbed the whole night, not sleeping at all. I tried to give her some tonic, but she wanted to be alert for them sharp-tongued sisters of hers. Not that it did her any good."

Biddy grew even more somber. "Day before last, all the household and guests gathered in the parlor to play cards. Lady Nancy was skittish as a mare foretelling a summer storm. I didn't find out what happened 'til later from a maid. It seems some friends of Lady Lillian were snickering at the next table, likely mocking our mistress, when one fella said something like, 'Yer so like yer dear mother, Lady Nancy.'"

Biddy looked around to assure they were alone, then lowered her voice further. "It seems our mistress stood up, knocked her tea to the floor, and called out ... well, 'screeched' was the word the maid used, 'I am not demented. I am of sound mind.' And slumped back into her chair."

"Saint Joseph, have mercy." Mrs. Bridge's shoulders drooped and her face paled.

Biddy grabbed her forearm. "Are ye well? I'll not distress ye further."

"I'll be fine. 'Tis best I know what happened."

"I was sent for, of course. There she sat, staring ahead with no life in her eyes at all." Biddy struggled to hold back her tears. "I took her to bed and dosed her good. Right before drifting into sleep, she said, 'We leave tomorrow.' The entire household was relieved to hear of that decision, ye can be sure."

A service bell rang. "That's for you, Biddy. Dry yer eyes and ..."

But Biddy was flying to her lady's side before the housekeeper could finish.

✠

Although Lady Nancy was propped up in bed, calmed (or drugged) and set to rights, Richard was aggrieved by her feeble appearance. More pallid than before the journey, her high cheekbones protruded over a wrinkled, sunken face. She was wasting away.

"Well, look at us both," Richard said once Biddy left the room. "We're each a bit worse for the wear." His mother looked at him dolefully, but made no response. "Such a pity your stay was so short."

"I needed to be home, Richard. There is no more desirable place than your own bed when you're ailing."

"I suppose not." He sat in the chair Biddy had placed beside the bed. "How are you, Mother?"

"As well as can be expected." Her glazed expression revealed nothing.

"I truly want to know." As she remained mute and expressionless, Richard became uneasy. What was going on in her head? Did he even know this person, his own mother?

He thought of Eveleen's emerald green eyes; they were open and honest. He felt he could soak up her very essence. How different it was to search his mother's eyes. There was a curtain there. No, more like a heavy oaken door preventing him from peeking into her soul. What was she hiding?

He took her hand in his. "Did something happen?"

She turned to him, her head tipped to one side. "Yes, Richard. I visited my family. We ate, we drank, we slept, and ... we laughed. And spoke of old times, the wonder of childhood and such."

"Did you speak of me?"

"Of course." She took back her hand and began cracking her knuckles. "Everyone wanted to know all about you."

Richard winced. "Must you?"

She looked at her hands, then laid them to her sides. "To be honest, I spoke of little else but you."

"With Grandfather?"

"Grandfather?" Her words came quickly. "We spoke of you, yes, and your desire to go to Trinity. I mentioned, in confidence, of course, that you and your father were at odds over this and ... well, he said he was sure the two of you would work it through."

"Work it through?" Richard's heart pounded. "Are you sure you explained the situation clearly?"

"Of course, Richard." Her voice wavered. "Don't you believe me?"

"I believe you, Mother. I'm disappointed, that's all."

More like crushed, disillusioned, defeated. His hammering heart and trembling limbs made it impossible to sit there. He leapt from the chair, nearly knocking it over. "Get some rest. I'll come by later."

He rang the maid's bell and strode toward the door.

"Richard?"

He turned to see Lady Nancy propped on her elbows, eyes wide and lips quivering. "Do you love me?"

He forgot himself momentarily and saw only the lonely, frightened gentlewoman whom he loved so dearly creaking open her oaken door. He rushed to her bedside, kissed her brow, and said, "I adore you. I cherish you. You are the most precious person in my life."

In Richard's mind, the little white lie was made righteous by the look of overwhelming relief on his mother's face.

As he left the chamber, a craving for solitude swelled within him. Sir Nathaniel and Alistair, who turned out to be better company than expected, had left only that morning, cutting their visit short out of respect for Lady Nancy's illness.

Richard climbed to his unofficial sanctuary, the Blue Room of the third story where he and Eveleen stole rare moments together. He had seen his love only fleetingly since he'd been struck, with no opportunity for even a word between them.

Yet, upon entering the room, there she sat, crouched before the hearth. He slammed the door shut and rushed to grab her into his arms. With abandon, he pressed his lips to hers like a ravenous man before a feast. Only when the pain inflicted upon his cheek became too unbearable did he release her.

"I've missed you so," he said, placing his hands on either side of her face. He kissed her again, more gently this time.

She giggled. "Ah, ye never checked to be sure I'm alone. 'Tis by the grace of God that I am." Growing sober, she inspected his face with her eyes. "Look at ye, then. I've been sick with worry. Maeve told me ... well, she made it sound so much worse." Pent-up tears seeped from her eyes.

Richard smiled as he cupped her chin. "And yet, you're crying. Do I look that bad? The stitches have held. I checked the glass before my mother's arrival and noticed my bruise has begun to yellow."

"Yer beautiful. So very beautiful." Her calloused fingertips stroked his face with a gentleness he didn't know was possible, stirring his loins.

He took her behind the lacquered folding screen for additional privacy. There, he kissed her eyes, her nose, and was running his tongue over her lips when the door opened.

"Eveleen, where are ye?"

Eveleen mouthed the name, "Maeve," and stepped from behind the screen. "Right here where I belong, cleaning the Blue Room."

There was a pause, then Richard heard Maeve say, "The door was shut."

Richard could feel his temperature rise. It was no business of that feckless hussy's. He felt small, like a petty criminal hunkered behind the screen. His humiliation swiftly turned to fury.

I am Mr. Richard Lynche, he mentally railed, future lord of Duncullen Estate. This is untenable.

"The wind, I suppose," Eveleen was saying. "What are ye needing?"

"Thought ye could use some help, but I see yer fine here," was the reply.

Richard heard the swish of Maeve's skirts as she left the room. He could barely contain his rage. That slatternly wench would rue the day she forced him to hide like a common thief.

After several minutes, Eveleen returned to their spot behind the screen.

Richard grabbed her arm. "What the bloody hell was that about?"

Eveleen's eyes widened. "Ye heard what she said. She wanted to help, but I needed none."

"Maeve—the one who startled you into dropping the porcelain bird. The one who battered you with lies about my condition. Now she comes prancing in here—for what? To spy on you?" He clenched his fists. "I'll allow no lowborn, potato-eating beggar to bring me down!"

Eveleen gasped and leaned back as though slapped.

He eased his grip and softened his tone. "I'm not speaking of you. Heavens, no. You're the exotic flower growing in a pile of dung."

She stiffened and he kissed her on the nose.

"Not to worry." He smiled. "With me, you'll rise from the dross of the provincial peasant. First, I'll teach you to speak clearly, without your lowly brogue."

She fidgeted. "I must return to work."

"Of course, my love." He kissed her on her forehead and held her in his arms until she broke loose and hastened away.

☦

"I've been waiting for you."

Sir Edward scraped back his chair, rose, and menacingly rounded his desk. All but Maeve's thudding heart froze inside the door of the study. The old man hadn't met her there for weeks. Why now?

In front of his desk, he propped his boot on the chair for petitioners and rested his forearms on his knee. "Do you think it was wise to cross me?" His cold eyes seemed to peer right through her.

"Cross ye?" Maeve could barely breathe.

"You bed my son behind my back and think I won't find out about it?"

"Bed Mr. Richard?" Maeve wagged her head back and forth. "No. No, milord. I've not spoken to him." In fact, when she realized he was behind the screen in the Blue Room, she could not escape fast enough.

Red-faced, Sir Edward pounded his fist on the desk beside him. "Liar! I have the word of a gentleman—a gentleman with knowledge of Richard's fleshly pleasures."

Maeve rushed to Sir Edward and dropped to her knees before him. "

"'Twasn't me, milord. I'm loyal to ye, ye know that."

His eyes seemed to flicker, giving Maeve hope she could escape his wrath. "We spoke of it, you and me, but I was awaiting yer nod, sir."

When he still made no response, she risked a peek under her lashes. "So long it's been since ye've wanted me, that nod never came."

"My business has taken me elsewhere." He removed his foot from the chair and sat in it. Lifting her chin, he said, "But I'm here now."

Maeve's heart slowed as she eased into the familiar role of seductress. Only until her money was saved.

Sir Edward placed Maeve on his lap and dipped his hand into her bodice. Although she knew it would be short-lived, she felt most in control when he wore that hungry-dog look. She leaned in to nuzzle his neck, then flicked her tongue in his ear.

Practically panting, he lifted her and laid her on his massive desk. He moved in close to her face and his eyes hardened. "If not you, then who is bedding my son?"

Maeve was rattled to the core. Who had been seducing who? His steely look bored through her defenses. She had to say something. But if he knew she'd seen them and said nothing, she was at the mercy of the bloodthirsty wolf. "I don't know nothing firsthand," she said. "But there's been talk. Gossip, mainly."

"And what, pray, is the gist of this gossip?"

"Well, that he might be sweet on the red-haired girl, Eveleen."

"Is that her name? Eveleen?"

Maeve struggled to read the man. Her survival depended on it. Was that a flash of lust? Curiosity? Certainly conniving. Just when she thought he had lost interest in her, he took her with unusual vigor, then sank into his chair, spent.

Maeve rose from the desk and began to put herself back together. Seeing the self-satisfied smirk on the old man, her whole body quivered. There was danger here.

"I think it's time," he said, his tented fingers pumping up and down. "Seduce my son and bring me reports." He cocked his head to one side. "Isn't that what you've been wanting?"

Maeve sensed a trap. How to answer? "I only wish to train him to be as powerful and high-spirited as yerself."

"Then so you shall. And you'll be rewarded well for your work." He laughed as though he'd told a wicked joke, and while Maeve couldn't see it, she giggled anyway.

✦

A few hours later, Maeve was surprised by a summons from Sir Edward. Being near him exhausted her. Surely, he wasn't up for more.

Once back in his study, she beheld in his stretched hand a most delicate pair of blue silk stockings embroidered in white.

"Will these do for your trouble?" His eyes narrowed. "They are yours, but I expect, upon demand, you will wear them for me."

She took them into her hands as though they were spun gold. Only in her dreams had she owned anything so elegant. "They are lovely, milord."

And a fine price they'd bring in Dublin.

Chapter Thirteen

She's in a frantic state, Mrs. Bridge. There's no calming her." Biddy was wringing her hands, at wits' end herself as far as Mrs. Bridge could see.

"Have ye looked everywhere?" the housekeeper asked. "'Twas not long ago we went through this same plight only to discover Mr. Richard was the culprit."

"Mrs. Bridge, I placed all our lady's purchases in her chest of drawers meself. Ten pairs of silk stockings she bought in Dublin and the pale blue were her favorite. They're nowhere to be found." Poor Biddy's bottom lip trembled. "Ye know how she feels about thievery. She insisted I raise me own skirts to prove I'd not lifted them."

"Oh, Biddy. The idea." Mrs. Bridge pulled the stricken young lass into her arms. Ye'll never find any to love ye more, ye old bat, she'd love to tell the grand lady.

Biddy pulled back and wiped her eyes. "She's insisting on a search of all the servants—from Hogan on down. Yer to search his belongings and he's to search yers."

Mrs. Bridge huffed. "We'll save that indignity for the last. Tell the mistress I'll begin with the maids and have Will go through whatever pittance the grooms may own." She started to go, then turned back. "And Biddy, don't take the lady's behavior to heart. 'Tis a mystery to me why she goes as mad as a sack of cats when the least thing goes missing, but ye know she loves ye above us all."

"Thank ye. I'll see to her now."

After bringing the bad news to Will personally, Mrs. Bridge mustered the help of Orla to go through the meager possessions of the maids.

"All this foolishness over the rantings of a—well, a very ill woman," grumbled Orla as she pawed through Fiona's cloth satchel.

Mrs. Bridge pulled Tara's scant effects from her bag and laid them on the table. An extra linen shift, a brown woolen skirt, and an old ivory comb with missing teeth. "Hush, Orla. The walls have ears."

As she placed Tara's possessions back into her bag, Mrs. Bridge looked up. The cook had grown too quiet. "Orla?"

"Oh, Lord Jesus in heaven." The plump woman pulled herself up with the help of the nearby table and looked at Mrs. Bridge with pursed lips. Reluctantly, she held up a pair of pale blue hose embroidered in white.

A large rock buried itself in Mrs. Bridge's stomach. With a clenched throat, she croaked, "Who?"

Orla brushed the tears that trickled from her eyes. She breathed deeply, then said, "Maeve."

"Oh, the fool. The wretched little fool."

✦

Maeve stood before the two women with jutted chin and frightened eyes. "What are ye doing rummaging through me things? I bought them stockings, I did, with me own money."

"No, ye didn't," Orla snapped. "They belong to the lady herself and ye know it. Lifted them straight from her chest of drawers. Ach, the boldness of ye!"

Maeve paled. "I didn't steal nothing. 'Twas a gift, is what it was. From a lad in town." She looked at Mrs. Bridge, eyes wide.

"I know how ye feel about followers and don't want to be dismissed, but I'm not a thief. Never a thief."

Orla snarled. "I've known ye for a backbiting shrew, but a good-for-nothing filcher? Yer a disgrace is what ye are."

Mrs. Bridge could feel the tension seizing her neck. "Orla, please. Let me talk to Maeve alone."

The cook's nostrils flared. "As ye wish," she said, and stomped out of the servants' hall.

"Sit," Mrs. Bridge told the lass as she lowered herself to a seat across from Maeve.

The girl's bluster disappeared. Instead, a vein in her neck thumped and she struggled to swallow.

Mrs. Bridge went on. "'Tis a serious charge, thievery. The mistress takes it to heart when one abuses her trust." The base of her skull throbbed and a tingling arose in her left arm. She stopped speaking and breathed deeply, hoping to ward off her affliction.

"I took nothing," Maeve blurted. "'Twas a gift, like I told ye."

"That's not possible. Lady Nancy bought them from a hosier in Dublin whilst she was away. Anyone can see they're of a fine quality no lad from town could afford."

Maeve's face crumbled and she broke into heart-wrenching sobs. "I am undone," she wailed. "I'm blameless, but what does it matter? I'm ruined. How could he've done this to me?"

Mrs. Bridge couldn't say what she'd expected of the lass, but it wasn't this. Her head began to pound, but it seemed nothing compared to the suffering of Maeve. With eyes blurred by tears, she reached for the poor girl's hand. "Maeve, if ye know something that will save yerself, speak up now. Whoever is to blame should take the punishment."

Maeve lifted her head and a sneer crept onto her lips. "The one who's to blame? That's a laugh, Mrs. Bridge."

"Tell me."

"What have I to lose now? I'm doomed." She wiped her cheeks with her sleeve and looked Mrs. Bridge in the eye. "'Tis the great lord of Duncullen himself that give 'em to me. A special gift, he said. And I a lackwit for taking it." Her eyes hardened. "If only I'd burned them. What could he have done then?"

Mrs. Bridge's mouth grew parched. Her face and neck baked with rage. She reached into the pocket tied to her waist and pulled out the stolen stockings. "The filthy rotten weasel," she mumbled, turning the offending hose over in her hands. Her anger bellowed, "Throw them into the fire!" That would serve the bastard right.

"Mrs. Bridge?" Maeve stared at her wide-eyed. "Yer face is purple. And yer hands."

The housekeeper saw she had crunched the stockings into her trembling fist. She set them on the table and wiped her palms across her skirt. "Orla knows ye had them. He wins again. There's nothing we can do."

Maeve bolted upright, knocking her chair to the floor. She spun in one direction, then the next. "Oh, Jesus in heaven, what'll I do? What's to become of me?"

"Sir Edward is too strong. He can do with us what he chooses."

Maeve grabbed fistfuls of her hair and crouched on the floor, squalling like a dying animal in a trap.

Mrs. Bridge's heart pulsed in her ears. "Ye won't be hanged, likely. Lady Nancy likes a good flogging. We'll all be forced to watch." Her vision blurred, partly from tears and partly from the agony in her head. Run! she wanted to scream to the girl, but it would go all the worse for her if she did. A hanging then, for sure.

Maeve twisted her head to face Mrs. Bridge. "Why? Why would he do it?"

"He wants something. Ye must be standing in the way."

Maeve's eyes flashed, then her head dropped. "I'd have gone quietly," she whispered, "had he told me."

Would ye? Mrs. Bridge wondered.

✦

Maeve's eyes were dry, which belied the crippling shame she had suffered. As she stood before Sir Edward awaiting judgment, she vowed she would hold her head high, worthy of her namesake, the stubborn and powerful Queen of Connacht. He'd get no wailing nor begging from her. She'd not give the back-stabbing toad the satisfaction.

She once thought she had Sir Edward wrapped around her finger. But even after his treatment of Richard, this treachery stupefied her. In a matter of hours, she went from cleaning ashes from the parlor's hearth, to Mrs. Bridge's confrontation over the forbidden gift, to standing accused before her own betrayer on the serious charge of theft.

Her emotions jounced like a cricket in a box. Despite her breakdown before Mrs. Bridge, she had pulled herself together and inwardly sworn she would defeat her enemies. Soon after, her resolve faltered, creating another wave of despair before she once again steeled herself for this hearing.

Maeve tried to catch Sir Edward's eye, looking for an ounce of regret in his expression. Yet, he refused to look at her face. He stared instead at the parchment before him as he read her sentence.

"For the heinous crime of thievery, you are hereby sentenced to ten lashes with the birch upon your shoulders."

The news, but more the coldness of the man, sickened Maeve. She'd been beaten and whipped many-a time and had the scars to prove it. Ten lashes were not many and the birch, a bundle of stripped twigs, was not as severe as the cat o' nine tails. She felt the merest satisfaction, though, when he failed to meet her gaze. He'd a touch of the shame, but no more.

"Hogan, send one of the groomsmen to fetch Ronan. The punishment will be applied at sunrise."

Panic bubbled within her. Ronan, Maeve thought. The burly oaf. He'd gladly rip the skin off her back for free. She had rebuffed Ronan's advances more than once and was sure Sir Edward's tenant and occasional flogger would not hold back.

Hogan stepped forward. "If you please, sir, Lady Nancy has requested that she be apprised of all details concerning the thief's sentence."

Maeve hugged herself, as though she could still her shuddering shoulders. The cold-hearted harridan chomped at the bit to see the stripes on her back.

"She has, has she?" Sir Edward sneered as though he smelled something rank. "Methinks the lady savors this too much."

Hogan bowed and left the study.

Sir Edward finally looked Maeve in the eye, but she could read nothing there. He nodded to the two groomsmen in the corner of the room. "Secure her in the barn until daybreak."

Standing as stoically as legendary Queen Maeve now seemed a fool's game. Relying on the scant hope gained by her light sentence, Maeve dropped to her knees and pleaded, "If ye cannot find me innocent, milord, find it in yer heart to pardon yer humble servant. Ye know I've been faithful, even devoted to ye." She avoided any allusions to her special favors. She was not reckless enough to besmirch her master before witnesses.

Sir Edward grunted in disgust before nodding to the groomsmen, who proceeded to drag her to her feet.

Terror filled Maeve with unusual strength, however, allowing her to wrestle free of the guards, rush to her judge and master, and fall to the floor. Wrapping her arms around his knees, she pleaded, "Milord, don't do this. Ye know me to be innocent."

His laugh chilled her to the bone. "Innocent? You've not been innocent since your head poked free of your mother's womb."

Without warning, the door to the study crashed against the wall, revealing the silhouette of a fierce-looking Lady Nancy. Maeve scrambled to her feet and backed away from Sir Edward.

The mistress stepped forward, nostrils flaring and red cheeks burning with rage. "Ten lashes? Am I to understand the pilfery of my most personal apparel warrants nothing more than this slap on the wrist?"

"Madam, you are speaking beyond your station. I suggest—"

"I suggest you act like the man of breeding you pretend to be and learn how to handle your inferiors."

Startled by the flash of pain in Sir Edward's eyes, Maeve dared not breathe.

Hogan stepped from behind his mistress. "Milady, may I escort you to your chambers?"

She ignored the butler. "Of course, the way you handled your own s—"

"Silence, woman!" Sir Edward's face was nearly purple. "One more word and I'll slice out your tongue."

"You'll slice out the tongue of your wife, but for this whore, only ten lashes." She spun, and with Hogan in tow, was gone.

Baring his teeth like a deranged animal, he turned and pointed his knobby finger at a cowering Maeve. "Thirty lashes," he bellowed. "With the cat."

"No, milord. No!"

"Get her out of here," he demanded and turned away.

The groomsmen hauled Maeve to the stable. There, they shoved her into an empty stall and tied her wrists to a metal ring on the wall. She sank to the floor amidst the muck and wept from a soft, vulnerable spot she'd burrowed deep within herself. Exhausted, she finally fell into a dreamless sleep.

⊕

"Maeve ... Maeve ..." The faraway sound of her name grew closer and closer. Someone yanked her shoulder this way and that.

"Huh?" She opened her eyes to Tara's puffy face illuminated by the glimmering moonlight together with the glow of her sister's lantern.

"Orla wouldn't let me come to ye 'til the evening meal was behind us." Tara's lower lip quivered. "'Twas never so quiet in the servants' hall, Maeve. All are muddled over ... well, ye know." Her shoulders shook with silent sobs.

"Ye can tell 'em I stole nothing. Me thrashing is a sham, but there's naught I can do." Her entire body ached from fatigue and the agonizing position she was forced into with her arms stretched over her head as they were. It was nothing, however, compared to the pain in her heart.

Tara's breathing stuttered as she tried to pull herself together. She left, returning with a small pail and milking stool. "Mrs. Bridge sent this stew—from the family's pot. Neither Orla nor Hogan agreed, but Old Bridge insisted." Tara shrugged. "Ye can't tell about some people, now can ye?"

"I can't eat that."

"I'm going to feed ye. 'Tis why I brought the stool."

"It's no good. Me stomach's a churning."

Tara began to sniffle again. "Bridge told me ye'd say that, but she said ye'll need all yer strength. For tomorrow."

Tears rolled down Maeve's face. "Thirty lashes, Tara. With the cat."

"I know. Maybe they'll not brand ye. Without the 'T' on yer thumb, ye can go to Dublin and perhaps find a new position."

Something in Tara's voice brought Maeve up short. "Ye'll come with me."

Her sister dipped a spoon into the pail and brought it to Maeve's lips. "I have a place here. What good would it do for us both to be on the roads?"

Maeve was dumbfounded. "Tara, 'twas I that got ye this position. Ye'd send me out alone? Maybe to starve?"

"Of course not." Tara looked down. "'Tis not the time to speak of this."

Maeve took the stew into her mouth and forced it down her clenched throat. They'd sort it out later, she persuaded herself. All would be right. With the stew, however, she swallowed something she'd never tasted before—a stark, utter loneliness.

✚

Eveleen's nerves weren't the only ones on edge. The servants' hall hummed with whispers of disbelief. When Tara returned from her visit to the stable, everyone stopped and stared. Dizzy with shock and confusion, all were keen to know how Maeve was faring. Was she showing her usual sauce or had she, at last, been humbled?

Tara, still holding the pail, looked from one to the other. She stuck out her jaw and announced, "She never done it. 'Tis all a sham, she says, and I, for one, believe her."

No one spoke a word. In silence, each of them, including Eveleen, set up her pallet and turned in. It was a long time, however, before Eveleen heard the sounds of sleep claim all in the room but herself. She tossed this way and that, her mind astir.

While she hadn't gotten on with Maeve, Eveleen could never wish such a fate upon her. The more she thought about it, the more the whole story rang hollow. After the uproar from the porcelain bird, Maeve knew too well the lady's fury over the merest hint of theft. Would Maeve then boldly pinch Lady Nancy's stockings? The lass was cruel and selfish, true, but not thickheaded. Something was amiss, and Eveleen found herself drowning in an unshakable dread.

⊕

Maeve lay awake, watching the moon 'til the morning's first blush.

Mrs. Bridge was the earliest to come to her. She had that pallid, pinched look she wore when her affliction was upon her.

"Beg for mercy." The housekeeper held out a ladle of water for Maeve. "'Tis no time for false pride. Not that the beast will give it, but ye can never be sure."

Fear welled up in Maeve, making it difficult to breathe, but she drank as well as she could.

Mrs. Bridge dipped more water into the ladle. "Take all ye can now. It'll be better for ye later. Will and I have gathered the lint and ointment for yer wounds. Grim, it'll be, for a few days, but we'll take good care of ye."

Overwhelmed by the kindness of the housekeeper, Maeve would have loved to squeeze Mrs. Bridge around the waist the way she'd hugged her mother as a wee lass. But with both hands bound, she could only ask, "Could ye move a bit closer?"

Mrs. Bridge obliged, allowing Maeve to kiss her on the cheek. Tears poured down the older woman's face. "We'll get ye through this, me and Will. Fear not, child." She petted Maeve's hair as Maeve always wished her mammy might do, then the housekeeper scurried from the barn.

Maeve watched for Tara, but her sister did not return. Instead, she was shaken by the sight of Ronan in the doorway. A beefy man with hooded brow and few teeth, his rough linen shirt did little to hide his brawn. With menacing eyes, he pulled a mean-looking cord from his canvas bag.

"Here's me little kitty." He lovingly ran his fingers down each of the nine knotted strands. "Ye were too good for ol' Ronan and now look at ye. Not to worry. Kitty will take fine care of ye, though she does bite a little." He laughed savagely at his own cruel joke.

Maeve's head swam as she struggled to breathe. "I'm dying," she said, panting.

"Ye'll not die." He stashed the cat o' nine tails back in its sack. "But ye'll wish ye had."

Ronan dropped the bag and entered Maeve's stall. His rank breath was overwhelming while, breathing heavily, he released Maeve's arms from the metal ring on the stable wall. Every movement brought an agonizing burn to her joints and muscles. The lout grabbed her elbows and thrust her arms to her sides. Maeve howled in pain, which prodded the flogger to even greater roughness.

Maeve stumbled from the barn with Ronan's calloused hands clamped on her upper arms. Scanning the courtyard, she saw every groomsman, maid, blacksmith, and laborer's eyes fixed upon her disgrace. Some eyes mocked, but most held pity. She spotted Tara, staring at the ground and hugging herself, rocking back and forth. Brea whispered to her sister, but Tara shook her head and would not look up.

Ronan shoved Maeve, causing her to stumble. His strong arms kept her from falling, but she was sure his crushing grip had bruised her. With the heavy oaken whipping post looming, she trembled from head to foot. Once again, she could not catch her breath.

As tears streamed down her cheeks, she chanted in her mind, I'm going to die, I'm going to die.

☦

The sun had barely risen when Eveleen, along with the entire staff, had been herded to the whipping post just outside the stables. Since she rarely had reason to come near this area, she shivered at the sight of the tall wooden pole splattered with darkened bloodstains, mostly from unruly tenants who had offended Sir Edward. Those occasions did not require Eveleen's attendance, but Maeve's offense reflected badly on the entire household and they all were forced to watch as a warning.

Eveleen's head snapped up as a snarling giant of a man drove Maeve from the stables, but none dared speak above a whisper. Eveleen heard a groom mumble, "Ye wait long enough, everyone gets what's coming to 'im."

She turned to glare at the foolish clod. Only a few feet away stood Tara, beside herself with grief. It broke Eveleen's heart, for she remembered well the pain of watching a loved one suffer. The helplessness, above all, gnawed at her heart.

At the post, Eveleen saw the man tie Maeve's hands to a metal ring, pulling the girl's arms so taut, her toes barely brushed the ground. Her stomach wrenched as her former foe's head drooped to one side.

A low murmur arose at the arrival of his lord and ladyship. Her heart skipped a beat to see Richard standing beside his mother, wearing a stern look. It was clear to her that he liked it no better than they did.

However, the sinister way Richard's eyes glowered above his stitched-up gash made Eveleen uneasy. She quickly realized he displayed a fury directed at Maeve herself, and not the injustice of her fate.

Fiona whispered into her ear, startling her. "Ye know where she got them stockings, don't ye?"

Eveleen shook her head.

"That one, right there." Fiona directed her eyes to the baronet and his family.

Eveleen's chest tightened. Holy God, could it be? "Which one?"

"The lord himself. A gift, it was."

Confused, Eveleen looked at Fiona.

"For letting him do what he liked," the girl said. "'Til he got tired of her."

Eveleen opened her mouth in shock, but Fiona had turned away. 'Tis the father, not the son, she shouted in her head. Never Richard.

Eveleen's head spun toward the whipping post as Maeve croaked, "Mercy! Milord, I beg ye, have mercy on me!"

All were silent, waiting for the master's response.

"Fifteen lashes," he announced. "But with the cat."

"Thank ye, sir." Maeve exhaled in a gush.

"No mercy for the whoring thief!" Lady Nancy demanded.

"Father," Eveleen heard Richard say, "will you slight my mother for the sake of this wretch?"

His voice tired, Sir Edward said, "I'll hear no more of this. My decision is made."

"Fifteen lashes it is," the flogger shouted as he ripped Maeve's blouse, exposing her nakedness. "And, milady, ye can be sure they'll be good ones."

He jammed a knotted rag into Maeve's mouth. "Something to bite down on in yer agony," he growled loud enough for all to hear, then stepped away.

✦

Maeve heard Tara's wail and the whistle of the whip before she felt the first bite of the lash across her back. She balled her fists and clamped her teeth onto the rag, surprisingly grateful for it. The cut stung bitterly, and yet, not as badly as she'd feared.

But as the whip hissed for the second slash, and the third, and the fourth, her flesh tore deeper and wider with every blow. Sweat from her brow stung her eyes while the coppery scent of fresh blood assaulted her nose. Slipping toward unconsciousness, her shoulders and back were aflame. Despite her gag, she yowled like the wounded animal she was until all, mercifully, went black.

Chapter Fourteen

Hold it together, Mrs. Bridge told herself. Her head was pounding like she'd been hit with a hammer as Will and Samuel carried an insensible Maeve to their cabin. Mrs. Bridge had tried to cover the girl with the torn blouse, but it kept falling away, exposing her nakedness.

Ronan was a beast to rip what little clothing the girl had. The nasty, vile creature disgusted her.

She ran ahead to open the door for the men. Pushing it ajar, she found Jack huddled in the corner beside the hearth. "What are ye doing there, son?"

He looked at her with a tear-stained face. "Is Maeve dead? I'm sorry I disobeyed, Ma, but I couldn't watch." His wide, childlike eyes squeezed her heart.

At that moment, Will and Samuel brought Maeve in and laid her on her stomach upon the pallet they'd prepared. She did not stir.

"Is she dead, Da?"

"Jack," said Will, "are ye ill, lad?"

"He's frightened," said Mrs. Bridge, under her breath. "As we all should be." She turned to Jack. "She's sleeping so she can heal, pet. The same way animals do."

"Head out to the pasture, Jack. Yer ma and I must nurse Maeve, and the animals need tending." Will turned to Samuel. "Take him to his calves."

Jack wiped his eyes on his sleeve and followed the groom out, only to run square into a frantic Tara. "I'm sorry," he told her, tearing up again.

But it was obvious to Mrs. Bridge that Tara saw and heard only her sister.

Jack looked befuddled and fretful.

"Off ye go then, Jack." Mrs. Bridge smiled to reassure the lad. "All will be well."

He nodded and stumbled from the cabin.

"Maeve, Maeve," Tara whimpered as she dropped to her knees by her sister's side and petted her sweat-soaked hair. "How could this happen? Look what they done to her, and innocent at that."

"'Tis good she's senseless as much pain as she's in," Mrs. Bridge said. "Leave us to tend her, Tara. I'll call for ye when she wakes, ye can be sure of that."

Will gently lifted the girl from the floor and guided her outside. Mrs. Bridge was relieved to hear Brea's soothing voice encourage Tara back to the Big House.

The housekeeper knelt beside Maeve and blotted the bloody wounds with a wet cloth. "Hand me the wool grease," she told Will.

He crouched beside her with the ointment pot. They gingerly spread the dressing over the cuts and gashes.

"Did ye see the look of her? Lady Nancy, I mean," Mrs. Bridge whispered. When Will didn't answer, she said, "For a gentlewoman and so meek at times, she seemed vicious almost. A thirst for blood there was in her eyes."

Will merely sighed.

"Don't tell me ye didn't notice. And all for something so trifling."

"How are we to know what's trifling to the rich? We all have our dark sides. Ye've got one yerself, Noreen."

"I suppose I do. As bitter as I am this moment, 'tis a blessing I've not the power to torture some I can think of."

Will looked curiously at his wife, then rose. "I'll get the honey."

"And the lint while yer up."

Standing before the cupboard across the room, Will stared out their door. "There's the jailor, Michael Critty, pulling up in his wagon. And what might his business be?"

Mrs. Bridge's head snapped up. "Surely not to brand the lass."

Maeve began to stir.

"I don't see why he would. We've all we need for a branding right here if it comes to that." Will's eyes showed pity at the sight of Maeve's back and shoulders with their deep gouges and torn flesh, now glossy with salve. "I'll bring the whiskey as well."

✢

"Richard!" his father thundered from the study.

He squared his shoulders. I'll be calm and reasoned no matter his bluster, he told himself. Breeding wins out.

Richard stepped through the doorway to find Hogan in the room, likely bringing the news. The butler bowed and stepped back, but did not leave.

"Hogan tells me Michael Critty is here, stating he was summoned—by me. I find that rather curious since I did no such thing."

Richard pulled himself to his full height. "It was I who sent for him. In your name, of course."

"Is that so? Refresh my doddering memory. Why was it I required the jailer? This would be good to know before I speak to him."

Stand firm, he commanded himself. "I believe it's clear for the benefit of all involved that the thief, Maeve, be transported for her crime. Mr. Critty is here to facilitate that."

"Transported, you say? To the colonies?"

"That's correct. In light of the mild punishment she was given for the flagrant theft of her ladyship's property, it would reinforce to all we rule that such corruption will not be tolerated."

A sneer spread across Sir Edward's face. "That sounded quite well-rehearsed. Bravo."

His heart pounding, Richard lifted his chin and stared his father in the eye. He'd not intimidate him this time.

Sir Edward rose, braced his hands on his desk, and leaned toward his son. "You sniveling little slug. We don't rule anything. I am in total control of all aspects of this estate until I take my last breath. And God help every creature on it when that happens."

Richard steeled himself for the tongue-lashing that was building.

"I will not be dictated to by you or your mother. That's where this whole thing is coming from, is it not? You certainly don't have the ballocks to dream up such a scheme, much less carry it out."

His own ire rising, Richard threw caution to the wind. "Do you think there's anyone—high or lowborn—on this entire estate who doesn't know why you're so lenient with this little whore?" He bit his tongue on, "You're making a fool of yourself."

His father turned that dangerous shade of red. "You puny, whey-faced maggot! One crack across the mug wasn't enough for you?"

As though a dam had burst, Richard's rage surged, washing away any desire for restraint. "I have another cheek. Perhaps you'll disfigure that one as well."

Sir Edward's face became grotesque with fury. He raised his fist above his head, screaming curses and insults while Hogan fidgeted, but Richard heard nothing.

A low drone reverberated through his head. Benumbed, as though in a dream, he glanced at Hogan, then back to his father, who now, to his horror, appeared to have an ivory-handled dagger thrust into his throat. Blood seemed to gush from the wound, cascading over the knife, down his drenched shirt into an ever-growing puddle on the floor. It pooled around Richard's own shoes.

What was happening to him? His father's gnarled face continued to yell and scream—all without sound. Richard watched, stupefied, as the scarlet cast seeped from the lord's face, as though through a hole in a bucket, until Sir Edward's entire head appeared as waxen as a corpse.

The bloodless head then burst into laughter, and his father, alive and well, left the study.

Richard's head began to clear when Hogan grabbed his arm and led him to a chair. "Sit down, Mr. Richard, sir. You're all washed out. I fear you'll faint dead away."

Richard sat, then looked toward his lap. "I've urinated on myself."

⊹

Will smiled as he watched Noreen Bridge set a pot of broth in the fire. He admired his wife's efficient, common-sense manner that hid, to most people, a burning passion. A passion he feared, however, should it ever be unleashed, for all on the manor knew they were at the mercy of their master's whims. This morning had been a stark reminder of that and he imagined a cold chill down many-a spine at the sight and smell of their powerlessness.

Maeve had been well-tended. Her wounds were dressed and covered with a protective layer of lint 'til she could scar. Mrs. Bridge had given the lass one of her own linen blouses, her very favorite since it had softened with wear.

"Would ye try to sit up, Maeve?" Mrs. Bridge asked. "Ye need to drink plenty of water for the healing."

"I will," said the girl.

Aware of the terrible bruising at the hands of Ronan, Will took her by the elbows as gently as he was able and helped her to the table. Once there, Samuel's voice startled him.

"Old Will, the master's calling for ye. He's with Michael Critty in the parlor."

"I'll be there directly."

Mrs. Bridge stopped him at the door. "I don't like the feel of this," she murmured, wary of allowing Maeve to hear.

"Nor I, but let's wait 'til we hear what he has to say."

✟

"Is the filcher suitably dressed?" Sir Edward asked upon Will's arrival.

"She is, milord. Noreen has fixed her up with lint and ointment. She was sitting up as I left her."

"Very well," his master said. "She is to be transported on the next passage to the plantations of Virginia. In the meantime, Critty here has room for her in his jail."

Will's gut sank. "Milord, perhaps a few more days to heal. She could not even rise without help."

"She'll rest a-plenty in the cage, sir," Critty said, far too eager to please as far as Will was concerned. Of course, the jailer would be paid well to keep Maeve.

"Her dressings need to be kept clean and changed every day or so," Will said, at his wit's end with worry.

Critty's jail was a filthy place, with men, women, sane and insane all crowded into the same place. The food was meager and wormy, bedding no more than a spot on the ground, for all money saved on barely tolerable conditions was cash in the jailer's pocket.

"She'll be in the clink, not the hospital," Critty grumbled. "'Tis yer decision, milord, to be sure, but in my experience, most of these criminal-types ain't that dainty."

Will wrung his hands as Sir Edward pondered a mite, then said, "One thing I'm sure of, she will not spend another night on my estate. The voyage to America will be difficult, to say the least. She may as well toughen up now." To the jailer, he said, "Take her with you after you go by the kitchen and eat a hearty meal."

"Kind of ye, sir. But I'll take a bite with me if it's all the same to ye. I've business to attend back in town."

Sir Edward nodded and dismissed them both.

"Get the wench up and ready," Critty told Will when they stepped outside. "I haven't got all morning." Then he headed to the servants' entrance.

Will rushed back to his cabin and burst through the door. At the sight of him, Noreen Bridge rushed to his side.

"We'd best talk outside," he mumbled, for Maeve sat pale and shaky at the table, trying to choke down some broth.

A few yards from the cabin, his wife hissed, "What is it? What's to happen?"

Will looked at her and swallowed. Tales of convict ships to the New World were frightful. Criminals were crammed into tight quarters below deck and rarely felt the sun on their backs for weeks or even months. Neither the food nor the lodging were fit for animals, it was told, and those that succumbed to such putrid conditions were tossed overboard as shark food. If the ship escaped foundering in a tempest, the threat of savage pirates was never far away. And all for a pair of hosiery.

"She's to be transported to the plantations," he said flatly.

"Lord, have mercy," Noreen moaned. She then grew angry. "Ye know she never done it, don't ye? The old bastard wants her gone for vile reasons of his own." Will saw the veins throb in her temples. "He's more dastardly than even I could have imagined."

"Critty's to keep her until her ship departs."

"In that hellhole? Surely, she's not to leave today?"

Critty strode from the kitchen with a round of soda bread and a slab of mutton. "I'm a busy man," he called across the courtyard. "Let's load her up."

Noreen Bridge was beside herself. "Jesus, Mary, and Joseph, what about Tara? She can say good-bye, certainly." She hailed a young groomsman. "Run to the Big House. Tell Orla to send Tara with all of Maeve's belongings." The confused lad stared at her. "Now!"

He wisely bolted.

Will followed his wife into the cabin. He gathered the lint, honey, and ointment pot they had set aside for Maeve. He gritted his teeth at the realization that it was more likely to end up for Critty's own use than for the tortured girl's back.

Mrs. Bridge sat across from Maeve, gripping the girl's hands and explaining her fate.

"No," Maeve sobbed, too weak to do much else. "No. It can't be. I am undone."

Her wretchedness filled Will's eyes with tears while he seethed in rare disgust for his master. Noreen was right. He brought despair on this girl for no more than his own, likely lewd, purposes. Sinful, was what it was. In truth, savage. And there was not a damn thing any of them could do about it.

"This cannot happen." Maeve's eyes were wild and her head spun this way and that, as though desperate for an escape. "The old man's a fiend! Satan himself!"

Mrs. Bridge's face was dark, but she said nothing.

Maeve's pleading eyes turned to Will as he stood by the door. He felt he had aged a decade since the break of day. "I'm heartsick for ye, lass. 'Tis a torment for us all."

"Tara," said Maeve. "I'll never make it without Tara."

As Will helped her up from the table, his stomach churned at the girl's distress. Maeve's tears fell to his arm like drops of acid burning their way into his soul. He ached to bundle her into their old wagon and race away to safety. Yet, they'd all be swinging from the gallows in the end.

Guiding her outside the cabin, Will could feel terror coursing through Maeve's veins as her muscles grew tense. He was not surprised when she pulled away and hied toward the brush like a hobbled cur after a beating, which, in a sense, she was.

Will didn't move, feigning shock. He could have held tightly, preventing her escape, but he did not. Instead, his heart cheered her on, as foolish as that was. He glanced toward Critty.

The jailor shouted, "Halt!" and reached beneath the seat of his wagon. Calmly, Critty pulled out a coach pistol and took dead aim.

Will hustled across the yard and grabbed Maeve's arms as kindly as he could. "He'll kill ye, for sure. We must go back now."

Maeve went limp and stumbled beside Will, a sheep to the slaughter.

When they reached the wagon, Critty laughed. "I'd not have shot the wench. What, and risk me guinea? I'm a better business man than that."

✟

Hearing the commotion, Eveleen ran to the parlor window, giving her a perfect view of the jailer's wagon. She held her hand over her mouth as that filthy man chained Maeve's hands and feet.

Heedless of the rules, Brea bustled into the room and pulled up beside Eveleen. "They're sending her off for a slave in the colonies," she said, her eyes red amidst her pasty face. She clutched her own arms as though she might crumble. "How could this be? What kind of people are these?"

Eveleen scowled. The very ones her da described.

✟

Maeve's heart soared to see Tara scramble from the servants' door with her small satchel of possessions. "Tara!" she called with all the force she could muster. "Don't leave me, Tara. Don't send me off alone!"

Tara stopped in her tracks and stood stark still. She let Maeve's bag drop and stared, her mouth agape. Maeve watched her turn toward Mrs. Bridge, who, with tears streaming down her face, wrung her hands.

"Say yer goodbyes, lass," the older woman told Tara.

With racing heart, Maeve called out her sister's name.

"I can't." Tara turned and, without another look, went back into the kitchen.

Maeve shrieked like a wounded animal.

"Shut yer gob, ye bloody slut." Critty snapped his horsewhip across her forearm.

Will Bridge called out. "Have a speck of mercy, man! The lass has been through enough."

148

"Ye know nothing, do ye, of how to manage scum like this?" Critty called to Mrs. Bridge, "I've no more time for this foolery. Give her the bag or we leave without it."

With tear-filled eyes, Mrs. Bridge ran to the bag, brought it to the wagon, and set it beside Maeve. "God bless ye," the housekeeper whispered, smoothing her hair. "May he keep ye safe all yer days."

With a couple of clicks from Critty, the horses pulled away, causing Maeve to lurch back.

A sudden bang caused all to look toward the slammed kitchen door. Maeve squealed as Tara, carrying her own satchel, trotted toward the wagon in silence. Once catching the cart, she flung her bag into the back and clambered on.

Maeve, as best she could with tethered hands, grabbed onto her sister like life itself, sobbing from her very core.

She heard Critty say, "Bridge, tell his lordship I'll tack this one onto his bill."

Tara did not speak. She did not move. Stone-faced, she stared toward the manor as though mesmerized while the creaking wagon tumbled down the road.

Chapter Fifteen

Tears washed over Eveleen's face as the jailer's wagon lumbered out of sight. Her stomach knotted while inwardly, she wailed in frustration. Innocent, she was, but what did it matter? The lady lied, the lord convicted, and the son ... what of the son? He glared with the cold, hard look, his only words calling for more lashes, greater cruelty. Eveleen shook her head back and forth.

"It cannot be true," she whispered.

"But it is true," Brea answered. "May God bless Maeve. And Tara, too. They'll need all the mercy they can get." She wiped her sleeve over her eyes and left the parlor.

For the first time since he discovered her crouched over the shattered porcelain bird, Eveleen was afraid of Richard. She craved a meeting in the Blue Room where he could explain himself, but at the same time, she shrank from such a confrontation. She had witnessed a darker Richard than she'd dreamed possible, a stone-hearted overlord who would cast Maeve—and perhaps herself—aside with merely a word.

Eveleen turned and polished the woodwork as though she could scrub these thoughts from her heart. For the rest of that day, she scurried from room to room, running from what she could not hope to escape.

⊕

Two days later, barely time for the household to catch its breath, Sir Edward summoned Mrs. Bridge to his study. He ran a finger over the mantle. "Filth," he spat. "Am I to wallow in filth now that the thief is gone?"

"I beg yer pardon, milord. We're short-handed, I'm afraid, 'til we've hired a replacement. Lady Nancy insists on interviewing each lass herself."

Sir Edward snorted. "She no longer trusts your judgement, I see. And with her shrewd grasp of human nature, I'm sure she'll successfully weed all potential larcenists from the lot." He picked up a pipe, lit it, and sucked on it noisily while Mrs. Bridge waited. "I don't want a new, inexperienced maid rummaging through my study. Assign the red-haired one."

Mrs. Bridge's breath caught in her throat. She coughed to cover her gasp. "Uh, Eveleen, milord? She's been here a few months, that's all."

Sir Edward glared at the housekeeper. "I've seen her work and that's the maid I'll have for my private study. You are dismissed."

Mrs. Bridge bowed and left. Not Eveleen! The master's interest in the cleaning of his study could mean only one thing. She had to find Will.

✟

"I gave me word, Noreen. I promised Paddy Scully I'd keep his girl from harm." Will paced before the cattle's feeding trough. "We cannot throw her into the claws of that lecherous wolf." He jammed his fingers into his hair. "Ye must do something."

She groaned. "He gave an order. How can I do otherwise?"

"Great God Almighty!" Will roared, causing the farmhands to stop and look.

"Ye know this is why Maeve is gone." Mrs. Bridge spoke through gritted teeth. "He gave her those stockings, had her whipped bloody at the post, and shipped off to certain death on the American plantations. All for his own lust. He wants Eveleen now and he means to have her."

Will looked her in the eye. "I gave me word. I'm all she has to keep her safe. That's what her da said when I took his little girl away. And it's true."

Mrs. Bridge's eyes widened and she put her fingers to her mouth. "What if I change her schedule? For her own safety, she could clean the room before dawn, before the old man is awake."

"In the dark?"

"It won't be easy, but a glass lantern or two should give enough light. That new stable boy, Doolin, can keep up the hearth fires during the day."

Will stared ahead, considering the idea.

Mrs. Bridge smiled. "What can the old goat say without tipping his hand?"

✤

Eveleen came away from her meeting with Mrs. Bridge perplexed. After all the horrible stories Richard had told of his father, she feared the man. But not until she'd witnessed his whimsical power of life and death over the entire staff had he terrified her. Now, to deal with his personal belongings each and every day left her in a panic. Although her sleep would be cut short under the new schedule, she was grateful she would not be required to see or speak to the ogre.

✤

A week after the flogging, Richard found Eveleen in the parlor. He closed both doors and pulled her away from the windows. "Where have you been?" he hissed into her ear. "Why have you not been by the Blue Room at the usual time?"

Eveleen saw frustration, but also anguish in his eyes. Face-to-face with the still-fiery gash on his cheek, her heart softened. She thought of the miseries forced upon her love's shoulders by his wretched parents and swept Richard's iciness at the flogging from her mind.

"With both Maeve and Tara gone, Mrs. Bridge changed me schedule. I clean that room during yer afternoon meal now."

He squeezed her arm. "Well, she'll just have to change it back. I cannot survive in this hellhole without you."

Eveleen squirmed and he loosened his grip. He glanced toward the closed door and stole a lingering kiss. His gray eyes softened. "I miss you," he said. "I don't care where or when, I've got to see you."

The familiar sense of well-being she'd always known in Richard's arms washed over her. "I start before sunrise now in yer father's study. 'Tis quiet. No one's about."

He pecked her on the lips. "Don't be surprised if you have an early visitor one day." Looking much lighter, he hustled from the room.

Eveleen basked in the warmth she'd missed these last days. He was her same sweet Richard. All was well.

✟

Orla shook Eveleen awake in the dark, drafty servants' hall.

"Ah, good morning," Eveleen whispered, propping up on one elbow.

"Good morning, is it?" Orla chuckled. "Not yer usual, 'It cannot be time already'?"

"Grumbling never changes things."

The cook stood over the girl, fists on her ample hips. "As hard as ye've tried to make it so." She shook her head and returned to the kitchen to bake the day's bread.

Eveleen scrambled to wash her face and stow away her pallet. For over a fortnight, Duncullen had been a cavern of despair and she herself was shrouded with heartache. After meeting Richard the previous afternoon, however, a sparkle of hope arose. Perhaps things could go back as they were.

He said he'd come by the study. She stifled a tell-tale smile. Maybe this day.

Carrying a scuttle of hot coals and a glowing lantern, she made her way to Sir Edward's study. Eveleen was always uneasy there. Even after she'd kindled the hearth fire and lit the lamp, the room spoke loudly of its master. Normally, she scampered about in order to finish as quickly as possible.

Today, however, she found herself lingering over the carved wooden panels that made up the walls, careful not to finish too soon should Richard arrive. Sweeping dust motes from the corner of the room, she felt a presence in the doorway. Her heart danced. Rising, she said, "Ye came."

A deep voice answered, "Not yet."

Eveleen was stupefied to find the portly silhouette of Sir Edward outlined in the doorway, wearing only his shirt and breeches. Head bowed, she mumbled, "Beg pardon, sir. I was looking for, uh, Mrs. Bridge." She hastened toward the door. "I'll take me leave now."

He slammed it shut, stepped into the room, and laid his hand upon her shoulder. "There's no rush."

The look in his eye confounded Eveleen, setting every nerve in her body on guard. She backed away, saying, "I'll just get me—"

He pressed his hand deeper into her shoulder, hurting her. "No. We'll talk."

Eveleen was unable to gasp any more than short, shallow breaths. That seemed to please him, somehow. He liked her fear of him, just like her drunken da.

"I understand you're keeping my son's cock warm."

She frantically waved her head back and forth. "No, milord."

The master moved his hand from her shoulder to the back of her head. "Ah, now. Don't be afraid. You'll not be sent packing for it. In fact, I commend him." His hand rounded her head and rested under her chin. "You're a fair piece of flesh, you are."

"Nooo," she whimpered. "Please, milord. No." Tears rolled down her cheeks.

"In fact, I'm surprised he's even able to perform." He tilted his head. "He is able to perform, yes?"

Eveleen, silently weeping, said nothing.

Sir Edward bent over and kissed her lips. "As sweet as I expected."

He smiled, but, to Eveleen, it was no more than a sneer. Every muscle in her body trembled. "In the name of Jesus, don't do this."

He drew back. "Don't do this? I'm here as a service—to you. Why should you settle for a spoiled namby-pamby like my son?" He raised one side of his mouth. "A lass like you needs a real man."

He snatched her by the arm and led her to his large oaken desk. There, he lifted her by the waist and set her atop.

What to do? What to do? She could think of nothing that wouldn't lead to Maeve's horrific fate—or worse, the end of a rope.

Standing before her, he lifted her head, then forced her lips open with his tongue. His rancid breath from rotting teeth caused her stomach to convulse. Lord God, save me, she pleaded. Please save me!

Chuckling, he lifted her skirts, then dropped his pants. Eveleen turned her head, too sickened and humiliated to look. Her whole body shook with sobs.

"When I'm through, there'll be no crying, I assure you. You'll be begging for more."

At the creaking of the door, Eveleen lifted her head. "Richard!" she squawked.

Sir Edward stepped back. "Have you come to see how it's done?"

Eveleen scrambled to push down her skirts and broke into loud sobs. "Thank the Almighty ..."

The words caught in her throat at the sight of Richard's contorted face. He wore the dark, menacing eyes of a dangerously wounded beast. In a slow, dreamlike state, Eveleen could see the veins in his neck throb just before he opened his mouth, unleashing a growl that rose from the deepest recesses of his gut.

He charged the room and clutched his father's throat, slamming the old man into the wall. Richard's teeth were bared as he squeezed tighter and tighter.

Sir Edward's eyes bulged and his mouth gaped. He hacked and hawked, struggling for breath, but Richard squeezed only harder.

"Richard, ye'll kill him!" Eveleen grabbed his arm and pulled as hard as she could. In his rage, he had the strength of a bull.

She called his name several more times before he turned toward her and released his father. Sir Edward dropped to the floor, gasping for air.

It was as though Richard awoke from a spell. His eyes softened at the sight of her and he gently laid his hands on her cheeks. "I am so sorry, my pet." His eyes filled with tears that did not spill, then he crushed her to his chest.

"Get out," Sir Edward croaked. "Both of you, out of my sight."

✦

In the Blue Room, Richard paced before Eveleen who had crumbled to the floor with her head in her hands. Her red, splotchy face broke his heart, but he was powerless to erase his father's depravity.

"Will I be dismissed?" she whispered.

He stopped mid-stride. "Dismissed? For his sins? I dare the bastard!"

"Hush, Richard. Ye'll rouse the household and I can stand no more trouble."

He reached out his hand to caress her dear head, but, with every nerve alit, he drew back. "I must get out of here. These walls are crushing me."

Eveleen looked him in the eye. "Go. I'll pull meself together. What else is there to do?"

That was precisely the problem. Richard could not think what he should do. He only knew he had to get air, to clear his head.

"Go," she repeated, rising from the floor. "I'm expected downstairs for me breakfast."

✦

In her cabin, Mrs. Bridge stopped preparing the morning meal to listen. She heard voices—agitated voices—coming from the direction of the stables. Too early, it was, for the boys to be stirring.

"Will," she said, "something's amiss."

Her husband sprang up in bed. "What is it?"

"There's a fuss in the stables. Ye'd best see to it."

Will scrambled into his clothing and bolted toward the voices. His heart raced when he recognized Richard's as the loudest.

What sort of troubles had they now before the sun dared peek its head?

Will strode through the open stable doors. There he found Samuel and the new boy, Doolin, stumbling to ready a skittish Black Bess. Mr. Richard, with his hair loose and clothing askew, was pacing back and forth, holding his head.

"Mr. Richard, sir," Will asked, "what's the meaning here? Is someone hurt or sick? I'll send Samuel to fetch the doctor."

Mr. Richard stopped in his tracks, his blood-red face twisted in anguish. "We don't need the blasted doctor. If these imbeciles would get this damned horse geared up, I could be on my way." He went back to pacing, flailing his arms over his head. "Are there no intelligent people in the entire Irish race?"

Will felt as though he'd been punched in the gut. "Of course, sir. Right away." He took the bridle from Doolin and whispered to him, "Yer a good lad, but I'll take over from here."

After expertly placing the bridle on Bess, he leaned over to check the tightness of the girth, but the reins were snatched from his hand.

Without a word, Mr. Richard vaulted onto Black Bess and spurred his horse through the doors.

☥

The cool morning air doused Richard's face as he and Bess raced down the rutted roads of Duncullen. The most vile, abominable sight he'd ever witnessed had wrenched away his breath. The house had engulfed him like a coffin. Even in the stables, he suffocated.

He leaned forward and kicked his horse, urging her on faster and faster. The misty darkness prompted him to stick to the path, enabling him to gallop as fast as Bess could take him.

Richard relished the moist air along with the exhilaration of speed, grateful for any relief he could find.

At a rise, he rode even lower in the saddle, spurring Bess up the incline. Then, without warning, he flew from his horse and hurtled to the ground. Lying in the wet grass, he glimpsed the hind end of a royal red stag followed by his courtiers as they leapt across the road. Startled by the deer, Bess had stopped dead in her tracks, causing Richard to be catapulted into the dry stone wall on the roadside.

Panting and dazed, he looked himself over. The instant he spotted a grisly gash in his biceps, it began to throb. He rose to his knees and covered the three-inch wound with his right hand to stave off the bleeding. When the red ooze seeped through his fingers, he tore off his waistcoat and shirt, then ripped off its sleeve. He wound it tightly around his arm, checking the flow of blood.

Bess puffed and pawed the ground. Richard saw the poor horse's nostrils flare as she stretched her neck between her front legs.

"We'll rest here, you and I," he told her, as he plopped onto the grass beside the road. His own breathing was labored and his head began to pound.

The image of his father's hairy arse, as he stood over … "Better my eyeballs had been ripped out!" he screamed, startling a flock of birds from their roosts. Outrage surged through his veins, forcing him to leap to his feet and, once again, pace up and down.

"He is not fit to be scraped from the shoe of a FitzAden, yet he debases my mother like she's worthless trash," he railed with only Black Bess to hear. "He debases me. And now he defiles Eveleen!"

He turned to the low wall and kicked the stones with all his might, as though the capstone were his father's skull. "I despise you, you repulsive pervert! With every fiber of my being, I despise you! You are not fit to live." He slammed his heel into the wall repeatedly until several of the stones loosened and slid to the ground.

Spent, his chest heaved as he dropped his head. "Everything he touches turns to dung." His eyes burned and his throat grew taut. Against his will, bitter tears rolled down his cheeks.

"Did he have to take it all? Could he not have left me the one resplendent thing in my life?" His sweet Eveleen. Desecrated.

When he lifted his arm to wipe his running nose, Richard noticed his injury was bleeding more heavily. He grabbed his shirt from the ground, ripped off the other sleeve, and wrapped a new layer of bandage over the wound.

The sun had sneaked into the eastern sky without his notice, shining through the morning fog with an eerie glow. Gingerly, he put on his sleeveless shirt and waistcoat, then picked up Bess's reins. "Come along, girl. We'll walk back. I'll not exhaust you again."

When he returned Bess to the stables, Jack rushed toward him and took the weary horse's reins. "Are ye well, Mr. Richard? Bess looks tired."

Richard patted her flanks. "She needed the exercise. You take care of her, Jack."

"I will." He frowned at Richard. "A ruckus, ye caused this morning."

Richard scowled. "That's none of your concern."

Jack opened, then shut his mouth. He damn well knows better than to talk back, Richard thought as he stalked from the barn.

Chapter Sixteen

There ye be!"

Brea stood in the doorway of the Blue Room. "Ye've missed yer breakfast and now yer noon meal."

Eveleen was crouched before the hearth, but the fire was cold.

"What are ye doing?" Brea snapped. The whole house seemed to be going mad. Mrs. Bridge was in a wild state with eyes that looked a bit crazy.

"Where is Eveleen? Does she make her own rules now?" the housekeeper had ranted, bustling around the servants' hall with no clear place to go. She charged Brea with finding Eveleen and now, here she was, swishing a poker around cold ashes and refusing to look her way.

She walked over and shook the girl's shoulder. "Are ye daft? Ye've been called for downstairs."

With the pale light from a single window, Brea could see Eveleen's eyes were red and swollen. She crouched beside her and placed a hand on her shoulder. "What's wrong?"

Eveleen sniffed loudly and ran her sleeve under her nose. "Not a thing. I'm a bit out of sorts, is all."

"Yer belly?"

"I've no stomach for food."

"And all ye want is to cry?"

Eveleen nodded her head. "I miss me ma."

"'Tis time for yer monthlies, I'd wager."

Eveleen's lips curved into a sort of smile. "I'd wager it is."

"Come." Brea stood and stretched out her hand. "Dry yer eyes. Mrs. Bridge is in a stew. A vexing day it is, here at Duncullen."

✟

Mrs. Bridge's head throbbed as she paced back and forth beside the servants' table. She fought the nausea that rose in her throat, having vomited twice already.

"Here she is," thundered Brea, causing Mrs. Bridge's head to reverberate with pain.

The housekeeper growled, "Yer not a field hand. There's no need to bellow like one." She spotted a wretched Eveleen hunched behind the girl. "Return to yer duties, Brea."

"Yes, Mrs. Bridge." The girl scampered away.

"Ida," she called to the new scullery maid, a scrawny, homely girl. "Weed the garden until I send for ye."

Ida, too, scuttled off without a word.

"Orla is not here, Eveleen," Mrs. Bridge said. "We can speak in peace."

Eveleen had not moved since she poked her head into the kitchen, and Mrs. Bridge had no patience for skylarking today. "Step forward, girl. I'll not shout at ye across the room."

Eveleen slinked closer, then sat in the chair Mrs. Bridge nodded to.

The housekeeper lowered herself into her own chair slowly, as though her heavy, oversized head would roll off if not perfectly balanced.

"I don't know exactly what's going on here, but I don't like it," she began. "Before the crack of dawn, young Mr. Richard creates a fray in the stables the likes of which I've never heard, bolting away on his horse, nearly knocking me Will clear off his feet. And not a backward glance did he give."

She noticed the girl's eyes widen, but no more. "Mr. Hogan informed me Sir Edward has holed up in his study all morning, refusing to see petitioners who seek his help." She paused for a split second before continuing. "He has asked for nothing but pot after pot of rum-shrub, I'm told."

No reaction.

"Which is why I wasn't shocked at the disgraceful condition of our master when he summoned me a short while ago. With great difficulty, he finally spit out that you are no longer to work anywhere near him or his personal belongings."

Eveleen's head popped up.

"What do ye say to that?"

There was no mistaking Eveleen's relief as tension drained from the girl's face and shoulders. "As our lord and master wishes."

"Ye've been careless with his things, he says," Mrs. Bridge went on, studying her closely. "I am to assign another girl." She had already picked Elly, a shy girl with a pocked face and none of the spirit Sir Edward liked in his conquests.

"And here sits yerself, missy, yer eyes—yer entire face a puffy mess." Mrs. Bridge frowned as Eveleen dropped her head. "I know something went on in that room. I mean to find out what it was."

"There's nothing to tell, Mrs. Bridge. I don't know what the master is talking about, but I respect his wishes. I'll never go near him again."

The housekeeper snatched Eveleen's wrist and held it in an iron grip. "Ye can tell me, lass. I'll not dismiss ye. Do ye think I know nothing of who our lord really is? That I am unaware of his lustful ways with young girls like yerself? And what are ye to do? Slap the codfish? Run to his wife with it? There's nothing the likes of us can do against a powerful man like that but stick together." She softened her tone. "And help each other where we can."

"There's nothing to tell. I was careless. It will not happen again."

"What of Mr. Richard? He has nothing to do with this? I'm no fool, girl."

Eveleen's lips quivered, then she looked Mrs. Bridge in the eye. "I know nothing of the actions of the young master. How could I?"

"I see." She nodded. "I really do see." She dropped Eveleen's wrist and sat back. "I tried to warn ye, didn't I? I tried to ... never mind." She closed her eyes, wishing to erase this day from her memory. "All I ask is that poor Will hears nothing of this. Can ye do that for me, at least? He promised your da he'd protect ye."

Eveleen stared at Mrs. Bridge. "And how would he be able to do that? He made a promise he had no way of keeping, didn't he?"

Mrs. Bridge's whole body sagged while tears sprang to her eyes. "Perhaps he did. But he made it in earnest and, well, I fear his heart will burst if he learns he failed his old friend in such a way. He's a good man, Eveleen, and I can't bear to see him hurt once again."

Tears dripped off the older woman's chin. "Explain to me what happened," she continued. "We both know there's little I can do, but I can do nothing if I'm blind to the situation."

"As I've already said, there's nothing to tell."

Mrs. Bridge scraped back her chair, rose from the table, and left.

✢

It was mid-afternoon and Richard had, by the grace of God, been left alone in the privacy of his chambers. There had not even been a summons by his mother. Probably not a good sign where she was concerned, but Richard considered it a blessing.

He tried to read, but couldn't concentrate. Eating and drinking were hopeless. He lay on his bed praying for sleep, but none came. He could find no escape from his misery.

A soft rap on the door shook him from his brooding. "I want nothing to eat," he called. "Go away."

It irked him to see the doorknob turn despite his instructions. "Are you deaf?" he barked, only to fall mute when his father slid into the room. How many times had Richard been commanded to appear before this man? Not once had his father come to him.

He leapt from his bed, tensed and ready for battle. Sir Edward, a scarf wrapped around his neck, stared back at his son through bloodshot eyes, wearing a face overgrown in gray stubble.

By God, he'd aged a decade. It was as though he was seeing his father for the first time and, for once, he was not afraid of this weak, broken-down buffoon. He could not muster one iota of pity for him. Only repugnance.

Finally, the old man spoke. "I didn't know."

"Didn't know what?"

Sir Edward flailed his arms as though summoning the words. "How you felt about the girl. I ... I thought she was a lark, a plaything."

"I have no idea what you're talking about."

"Don't lie about that, son. You're in love with her."

Richard's hatred for his father billowed inside him. "Now you call me son? And how could you possibly know my feelings about anything?"

"I'm not so old that I couldn't read it on your face. Had I realized, I'd never have touched her. You must believe that."

"Must I? I'm not the fool you take me for. Have always taken me for. My feelings mean nothing to you. They never have."

"I'm sorry."

Richard's mouth dropped. Not once had he heard those words slide through his father's lips. Yet, he would not be mocked again.

"I care nothing for the girl." He heard his voice crack and cursed himself for it, yet he knew too well how an admission of the truth could be used against him.

"Don't say it, lad." His father's eyes grew soft and moist, rattling Richard to the core. "It's been so long since I've felt such a passion, it's a wonder I even recognized it. But it all came back to me in a rush—the light heart, fluttery stomach, and that lustful energy." He shook his head. "All that makes life worth living."

His eyes pleaded with Richard. "I won't take it from you—not intentionally."

"It's too late for remorse."

"It was not consummated, Richard. She's yours. I'll have no more truck with her. You have my word."

Without responding, Richard pivoted and strode across the room to the window. His eyes filled with unwelcome tears he forbid his father to see.

"I'm sorry," Sir Edward repeated to Richard's back just before the door clicked shut.

⊕

Richard struggled to focus on memories of Eveleen giggling beside the Multeen, pulling in trout after trout. Or her eyes alight as she lay beside him, listening to his dreams. A goddess. His Aphrodite.

But a worm had burrowed into his brain, devouring those lovely images, then spewing a much uglier one in their place. He was tortured by the vision of Eveleen flat on her back, skirts thrust over her belly, her skinny white legs exposed before his father's beastly appetite.

Over the next week, Richard's nights remained sleepless, he refused to eat, and Eveleen—his stomach twisted at the sight of her. He found himself planning his day to avoid her. What could he say? What could he do? To see her, but even more, to touch her was too painful.

Once, while she was sweeping the ashes from the parlor's hearth, he stalked in, then froze. Stunned to find her there, he pivoted and retreated.

"Richard," Eveleen called in a loud whisper. "Mr. Richard," she corrected herself.

He took a deep breath and turned.

"I ... I wanted to thank you. For saving me." Her eyes were swimming with tears. "I was nearly ravished. Every day, I thank the Almighty ye came by when ye did."

"I thank God as well." He bit his lip and looked at his shoes. "I'm going to need some time to sort things out."

He glanced to see her reaction. Oh, Lord. She was crying. He walked to her and took her hand. "You did nothing wrong. I know that. But my father's treachery has wounded me deeply and ... well, I'll need time to heal." He dropped her hand and took a step back. "You understand that, don't you?"

"Of course, my love," she said, wiping rivulets from her chin. Then, in a child's voice, she asked, "Do you still think I'm pretty?"

Richard's heart beat against his ribcage like a sledgehammer, causing him to place his fist on his chest as though he could still it. He forced the words through his mouth. "Eveleen, you will always be pretty."

Before she could ask another torturous question, he spun on his heel and left the room. In the Great Hall, he leaned against a pillar and tried to catch his breath.

This was not his fault. The worm. It gnawed his brain, tormenting him day and night. It was taking over his life, boring through any chance of happiness.

There was no other way. The worm would be expunged.

✝

It repulsed Richard to sit in the Lynche box pew at Saint Aidan's with his father in attendance. He looked across his mother to see Sir Edward picking at his fingernails, paying no more attention to Father Healy's homily than the mouse that scuttled across the floor. The miscreant diminished their church and the entire faith by his presence.

Pale and listless, Lady Nancy was nodding off, barely able to hold up her head. Richard realized even he was too restless to focus on the morning's message. A fine example by the baronet and his family.

He picked up his missal and flipped it open. Often, in his boredom, he randomly opened the pages to see what message God might have for him. Psalm Fifty-eight.

> Do ye indeed speak righteousness, O congregation? do
> ye judge uprightly, O ye sons of men?
> Yea, in heart ye work wickedness; ye weigh the violence
> of your hands in the earth.

Richard audibly gasped. He looked to his right, but neither parent showed any sign of noticing. Wide-eyed, he looked back to the verse. God's hand had led him to this scripture. Clearly, Sir Edward, a hypocrite whose presence in this church feigned righteousness, wrought violence upon everything and everyone he touched.

> The wicked are estranged from the womb: they go astray as
> soon as they be born, speaking lies.
> Their poison is like the poison of a serpent: they are like the
> deaf adder that stoppeth her ear;
> Which will not harken to the voice of charmers, charming never so
> wisely.

He read the lines over like a fiend, becoming more engrossed in what God was imparting to him.

> Break their teeth, O God, in their mouth: break out the great
> teeth of the young lions, O Lord.
> Let them melt away as waters which run continually: when he
> bendeth his bow to shoot arrows, them be as cut in pieces.
> As a snail which melteth, let every one of them pass away: like
> the untimely birth of a woman, that they may not see the sun.
> Before your pots can feel the thorns, he shall take them away as with
> a whirlwind, both living, and in his wrath.

Richard gobbled up King David's pleas like a starving man. Yes, Sir Edward Lynche, lying and malicious, should dissolve like a slug into a smear of slime. If only he'd been born dead! God hated his evil as much as he himself did.

> The righteous shall rejoice when he seeth the vengeance: he shall
> wash his feet in the blood of the wicked.
> So that a man shall say, Verily there is a reward for the righteous:
> verily he is a God that judgeth in the earth.

Richard's fingers tingled. "He shall wash his feet in the blood of the wicked," pounded in his head over and over. Terror-stricken, he remembered the vision of his father's life blood pouring from the knife wound in his throat, submerging Richard's feet in sticky, scarlet ooze.

His heart raced. What did this mean? "When he seeth the vengeance ..." Is that what his vision was about? Vengeance toward the serpent who cares only for the evil he spreads over the earth?

And when he saw his father's listless corpse hanging from the rafters? Was that, too, a message from the Lord? Another verse came to him: "Whoso sheddeth man's blood, by man shall his blood be shed: for in the image of God he made man."

Genesis 9:6. The verse that commanded humanity to kill the destroyers of life. Those like his father.

The hair on the back of his neck stood on end as God's true meaning came to him. His hands shook and his head swam. He felt like a person apart, watching himself in the pew. His missal slid to the floor with a resounding thud.

Father Healy stopped his sermon and the entire congregation turned to look. All waited while he scrambled to retrieve his Scriptures.

Once the service resumed, Lady Nancy reached for his hand. "Are you unwell? Your hand is like ice. You look positively bilious."

He snatched it back. "I'm fine, Mother." Or he would be.

An odd sense of relief overcame him now that he knew what he must do. Richard was aware that their translation was from the Greek, which stated the sixth commandment as "Thou shalt not kill." But Father Healy had told him of the original Hebrew which actually said, "Thou dost not murder."

This was not about murder. This was a mandate from God.

Chapter Seventeen

Once Richard understood what he was ordained to do, he became analytical and detached.

First, he knew that, while his deed would fulfill God's will, he trusted no one to be intellectually capable of comprehending his motives. In Clonmel Grammar's library, he remembered finding an analysis of Phillip Massinger's 1639 drama, *The Unnatural Combat,* in a dusty old tome. The play was believed to be based on Italian gentlewoman Beatrice Cenci, who killed her father to stop his despicably incestuous acts upon her. Yet, the Pope himself had ordered her beheading. Richard expected no better upon the discovery of his own virtuous mission.

He must succeed in the undertaking while bringing no suspicion upon himself. Therefore, it would be poison. Arsenic was not only odorless and tasteless; it could be easily obtained. Just a little in his father's morning tea and none would be the wiser.

But how little? And what were the symptoms? How long would it take the miscreant to breathe his last and terminate his evil presence on this earth?

Richard's stomach wrenched at the fear of a misstep due to his own ignorance. Yet, he dared not speak of it to anyone, lest he raise suspicions after his father's grisly death. It would be grisly, would it not?

Arsenic, he thought. Called the "Poison of Kings" since it had handily dispatched many of Europe's crowned heads. The irony made him laugh. Sir Edward would finally achieve the social parity for which he'd always strived.

✿

Acquiring the arsenic would be the easy part. The hours he'd spent as a boy with Jack and Old Will would pay off. Once his former playmate, Denny, had succumbed to the fever, Richard was permitted to play with Jack, who, though a few years older than he, was considered harmless. They were nearly always under the heedful eyes of Old Will, keeping them free from mischief.

Richard smirked. Old Will had unwittingly taught him the very skills he'd need to dispatch his father to the agonies of hell.

He remembered how he and Jack sat statue still on a bale of hay, watching the overseer stretch for the apothecary jar on a high shelf. Old Will would remove the cork and carefully sprinkle it into a dough of oatmeal, butter, and honey. Wearing special gloves, he then rolled the mixture into pea-sized pills and threw them into dark corners where rodents lurked.

"Stay away from this, lads," he used to warn them. "Ye see the gloves I wear. The poison can seep through yer skin and cause a raging illness. Or even kill ye if ye get too much."

Richard smiled at the memory. Old Will, he thought, you have proven yourself indispensable.

While his father deserved no more than the rats, Richard would be mixing the white powder into a cup of tea instead of oatmeal. The challenge was to obtain the poison without being seen.

On his side was the unfailing daily routine of the household staff and his parents. His father customarily ate breakfast at ten, followed by meetings with tenants and townspeople. His mother, like Richard himself these days, ate in her chambers. The staff, including the stable hands, ate a noontime meal in the servants' hall. On this day, they were his primary concern.

After his breakfast dishes were cleared, Richard pulled on his knee breeches with the buttoned pockets and an old frock. Reaching into his chest of drawers, he retrieved a small leather coin purse. The gift from years ago, the giver long forgotten, would be disposed of once it served its purpose.

From his window, he watched the last straggler from the fields make his way into the kitchen. Richard then sneaked downstairs to the library and left the house through a pair of French doors that led to the gardens.

Thinking he'd been calm and methodical, Richard was stunned to see his hands quaking as he stood on the terrace. Either be nonchalant, he berated himself, or slither back inside, you coward!

After several deep breaths, he clasped his hands behind his back and wended his way toward the stables.

Despite his best efforts, every nerve was exposed. The screeching of crows clawed at his eardrums. He flailed at the touch of a dragonfly and had to command himself not to cut and run. Once inside the barn, the whinny of a mare rammed his heart into his throat.

Although time was short, Richard made his way to Bess's stall and stroked her nose, soothing the unruffled filly. Within minutes, his own heart slowed and muscles relaxed.

"It is what God ordains," he reminded himself, stepping into the barn's alley.

Wrenching his eyes from the rafters, Richard strode toward the shelf containing the poison and removed the translucent apothecary jar. After pulling some old riding gloves from his pocket, he struggled to put them on. He'd grown in three years. No matter. Like the coin purse, they would be burned.

From his right pocket, Richard remove the purse. Setting all on Old Will's workbench, he lifted the bottle, pulled the cork, and tipped the jar toward the purse. How much? He wanted enough to do the job, but if too much was missing, wouldn't that raise suspicion? Richard's ears echoed with the boom of his thumping heart.

Do it!

He shook the bottle, emptying an unknown amount of arsenic into the pouch, yanked its drawstrings, and jammed the purse into his pocket. Frantically, he grabbed the cork, wedged it into the bottle, and stashed it back onto the shelf.

He gasped when he realized the bottle had left a clean circle in the midst of the dusty board. He gently lifted the vial and set it within the ring. Relieved, he exhaled in a huff which sent a billowing cloud of dust into the air.

Drawing breath, he felt a suspicious tingle in his nose right before he heartily sneezed. God's nails! He'd inhaled the poison.

"Who's there?"

Old Will. Scrambling from the workbench, Richard ripped his gloves from his hands and jammed them into the same pocket as the purse, creating a noticeable bulge.

"Ah, Mr. Richard, sir. 'Tis you." Old Will tilted his head. "Did ye lose track of yer day? All the lads are eating dinner now, but I can ready Bess for ye if ye like."

"Uh, no. Well, yes, ready the horse." Richard's struggle to remain composed seemed insurmountable. He shifted his weight from one leg to the other.

Old Will cocked his head to the other side. "We've not seen much of ye lately, sir. Black Bess has missed ye, to be sure. Grateful she'll be for a bit of a blowout."

"A blowout?" Richard studied the old man intensely, searching for any hint of suspicion. "I'll not ride her as hard as I did last time."

"Of course not, sir."

Richard was sure Will had glanced toward his bulging pocket before turning his attention to Bess. He knew something! Like a skyrocket, Richard's heart rate surged. His stomach churned and threatened to heave. He'd snorted the poison. He had to vomit.

He ran out to the far side of the stables and retched into the high grass. His throat burned, convincing Richard that arsenic dust was stripping his esophagus. A cruel joke! He would send his own soul to hell! He jammed his finger down his throat as far as he could reach, then spewed the remaining contents of his stomach. His empty stomach started to spasm on its own, bringing up only acrid bile. When he finally stopped, he tumbled to his side, the muscles in his gut aching.

"Mr. Richard!"

Richard lifted his head to see Old Will rounding the corner of the stables. He climbed to his hands and knees.

"What in the name of Old Saint Peter?" Old Will hooked his hands under Richard's arms and helped him to his feet.

"I'm ill, is all." Richard's head was spinning. "I'd best retire to my chambers. Bess will have to wait."

"Of course, sir. Let me help ye." Old Will looked down. "Ye've dropped yer gloves."

Richard tensed and slapped his pockets. Nothing. It couldn't be!

"Stand back," he barked at the overseer. "I'll get them myself."

He dropped to the ground, grabbed the gloves, and crawled this way and that in a frantic search for the pouch. Drenched in sweat, he leapt to his feet and ripped the button from his pocket. Thrusting his hand inside, he fingered the cool leather of his coin purse.

His shoulders slumped and he pulled in as much air as he could manage. Panting, he turned toward Will to find the old man's mouth agape. Wiping the sweat from his brow, he lumbered toward the house.

"I need no help."

✟

Richard lay on his bed and waited to die.

He stared at the top drawer of his dresser. There, after slinking back to his room, he had tucked the poison pouch under his newest pair of leather gloves. His old gloves he'd stashed under some shrubbery as he staggered past.

His stomach rumbled and groaned while he swallowed bile and the bitterness it represented. Was God a cruel prankster who took pleasure in mocking his virtue, just like his father?

Richard moaned as he silently prayed. Oh, most powerful God, why, in your wrath, do you smite me? I am like your faithful servant, Abraham, ready to obey your most macabre command. You instruct me to sacrifice the evil-doer, yet you snuff out my own flame instead.

"Mr. Richard."

Ugh. Hogan. Richard continued to face the wall. "Can I not die here in peace?"

"Of course, sir. Old Will mentioned you had fallen ill and I came to see what might be done for you."

"What might be done for me is to be left alone."

"Right you are, Mr. Richard. A long sleep will do the trick."

A very long sleep, indeed.

✟

It was dusk before Richard, to his surprise, awoke with an aching hunger in his empty, but functioning stomach. He bolted upright and rang the servants' bell.

Young Doolin must've been assigned the hall chair outside his chamber judging by the speed with which he burst through the door. "At your service, sir."

Richard almost laughed at the boy's eagerness. "Inform Hogan I'll require a plate of meats and cheeses from the kitchen. Tell him I am much improved. The sleep he recommended served me well."

"That I will, sir." The little fellow spun like a top toward the door.

"Wait," Richard called. It was clear the anxiety of his mission had been overwhelming. If it was to be completed, it had to be right away. "I need Hogan to deliver a message to my father."

"Sir?"

"I would like to meet Sir Edward in the breakfast room at his usual time—ten o'clock tomorrow."

With a quick bow, the boy was off.

"My Lord and my God, Your will be done."

✟

Richard was already seated at the breakfast table when Hogan and one of the kitchen maids brought in cold meat, cheese, and fish.

"Mr. Richard," Hogan said with his usual unflappable composure. "Please forgive me. I was told you would take breakfast at ten with your father."

"You were told correctly," he answered, his hands in a white-knuckled clasp beneath the table.

"Bring the toast, butter, and marmalade," the butler mumbled to the maid, who quickly left the room.

"Hogan, I have my future to discuss with my father and I will need total privacy," Richard said. "I pray you will understand and leave us in peace when Sir Edward arrives."

"Once I have poured ..."

"No." Richard stuck out his chin. "I will pour the tea. Once you bring the urn, you are dismissed."

Only Hogan's flared nostrils conveyed any surprise at the unusual demand. "As you wish."

All the previous night, Richard had lain on his bed and mulled over the timing of his task. Once he dismissed the servants, how close to the hour of ten should he prepare the fateful cup of tea? Too late, and his father could catch him in the act. Too early, and the tainted tea would go cold, only to be poured out by his father for a hotter cup.

While his father was punctual, he could not be counted on to enter at the precise striking of the hour. When the mantle clock showed five minutes before ten, Richard took a deep breath and put it in the hands of fate. If the tea was poured out, he would just have to make a new attempt tomorrow.

He rose from the table and walked to the sideboard. He set two cups side by side, considered them, then moved his own several inches from his father's. Struggling to keep his breathing steady, he removed the leather pouch from his pocket and pulled the bag open. He sprinkled a few grains of white dust into his father's cup, then stared, contemplating it.

"Ye'll need more than that, I'd say."

Richard's heart froze as he whipped his head toward the voice.

Mrs. Bridge took a few steps closer. "That'll make him sick, if that's what yer after. Otherwise, ye'll need a stronger dose."

In a futile effort, he stuck the pouch behind his back. "I ... I don't know what you're talking about." He glared at the housekeeper as she came ever closer.

"I believe ye do. If it's dead yer wanting him to be, ye'll need a bit more of that powder." Mrs. Bridge picked up the teapot and filled half the cup. She cocked her head. "Well?"

Richard realized he was gawking at her with his mouth hanging loose. He closed his lips tight, pulled the leather pouch from behind his back, and emptied all of the poison into the cup. With the teaspoon, he stirred frantically with one eye toward the clock.

"Now," said Mrs. Bridge, "when the old man arrives, fill the cup the rest of the way. It'll be plenty warm." She even smiled. "An old server's trick."

With that, she slid out the servants' door with little time to spare. Richard had barely jammed the coin pouch into his pocket when his father burst in the room.

Seeing his son, Sir Edward stopped short. "You came. I wasn't sure you would."

Richard, hands trembling, filled his father's cup with hot tea. He lifted the saucer and cup and placed it before Sir Edward. "I would like to discuss my future with you. Privately. I have dismissed Hogan, so I will serve you myself." He returned to the sideboard. "What would you like?"

Sir Edward lowered himself into his chair at the head of the table. Richard steeled himself. He refused to wither under his father's scrutiny.

"The food can wait," Sir Edward said. "You're as skittish as a head-shy foal. Sit down here and say your piece."

Richard stole a backward glance before he poured tea for himself. Sir Edward had not touched his cup.

"If you insist on this unnecessary degree of privacy, can you at least pour a simple cup of tea with some modicum of haste?"

Richard's cup and saucer rattled and clinked as he struggled to breathe.

He screamed in his head, He's picking it up.

Sir Edward placed the rim to his lips, then glared at his son. "Sit. Now."

Mentally fortifying himself once again, Richard obeyed. He lifted his own cup and sipped, hoping to encourage his father to do the same.

Sir Edward blew into the tea, then slurped loudly.

Richard's heart pounded in his ears. This was the test. Was it truly tasteless? He forced himself to speak, but to his own ears he sounded far away. "I'd like to discuss the Grand Tour."

His father set his cup down showing no signs of distaste. "This is not what I expected."

"I'm nearly a man now and it's time for me to expand my horizons. See the world." He was speaking far too quickly, but could not slow down. "You and I have been at odds over this, and other things I'd rather not discuss. I will not discuss them. In any case, I believe it would do my mother, the household—all of Duncullen—some good if we were apart for a period of time."

He had practiced this fake speech over and over as he lay in bed, but it was coming out in a rambling, disjointed manner.

"Slow down. Drink your tea before it gets cold. Let's sort this out."

His father's reasonable tone was unnerving him. His hands trembled as he sipped.

Sir Edward took a large gulp from his own cup, then drained it. He rose, walked to the sideboard, and retrieved the pot for a refill. After serving himself, he poured a bit into Richard's cup. "It's not too late to join Alistair's group. Moore has hired

Gerald Stewart as bear-leader. The man's from London and has led several of these excursions. He comes highly recommended."

Back at the sideboard, Sir Edward picked up a plate and began piling meat and cheese onto it. He grabbed a piece of toast and proceeded to spread a thick layer of orange marmalade. "This pleases me, Richard. But I can't for the life of me understand your insistence on privacy." He took a bite of his toast, looked at his son, and spoke with a full mouth. "You're a strange lad. Too much like your mother."

He prattled on for what seemed an eternity about the coach he would rent, which servants he could spare to accompany Richard, and the itinerary they'd likely follow, but Richard could not have repeated a word of it.

Every tick of the clock seemed like a moment; each moment was a week. Finally, when his father took a breath and rang the bell for Hogan, Richard stole a glance at the time. Could only twenty minutes have passed? And no adverse symptoms. If something didn't happen soon, Richard feared he'd collapse into a puddle of urine.

The butler arrived almost immediately, stood by his master's side, and awaited instructions.

"Richard has informed me he will be joining the Grand Tour. Since the group he will accompany departs in a month's time, I will need the morning to make arrangements. Do we have petitioners today?"

"Just two, milord. Young Tom Kelly requests permission to cut a sturdy tree from your forest in order to build a new water trough. His has rotted through."

"He has my permission. Send him on his way."

"Barry O'Brien is asking you to intervene in a property dispute. He claims Jimmy Hayes has broken his hoe and will not replace it."

"Harold O'Brien? From Cahir? I thought he was dead."

Richard snapped to attention. His father's eyes were cloudy and his skin had paled.

"Yes, milord. Harold is deceased. It is Barry who wishes to see you." Hogan frowned. "Are you well, sir? You're looking poorly."

Sir Edward clutched his stomach and howled in pain.

It had started. Richard leapt from his seat and feigned concern. "What is it, Father? Something you ate?"

"Oooh," the old man moaned. "The room is spinning. And my throat! My throat is on fire."

"Send for Dr. Quinn," Richard ordered the butler with very real panic in his voice.

Hogan called through the servants' door and returned to his master, who continued to clamor and howl. Without warning, Sir Edward slumped to one side and spewed his morning meal before Richard and Hogan, then dropped his head, insensible.

Richard gagged at the sight and stench of the bloody vomit.

"Great God! Sir Edward, can you hear me?" Hogan stepped in and lifted his master's head. He looked at Richard, his eyes wide with alarm. "He's clammy as a dead perch."

"We must get him to his chambers."

At that moment, the servants' door flung open allowing Will Bridge, followed by his wife and two groomsmen, to pour into the room.

"What's happened?" Mrs. Bridge's eyes were wide in apparent shock and concern. Dropping her act for not even one full second, she shot a knowing look at Richard.

It was done so quickly and seamlessly that Richard wasn't sure if he'd imagined it, but his stomach twisted in distress, all the same.

"Samuel's off for the doctor," said Old Will before he and the two young bucks lifted Sir Edward and carried him to his bed.

As they passed Lady Nancy's chamber, she burst into the hallway, followed by Biddy. "What's become of my husband?" She grabbed his cheeks in her two hands and called, "What is wrong, Edward? You must wake up. Wake up!"

Biddy held her lady firmly by the shoulders and led her from the struggling servants. "Let them put him to bed, milady. All will be well."

Lady Nancy broke from her maid and latched onto Richard's arm. He gritted his teeth, too on edge to deal with his mother's dramatics now.

"Mother, Biddy is right. Father was fine until he ate breakfast. Perhaps some of the food disagreed with him." He peeled his mother's hands from his arm. "Dr. Quinn has been sent for. I'll come for you if there's more news."

"Come for me? I will be at my husband's side and no one will stop me, Richard. Not even you."

Richard sighed. A strange time for wifely devotion.

The procession entered Sir Edward's chambers and, still insensible, he was laid upon his large bed. The two groomsmen were excused. Richard and Hogan posted themselves bedside while the others stood farther off, waiting and wondering. Biddy led the addled Lady Nancy to the small wingback sofa in the corner of the room.

Is it over? Richard wondered. Then his father emitted a low moan. Sir Edward shifted this way and that before opening his eyes, although they were unfocused.

"Noreen," he croaked, then clutched his throat. His face twisted in pain. "Noreen."

Will turned to his wife who'd come little farther than the door. Richard was sure he'd seen a flash of fear in the overseer's eyes.

Will spoke in a low tone. "Noreen?" He nodded toward his master.

Her lips pursed into a thin, straight line, she shuffled closer to the sickbed.

Now seeing her, Sir Edward stretched out his hand. Mrs. Bridge took it as one might a festering sore. "Noreen," he whispered, "where is my beautiful Nancy?"

She dropped his hand as though it had bitten her and stepped back. "Milady?"

Lady Nancy scuttled to the bed and leaned over her husband. "Edward, I'm here." Tears ran down her cheeks, leaving Richard completely baffled.

Sir Edward fixed his gaze upon his wife. "If only ..." He winced in pain as he gasped for breath. "If only you ... had loved me." He struggled for every word. "Instead of my money."

"Edward!" She opened her mouth to protest further, but Sir Edward waved her away. Sobbing into her linen handkerchief, she rushed back to the sofa and comfort of Biddy.

Sir Edward twisted his head until he spotted Richard. "Away!" he croaked, chasing everyone from his bed. "My son. I want my son."

Richard crept to his side. *He's so weak,* he thought, stunned by the old man's ashen face and dark, sunken eyes.

With great effort, his father motioned for Richard to lean over him so he could speak in his ear. Richard shivered at the touch of his father's cold lips.

"You ... poisoned me."

Richard's heart raced like a Thoroughbred. Speechless, he could only wheeze.

His father pulled in as much breath as he seemed able. "Still the coward," he said, before closing his eyes.

Richard rose. His heart hurt and his throat closed. Never had he experienced such anguish.

Within minutes, Hogan leaned over, listening for his breath. "He's gone."

Lady Nancy noticed her son as though for the first time. She tilted her head. "What did he say to you? His last words."

Richard rose to his full height. His lips trembled.

"That he was proud of me. That he loved me."

Chapter Eighteen

Richard could barely breathe as the hoary Dr. Quinn examined his father's corpse. Neither his mother nor the staff showed any signs of suspicion, yet his father had figured out the truth. How could he know?

"Gastric fever." The doctor shook his head. "I always thought it would be the gout that got him." He squinted at Richard. "There were some unusual bruises around his neck. Do you know where they came from?"

Richard's heart thundered, but he did all he could to remain expressionless. "I don't. He'd started wearing a scarf more than a week ago, but I never asked why."

Dr. Quinn looked uncomfortable, like he'd said too much. "Of course not. They were not recent, so it does not change the cause of death, in any case." He sighed. "I'm sorry I was unable to arrive faster, but there was not much I could have done."

"I understand." Despite his relief, Richard wanted to laugh at the self-assured old man. Gastric fever, was it? he thought. You withered old buffoon.

He dared not get too cocky; he had one more obstacle to overcome. If Father Healy had any misgivings concerning the nature of Sir Edward's death, he was required to contact the coroner forthwith. An inquest would follow.

Within a few hours, the clergyman arrived and conferred with the doctor. Richard watched him nod his head in agreement, then shake it in commiseration. Meanwhile, Richard paced the room, straightening artwork and fiddling with figurines his father had collected over the years.

Father Healy finally approached Richard and placed a hand on his shoulder.

"You are understandably distressed. But remember, your father no longer walks by faith. He now walks by sight."

"Yes."

"'We are confident, I say, and willing rather to be absent from the body, and to be present with the Lord.'"

"Second Corinthians," Richard said. To this ninny babbling inapt platitudes, he went for enlightenment. Yet, this ninny would determine whether Sir Edward's demise resulted from foul play or natural causes.

"While your father's death was sudden, in a sense, we must remember his earthly habits were such that we cannot be totally shocked." Seeming to realize he may have spoken ill of the dead, the minister added, "God rest his soul."

Whether giddy from relief or trepidation, Richard tried to stifle a laugh. He panicked when a whinny escaped his throat.

However, good fortune followed him and the minster's eyes revealed only pity. "Do you need a few moments to yourself, Mr. Richard? I hate to distress you further, but we must see to the reading of the will as soon as you and your dear mother are able."

Richard bit his lip and donned a gloomy look. "No, we should put this behind us."

Within an hour after Dr. Quinn had taken his leave, Richard and Father Healy joined Lady Nancy in the parlor. Already attired in silk mourning clothes and clutching a handkerchief, his mother positioned herself on the settee. Biddy stood stoically behind her.

Richard studied his mother's eyes and, as he feared, they were glassy. While Hogan poured tea, Richard sat beside her and inhaled her familiar rose water perfume. Somehow, this comforted him and he took his mother's hand.

Father Healy sat across from them. "I have here Sir Edward's last will and testament which was left in my care."

Lady Nancy whimpered and squeezed Richard's hand. "I don't know what's to become of us."

The minister glanced at her, presumably to determine her state of mind, then broke the seal on the document. As his eyes skimmed the parchment, they grew wide.

"Well," he said, "it appears Sir Edward has designated Sir Nathaniel Moore as both executor and trustee of his estate." He looked at Richard. "Until such time as you are of legal age, of course. You're seventeen now, are you not?"

Richard nodded and turned to the butler. "Hogan, has a messenger been sent to Sir Nathaniel?"

"One has, Mr. Richard. And another to the relations of Lady Nancy."

"Very good." He looked to the minister who, wearing a sullen expression, stared at the document. "Go on, Father Healy."

"Forgive me, but somehow I assumed I would be called upon to perform those duties." The clergyman read the entire will aloud which, at first, was as expected. Richard would inherit the estate and its titles once he reached twenty-one. Sir Nathaniel, as trustee, would run Duncullen for the next four years, overseen by the Court of Chancery. It was no surprise that Hogan was bequeathed the customary two pounds for long and faithful service. The butler dutifully expressed his gratitude.

Yet, even Father Healy's eyebrows rose when he read, "My dear overseer, Will Bridge, and his wife, Noreen Bridge, will be employed by Duncullen into old age. Once no longer able to perform their duties, they will continue to live on in comfort until their deaths. At that time, their son, Jack Bridge, will remain in their cottage where all his worldly needs will be met until the end of his days."

Lady Nancy squirmed and huffed. "I don't understand, Richard. I don't understand this at all."

He patted her hand. "It's fine, Mother. All is well." It seemed overly generous to Richard, too, but it didn't distress him.

The will next turned to the funeral arrangements, mostly standard, that Sir Edward had laid out. He would have all the trappings allowed by law for one of his stature. He described the types of clothing required by the gentlemen and ladies who attended as well as where and how he would be interred. Money had been set aside for traditional mourning rings and black gloves for the mourners, as well as the fine selection of food and drink for those in attendance.

Then came the thunderbolt. "I have also set aside moneys to be used for the customary wake for the common folk. There is to be whiskey and smoking pipes for all my servants and tenants to enjoy. Michael Halligan, the fiddler, should he still be among the living, will be hired to play into the night so that dancing and games may be enjoyed in the barn. In return for this, I request each to wear a crepe armband in my memory and to offer a prayer for my soul."

Father Healy paled. "This cannot be."

"I'll not allow it!" Lady Nancy squealed. "It's a disgrace to our name. Richard? We won't have it." Tears seeped from her eyes and rolled down her cheeks. "What will my father say?"

Richard fumed. "One last spit in our faces. Another example of his contempt for all that is decent."

Father Healy stood. "I cannot be part of such heresy. The bishop forbids it." His voice rose in thinly veiled outrage as spittle flew from his mouth. "Not even the Popish priests or bishops countenance this unholy—these pagan rituals. They are condemned everywhere."

"We'll ignore it," Richard said. "The man was a beast. We just won't honor such rubbish."

The minister closed his eyes, breathed deeply, and lowered himself into his chair. "Let us remain calm. I know you are distraught, but we must not say things we will later regret. It is the purview of the executor to fulfill your father's wishes. Sir Edward, unfortunately, has been very definitive in his instructions with little room for interpretation. However, we shall present this dilemma to Sir Nathaniel."

Following a prayer, Father Healy stood and bowed to Lady Nancy as though preparing to depart, then stopped. "Ah, Mr. Richard, I nearly forgot. Your father wrote you a separate letter, which he entrusted me to give you unless I received further instructions. Which I have not." The minister reached into his pouch and pulled out a sheet of parchment, folded and sealed.

He handed the letter to Richard and said, "It was Sir Edward's time. We don't always understand the ways of the Lord, but we have peace knowing there was an empty space in heaven that only your father could fill."

Unable to speak, Richard clamped his teeth onto his bottom lip and looked away.

Father Healy's mouth dropped. He bowed his head, mumbled something akin to, "Well then," and fled the room.

Fury filled Richard's eyes with tears. He looked at the letter in his hand. It felt vibrant, alive. To read it, he'd require privacy.

"Hogan, have we a good fire in the library?"

"We do, Mr. Richard."

"In that case, I too, must take my leave of you, Mother." He kissed her hand and left the parlor.

AROON

✠

Richard settled into the upholstered armchair before the hearth and broke the seal on the mysterious letter. A tingle ran up his arm and his stomach twisted. After a deep breath, he unfolded the crisp parchment. The sight of his father's handwriting left his mouth dry.

To my Son and Only Heir:

If you are reading this letter, I have perished without achieving my most desired goal: Ensuring you are man enough to fill my shoes. Or at least that you do not squander all I've worked for until you can produce a son who is more capable.

I blame your mother for this.

Due to such an unfortunate occurrence, I can only attempt, through this short missive, to relay the issue that concerns me most. Your unmitigated arrogance. You and your mother fling your FitzAden name around assuming the mere mention of your pedigree will solve all your problems. You will shortly find out it cannot.

I am certain you, your mother, and Father Healy are seething over my demand for a traditional wake. I believe I can hear the three of you from my grave.

Shut your gobs for a moment and hear what I am telling you.

You are inheriting more than money and title. You inherit the responsibility of people barely able to care for themselves, yet they perform the backbreaking labor that allows you to live as you so blatantly feel entitled. Like loyal puppies, they will follow you as long as they see some sign, no matter how small, that you care about them and their daily struggles. You can kick a dog, yes. As long as you give it the occasional pat on the head.

So at my funeral, do not ignore their customs, no matter how distasteful to you. This bone we throw will smooth the way as you become their new master. But it will hardly be enough.

191

Their problems will be a petty nuisance to you. Show firmness, but also concern. During a bad harvest, make sure their children are fed before you scoop up your rents. Make an appearance at fairs and festivals, patting each man on the back and calling him by name.

I have heard your mother say too many times they are little more than animals. That may or may not be true. But remember, they come from warrior stock which simmers below the surface.

Ignore my advice at your peril.

Your father,

Sir Edward Lynche, Bt.

Richard bit too deeply into his lip, then licked the blood from his teeth. He spoke aloud, as though the spirit of his father lingered in the room. "So this is your plan. From the fiery pit where your soul resides, you try to drag me into the mire you wallowed in. Never fear. Duncullen will no longer be the laughing-stock of the aristocracy under my rule. And as for your advice ..."

He crumbled the letter into a tight little ball, then pitched it into the blaze before him. Smirking, he watched his father's words go up in smoke.

✦

Mrs. Bridge barked orders to the maids like a general on a battlefield. She pointed to three of them. "Prepare all the rooms for guests. Leave not a speck of dust anywhere. We'll not be disgraced at a time like this. You lasses there. Cover the mirrors and turn the pictures toward the walls. And in the parlor, everything must be draped in black."

The staff itself already wore the required black armbands. Orla had those in the kitchen creating a feast fit for a man of Sir Edward's stature, most of which would be served to the attendees of standing. Lesser foods, particularly the traditional rolls of bread, were made for the townsfolk and tenants. Outside, grooms readied the grounds for the mourning coaches and dozens of horses expected to arrive.

Only Eveleen remained, awaiting instruction. "Come with me," Mrs. Bridge told her. "We will prepare the body for burial."

Blood drained from the girl's face. "Ah no, Mrs. Bridge. I cannot do it. I'll sweep every hearth and empty every chamber pot, but this I cannot do."

"It'll be you and me to start," the housekeeper said, as though Eveleen had never spoken. "Two of the tenants' wives will join us shortly."

The young maid dropped to her knees, her hands clasped as though in prayer. "I'm begging ye, Mrs. Bridge."

"Get up. We've no time for that. The very reason ye cannot bear it is why I require it." She pulled on Eveleen's elbow, lifting her to her feet. "Get some fresh water and meet me in the master's chambers."

☦

The door creaked open and, head down, Eveleen shuffled in with two pails of water.

"Put them on the floor beside the washstand," Mrs. Bridge said as she closed the chamber door. Grabbing a straight-back chair, she jammed it beneath the doorknob, locking out all others.

The body was already stripped where it lay, with the distended stomach of one who ate too well while others around him starved. Its skin was pasty and lips already blue.

Mrs. Bridge sighed and nodded to Eveleen. "Stand beside me. We don't have much time. Even now, the neck is starting to stiffen."

Sobbing, the young maid moved beside the bed next to Mrs. Bridge.

"What do ye see?" the older woman asked. When Eveleen responded with ragged breathing, Mrs. Bridge answered her own question.

"I see one who became a powerful man with his titles and money. A man who was charged with protecting those beneath him, but instead abused them time and again. Now he must appear before the Lord, just as ye see him here. No money. No power. No titles. What good are those things to a man when he stands before the Almighty in judgment?"

She took a deep breath and softened her voice. "He can hurt ye no more, Eveleen. He can hurt no one. He's as stripped of his power as he is of his garments."

Mrs. Bridge leaned in close to the body and delivered her words in a furious whisper. "Ye wretched pig of a man. What will ye tell yer Maker? Of all the children ye fed—once their widowed mothers whored themselves to ye? Of the countless young virgins ye molested? Of the son ye belittled? The wife ye tormented? Yer a bloated sot of a man, no better than any drunkard begging in the village square."

She worked up a wad of phlegm and hawked it onto the dead man's face. "That's for Maeve." She spit again. "And for Tara. May they survive their terrible voyage only to suffer as slaves on some dismal Virginia plantation." She spewed more spittle over his nose and brow, on his cheeks and chin, calling out the names of the poor lasses over the years, befouled by the unquenchable lust of the cold carcass before her.

Finally, her mouth parched, she turned to Eveleen. "Now for yerself."

"I ... I can't."

"Oh, ye can. Look at the bruises on his neck. I don't know how they got there, but damn him, I know why."

Fresh tears rolled down the girl's face, but Mrs. Bridge only glared, her arms crossed.

Eveleen's lips trembled, her face pale and puffy from weeping. She began working her cheeks, pursing her lips, and sucking up saliva. With new steel in her eyes, she turned to the corpse and flung all of her slaver onto his clammy chest.

Open-mouthed, the young girl panted from the effort, but wore an expression of deep satisfaction.

Mrs. Bridge coughed up one more gob of slobber and hurled it with great force onto the swollen remains. "And that one is for me. May ye rot in hell!"

Both women jumped at the rattling of the door. "Mrs. Bridge! 'Tis Polly Egan and Katie Dunne here to prepare the dead. Let us in."

"Of course," called Mrs. Bridge. "Quick, wipe him off," she whispered to Eveleen before clumsily rattling the chair to open the door. "Forgive me caution. I could not bear it if Mr. Richard were to happen upon us. He's taking it so very hard, poor lad."

As the women entered, Mrs. Bridge turned to find Eveleen calmly nodding to the new arrivals as she swabbed Sir Edward's face and chest. Mrs. Bridge risked a lop-sided smile.

Ye've got mettle, lass. Ye'll be right.

Chapter Nineteen

During the two hours it took to prepare Sir Edward for burial, servants transformed the parlor by draping all, including the table that would serve as a bier, in black cloth. Candles in tall taper holders surrounded the table.

Mrs. Bridge followed two strong farm hands as they carried Sir Edward, dressed in his finest, into the parlor.

"Set him here, lads." Old Will pointed to the table. "The cabinet maker is constructing the coffin. Once it's finished, you can come back and chest Sir Edward."

"I seen it," said one fellow to the other. "A fine piece of furniture, it is. Elm wood, held together with a double row of brass nails."

"Enough of yer jawing," Mrs. Bridge chided. "How in God's name did ye get his clothes so rumpled?"

The talkative one made a cursory attempt to straighten his sleeves, then the two hustled out. Mrs. Bridge sighed, and arranged his attire in a more presentable manner.

Hogan appeared at the door. "Mr. Richard requests your presence in the library."

"Mine?" Mrs. Bridge asked.

"Both of yours," he answered, then whispered, "They've read the will. The old man left me a bit and mentioned you both as well."

"Well," Mrs. Bridge replied, "we'll not dawdle, then."

⊕

Mr. Richard sat erect with chin held high in the throne-like library chair. There was no sign of the bereaved young man Mrs. Bridge had described to the tenants' wives.

"Close the door, Old Will," the young heir said. "This is a private issue."

Will obeyed and returned to his wife's side. They watched Mr. Richard, whose mind seemed elsewhere, and waited for him to begin. Old Will coughed.

Mr. Richard snapped to attention. "Yes. We have had the reading of the will, and you both, as well as Jack, were specifically mentioned by my father."

He watched their faces, apparently looking for a reaction. However, the Bridges were professional servants who no more changed their expressions than did the corpse in the parlor.

"You are both to be employed here for the entirety of your lives. When you become older and infirmed, your cabin will remain yours until you breathe your last. As for Jack, he, too, is to live and work here in full comfort until his dying day."

Mrs. Bridge looked to Old Will who nodded, his eyes brimming with tears. "That's fine," he said. "Real fine. I've been with yer father since we were lads, but I never thought ... well, 'tis a fine thing."

"Thank you, Mr. Richard," Mrs. Bridge mumbled. Something inside her, she realized, had changed and she could not grovel.

"Old Will, how are the preparations coming?" Mr. Richard asked.

"Gerald Hayes, the blacksmith, and meself went to town and purchased all that's needed. We'll not let ye down, sir."

"I know you won't, Will. You, of all people, never have." He blinked a couple of times. "You may continue with your work now. That's all I have to tell you at this time."

The servants turned to leave.

"Not you, Mrs. Bridge. I have one more thing to discuss."

Will nodded and went on his way, closing the door once again. Mrs. Bridge turned toward the young man, hands folded before her.

Mr. Richard opened his mouth to speak, closed it and sighed.

Boldly, Mrs. Bridge broke the ice. "Truly, sir, there is nothing for us to discuss."

"Really?"

"The secret stays between us two. Think about it. If I were to go to the sheriff, you merely explain me own part in it. Surely, ye'd be believed. I mightn't be believed, but I can put enough doubt in the minds of others that yer good standing would be ravaged. Tell me, what good would it do either of us to speak of it again?"

The tension in Mr. Richard's jaw and shoulders thawed. "That's settled, then."

When the housekeeper turned to leave, however, he stopped her. "One more thing before we put this away forever. My father ensured you and your family were provided for. For the rest of your lives. And yet you hate him so."

Mr. Richard squirmed when Mrs. Bridge overstepped her station and stared straight into his eyes. "All is done for the sake of Jack."

His brow furrowed. "Jack?"

"What else would you expect a man to do for his own son?"

✟

Stunned by Mrs. Bridge's revelation, Richard's head sagged into his shoulders. He could not digest her news. He had a half-brother, one he loved dearly. Never as an equal, though. Jack was dimwitted, of course, and his mother was of inferior stock.

His father with Mrs. Bridge? The very idea was disturbing. What then of Old Will? Did he know Jack was not his son? A wave of sadness washed over Richard. Old Will was baseborn, but he was a good man and a fine father. Yet another had sired his son. Nothing made sense.

All the ironies wrapped around each other, causing Richard's head to pound. A man with no son bestowed unconditional love beyond what Richard had ever seen while Edward Lynche, a man of stature with two natural sons, was an abysmal failure. Richard's eyes widened. Could there be more? How many brothers and sisters did his father leave in his wake?

Richard could not sit still. He leapt from his chair and paced the room. Even dead, his father'd flipped his world on its head. Mrs. Bridge, Old Will, even Jack, would never be the same to him again.

He made his way to his mother's chamber, although he realized she was likely asleep.

Biddy answered his knock. "Mr. Richard, 'tis a fine thing yer here. Lady Nancy is much aggrieved. Heartbroken, she is."

"Oh, Richard," called his mother from her chaise longue, reaching her hands to him. Her face was puffed and swollen; her lower lip trembled. Most startling to Richard was the terror in her eyes, like an orphaned child.

He went to her side and took her hands.

"What's to become of us without your father?" she wailed.

Her panic confused him. "You're not alone. I'll take care of you."

"You?" She snatched back her hands. "You know as much of running an estate as Biddy does." She thrust her face into her palms. "We're doomed to ruin and disgrace. While your father was a lout of a man, he kept us without a financial care in the world. But now—"

Richard stood and clenched his fists. "Never fear, Mother. Sir Nathaniel will hold us together for the next four years. You needn't concern yourself until then."

He strode from the room before he said something he'd regret, but couldn't help thinking, I did it for you, you ungrateful witch.

✦

As evening approached, the servants had transformed the estate into a proper house of mourning. All was draped in black and they'd set food inside and out. Richard spent much of the afternoon greeting family and friends as they arrived, accepting their condolences.

"Please excuse Lady Nancy," he explained to each. "She is greatly distressed. Inconsolable, really."

They each clicked their tongues, shook their heads, and lamented that Sir Edward's passing was so sudden and unexpected.

It didn't take long for the Big House to stifle Richard, who snatched the first opportunity to escape. He wandered through the courtyard, briskly nodding to servants and tenants who offered sympathies.

Entering the barn, he froze when he spotted Jack, all alone, brushing the nag he sometimes rode. Richard's throat closed up. He was the same old Jack. Somehow, Richard thought he'd appear different.

His half-brother looked up. "Mr. Richard!" He dropped the brush and ran toward him. Touching his arm, Jack peered at him with soft, gentle eyes that could never have come from his father.

"'Tis a sad day for us all. The Lord took yer father from ye, but He carried Sir Edward straight to heaven. Yer da don't suffer no more. He's happy."

Richard's tears came quickly now. What was it about Jack that made him crumble? He steeled himself to keep from collapsing into Jack's arms.

"Cry all ye want." Jack's own lip quivered. "Tears are made to wash away yer sorrow. The more sorrowful ye are, the more tears ye need. That's what me ma says."

Richard nodded. Then Jack did something only he'd dare do—he took Richard and folded him into his arms.

Richard rested there and sobbed silently. He had a big brother.

"Oh! I beg your pardon."

Richard yanked himself away from Jack and straightened his shoulders. He turned to see Alistair Moore, who seemed unsure where to look.

Richard frantically wiped his eyes. "Alistair, you've arrived. Please forgive my neglect of you and your family." He strode toward the barn door.

"Hold up," Alistair said. "No need to rush inside. It's only my father and me. He's presently occupied, scrupulously poring over your father's will." Alistair's usual smirk became serious. "I'm sincerely sorry about your father. I know he could be annoying, but ... well, now he's gone. I don't know what to say."

"There's nothing to say." Richard moved as though to leave. "I need to discuss something with Sir Nathaniel."

Alistair grabbed his arm. "I've been worried I did the wrong thing when I spoke up, but now I'm glad. Considering he died with a higher opinion of you."

Richard cocked his head. "Whatever are you talking about?"

"When I was here last. Your father put the screws on me before I left, trying to elicit any secrets I might have learned."

Richard's heart pounded. "And?"

Alistair winked. "I let him know you are not the virginal feather he seemed to think you were."

"How did you do that?"

"I mentioned a certain maid whose name I knew not." Alistair smiled. "I feared I spoke too much, but now I'm relieved. He knew better of you before he died."

The stupid bloody bastard! Richard wanted to slap that complacent grin off the bumbler's face. When he saw that he was wringing his hands, he stashed them behind his back.

Alistair looked bewildered. "Oh. Of course, you're upset. I was a fool to speak so boorishly at a time like this. Please forgive me."

"Think nothing of it," he growled and left the barn.

※

Once inside, Hogan directed Richard to Sir Nathaniel who'd taken over the study. The older man looked a little too comfortable behind his father's large desk.

"Sit down, my boy." He directed Richard to the chair used by petitioners. "My sympathies on this tragedy. He left us too soon. Far too soon."

"Yes." Richard was furious at Sir Nathaniel's blatant condescension. "Congratulations on your role as my new lord and master," he blurted.

Sir Nathaniel glared. "That's not how I would describe the burden your father has placed upon me. Due to my admiration for Sir Edward, I will do my duty toward you and your mother to the best of my ability."

Richard slumped. "Forgive my outburst. This day has taken a terrible toll on me."

The older man's face softened. "Of course." He looked back to the parchment before him. "Most of the arrangements your father has requested are well on the way to fulfillment. Your staff here is first-rate, especially Hogan."

"What will you do about that ridiculous wake my father required?"

Sir Nathaniel raised his eyebrows. "Do? Why, he shall have one."

"Surely not! We'll be a laughing-stock. Father Healy cannot even perform a funeral under such circumstances."

Sir Nathaniel stared at Richard, as though trying to figure something out. "A laughing-stock, eh? I wondered why Edward chose me as executor and trustee instead of one of your illustrious relatives. Now I see. Your father understood what his people needed from him and so do I. Therefore, I will respect and satisfy those requests. If you want to successfully rule this manor, you'll respect them, too."

The same drivel as that blasted letter. "And what of a minister for the funeral service?"

"There will be no alcohol served the morning of the funeral itself. That is the only requisite Father Healy must fulfill. The rest is of no concern to him or the church. Although you'll never convince them of that."

Richard stood. "I have only one more question for you, then. How are we to eradicate the ignorant superstitions and idle ways of the Irish if we condone this barbaric behavior? Are we under no moral obligation to even attempt to civilize them?" He swallowed before continuing. "What would your father, renowned for hunting down and imprisoning priests, think about that?"

Confident his retort had hit its mark, he strode from the room.

Chapter Twenty

In the late afternoon, Lord Ethan de Barnefort, the Viscount Kilmullah, and his wife pulled up in their carriage outfitted in funeral black. Upon greeting his uncle and aunt, Richard learned that Jonathan, their elder son, was mysteriously indisposed and could not attend. Nor could his grandfather or any of the other FitzAden relatives. They sent only excuses and their carriages to be used in the funeral procession.

The younger de Barnefort, Thomas, stumbled out of the carriage with his plump wife, Anne.

Furious, Richard stormed into his mother's chamber, ready to rail about these blatant slaps in their faces. However, it seemed she'd already received the news of her family's uncivil rebuff. He found her sobbing with her sister, Lady Lillian, and Thomas's Anne, who clucked and fussed over Lady Nancy like a little round hen. With a bow, Richard dismissed himself.

☩

Dusk found Richard accepting the consolations of local gentry, tenants, and townsfolk as he stood beside his father's coffin and his own pretentious family.

Seething with contempt, he scowled at his mother, puffy-eyed, seated next to him with her handkerchief dramatically clutched to her cheek. Behind her stood Lady Lillian, her stalwart support, a gloved hand laid upon the widow's shoulder. Richard did not miss the subtle flinch at her sister's touch.

Next was his Uncle Ethan, with eyes half-closed from the tedium and nostrils flared as though smelling something crude and distasteful. Then Thomas, second son and heir to nothing, whose dull eyes showed a distinct lack of intelligence.

Richard glanced at his father's waxy corpse. In his limited experience, dead bodies were grotesque variants of their former selves. Yet there his father lay, an ashen, sleeping version of his living self. Richard's lower jaw trembled as an icy hand gripped his heart.

Was he truly dead or was this another eerie vision? Could his overpowering presence be erased with no more than a pinch of powder in his tea?

A faraway voice called him back. "Mr. Richard. Mr. Richard, sir?"

He blinked. "Wha—?"

There stood Gerald Hayes, the smithy, reaching out to him with blackened hands. "Ye look a mite pale, sir. Do ye need to sit down?"

Others surged forward, expressing concern.

Richard felt faint-headed in the crush of people. "Step back! I am fine."

"Give him air, then," Gerald said, and the horde of warm, malodorous bodies receded.

Richard forced himself to breathe slowly and evenly.

"Ah, ye gave us a scare, sir." The blacksmith offered a little nod and mumbled, "I'm sorry for yer trouble." He then moved to kneel before his former master in prayer.

Above the murmur of the mourners, Richard soon heard a wavering voice call out, "I heard the banshee last night, I did. She was keening in the woods by me home, warning of Sir Edward's passing."

"Hush, Grandda," scolded a young lass. "Everyone can hear ye."

Richard shuddered. He was well aware of the ancient Irish legend where the banshee wailed in the woods when murder was afoot. He breathed deeply and warned himself to hold it together. It was merely a primitive superstition.

Old Will stiffened as he stood by the exit door of the parlor. He shot Richard a worried glance, then hustled the people through the line. "A pipe of tobacco there'll be in the barn," he told each of them.

Sitting beside the hearth was Alistair. He caught Richard's eye and grinned in his lopsided way. Richard raised his eyebrows and sighed.

Somewhere in the procession of mourners, a hunched old woman in a tattered scarf began the high-pitched wail of death that fell to a low moan. Two other women swayed and keened along with her. The primeval lament invaded Richard's body and caused his bones to tremble.

With the eyes of a cornered animal, Lady Nancy clutched her sister with both hands. "Make them stop. I won't have it. Make them stop."

Lord Ethan barked, "Enough! Remove these women."

Husbands and sons ushered the wailers outside. Yet, Richard could not relax. He was clutched in an aura of the supernatural. Were there spirits? Did they know?

The murmuring in the parlor switched to a frozen silence, as loud as a clap of thunder. The gathering stood motionless, looking in awe toward the entrance hall.

Richard's heart pounded in terror as a clump-shuffle, clump-shuffle sounded on the wooden floor in a painstakingly slow approach. When the mysterious being finally appeared, Richard stepped back as though struck and let out a shrill yip.

His head spun toward the coffin to assure himself the corpse rested there still, for before him stood a dirty, ragged version of his very own father limping forward with the help of an oaken shillelagh.

The man of the same height and build, high forehead, and aristocratic nose of the Lynches peered at Richard with his father's familiar look of disdain. This man, however, had long, stringy hair covered with a dusty tricorne hat that looked like rats had feasted on it. His ruddy face was stubbled with gray and his threadbare, patched clothing hung loosely from his frame.

Yet, all the common folk bowed their heads ever so slightly. A sign of reverence?

"Identify yourself," Richard said, attempting to recover from his womanly shriek.

The man dipped his head and said, "I am Cornelius Lynche, rightful heir to Duncullen and all its environs." He nodded to Richard's mother. "She recognizes me."

Lady Nancy sniffed and turned away.

"And there lies my cousin," Cornelius Lynche announced to the room. "May he burn in hell!"

A gasp rose from the crowd.

Lord Ethan snapped out of his apathy. "You miserable, foul-smelling villain!"

"So you say," the stranger shot back. "I say Edward's father, Old William Lynche, turned his back on Almighty God and the one true church for no more than a few quid."

His voice rising, he addressed the entire room. "He betrayed his own brother, my father, the first-born. William had my da kicked off our land. This land. He left his own kin homeless, penniless."

He pulled a tattered parchment from his pocket and held it up. "I carry the deed to Duncullen right here. When I showed this to Edward, my cousin, lying dead this night, he laughed and threatened to banish me to the colonies if I ever again set foot in my own home."

"That scrap of paper is meaningless," said Lord Ethan, "and you know it."

"To the English, it has no legal standing. But the Irish see it different. I come tonight to see the spawn of Edward, and find out what kind of man he be. Is he more English? Or does his Gaelic blood stir at the injustice his forebears suffered?"

Richard rose to his full height. "Until this moment, I had no idea of your existence. But it is clear your father was ignorant."

The tenants and townsfolk shuffled uncomfortably. To Richard, they clearly felt some sympathy for this man. He did not want a row at his father's wake, yet this pretender had to be put in his place.

"Your father had the same opportunity as his brother to cast off the superstitious chains of the Roman Church, yet he unwisely chose not to do so. Now look at you. Is that my fault? Or my father's?"

Richard looked around. Some of the people kept their eyes downward while others sneered with furrowed brows. With whom were they unhappy? Surely not him.

"I seek only justice," the man said.

"Justice?" Lord Ethan called out. "Your grandfather made a poor choice and you must live with the consequences. Be on your way. If you'd rather, you can kiss the clink."

Richard felt the burn of his so-called cousin's stare.

"Never fear. I'm leaving," the beggarly man said. "I know what I came here to learn. Edward's son is even colder of heart than his father."

Appalled, Richard shouted, "Get this creature out of here!"

Two servants stepped forward, but the man waved them back with his walking stick. "Call off your hirelings. I'll see myself out."

He slowly hobbled through the exit door.

"Sir Nathaniel," called out his mother, "I hold you responsible for this calamity. We warned you about allowing this ridiculous wake."

The room crackled with tension. The fray Richard hoped to avoid seemed imminent. "Mother, you are distraught. Biddy, escort Lady Nancy to her chamber for some much-needed rest."

Biddy helped the pale, trembling gentlewoman to her feet and led her away. Lady Lillian followed with an unmistakable look of relief.

The roomful of mourners quickly emptied as each kept their condolences and prayers uncommonly short.

Once the last had passed through, Alistair approached Richard and pulled him to one side. "Let the servants stay with your father now. Come with me."

✠

Gratefully, Richard followed his friend into the courtyard. Small groups of men puffed on the traditional tobacco pipes they'd been given and slurped their cups of whiskey. Animated storytelling and raucous laughter gave an air of merriment to the occasion. As each group caught sight of the young gentlemen, they adopted a more solemn bearing.

"Don't mind us, fellas," Alistair told them. "Finish your tale." He looked to Richard. "Let's go to the barn where the real fun is."

Richard heard the fiddle music he'd thus far been too distracted to notice. Although the crass behavior disgusted him,
his curiosity was overpowering.

"Just slip inside," Alistair said. "If they notice us, they'll
stop."

They slithered into the barn and stood in a shadowed area.
"This is more like a festival than a funeral," Richard whispered.

Alistair put him off with a shake of the head and tapped his
foot to the fiddler's jig. In the center of the stable, several young
men hopped and stomped to the music. But one, whose feet were
fast as lightning, stole the attention of the entire crowd who
whooped and clapped as the fiddler played faster and faster.

During the dance, Richard spotted Eveleen standing with
three other maids. So lovely she was in the light of the burning
lamps, his eyes grew moist.

I've missed you so, he thought, surprising even himself. He
realized an overwhelming loneliness had crept into his being. It
was unbearable.

The other maids clapped and chattered, pointing to the danc-
ers in delight. Eveleen smiled and nodded, but the familiar glow
was missing from her eyes.

When the fiddling stopped, the revelers pushed forward a
boy of about ten with a snub nose and straw-colored hair. He
tried to escape, ducking under the arms of the crowd, but someone threw him back into the open space. He sighed while by-
standers called for a song. When he opened his mouth to begin,
a hush fell over the barn.

Richard was stunned. It was the clear soprano of an angel.

Alistair whispered, "Shule Aroon. Walk My Love."

How would Alistair know that? The Gaelic language was
banned over a half century earlier. The boy's voice echoed
through the rafters.

Shule, shule, shule aroon

Shule go succir agus, shule go kewn,

Shule go durrus oggus aylig lume,

Iss guh day thoo avorneen slawn.

Alistair translated. "O come, come, come, O Love. Quickly come to me, softly move. Come to the door, and away we'll flee, and safe for aye may my darling be."

His heart aching, Richard looked from the shadows to Eveleen. The boy seemed to have chosen the song for them.

"I'll sell my rod, I'll sell my reel. I'll sell my only spinning wheel to buy my love a sword of steel," Alistair softly translated. "I'll dye my petticoats. I'll dye them red. And 'round the world I'll beg my bread. Until my parents shall wish me dead."

As the last notes died away, Richard struggled to find his voice. "The Irish are quite dramatic."

"Mmm? If you say so."

⚚

Eveleen fought to hold back tears throughout the lad's tender song. Yet, she saw burly farmers and hardened laborers wiping their eyes with their sleeves.

Ronan, Sir Edward's flogger of choice, sniffed loudly. He then stood on a bale of hay and announced, "Enough heartache. 'Tis a game we need to lift our spirits."

A younger, homelier version of Ronan, likely his brother, pushed his shoulder, winked, and said, "Frumso Framso."

Brea, Elly, and Ida tittered as one of the groomsmen dragged a stool to the middle of the stable floor and shoved Ronan onto it with little resistance.

The fiddler stepped forward and, in a booming voice, asked the required question. "Who do you want for your dance?"

Ronan recited, "A nice girl to be talking to."

"Name her."

He scanned the crowd and pointed to Eveleen. "That one."

Eveleen felt heat surge into her face as the maids around her giggled and pushed. "It's you, Eveleen. He wants you."

She dug in her heels and shook her head. "No. No, I can't."

The girls and several others thrust her before the hulking oaf. His leering face disgusted her.

After clearing his throat, he stood and spat onto the hard dirt floor. Then he grabbed Eveleen by the shoulders and planted a robust kiss squarely upon her lips.

A good-natured roar arose from the circle as the kiss went on and on. Eveleen tried to pull away, but the muscular whip-wielder held her firmly. Her squeal was muffled by his crusty lips.

When he finally released her, she turned away. To her astonishment, just out of the shadows in the corner of the barn stood Richard, his face twisted in rage. She screamed his name in her head, barely able to prevent the forbidden utterance from escaping her lips.

Without a word, the young master spun on his heel and stomped from the stable.

Eveleen realized everyone was standing in stunned silence at the unexpected interruption. Once Richard was out of earshot, Ronan placed a hand on her shoulder. "Don't worry about him. The old man has willed us this wake in his final testament. There's nothing the young silk-stocking can do about it."

Shaking with frustration, Eveleen cringed at his insolent words. This man was a complete buffoon.

The ugly brother said, "That's who we'll have to deal with when he comes of age. May the Lord help us all. He's got none of the common sense his father had." Then, after a reverent pause, "God rest his soul."

Eveleen could not hold back. "His father, ye mean? Ye know nothing of Sir Edward's wicked ways. Ask any of the maids what a fine master he was."

Ronan shrugged. "So he appreciated a pretty young lass when he saw one. Ye can't fault a man for that." His eyes undressed her from head to foot. "I'm appreciating one right now."

Eveleen glimpsed as Jack, who'd been watching from inside a stall, approached. "Ye'd best keep yer eyes and hands to yerself," he told Ronan.

The brute snorted. "Don't stick yer nose where it don't belong, Jack. I don't want to hurt ye."

Jack held his ground. "I'm warning ye, Ronan, for yer own good. Leave Eveleen alone."

Ronan cocked his head. "Yer warning me?" His eyes widened. "Oh, I see. Yer sweet on her yerself." He released Eveleen and spoke to Jack as one would a child. "Well then, I'd best look elsewhere, hadn't I? I wouldn't want to wrangle with the likes of you." To the onlookers, he said, "There's plenty here just as pretty and more willing, I'll wager."

Eveleen pushed her way out of the crowd, her cheeks streaked with tears of anger and frustration.

⊕

Alistair watched the red-haired girl dash from the barn in evident distress. It was her. Aphrodite.

"Who are ye, there in the shadows? Show yerself," called out Ronan.

Alistair stepped forward. He fought the urge to chuckle at the shocked looks of the local mourners. "Mr. Alistair Moore, at your service."

"Begging yer pardon, sir," Ronan's unimpressive younger brother said. "We'd no idea 'twas yerself in that corner."

"I didn't want to interrupt your grief. But now that I'm exposed, I see a wrestling contest at the far end of the stable in which I'd love to partake."

A roar of approval rose up from the men as they patted his back and followed him to the makeshift ring. Where, of course, Alistair won every match.

⊕

By midnight, Halligan had packed up his fiddle and the mourners had drifted home. Guests of the family—the de Barneforts and a few local members of the gentry—were tucked into their rooms. Alistair stopped outside Richard's chamber to see if, after the night he'd had, he wanted to talk.

He smiled. For the bookish type, the fellow was afire inside. To his disappointment, he heard only heavy breathing within Richard's chamber.

With no more excuses and no suitable company, Alistair made his way to his room. After seven wrestling matches, he could not even consider crawling into bed. He threw open the draperies to let in what moonlight the clouds would permit and, brimming with energy, paced the room. He crouched before the hearth and poked at the glowing embers, watching the sparks float through the air until they died out. For those that didn't, he leapt up and stomped on them.

Deciding the room's air was too stagnant for sleep, he threw open both windows and stuck his head outside. Aside from the normal night sounds of country living, Alistair heard something out of place. Murmuring followed by soft chortling. Who?

He then realized his room was directly above the parlor, where a handful of servants were tasked with watching over the dead through the night. Eager for some company, Alistair decided to join them.

He crept down the main staircase and, in stocking feet, tiptoed toward the parlor. Deciding how and if he should intrude, he listened at the door. He recognized the voice of Samuel, the long-legged footman who served him those potent whiskeys on his last visit. Old Will, the overseer, was there, too, along with Hayes, the blacksmith from the viewing.

He knocked gently so as not to spook the men. It was a strong-willed man who would not jump at a sharp, unexpected sound in the presence of the dead.

"Enter," said Old Will.

Alistair stepped in to find the three servants sitting in a small circle before the coffin. A box was between them, serving as a card table. Beside them lay Sir Edward with a fan of cards stuck between his fingers and a pipe dangling from his cold mouth. Anyway, it wasn't lit. At least, he didn't think it was.

Seeing Alistair, Old Will jumped from his chair. "Mr. Alistair, is there something yer needing?"

"A little company," he answered. "I cannot sleep, I'm afraid."

In the light of the lantern, Alistair saw Samuel rip the playing cards from the folded hands of the corpse. "You're playing whist. And I see Sir Edward makes up the fourth."

The men kept their heads down.

"He's having a smoke with the three of you as well."

All looked up in alarm and Samuel snatched the pipe from the deceased.

With mock gravity, Alistair said, "Now, Samuel, you'd not take away a gentleman's last smoke, would you?"

The servants visibly relaxed and laughed. "No, sir," said the blacksmith, Hayes. "Put that pipe back in Sir Edward's mouth, boy, or there may be hell to pay around here."

"Considering the hell he was capable of when alive." Alistair nodded to the corpse. "If our distinguished host doesn't mind, I'll take his hand of cards and give him a break."

"How about a pipe for yerself?" asked Old Will, reaching for a fresh one in his pocket.

"It would be an honor." Alistair took the pipe in his mouth and leaned forward for a light. He sucked in several deep breaths until a halo of smoke emerged from the bowl. "A nice blend."

"That it is," said Hayes, puffing on his own.

"And how about a nip of fine poteen?" asked Samuel.

"Oh ho ho," said Alistair. "I'll pass on that. Somehow you got the best of me on my last visit. I don't like to make the same mistake twice."

"Aw, Mr. Alistair," said Samuel. "I'd do right by ye, sure."

"All the same, this pipe will do me just fine. But you fellows enjoy your poison. It promises to be a long night."

They all took a swig and turned their attention to their cards and makeshift table where they threw down and scooped up trick after trick. It didn't take long for the three Irishmen to relax and resume their reminiscences of Sir Edward.

"Yer right, sir, about the hell Sir Edward could raise," said Samuel, with a slight slur to his voice. "About six months ago, it was. I had a terrible night. Bad dreams."

The blacksmith shook his head in sympathy.

"Well, I finally slept, but it was too soundly. For when I woke, 'twas to a risen sun and the giant figure of Sir Edward looming above me. I say giant because he seemed to grow a full twelve inches when he got riled."

Old Will laughed. "That he did."

"Up he yanks me from the hay with the strength of a boxer, booming all the while that his horse ain't ready to ride. He drags me out to the yard and stands me before the whipping post, shaking me arm and making his harsh threats. Well, I won't tell ye what happened next. Let's just say, he cracked a slick smile and said, 'I see I'll have no further trouble out of ye.' And he was right!"

"Oh, a frightening figure, he was," Hayes added. "Me poor little apprentice, Jimmy, shivered and hid at the sight of the man. It once took me two hours to find the little chiseler."

"But you fellas should have seen him in his younger years," said Old Will, with the unfocused eyes of one lost in his memories. "He was quite the young blade, I tell ye."

He took a long swig of his whiskey. "I was a few years younger than he was, and he took me everywhere with him. But this once, he bade me stay behind. 'Twas a trip to Dublin and he was gone a month's time."

Will smiled. "The old man, Sir William, got a message and had us clean the place spic-and-span. 'Edward's bringing home someone special,' was all he'd tell us. The lad's mother, Lady Jennifer, had passed by this time. She was a fine one."

Seeing he'd drifted in his memories, Alistair prodded him. "So who did Sir Edward bring home?"

"Ah, up pulls the carriage," said Old Will, "and who should alight but the young and handsome Lady Nancy. The son of a gun had brought home a bride. Everyone was glad to see a lady in the house—except the young lasses who had their eye on him, of course."

They all laughed, but Will became sober.

"The part I remember most is the bright, glowing face on him. I don't believe I ever saw, before or since, a young man more beguiled by a lass."

"What happened?" asked Samuel.

Old Will let out a long sigh. "I should have known the minute she stepped out of the carriage. She looked like she'd been dropped into the midst of a bog. Which, I guess to her, she had. But she never could warm up to the place. Or to Sir Edward, neither, especially after young Richard was born."

The overseer waggled his head. "Listen to me gossiping like an old granny." He held up the bottle of poteen to toast his old friend. "To Sir Edward, a fine lad, a good one, until ... well, let's just say time sucked the pleasure out of life."

They all got quiet for a while. Alistair looked at Sir Edward and felt a bit sad for him. Then he peered into his own future and grew sad for himself.

Chapter Twenty-one

In the morning, Richard joined the guests in the breakfast room. After a restless night, he found himself in the chair where his father had drunk poisoned tea only twenty-four hours before, causing Richard's nerves to grow even more skittish. The others offered what comfort they could, assuming his anxiety stemmed from grief, not guilt.

For what should he feel guilty? Following the wishes of the Almighty Lord? Sparing his mother the daily torment that was destroying her mind? Or saving Eveleen from his lecherous clutches? His face grew hot at the memory of that boorish beast, Ronan, befouling Eveleen with his kiss.

Those smutty games the Irish played! They were a savage race, no more refined than animals. It infuriated Richard beyond reason that he'd been forced to stand and watch, powerless in the face of her debasement.

"Oh, Richard dear, my heart breaks for you," said his houseguest, Lady Eleanor. "Soon this sorrowful day will be over and you can begin to heal from your terrible and sudden loss."

She seemed sincere in her sympathy, which made sitting before her even more untenable. "Thank you, Lady Eleanor." He turned to the table at large. "Perhaps you will all excuse me. I'd best go over today's arrangements with Sir Nathaniel."

"Of course," they all murmured as he took his leave.

He made his way to his father's study, now Sir Nathaniel's study. His fist was poised to knock when he heard Uncle Ethan's baritone voice.

"It's all settled, Thomas," Richard heard him say. "Moore has agreed to the entire arrangement."

"Why would he do that?" His cousin's usually pleasant voice was tight.

His uncle chuckled. "One needn't talk long to a man to determine his weaknesses, son. The sooner you hone your powers of discernment, the sooner you will find success."

Thomas sighed, rather loudly.

"Like most baronets," his uncle went on, "he is eager for a seat in the House of Lords. A wink, a slap on the back, and a hint that pleasing the right people could lead to a barony turned Moore into quite a congenial fellow."

While Richard despised eavesdropping, he could not stop himself. Am I going mad? he wondered. I see conspiracies around every corner.

"You can put away your look of contempt, Thomas. This is your last chance to avoid an exile in the colonies, managing rice plantations in a dismal swamp. You're thirty years old and I have no title or land to pass on to you. Jonathan gets everything."

"I could not be more fully aware of my situation if it were tattooed on my right hand."

Lord Ethan's tone softened. "We want you and Anne with us in Ireland. We want to bounce your children on our knees. Am I to be condemned for that?"

Thomas's voice rose. "How will my management of Duncullen make any difference?"

Richard's breath caught in his throat.

"The lad will be of age in four years," Thomas continued. "What is the point of delaying? This is no solution I can see."

Lord Ethan groaned. "No, not that you can see. I have it on good authority—the butler—that just yesterday, the boy expressed an interest in the Grand Tour. That's a year or maybe two on the continent where only God knows what might happen to him."

Thomas's voice became strident. "What are you saying? I'll not be a party to any underhanded attempt to harm Richard."

His uncle's voice grew quieter and Richard struggled to hear over his pounding heart.

"Calm down. And stop reading those blasted novels. They're softening your brain. No one is going to harm the lad. Yet, two years is a long time. Things happen. He might catch a terrible disease, or in a drunken stupor, bash his head on a cobblestone in Venice."

Richard had no doubt of Thomas's sarcasm when he said, "One can only hope."

"You're being naïve, my boy. I didn't say I hoped such would occur, just that you'd be in an excellent position, assuming you're running the estate with competence and success, to have a title bestowed upon you." He paused. "Not this one, of course, but a new title to the same lands."

A shuffling of feet.

Uncle Ethan sounded a little more pleading when he said, "We'd be doing Richard a favor, perhaps. The boy has shown little or no interest, I'm told, in the customary pleasures of a country squire. He has a passion for academia. He may be better suited to the dark halls of Trinity or Oxford. Have you thought of that?"

"Perhaps," Thomas said.

"And here you'll be, ready to serve the king in his stead. You saw the reverence the people still showed that beggar last night. A weak master could lead to insurrection. Disastrous for all concerned." There was a pause, then Lord Ethan said, "I admit, it is a small chance that you can stay on here at Duncullen. But the chance exists, so why not take it? At the very least, you will be better prepared to run our plantations."

Richard was boiling inside and could stand no more. He pounded on the door, and as a ruse, called out, "Sir Nathaniel, a moment of your time."

Lord Ethan pulled the door open. His two kinsmen stood before him, the younger looking sheepish while the elder stared him in the eye, remorseless and cocksure.

✦

Sir Edward's funeral was held on an otherwise unremarkable Irish day. The skies were heavy with clouds and a steady drizzle set a suitably somber mood. Following the service, mourners took their leave throughout that day and the next, until only Sir Nathaniel, Alistair, Uncle Ethan, and his family remained.

Two days following the funeral, Sir Nathaniel broke the news to Richard in the study with Uncle Ethan and Thomas in attendance.

"I think it for the best that, until you reach majority, Mr. Thomas de Barnefort conduct the day-to-day affairs of the estate. Under my supervision, of course."

Every nerve in Richard's body buzzed. He kept his teeth clamped to his tongue to prevent blurting his true sentiments.

Sir Nathaniel frowned. "You're still a lad, Richard. Seventeen. You must submit to the wisdom of your elders."

He bit down harder. If the definition of wisdom were a lust for power and money.

Uncle Ethan placed a patronizing hand across his shoulders. "This is what your father would have wanted." He winked. "It's your time to sow wild oats. Enjoy life without the cumbersome burden of responsibility. We'll hitch Thomas to that yoke."

Seated behind the desk, Sir Nathaniel folded his hands. "It's settled, my boy. Your uncle is right. Take advantage of these final years of freedom. Go to the continent. Join Alistair on the tour."

Richard drew in enough air to fill his lungs, then, slowly breathing out, looked from one to the other. "I appreciate your kind consideration of my last years of youth, but fate has dealt a terrible blow to me and my mother. I cannot run off to the continent." He nodded to Sir Nathaniel. "And continue to let my father down. It was always his dream that I should walk in his footsteps, and I foolishly rejected his instruction. No more."

Richard directed his attention to Thomas. His voice trembled with rage. "My dear cousin, I will stay here at Duncullen and, under your able tutelage, make my father's holdings the finest in all Tipperary."

Thomas's eyebrows rose as he grasped Richard's hand. Misinterpreting his quavering voice, his cousin said, "You are a credit to your father. I know he watches over you this day with great pride."

Richard did not miss his uncle's smirk nor the exasperated sigh of Sir Nathaniel. As for Thomas, Uncle Ethan may have been right. He was unbelievably naïve, yet Richard took an instant liking to him.

⊕

The next day, Uncle Ethan and his wife departed, leaving Thomas and Anne behind. Anne had so filled Lady Lillian's ears with instructions concerning the transfer of their possessions, Richard thought the lady might forego the carriage and gallop off on the nearest steed.

That afternoon, Sir Nathaniel and Thomas spent hours going over Sir Edward's books, riding the grounds, and interviewing

Old Will, Hogan, and other servants. They excluded Richard from these sessions, a slight that left him seething.

When Richard had readied Bess for an afternoon escape, Alistair insisted on riding along, an unwelcome intrusion on Richard's much-needed solitude.

After cantering for several minutes in silence, Alistair said, "I saw her."

"What?"

"Aphrodite. I saw her."

Richard's stomach twisted. "I don't know what you're talking about."

"She's red-haired. And quite lovely."

Richard grunted and looked away at some grazing cattle.

"The one that clodhopper kissed the other night, right?"

Richard turned to glare at Alistair, but saw no mockery or malice in his friend's eyes.

"You know she didn't want to do it, don't you?" Alistair went on. "She was humiliated by the oaf. It's part of the game to resist, so no one thought anything of it. I could see it on her face, though. She was revolted, actually."

"It makes no difference to me."

Alistair sighed. "Your beet-red face tells a different story. You're a fine fellow, Richard, and one of the rare Clonmel Grammar alumni I count as a friend. I must say, though, that temper of yours will be your downfall."

Richard felt immense relief from Alistair's words. He could not lose Eveleen after all he'd been through. He had no intention of discussing her with Alistair, however, and closed the subject by setting his eyes forward and gripping the reins tighter.

Alistair could not keep his mouth shut for long. "I hear you're going to stay here and become Ireland's premiere baronet."

Whether his friend intended it or not, Richard felt mocked. "I have a responsibility, Alistair, which no one thinks I can handle. I am not every landed father's ideal heir as you seem to be."

"Oh yes, the same self-pity you spouted last time I was here. I told you then all is never as it seems."

No, it isn't, Richard inwardly groaned. Who'd have guessed the Pandora's box of troubles his father's death would unleash?

"I, too, face these same responsibilities, do I not? While you think they will be airy and effortless for me, I assure you, you are much mistaken."

Something in Alistair's voice caused Richard to pull up Bess's reins. "What are you telling me?"

"You are concerned because you lack the know-how and skills of a country squire. These can be learned, even mastered. My lack is much more complicated." His intensity took Richard aback. "I'm trapped into this life and I hate it. I love riding, racing, wrestling—all those things at which I excelled in school. What I despise is putting myself above the rest."

Richard was confused. "Rest of whom?"

He waved his arm. "The rest of those around us. The people." His brow furrowed with emotion. "We're the lucky ones. We were born with more—more money, more power, more schooling. But we're not better human beings. Not in God's eyes."

"That is God's plan, Alistair. We were born with these advantages because we are better. Some are born to rule and some are born to serve."

Alistair sighed. "I know the doctrine. Like you, I've been catechized in it since birth." He looked down. "I just can't swallow it. It leaves a bitterness on my tongue." He twisted his head toward Richard. "It feels wrong."

Richard studied Alistair for a moment, who seemed genuinely troubled by these thoughts. "I don't know what to say. Maybe the Grand Tour is what you need. Perhaps you're not ready to accept the yoke of responsibility, as my uncle calls it. It'll come, Alistair. It'll come."

Yet, seeing the pain in his friend's eyes, Richard wondered if it would.

Three days later, as the Moores were taking their leave, Alistair pulled Richard aside. "I'll not see you before I go abroad. We leave in three weeks. But I'll send you a note from time to time. Just to make you jealous, of course."

"You said I was one of your few friends, Alistair. You are my only friend. I'll look forward to your letters." Richard remembered Uncle Ethan's near-wish that he crack his head or catch a disease. "Be safe. Have fun, but be safe."

Alistair laughed. "You can count on the fun part. I'll leave my safety in God's hands."

The Moore carriage pulled away from Duncullen and the two friends set off on very different paths.

Chapter Twenty-two

A fortnight had passed since Sir Edward's funeral, and Duncullen remained heavy with sorrow. Eveleen had hoped things would improve between her and Richard, but they became even worse.

The gossip in the servants' hall, however, remained constant. Lady Nancy, it was said, was inconsolable. When awake, she cried and moaned that they would soon be destitute, at the mercy of unloving relatives. Biddy dosed her well with laudanum, which left her dazed or asleep much of the time.

Mr. Richard was as tense as an overwound pocket watch. He spent his time alone, riding and reading. When dealing with servants, inside or out, he barked orders and took them to task for the most minor of errors. Only Jack was treated with the easy kindness the others missed.

He shared stolen glances with Eveleen, but no more.

An hour past the midday meal, Eveleen dragged her broom across the library's rug. She felt peevish and drained, as she had for a while now. Having not bled for two months, she felt a nagging worry she could be with child, but shoved those thoughts from her head. After all, the ordeals of Maeve's whipping and exile to America, Sir Edward's humiliating assault, and the uproar created by their master's sudden death were enough to stop her monthlies, weren't they?

What of Richard? He was changing, like everyone said. While there had been little opportunity for them to meet, his glower at the sight of Ronan's kiss haunted her. He hadn't even tried to speak. Instead, he walked away that night, and he had stayed away.

She wailed in her head, We are married in the eyes of God, are we not? Can he dismiss me so easily?

"Eveleen."

Startled, her head jerked up and her hand flung to her heart. At this reaction, Jack stumbled back a few steps.

"Sorry," he said, eyes wide.

"Oh, Jack." She giggled nervously. "I'm fine. I was lost in me thoughts, is all."

"'Tis Mr. Richard," he said, wringing his hands. "He wants me to sneak ye out and bring ye to the river." He swallowed. "I'm not good at sneaking, but Mr. Richard told me to do it."

Eveleen's heart pounded. "If that's what he ordered, we'll have to try. Maybe through there." She pointed to the French doors. "Where is yer ma?"

"In the kitchen with Orla." He walked to the doors and opened them. "We'll have to go fast."

"That we will," Eveleen said, gathering her skirts about her.

✦

Out of breath from their tramp through the woods, Eveleen panted at the edge of the clearing.

"Here she is, Mr. Richard," Jack called out.

Richard's face lit up at the sight of her; his smile caused Eveleen's heart to flip. She'd missed him so.

"You've done well," he said to Jack, his eyes never leaving Eveleen. "You can go back now. Our secret?"

"Our secret," Jack promised and was gone.

Despite the familiar longing on Richard's face and her own immense desires, Eveleen held back. Why had he summoned her? They'd been apart for so long.

"I've missed you," he said.

Her eyes searched his face, but she found only sincerity. "Me, too."

"The world has turned upside-down." He ran his hand against the back of his head, reminding Eveleen of a confused little boy. "I feel so all alone."

"I'm here."

He held out his arms. "I ... I need you to hold me."

She needed no more and dashed across the clearing into his waiting arms. Her head against his chest, Eveleen inhaled his warm, familiar scent while Richard's heartbeat thumped in her ears. Tears of relief washed her cheeks. She'd feared she'd never have this again.

He lifted her face to his and kissed her passionately. Together they fell to the ground and the old desire welled within her. Their kisses became frantic and heated, as though each needed the other for survival.

Breaking away to catch his breath, he gently wiped her face dry with the sleeves of his jacket. "I love you, Eveleen. I almost forgot that, but I love you."

Her heart swelled until she thought it might burst. "I was so afraid."

"Of what?"

"That you—that you no longer wanted me."

He pushed her hair from her face. "I'll always want you. I may not be able to have you, but I'll always want you."

She frowned. "You already have me, Richard. I'm devoted to ye. Do ye doubt that?"

"No." He sat up. "That's not what I mean." He pursed his lips and stared at his hands. "God forgive me, but I thought things would be easier for me, for us, without my father in the way."

Eveleen dared not say it aloud, but she'd thought the same thing. "Surely, ye'll go to Trinity now. Mr. Thomas is here for four years, they say. Yer free." She started to add "to take me with ye," but the look of despair on his face made it catch in her throat.

"Everyone's against me, Eveleen. I trust only you. And Jack."

"I don't understand."

His face hardened. "Well, my wonderful father left a fine letter urging me to keep his estate together until I could produce a more capable heir. My mother is beside herself that my incompetence will land us, impoverished, at her father's doorstep. Surely, you've heard that a shabby distant cousin of mine is claiming my birthright while the Mr. Thomas you so blithely recommend plots against me as we speak."

Eveleen was confused. "It cannot be."

"But it is. Dare I leave Duncullen for even a short time while conspirators undermine me at every turn?"

Her mouth grew parched. She'd been longing to be together in Dublin. "What about us?"

"Us?" His eyes narrowed. "I dare not venture forth on that front. I'd be playing right into Thomas's hands. Marrying you is illegal, of course. Uncle Ethan would love it."

Eveleen felt sick. "Richard, we are married. We wed on this very spot before Almighty God."

His mouth dropped. "Of course, we're married. I was speaking in terms of the laws of man, not the eyes of God." He kissed her tenderly. "I meant every word I said that day and I still do. I just don't know how we'll manage it right now. Being openly together, I mean. I need to cement my position here. Then we can work it out."

She eyed him for a moment, then looked away. "I'm not sure we have time."

"Of course we do. We're young yet."

Eveleen's hands grew cold with fear and her lip trembled. "Richard, I may be with child."

He clambered to his knees. "What?"

She sat up and studied her hands. "I've not bled for over two months. That happens sometimes, so I try not to worry. But me breasts are full and tender, and me stomach is queasy much of the time."

He leapt to his feet and began pacing. "This cannot be. You can't do this to me now, Eveleen. Of all the times, you cannot do this to me now."

"I've not done it to ye." Tears dripped from her chin. "Ye done it to me."

"What will we do?" Richard frantically waved his arms in the air.

"Ye must marry me by law. Else our wee one'll be a bastard." Eveleen cringed at the disdain on his face.

"I cannot marry you," he fumed. "It is against the law. Haven't you listened to a word I've said? I will lose everything. My mother's greatest fears will be realized. This cannot happen!"

With that, her world crumbled around her. Heartbroken, Eveleen openly wept, but Richard seemed not to notice. He paced and ranted as though mad. When his words became too unbearable, she blocked him out.

All at once, he stopped. "Pennyroyal. That's what we need."

She snapped back to attention. "Pennyroyal?"

He ran to the bank of the river. "I thought so. Some is growing right here." He pulled up several plants.

Eveleen stood. "What are ye doing?"

"I have it on good authority that a tea brewed with pennyroyal, drunk for several days, will eliminate this problem altogether."

"Eliminate?" Eveleen felt an odd sense of protection for the new life inside her. "Ye want me to kill our baby?"

He brought the plants over and shoved them into her hands. "You're not even sure there is a baby. It's simply a precaution, nothing more."

"But if there is—"

He placed his finger on her lips. "This is not the right time for a child. Surely you can see that. If we have one, it will need a good home, plenty to eat. I'm not sure I can provide even that at this point." He closed her hand around the herb. "Of course, we'll have children, but not now. When we can accept our son publicly with open arms as the rightful heir to Duncullen, we will have our child."

Her eyes stung. "Ye would keep Duncullen at the cost of this child?"

Richard's face reddened. "Don't turn me into the monster here. You spoke not a word when you were fertile. You let me think all was well."

She flung the pennyroyal to the ground. "I didn't know meself! How could I tell ye?"

He grasped her by the shoulders. "Duncullen is all I have, Eveleen. Being the lord of this baronetcy is what I was born to do. Even Trinity is out of the question if I lose all here. Can you understand that?"

Tears of rage or sorrow spilled from his eyes. Either way, they melted Eveleen's heart. She kicked at the strewn pennyroyal. "Ye cannot use the plant straight from the ground. It must be dried."

Her emotions were a jumble. Maybe he was right. Perhaps there wasn't a baby at all. Perhaps she could drink the tea, make Richard happy, and nothing bad would happen.

She was unable to speak above a whisper. "There's some that hangs in the kitchen."

Richard snatched her into his arms. "Oh, my darling. You'll see. This is the right thing to do. I love you so!"

"I've not yet decided, Richard."

He kissed her tenderly. "If you love me, you'll drink the tea."

✝

I am a fool.

That evening, Eveleen lay on her pallet, dread weighing upon her stomach like a rock. The love she and Richard felt for each other had seemed like a Cinderella story come to life. How many nights had she lain here, dreaming of the day she and her beloved could stand side by side as Lord and Lady Lynche of Duncullen? She pictured her mother and sisters safe and happy in the upstairs rooms. Not the Blue Room, of course. That would always be their special sanctuary.

She could see herself describing the plight of poor tenants while a tear escaped Richard's eye. Because of her, he would finally understand their dismal dilemma. How distraught he'd be as she related the death of her poor brother—how Ned's stomach bulged, his hair sloughed off, and he lay moaning by the hearth 'til his wee heart just quit. Richard would wipe Eveleen's tears as she told the tale and promise no child would suffer so under his protection.

Now, if indeed she was with child, Eveleen knew her dream would never come true. Not even his own child would he protect. Deep inside, though, she knew Richard was right. What reception could she expect from Lady Nancy when Eveleen stood before her with a babe in her belly?

She had grown old in the last weeks, she felt, observing first-hand how the highborn so deftly dealt with the likes of her. Off to the plantations she'd be sent, on a rat-infested hulk.

Would Richard stand tall, defending her to one and all? Or would he let her go? The truth sank into her heart like a bayonet. She could not say for certain what he would do.

☧

Early the next afternoon, Eveleen stood before the kitchen fire, waiting for a pot of water to boil. On the table sat a drinking bowl containing the dried pennyroyal she'd pinched. She turned her back to it, unable to look at the death-inducing herb. It could as easily have been a bowl of stinging thorns.

The watched pot simmered too soon, and she poured the bubbling water over the dried weed. Its sweet, minty aroma billowed from the bowl. As though in a stupor, she sat and waited while the witch's brew steeped.

Orla's voice snapped her from her reverie. "What is it yer doing with Sir Edward's pennyroyal, Eveleen?"

"Well, 'tis me head is what it is," she said, stumbling over the excuse she'd planned. "More me stomach, though. I haven't felt well for a while now."

"Yer looking right feeble, ye are. I kept the pennyroyal for the old man's gout, but he won't be needing it where he's gone." She leaned forward and said in a low tone, "An icy cup of rum shrub is what he'll need, but I doubt he's getting any of that either."

Eveleen tried to smile.

Orla shook her head. "Ah, poor sick lass. Drink it down. May it be the cure ye require." She turned to leave, then stopped and added, "Only the one cup for now. It can botch up yer monthlies and bring on the cramping if ye take too much."

"Just this one," Eveleen agreed as the cook walked away. She lifted the bowl and pressed her lips to the rim, stopped, and set it down.

'Tis for the best, she chided herself and raised it to her mouth once again.

Unbidden, the memory of her youngest sister, Katie, surfaced, when the midwife first placed the child in her arms. In her mind, she could see the wrinkled little head topped with a shock of black hair. Her eyes were a dark, dark blue, as shiny as glass marbles.

Remembering, she could almost feel the skin of the infant's cheek, softer than anything she'd ever touched. Eveleen had gently brushed the puckered lips with her finger and gasped when the baby began sucking.

"Ma," she'd called out, "she's already hungry."

Little Katie was a sweet baby who snuggled with Eveleen night after night, usually for protection from Da, but also because of her warm, gentle heart. A wee angel grew inside her now, wanting nothing more than to be born and loved!

She leapt from the bench and dumped the pungent tea into the slop bucket. In despair, she sobbed from deep within.

I love Richard, she bemoaned. I do. But I will not kill this new life within me. May Richard forgive me and may God give me courage.

☦

Noreen Bridge lay in peace and comfort beside her husband while Will's gnarled, calloused hands tenderly stroked her cheek. She felt warmed by his soft gaze in the firelight.

"Ye've not had a headache in more than a fortnight," he whispered, just loudly enough to be heard over Jack's snores. "With all that's gone on, I'm surprised. Very pleased, to be sure, but surprised."

Noreen smiled. "Ye need not be, Will Bridge. For surely ye know the millstone that's been lifted from me heart."

"I don't know. What burden was it that afflicted ye so?"

With a tight jaw, she said, "That loathsome cur is finally where he belongs—lying stone cold in his grave. I am done with him."

Will's eyes sagged. "Sir Edward?"

"That bastard is out of our lives, and I don't mind saying I helped him out the door."

"What do ye mean?"

Noreen Bridge's stomach twisted at her husband's pained expression. She placed her hands on the sides of his jaw. "Yer the greatest love and best friend of me whole life and I'll tell not another soul what I'm telling ye." She took a breath. "Richard was in the breakfast room with yer rat poison."

"The pellets?"

"The white powder. He was sprinkling it in the old man's tea and I caught him. 'Twas meself that urged the lad to add enough to snuff the fool out. No need to merely sicken him."

Will's eyes grew in horror. "Oh, sweet Jesus in heaven! Mary, Mother of God!"

A series of snorts interrupted Jack's rhythmic snores.

"Hush, Will. Do not wake the boy."

"Why did ye tell me this, Noreen? For the love of God, what have ye done? Ye committed murder. A mortal sin."

Noreen felt her blood rise. "A mortal sin, is it? Ye know what an evil blackguard he was. Ye witnessed for yerself how he treated Maeve and worse yet, Eveleen. How he abused his own flesh and blood. Little wonder the boy'd had enough." Her lip trembled. "Have ye forgotten what he done to me?"

The warmth drained from Will's eyes. He retreated from her and her heart wailed in agony. When he spoke, his words sliced like a razor.

"'Tis the depth of yer feeling for Sir Edward that stings so sharp."

"Depth of me feelings? Will, 'twas me hatred of the man that boiled me bile and laid me low with anguish and misery. At long last, I am free of him."

"Aye. Yer finally free of him. It seems he's had yer heart in chains all this time. Ye couldn't let him go, could ye?"

"I don't know what yer talking about."

"I can see that ye don't. Ye believe yer hate is the far side of love when in truth they're near one and the same."

"Yer making no sense."

"Passion is what I'm talking about, Noreen. Love and hate sit side-by-side, with only the thread of a spider between them. So fragile, a breach of that thread can turn the greatest love to a malignant fury, as it has done to you. But, make no mistake, the passion is the same."

"I love ye, Will. Ye know that."

"We have a good life and a son we've raised together. But yer zeal, ye saved for him."

"What would ye have me feel for the scum of the earth?"

"Nothing. The same as he felt for you, after all. I'd have ye feel nothing for the man."

The familiar tightness gripped the base of her skull. "Ye may be a saint, Will, able to forgive and forget. But I remember all too well how he vowed his love for me, placed a babe in me belly, then passed me on to his hired hand like an old rag.'"

Will winced. "Is that how ye see me? I've loved ye since ye first glided through the Big House, the most bewitching colleen on the face of the earth. 'Twas no surprise when ye fell for Sir Edward. I was a shy, gawky clumperton and he was ... well, he was Sir Edward."

"I never saw ye that way."

Will chuckled. "Ye never saw me at all." He sighed. "Once he brought Lady Nancy home, his face lit with love, I worried for ye. 'What's to become of Noreen?' I asked him. To this day, I cannot believe me brass. But he bit his lip and told me ye were in the family way. He said he didn't know what to do."

He wiped some tears from his chin. "'I'll marry her,' I told him, 'if she'll have me.' Ye see, he didn't pass ye on. I'd prayed every dawn and dusk that ye'd turn to me. 'Twas God's mercy that yer me wife. Me greatest day was when Sir Edward pulled up with Lady Nancy."

"The day ye married me was me own best day." She leaned in to kiss Will, but he shrank back.

"I thought I could make ye forget Sir Edward, but I couldn't. Only his murder could purge him from yer heart."

"No, Will." She reached for him, but he moved her hand away.

"Neither you nor Mr. Richard have anything to fear from me. We'll never speak of this again. I'll not see the mother of me son hanged. For he is me son, Noreen. Edward planted the seed, but 'twas I who loved and nurtured it. Never forget that."

"I never do," she started to say, but he turned his back and faced the wall.

Chapter Twenty-three

Alone in his chamber, Richard sat before his open copy of Plato's *Republic.* The words swam before his eyes, ruining all attempts to read the great philosopher.

What had become of his dreams? His life?

A deep loneliness swamped Richard. "I am an orphan," he whispered, "if not in fact, then in reality. Mother wades through the muck of her private misery, while I can neither understand nor offer assistance. She is of no use. She is not there."

He smirked. "My father is where I put him. In the ground."

A soft wisp of laughter brushed Richard's ear, causing an electric jolt through his body. Twisting his head in all directions, he found it as he'd thought. No one was there.

He lifted his book to refocus on what he no longer considered feasible—a utopian world. What rubbish! Unless ancient man was a far nobler creature than walked the earth this day, it was no more than Plato's delusion.

Wait. He definitely felt it. A distinct presence hovered behind his right shoulder. He spun. Not there. He wheeled to his left. Nothing. A low chortling. He could feel it more than hear it. The wind?

Richard leapt from his chair and rattled each window. All were secured. Goose skin covered his forearms. The hairs stood erect. Was he going mad?

Returning to his desk chair, he realized the presence remained, stronger now. He shivered, yet beads of sweat dotted his brow.

"Who are you?" he ventured in a harsh whisper. "What are you?"

Breathy laughter swirled in circles around him. He did not hear it as much as felt it. "Who do you think I am, you waste of a prick?"

The mocking snickers grew more pronounced. They pounded against his heart and in his ears like a drum.

"You were so clever," the voice laid on his heart. "Or so you thought. Look at you now. What did your patricide bring you?" A loud howling of merriment clanged in his head.

"Enough!" he yelled. "You're dead. You cannot touch me."

The taunting guffaws continued.

Richard sprang from his chair and pivoted about the room, in search of the invisible culprit. "Silence! Silence! Stop laughing at me."

A loud knock on the door broke the spell. The presence evaporated and Richard stood, gasping for breath, in the middle of the floor.

The knock repeated and he bade the petitioner to enter.

The plump form of Anne de Barnefort crept into the room. "Am I interrupting you?" She scanned from wall to window, and seemed barely able to resist a squat down to check under the bed. Her eyebrows flew up toward her hairline. "I came at this time to catch you alone, but ... I could have sworn I heard voices in here."

Oh, Lord. What would she report to her dotard of a husband? Richard reached for the open book on his desk. "Please forgive me. I didn't think anyone would hear me." He grinned as charmingly as he was able. "At times, I like to read my books aloud, as though I'm acting them out. A secret desire for the stage, I suppose." He put his finger to his lips. "Don't tell anyone."

Anne's laugh pattered like rain on a roof. She waved her hand at him. "Your secret is safe with me. I shared the same fantasy as a girl."

Richard closed the book and tossed it onto his bed. He directed his cousin's wife to a chair beside the fire and sat opposite her. "To what do I owe this unexpected visit?"

Eyes wide, she looked at Richard and sighed. "I'm in a quandary. About my role here, I mean. It's clear what Thomas needs to do. He is in charge. He makes all the decisions about managing Duncullen." Her lips pursed like a china doll's. "Oh, he must go through Sir Nathaniel, certainly. And you, dear Richard, are under his able tutelage, in hopes of taking over one day."

Hopes? "I am aware."

She giggled in her distinctive rat-a-tat way. "Of course, you are." She clasped her hands and placed them on her lap. "My concern stems from my responsibilities here. Your esteemed mother is the lady of the house and, as such, has dominion over the household staff."

"I would agree with that."

Anne opened her mouth, then closed it with a noisy sigh. "The dilemma for me," she finally said, "is with which things do I burden the grieving widow—a burden many would say is more than she can bear—and which do I lay upon myself?"

He grew concerned. "Is Mother unable to make even the most mundane of decisions?"

Anne's mouth made a small O. "She does so, Richard, with the strong guidance of Mrs. Bridge. A most competent housekeeper, I must say."

"Then I don't understand."

She leaned in conspiratorially. "It seems yesterday afternoon, I was looking out my chamber window. It was such a lovely day and I was thinking what a fine garden you could build on the south lawn. It's no more than a wooded area now with scrubby underbrush. It would make a most majestic garden. Don't you agree?"

"That is not in her ladyship's purview."

"Of course not. The point is, while I was enjoying my inspired vision, I saw two of the servants sneaking across the courtyard into the woods. Naturally, they will have to be dismissed. Now, is that something I should discuss with Lady Nancy or would you advise I handle that myself?"

A rock thumped to the bottom of Richard's stomach. He struggled to catch his breath. "Which of the servants do you think you saw? Can you identify them?"

"It wasn't that difficult, actually."

His mind raced. "You were quite far away, were you not? We would want to avoid an inaccurate identification."

"Of the female, I am sure. Only one has hair as red as hers. The male I believe to be Jack, the son of the housekeeper." She lowered her voice despite the fact they were quite alone. "He is, in fact, a halfwit, more child than man. What kind of woman takes up with one such as he?"

"I, too, would be astounded should that prove to be the case." He had to stall. "You are quite right. It would unnecessarily upset my mother at this time. Jack and I were childhood companions. Let me look into it myself."

"I would not encumber you, dear Richard, with a lady's business."

"This once, dear Anne. This once."

✚

Thomas de Barnefort studied the large parchment rolled out across his desk. At a knock on the door, he called out, "You may enter."

In bounced his rosy-cheeked wife who flittered across the room and stared at his unfurled scroll. "What's this, Tommy?"

"It's a plat. A map of the baronetcy of Duncullen."

"Oh, my goodness. What are all those little boxes?"

"Those are the plots rented out to each tenant. See here?" He pointed to a snake-like drawing through the middle. "This is the Multeen."

"Where are we? Point to the Big House."

"We're here. Not far from the river." He looked up. "Annie, there is so much I can do here. Uncle Edward was stuck in the past. There have been countless exciting improvements in the field of agriculture. Richard and I can turn Duncullen into a show-place."

Anne frowned. "I almost forgot, Tommy. That's why I came by. I went to Richard's chamber to ask him something and I heard him shouting in a most distressed way."

"Really?"

"Yes. He was crying out, 'Stop laughing at me.'"

"I was unaware of any visitors today."

Anne huffed. "There are none, Tommy. That's the point. He was alone." She peered into her husband's eyes, indicating she expected his full attention. "That's not the worst. Before that, I'm sure I heard, 'You're dead. You cannot touch me.'"

Thomas stood quietly, taking it all in. "Are you certain he was alone? A servant, perhaps?"

"I knocked, and he bid me enter. Naturally, when I saw no one, I questioned him. 'I thought I heard voices,' I said. He claimed to be reading aloud from his book."

He shook his head and chuckled. "There it is. A simple explanation, as always."

"Not so simple. He lifted his book from the desk and tossed it onto the bed. I glimpsed the title. *Republic* by Plato. I personally have not read it, but how much of that book can be considered drama?"

"Hmmm." Thomas recognized a familiar twinkle in Anne's eyes. "Now don't read too much into this," he warned. "We both know the wild rides your imagination has taken in the past."

Anne giggled. "Don't read too much into it? Tommy, you're so comical."

Thomas winced. "In all seriousness, I'd prefer not to be judged on what I might do when I assume no one is watching or listening. Wouldn't you?"

She poked out her lip. "It's perfectly clear to me he was arguing with the phantom of his own father. What other explanation could there be?"

"Any number of them, my love. Have you considered he was enacting a story he'd committed to memory?" He plopped into his leather chair. "I was giving the lad space to grieve in peace, but perhaps it's time he re-join the world. I'll get him to look over this plat with me and we can share ideas."

"A garden, Tommy. Off the south lawn." Anne pointed to the precise spot on the map. "Between here and the river."

He smiled. "A capital idea."

✦

Richard paced the portico. Thankfully, Thomas and Anne were spending the weekend with Thomas's former classmate who lived a few hours' ride from there. The Sunday afternoon outing for the servants had finally arrived, but they were taking their own blasted time in pulling out of the courtyard.

One of the stringy-haired ninnies who worked in the kitchen scuttled toward the wagon, stumbling over her own skirts as she ran. Frustration lit Richard's head like a burning ember. "Get yer skinny arse in the wagon, you bloody nitwit!" he mumbled.

His pulse throbbed in his temples as two groomsmen dragged her clumsy bag of bones onto the bed of the cart. Old Will slapped the reins and the wheels of the wagon lazily began to turn.

"Sweet Jesus in heaven," Richard growled, then strode into the house. He leapt up the staircase two stairs at a time, eager to the point of bursting for his meeting with Eveleen in the Blue Room.

He stopped outside the door, took a deep breath, and entered. There, he was taken aback to see his love sitting on the wing-back chair beneath the window, curtains pulled back for light. He had never seen her, nor any servant, hazard uninvited the use of family furnishings. He frowned, slightly disturbed by her presumption.

Yet, her peaked complexion was as unsettling as her behavior. Eveleen stared at her folded hands, barely lifting her eyes at his entrance.

He rushed to kneel beside her. "My dearest, are you unwell? I know you're grieved by what must be done. Is melancholy the cause of your pallor?"

She sat in silence, her eyes filled with tears.

Richard whispered, "Is it done?"

The shaking of her head was scarcely a twitch.

"Will it take more of that vile tea? Perhaps it was nothing." He sighed. "It distresses me that you must go through this."

She looked up, her eyes red. "I love ye, Richard, more than me own life."

He stroked her hair. "And I love you, my sweet. You are the best thing in my whole world."

"I would die for ye. I hope ye know that."

"I prefer you alive." He smiled, hoping to lighten the mood.

"I want ye to know I tried. For you, I tried." Her eyes pleaded with him. "I couldn't do it." Her words gushed forth in a torrent. "I'd give me life for ye, please believe that, but I cannot harm our wee babe who asks for no more than to be born, to see the light of day. Ye understand that, don't ye?"

Richard's mouth dropped open as his heart began to pound. He could not get enough air into his lungs. "You what? No, I don't understand. I told you I would lose everything, did I not? Did you not understand me?" He lunged toward her. "DID YOU?"

She recoiled, her eyes wide. "I understood ye, I did. But don't ask me to do this." She snatched his hand and squeezed it. "Anything else, Richard, but not this."

He flung her hand away, stood, and spun all in one motion. He did not know if his body could contain this rage. Sound was muffled as the room took on a pinkish hue. He strode toward an ebony chest and kicked it, splintering it into a hundred pieces.

Eveleen cringed, drawing into a ball in that damned chair.

The bloody brass of her. Richard stomped over and yanked the girl to her feet. "I'm not asking you to drink that tea. I'm ordering you to drink it, if I have to take you to the kitchen and pour the scalding liquid down your throat myself."

"I cannot."

He shook her. "Right now! You're going, do you hear me?"

Like a beggar's brat, she dropped to the floor in a dead weight. "Ye cannot force me. I won't."

He released her arm as though it were vile to the touch. Panting, he paced the floor. "Why are you doing this to me? What have I done to deserve such contempt?"

"Nothing. I love ye."

"Stop saying that! You don't love me. It's all a lie. If you loved me, you wouldn't drag me, my mother, and everything I stand for into the sludge. And for what?"

"For the wee—"

"Don't even say it! You'd destroy me for a creature barely formed, that may not even exist." The repugnant thought that invaded his mind flew from his mouth. "Who's to say the entity is even mine? I've no idea with whom or how many you've whored. How about the brute at the carnival that masqueraded as my father's wake?"

He crept up to her, knelt down, and spit his words directly into Eveleen's face. "Or my father himself? Are you carrying my child, or my brother?"

Richard felt the sting of Eveleen's slap before he saw it.

"You hit me." Landing precisely where his father's blow had struck, the same insult and humiliation spewed over him again.

"I'm so sorry, Richard, but yer words were too ugly. Ye know they're not true. Take them back." She dropped her face into her hands.

Somehow, Richard could hardly hear her gut-wrenching sobs. It was too much. He was drowning in the torment he'd suffered from his father, his mother, uncle, Sir Nathaniel, and now Eveleen. Was he no more than a spineless whipping boy for others to abuse?

The truth seeped its way into his consciousness with all its rawness, its depravity. Not about the father of this supposed baby. It was his. He knew that.

The truth was about himself and his place in the world, including the folly of his love for this lowborn servant who had tricked him into believing she was any more than that. And worse, that she'd loved him as he loved her.

Richard felt naked and demeaned as he sat on the cold, wooden floor. Agonizing thoughts tumbled through his mind.

I have been a fool and everyone's laughing, mocking. Everyone. Especially my father. Even from the grave, he jeers.

"All must find you clever," he said, his voice subdued. "You've managed to dupe the young master into falling in love with you."

Eveleen grew quiet. "What are ye on about?"

"I must have come across as quite naïve, a simpleton that you could maneuver me so."

"No."

He felt nauseous, and his head pounded. With shame? "What have I done so very wrong? To love you with every corner of my heart, every cell in my body? Is that my crime?" His stomach twisted. "I cherished you. I held you above my own family, risked my good name for you. Why wasn't that enough? Why am I not enough?"

He broke into silent sobs, wrapped in a loneliness he once considered impossible.

Eyes closed, he felt the gentle stroke of Eveleen's calloused hand tickle down his injured cheek. He grabbed her and crushed her against his body, as though for dear life. With the beating of her heart against his chest, he felt the comfort she'd always provided, a comfort he'd craved even as a young child.

Almost involuntarily, he opened his mouth to say, "I love you," when he remembered. He grit his teeth and thrust her away, causing her to fall back on her elbows.

"Does your guile know no bounds?" he screamed. "You disgust me. Get out of my sight!"

She gaped at him as though he were demented.

"Am I the one who is mad?" he continued. "You bewitch me with your wiles, then declare yourself to be with child. Only your word makes it so. Why should I believe you? So I can be destroyed through your blackmail?"

Eveleen let out a wail that raised the hairs on his neck.

Shaken, he lowered his voice, which shook with rage. "The profound love I've had for you pales in the torture of your betrayal. Have the child, if a child there is. Tell the world it's mine. I'll deny it. It's my father's, I'll say, with whom you've prostituted yourself. No one will be surprised at that. Now, with his demise, you are trying to fleece me in his stead."

"Richard, never could ye do such a thing."

"Who will be believed? I assure you, it will not be you."

She rose to her feet and stood before him, looking so small, so defeated. Her eyes were flushed with pain. His heart ached, but he could not permit himself to waver. Her power over him was too strong.

"Go," he said. "I am done with you."

✛

"I cannot believe you didn't see it for yourself." The sun high in the sky, Anne and her husband stepped from the carriage. "It was the talk of the gathering."

Hogan, who stood waiting outside the carriage, bowed. "Welcome back to Duncullen, Mr. Thomas, Miss Anne."

"Thank you, Hogan," said Thomas. "It's a relief to be back."

"What is the meaning of that?" asked Anne. "Indeed, it's a pleasure to be back, but a relief?"

Thomas sighed. "All the intrigue. No more than gossip, really. Who's flirting with whom? What was said where? It's draining."

"Young Mr. Wright kissed Lady Tallingham directly on the neck. With her husband only yards away. I saw it with my own eyes."

"So you said. Are you certain the lad did not merely whisper something into her ear? 'What a lovely reception' or some such."

Poor Thomas, Anne thought. Duncullen was turning him into an old man. Then she noticed his eyes brighten.

"Oh." He was looking ahead. "There you are."

The future lord of the manor stood on the portico, his hair uncombed and his sunken eyes bleary.

Anne scooted up the steps. "Richard, are you ill?"

"Recent events seem to have crashed upon me," he mumbled. "It's all too much."

As Thomas approached, Richard stretched his lips into a weak smile directed at one, then the other. "Without the good cheer of you both, I'm afraid I've been rather melancholy."

Anne latched onto his hand. "Oh, dear boy, we would never have gone had we known." She whispered to her husband through clenched teeth, "I told you so."

"Forgive me." Thomas clapped Richard on the back. "This very day we begin our plans for Duncullen. Together."

"Any distraction would be welcome," Richard said. "But first, Miss Anne, if I may have a word with you concerning household matters."

"Of course."

Thomas headed into the house. "I'll be in the study when you're ready."

Anne tilted her head. "Shall we sit inside?"

Richard heaved a sigh. "This will take only a moment. I've looked into the matter you brought to my attention. The one regarding servants you saw from a window."

"Yes."

"I don't know precisely what has gone on between them, but the two did sneak into the woods, as you said. I cannot bring myself to believe it was a dalliance, as such, but it's unacceptable nonetheless."

He breathed deeply before continuing. "Jack is under the protection of my father's will. He is guaranteed a lifetime position here."

Anne would have thought it impossible, but his eyes darkened even more. "The girl—" His voice cracked. He swallowed, then forged ahead. "The girl is under no such provision. She must be ... sent away, back to her family."

When tears fell from his eyes, he swiped at them as though they burned like acid. "If you would handle this, I would be grateful. It would distress Mother unnecessarily, as you said."

"Of course, Richard. Don't give it another thought."

He spun on his heel and strode away, but stopped at the main door. Turning back, he said, "Today. She should leave today."

Anne opened her mouth to offer further comfort, but he stumbled through the entryway into the darkness of the house.

Her eyes widened with surprise. "Well."

✚

Miss Anne looked up from her writing table. "Ah, Mrs. Bridge. I see Elly was prompt in giving you my message." Her stern eyes belied the smile she wore. "I must say, for the most part, you run and orderly, well-disciplined household."

"Thank you, Miss Anne." Surely the woman didn't call her all the way upstairs for that.

"With the glaring exception of the red-haired maid."

This stopped the housekeeper cold. "Do ye mean Eveleen, Miss?"

"That's the one. She is to be dismissed immediately."

251

Mrs. Bridge's stomach wrenched. Saint Joseph, give me strength! she screamed in her head. Outwardly, she waited, stone-faced, for the woman to explain herself.

"With my own eyes, I saw the wench scurry into the woods following a certain young man. In the middle of the afternoon. Scandalous!"

Mrs. Bridge slowly blinked and pursed her lips. Young man? Could it be Mr. Richard? "I would like to find out if there is some sort of explanation. May I question the maid first? She's one of our hardest workers."

Miss Anne glared. "Do you believe me an idiot? That has already occurred. The young master, Mr. Richard himself, has ordered her discharge and he wants it done immediately. Return the strumpet to her family without delay."

"Yes, Miss Anne." Her mind whirled. Whatever was this about? It was Mr. Richard she'd fretted over, so who was this lad she supposedly followed. And how could she tell Will, poor fella? It would tear his heart out to face his old friend with this.

Miss Anne's icy voice cut through her reverie. "Be off with you."

✢

Slowly, Richard cracked the door to his mother's chamber and peeked inside. She lay propped on the bed, her hair loose and flowing over the many pillows cushioning her head. Haltingly, she twisted in his direction.

"Who is that?"

"It is I, Mother."

"Richard? Come closer."

He obeyed. A shiver ran down his spine at the sight of her pale blue eyes, with pupils the size of pinheads. Scratch marks covered her arms and chest.

She smiled weakly. "Don't stare, son. My skin is so itchy at times, I could tear it off." She tilted her head. "What's wrong? You look sad, like you did as a boy when something hadn't gone your way."

Before him lay the once-elegant lady who'd read whimsical rhymes and sang sweet songs to ferry him to sleep. How many times had she kissed his elbows and blotted his tears, reminding him to be a strong little man?

"What's happened to us?" he asked. "We were beautiful once." Melancholy enveloped him like a shroud and he sank into the bedside chair and wept.

Lady Nancy propped herself on one elbow, stretching her other hand to pet his bowed head. "You still are, silly. My dear, sweet prince."

She softly crooned, "Lavender blue, dilly dilly. Lavender green. When I am king, dilly dilly, you shall be queen."

Oh Lord. Not this song. Richard's heart broke into a thousand pieces as his mother sang the lullaby that had once brought him so much comfort. He lifted himself from the chair and laid his head upon her shoulder, and she snuggled him against herself, stroking his cheek.

"Who told you so ... dilly, dilly ... who told you so?"

Richard felt her chest struggle to rise and fall. "'Twas my own heart, dilly ..."

Richard lifted his head to alleviate the pressure he'd caused, but his mother was panting now.

"Oh ... dear," she huffed. "I can ... scarcely ..."

Richard stood and stroked her head this time. "Not to worry. Rest now."

She closed her eyes as her chest continued to heave. "My mother used to ... sing me ... that song."

Richard whispered, "So did mine."

Chapter Twenty-four

Eveleen peered uneasily into Mrs. Bridge's cabin. Ever since Biddy'd ordered Eveleen to the housekeeper's residence, her stomach had been in knots. How well she remembered the last miserable conversation the two shared in private.

"Naught ye'll get from the lord's son but the big belly," Mrs. Bridge had told her, "or the clap. Probably both." Something like that.

Could she possibly know? It did not ease Eveleen's mind to see a grim Mrs. Bridge standing by the hearth, wringing her hands.

"Come in, lass." The housekeeper's voice was somber. "Better, it is, to do this in private."

Eveleen's heart pounded and her fingers grew cold as she crossed the threshold. Feeling lightheaded, she rested her hand on the wooden table, steadying herself.

"Sit down."

"I'll stand, if it suits ye either way." Eveleen felt herself swaying from side to side.

Mrs. Bridge breathed deeply. "I don't know what else to do, but to say it out. Yer to leave Duncullen, Eveleen. Today."

"Wha--?"

"Miss Anne claims you ran off into the woods with some fella. Could that be true?"

The world grew hazy, as if in a dream. "Some fella? I—I don't know." Her voice sounded far away as she stared at her hand on the table.

Mrs. Bridge's tone turned harsh. "Ye don't know if ye sneaked into the woods like some tawdry moll?"

"I need to talk to Rich—to Mr. Richard."

"Oh, lass, what have ye done?"

The words tumbled from Eveleen's mouth. "Mr. Richard will set this straight. Just go to him. He'll explain it all. Ye'll see."

"'Twill not be possible. According to Miss Anne, 'twas himself who ordered ye away."

Eveleen's head shot up. "That cannot be true. Let us ask him, face to face. He'll have calmed down by now." Nothing was real. She seemed to watch herself from a separate body as the world spun around her. Jesus, help me, she prayed. I'm going daft.

The next thing she knew, Mrs. Bridge was lifting her from the floor onto the bench beside the table. To her mind, a thick fog had saturated the cabin.

"I can't go home," she mumbled. "Not like this. I cannot."

⸙

Consciousness slowly seeped back to Eveleen as she lay on a cot, bewildered by her whereabouts. Nearby whispers swirled in her brain.

"I tried to speak to the haughty little prig, but he refused to see me."

"Hush, Noreen. Eyes and ears are all about."

The Bridge's cabin, she realized. How strange that she'd fallen asleep.

"I don't give a care who hears me. So disgusted I am, I could spit on his shoes."

Who? Then, with a blow to the gut, Eveleen remembered. Richard was sending her away. Whatever would she do? She struggled to make sense of it. Wait. She almost smiled. Foolish girl, she thought, 'twas a dream. Ye drifted to sleep and had a dreadful nightmare, no more.

"Will, our worst fears may be true," Mrs. Bridge was saying. "Orla saw the lass in the kitchen only last week. Sipping on pennyroyal tea, she was, claiming a sour stomach."

"Jesus."

"Young fool. Remember Maureen Riley's newborn? The wee fella reeked of pennyroyal when he popped out, fat and healthy."

Old Will's voice was shrill. "If Mr. Richard wants to act like a man, he must own up to his responsibilities. He can't just set the girl on the road and forget her."

Eveleen's eyes burned. Lord, have mercy. It was true.

"I aimed to tell him so meself," Mrs. Bridge went on, "but holed up in his chamber, he is, refusing to talk to me or anyone else."

With time, he'd calm down. They were married, for the love of God!

"Go to him, Will. Maybe a good man like yerself can get through. We've got to try."

A glimmer of hope trickled into Eveleen's heart until a knock thumped on the door.

"Mrs. Bridge."

At Brea's distressed voice, Eveleen bolted upright.

"Here are her things. Miss Anne's sent word. She's to be gone within the hour."

✦

Old Will had hitched the wagon and stashed Eveleen's scant belongings in the back. A few of the maids and grooms made their way to the Bridge cabin to squeeze her hand and wish her Godspeed.

Only Brea and Jack looked like they might miss the girl. The solemn expressions of the others seemed more to reflect their own uncertainties. They knew little of Mr. Thomas de Barnefort's ways while Mr. Richard's fickle behavior kept them off kilter. More than one whispered, "Who will be next?"

Will stood in the doorway, his heart torn to shreds. He'd give his right foot, he knew, not to face Paddy Scully like this. His friend had given him a sacred trust, his own child, and now Will must return her ravaged by one of the very people Paddy despised.

Even his own family had been thrown upside down. He and Noreen spoke agreeably to each other and continued to lie together, but he rarely touched her. He could not forget her words, which constantly clanged in his head: "He passed me on to his hired hand like an old rag."

Noreen interrupted his thoughts. "Will, can ye step inside? I've something to say before ye set off."

Once out of earshot of the others, she gazed at him with pained eyes and pursed lips. "I don't know if 'tis the right time or 'tisn't," she began, "but it hurts me so to see ye go off this way. I know how ye feel about Eveleen and yer word to her da. Plainly, yer sickened inside."

Will nodded and shuffled his feet, his anguish increasing by the minute.

"I gave a lot of thought to yer words when we last spoke. And while they held some wisdom, to be sure, I have to say ye got it wrong."

His head snapped up.

Noreen lifted her chin. "Aye, Will, yer wrong this time. Ye said me hatred of Sir Edward was a hair's breadth from love. That they're both passion, one and the same. Well, 'tis not true."

Will frowned, curious now. "Go on."

"I admit I'd have been a better person if I cared not a jot for the old man, if his actions meant nothing to me. I wish the pain I felt could've been wiped clean, but it wasn't. All these years, I stood by and watched, time and again, as he stole the dignity and decency from everyone he touched. I despised him for me-self, true, but me hatred grew with each new victim."

"Noreen, 'tis a hard journey I take, and me heart is near to bursting now. Could this not wait?"

His shoulders slumped in frustration as tears spilled from his wife's eyes.

She ran her sleeve across her nose. "I'm botching this up, to be sure. That's not even what I need ye to know." She sniffed loudly and swallowed. "There's another kind of love better than passion. Something stronger and deeper, the kind of love I have for you." She stepped closer to Will and searched his eyes. "A love that comes from years of trust, knowing yer there for me through thick and thin. Not once have ye let me down, Will Bridge. Never. Not even now."

She breathed deeply and lowered her voice. "Ye took a lost and broken girl, much like poor Eveleen out there, and put her back together, piece by piece. Ye made her stronger than she was before. Ye took her son, a lad others would scorn or abuse, and made him yer own. He's the fine man he is today because of you, Will. He needed a solid and steady father, and there ye stood."

Will swallowed. Noreen took a breath and went on.

"Ye believe in me and so, I believe in meself. With you, I'm not afraid. Ye know me like no one else, the good parts and the bad, but ye love me still. At least ye did." She took his hand. "And aye, me stomach turns to pap when I catch ye watching me with yer soft, loving eyes. I tingle all over at yer gentle touch.

Please believe me. No amount of lust or passion I felt as a lass can come close to what I feel for you, Will, and no one but you."

She wiped the tears from her chin with her apron. "I don't know if that's the kind of love ye need from me, but it's what I have to give."

Swelled with emotion, Will pulled his wife into his arms. He poured all the devotion he felt into a hot, crushing kiss. Her warm tears sloshed together with his, and yes, he felt her passion.

Breaking off, he said, "I thought I loved ye as much as me heart could stand, so how can I love ye twice as much right now?"

They had only moments, but, for that short time, they were the only two in the world. Jack's voice brought them back to their ugly reality.

"Ye want me to ride with ye, Da?"

Will turned to his son. "No, lad. 'Tis something I must do meself."

Jack frowned as he looked from one to the other. "What's wrong?"

"For once, son, something is right." Will pecked Noreen on the lips, squeezed her hand, and headed for the door.

✛

The creaking and moaning of the cart's wheels were broken only by the clomp-clomp of the piebald horse pulling them along the road to Kilmacthomas. Will kept an eye on the low, dark clouds blanketing the hills to the west. They had yet another hour's travel and he hoped to avoid the downpour that threatened.

Little had been said by Eveleen or himself as they plodded along the rutted track, each lost in their own thoughts. Twice, he'd had to pull up while Eveleen puked in the hedgerow that lined the lane. She spewed with such force the first time, Will couldn't imagine what she'd had left for the second. By the violence of her retching, it seemed she was vomiting up her very bowels.

Will's shoulders hunched forward. Dread pressed down upon him, heavier with each thud of Pete's hoof. He had let down his oldest friend in the worst possible way, and it took every fiber of his courage to continue down this road. He was overjoyed that Noreen had lifted the pall from his heart with her sincere declaration of love. But, until he faced Paddy with this calamity and begged forgiveness for his failures, that happiness would have to wait.

Not that he expected to be forgiven. He glanced toward Eveleen and his spirits sank even lower. The girl's face resembled two black coals sunken into a bowl of wet flour. Her shoulders shook with silent sobs. Will removed his coat and placed it over her shoulders. She faced him, nodded, and stared ahead, reminding Will of a murderess he once saw as she approached the scaffold for her hanging.

When the hovel at last came into view, an agonizing burn rose from Will's stomach to his jawbone. The lad—Nolan, was it?—called inside, likely announcing their arrival.

Paddy stepped over their threshold into the yard, looking far older than his years, but sober at least. His bedraggled wife crept out behind him, followed by the unkempt boy and little girls. Eveleen let out a squeak, then bit her lip. Was it joy or distress, Will wondered, or both? He rolled the cart into the yard, then pulled up on Pete's reins.

"Eveleen!" called the older girl and the children ran to greet their sister. Eyes down, Eveleen cautiously stepped from the cart, and held each child in turn. When her mother, Mary

Scully, neared, Eveleen grabbed her close and held on as though drowning.

Meanwhile, Paddy approached and grabbed the horse's harness. His frown and tone of voice revealed his confusion and concern. "What brings ye here, Willie? Word came the old man at Duncullen gave up the ghost. Don't the young buck need good help?"

Will glanced at Eveleen, who listened keenly as she chewed her fingers. Weary, he could put no spirit into his words. "Everything's changing, Paddy. Her ladyship's illness is made worse with grief and a young cousin's wife has taken on her duties."

Paddy's frown deepened. "And?"

Will swallowed. "Miss Anne has found Eveleen's work unsatisfactory."

"Unsatisfactory? The girl can outwork any draft horse. She hasn't a lazy bone in her body. What sort of rubbish is this?"

The burn in Will's throat and chest grew sharper. "The young wife is new to this sort of thing."

Paddy scowled. "I see after twenty more years of life, Willie Bridge, yer no better liar than ye ever were. What's really going on here?" He turned to Eveleen. "Girl, what have ye done to get sent home, hanging yer head in shame, as ye are?"

Eveleen kept her head low. She was struggling to breathe, stuttering as she inhaled.

Paddy glanced at Will, then back to his daughter. "Yer still the innocent I sent off from here, are ye not?"

Eveleen covered her face with her hands and broke into heart sickening sobs. Will felt tears well up behind his own eyes, watching Paddy Scully finally realize the truth.

"What have ye done?" he bawled at the top of his lungs, causing Eveleen to slink to the ground in a heap. Mary Scully let out a squawk and lifted her daughter, wrapping Eveleen in her arms.

Paddy spun to face Will. "Who done it? The rogue will marry her, by God!"

Will forced himself to look his friend in the eye and shook his head back and forth.

"NO!" Paddy bellowed. "Not the old man. The filthy, bloody bastard!"

Eveleen looked up. "No, Da. I done nothing with Sir Edward. I swear to ye."

"'Twas his goddammed brat, then! Yer no more than a whore, do ye hear me?" He slapped her face, sending her sprawling to the ground.

The girl's mother dropped to her knees and scrambled to the girl. "Are ye with child, then?"

Eveleen wiped her nose with the back of her hand. She nodded.

Mary Scully's head sank into her shoulders. "Jesus in heaven, save us."

Paddy leaned toward the two. "Where do ye plan to go, ye dirty slut! Ye've been driven from yer fancy manor house. By God, ye'll not stay here to ruin our good name."

Will sucked in his breath. "Have mercy, man. She's yer daughter all the same. Ye can't send her away."

Paddy turned his fury on Will. "What do ye know of it with yer nitwit of a son? I got two more lasses here—good, decent girls who'll make fine wives one day. But not with their bawd of a sister dragging them into the muck." He spun to face Eveleen and jabbed his finger at her. "Ye disgust me. Get out of me sight. Yer not me daughter. Yer no more a Scully."

Mary wailed and gripped Eveleen in despair. The little girls held each other and sobbed along with their mother. Only the boy, Nolan, stood tearless. Will saw that his lower lip trembled, but his eyes were narrowed and dark, saturated with malice. A malice clearly directed at Will.

At Paddy's lowered voice, Will tore himself away from the boy's venomous gaze.

"Be on yer way, Will Bridge. Back to yer plum job with yer nose stuck up the English arse. Yer a worthless cur of a man, gelded years ago by English vermin."

"I'll not leave Eveleen like this," he answered.

"She's of no concern to ye now. Not that ye showed proper concern when it was needed. I don't have much, but I have this plot of land. Get off it!"

Will walked to Eveleen and lifted her to her feet. "Come along, lass."

"I can't go back," she whimpered.

"And ye cannot stay here. We'll sort it out. Come."

He held her by the elbow and guided the distraught girl to the wagon. Mary followed the two. Will steadied Eveleen's arm to help her into the cart.

"Wait!" called Mary. She grabbed her daughter's face and kissed her over and over.

"Mary," called her husband, "get away from that wench. She is not our Eveleen. Our little girl is dead."

Mary wailed and clutched Eveleen to her as though she'd never let go.

"Mama," Eveleen cried, "let me stay. I love ye, Ma. Let me stay."

A threatening tone entered Paddy's voice. "If ye know what's good for ye, Mary ..."

With that, Eveleen pulled away from her mother and climbed aboard the wagon. Will rounded its bed and hauled himself into the driver's seat.

"Don't go, Eveleen," pleaded the little girls. "Please stay with us."

Paddy and Will looked each other in the eye. Will caught a glimpse and no more of the agony beneath his friend's contempt.

"If yer taking her, go," Paddy said. "Ye've caused enough suffering in this family. Get the hell out of here! Mary, I told ye to come back."

Will snapped the reins and the cart slowly rolled down the road. Just when he thought he could bear no more heartache, he saw that Mary was trotting alongside them, gripping Eveleen's hand and crying, "I love ye, me sweet darling. I'll always love ye."

"Mary!" Paddy yelped.

Eveleen glanced at her father. "Ma, he'll hurt ye. Go back now."

Her mother kissed her daughter's hand a final time, then let it go. Will marveled at her courage as she stood and watched the wagon roll away, ignoring her husband's repeated threats.

"Goddammit!"

Paddy had kicked their old fencepost almost to the ground, then tramped down the road, away from the house. Will craved a swig of poteen himself.

The wagon continued down the road, but Mary never moved. They reached the curve from where the Scully home would no longer be visible, and there she stood, her head leaning to one side as she watched her daughter ride away from her life. Likely forever.

✚

Richard listened to the creaks and moans of a settling house. Restless, he stumbled from bed, lit the lamp on his desk, then clicked open the pocket watch that lay there. Six o'clock. Another hour or so until sunrise.

Like so many nights before, he'd been awakened by a terrible nightmare. The dreams were not the same, but all were gruesome. In this one, he was on a foxhunt with dozens of others when he came across the prey, dead on the ground and crawling with flies.

Deciding it should be buried, he looked around for a servant, only to find everyone had disappeared. Now alone in the woods, he said aloud, "I'll do it myself."

He'd begun digging the hole with a shovel that had mysteriously appeared, as they do in dreams, when the spade struck something solid. He scraped the dirt away, only to uncover a body. Peeling back the rotting shroud, he exposed Denny, the servant boy who'd, years ago, perished after his brutal flogging. Richard's heart shot to his throat when the dead boy's eyes snapped open. Denny sat up, looked at Richard, and said, "Do ye want to play a game, then?"

The dream awakened Richard with a start, and he'd been unable to go back to sleep, let alone escape the memory of Denny's pasty, decaying face as he lurched upward from his grave.

Thinking he'd go mad confined within his chamber, he threw on some clothes and headed toward the stable. Black Bess always had a calming effect.

There he met Old Will, slinging hay into one of the smaller carts. "I wondered if I'd find anyone up and about," he said to him.

"Right."

Will's voice was uncharacteristically flat. Even in the lantern light, Richard could see the old man's face sagged and his mouth turned down. "Are you unwell, Old Will?"

"I am. Me body is drained and me soul is brimming with sorrow." He tilted his head and looked Richard in the eye. "Perhaps ye'd walk to the pasture with me? I need to speak with ye, if yer willing."

Richard stiffened. "Does it concern my orders of yesterday?"

"It does."

"Have they been carried out?"

"That's not simply answered, I'm afraid." Will lifted the handcart and pulled it out of the barn.

Richard bit his lip as he traipsed through the grass alongside the overseer. I'm no longer the boy who trailed you like a lost puppy, he mentally informed Will, as you'll soon discover.

He pulled back his shoulders. "The order was straightforward and clearly stated. I see no reason it couldn't be carried out—simply."

Despite his bravado, he felt a sense of panic, and maybe even chagrin, before his old friend.

"Mr. Richard, I'm not a man of yer quality and standing, but a part of me still sees ye like me own son. Please take no offense at that. I've no delusions of where I stand in this world."

Richard fretted over where this was heading. "You've always known your place."

Old Will stopped, set the cart down, and turned to face Richard. "Yesterday was one of the worst days in me entire life. Taking that lass back to her da in the condition she's in filled me with shame. Shame for me, and aye, shame for you."

Richard was taken aback, unsure if he was offended or embarrassed. "Why, uh ..."

Will held up his hand. "No need to pretend otherwise. Eveleen said nothing, but 'twasn't hard to guess." He rubbed his hand across his mouth and chin. "A wretched and sorrowful journey we took, lad. Her ma was heartbroken, but her da—well, her da was destroyed by it."

"The initial shock, I imagine. I've heard he's a hard man." Remembering Eveleen's painful stories of her father, Richard felt a softening toward her, so he quickly braced himself.

"He is. And like a hard, brittle branch, he did not bend. He broke." Will picked up the cart and tromped toward the pasture. "He won't have her back, Mr. Richard. He's turned her out. She has no home now, nowhere to go."

"When he calms down, he'll reconsider."

"I fear ye have little understanding of a man like Paddy Scully. He's been beaten down all his life, one way or another. All he has left is his pride. He'll not easily let that go."

Richard mulled over the next question. He didn't want to care, but he had to ask. "Where is she now?"

"I couldn't leave her there. I mean ye no disrespect, Mr. Richard. I tried to obey yer order, but there she was, lying on the ground."

"On the ground?"

"Her father's rage got the best of him." He looked Richard square in the face. "She's in me own cabin, safe for now. I told her we'd work something out."

Richard's heart fluttered like the wings of a moth around a flame. His weakness at the thought of Eveleen close by enraged him. "She is not welcome here. I don't know where she will go, nor do I care, but she will not stay here."

Frowning, Will looked confused. "She's carrying yer child. What would ye have her do?"

He staggered back and pointed. "Don't say that! You have no idea whose child that is. Eveleen is a liar and a traitor! A back-stabbing bitch of a girl!"

Old Will spoke just above a whisper. "Ye know that's not true, lad. She's a poor girl who fell in love and made bad choices. Surely—"

"Are you calling me a liar? You forget yourself, Will Bridge."
He lifted his chin. "In fact, as future lord of this manor, you do
not refer to me as 'lad'."

Will's shoulders sagged even further, and, while it hurt
Richard to see it, he could not back down.

"Mrs. Bridge told me ye know Jack's yer brother. So ye also
know that yer father saw to his own child."

Growling, Richard shook his balled fists in frustration. This
unflattering comparison to swine like his father was more than
he could stand. Why did everything have to be so hard? He deserved none of this! He paced back and forth, unable to reason
or even form a thought, it seemed.

"What would ye have me do?"

"A small cottage on the edge of the village, perhaps. We could
provide for her and the child, and she could do some work for
the estate. Sewing, perhaps. Or carding wool."

"So she can flaunt her little brat, humiliating me in my own
home?"

"I'm sure she'd agree to keep mum about that. She has few
choices right now." Will thought for a moment. "We could spread
word that she courted some rogue passing through, secretly of
course, who then ran off into the night, leaving her ruined."

Richard saw all too clearly the excruciating anguish he'd
suffer should they ever meet by chance. At the same time, he
couldn't allow Old Will to think him more heartless than his
father.

"She must swear—on a Bible, if necessary—that we will never come across one another, not even in passing. She will turn
away, hide, whatever it takes. I refuse to ever lay eyes on Eveleen
Scully again."

Chapter Twenty-five

Eveleen crouched as close to the Bridge cabin's door as she dared. A soft rain pattered outside and she yearned for the fresh scent of newly-moistened soil. Yet, Will made it all too clear that she must remain hidden. Richard had banished her from his sight.

Will's sorrowful eyes betrayed his smile. "Be mindful, lass. Show not an eyelash. The young master's heart is unsteady and ... well, 'tis best ye stay put."

Anger flashed through Eveleen. The young master's poor heart was unsteady. What of her and the baby? She struggled to choke back her wrath, for what good did it do? Never had she felt so completely helpless. Her only chance to avoid the life of a beggar, or worse, was to abide by Richard's wishes—never to be seen by him again.

Deep in her heart, though, she would not accept that. He'd remember, soon perhaps, that they were fated to be together.

Old Will and Mrs. Bridge had set off in their wagon not long after daybreak. Jack was tending livestock and Eveleen sat suffocating, bogged down in her misery. Her heart clamored for freedom, begging her to break out of the stale, stifling cabin and run through the mist over fields and forests until she reached the Galty Mountains. She imagined the rain cleansing her of this ungodly wretchedness.

The noonday sun was peeking through the clouds when Will and Mrs. Bridge returned. Mrs. Bridge spoke carefully. "We've found yer dwelling. On the edge of the village it sits. One room, of course, built of wattle and daub."

"Seems Little Jimmy White finally gave up the ghost," Will added. "He was a fine tapster in his day, 'til he started sampling more than he poured." He shook his head. "Drank himself to death, he did."

Mrs. Bridge frowned at Will. "Nonetheless, Maggie White has gone to live with her sister and their cabin's vacant." She grimaced. "I've looked through the place. The man was a filthy oaf and his wife no better. Ye'll not make it livable by yerself. Miss Anne won't like it, but I'm sending Brea along to help."

✛

Later that afternoon, Will drove Eveleen and Brea to the Village of Duncullen. Onto the wagon, he'd loaded a small, rough-hewn table and bench that had been stored in the barn's loft, along with an old iron pot. He brought fresh straw for floor cover and padding for her pallet. It was not much, but Eveleen was grateful for his efforts.

Brea was only too happy for the afternoon away. Will promptly returned to his duties while the girls got the windowless cabin ship-shape, even building a small peat fire in the middle of the hard-packed dirt floor.

Eveleen forced a smile. "Well, no more hearths to sweep out, at least."

Awaiting Will's return, they stood outside the tiny house to take advantage of the waning sunlight.

Brea's hand flew to her mouth. "Oh, no. There she be."

Eveleen looked around. "Who?"

Brea nodded to the haggard old woman stumbling toward the entrance of the cabin next door. "The shrew who bedeviled Maeve. Ye remember—no, ye weren't in town with us that day."

She stepped closer to Eveleen and lowered her voice. "Tara and me were peeking in the shop windows when we missed Maeve. We went back and, there she stood, like death itself while that witch was mumbling to her."

A shiver ran up Brea's body. "Not even to Tara would Maeve tell what was said, but she was shaken for days and days."

"Watcha staring at?" the old woman screeched as she hobbled toward her door. "Saucy young wenches."

Then she stopped and stared. "Yer from Duncullen, eh? Two more simpletons thrown out by those blackguards, the Lynches." She threw her head back and laughed. "The son, he's gone to the diet of worms."

"No," Eveleen called. "'Twas the father."

"Don't tell me!" the old crone scolded. "I seen the bastard in the box. Stumped all the way to the Big House, I did, to feast me eyes on him."

"'Twas Sir Edward who died," Eveleen said, as gently as she could.

"Aaah," the woman growled, "that's who I mean. Old William Lynche was who I bedded. Mr. Edward was no more than a lad." An evil grin lifted her wrinkled cheeks. "Both of them rot in the grave, but Winnie Dunn's still here."

She pulled out a brown bottle from her skirts and guzzled it. "Let me guess. 'Twas the wee pup this time." She chuckled. "They tried to breed the lechery out of him, but he's still a Lynche." She looked from one girl to the next. "Which of ye's been poisoned? Or is it the both of ye?"

Brea gasped and Eveleen's heart pounded as she took a step back.

The old harridan cackled, then shook the last drops of her flask into her mouth. "Moll, fetch me another bottle!" She squinted at Eveleen and Brea. "Damn that Jimmy White. Where'll I get me grog now?"

A young woman with sunken eyes and hair as black as soot stumbled to the door. Eveleen smiled and opened her mouth to speak, but with the girl's nasty scowl, she swallowed her greeting.

Leaning on the doorjamb, Moll grumbled, "Get yer bawdy arse in here, Winnie. I told ye I'd take care of ye."

Winnie shuffled into the blackness of their hovel.

Brea was close to tears. "Oh, Eveleen, whatever will ye do with those witches as neighbors? How else could the old hag know where we come from?"

"Our dress."

"She's a witch, to be sure." Brea peered down the road toward the manor. "Where is Old Will?"

As though Brea had conjured the overseer herself, his wagon rolled into sight. He brought a stash of potatoes, wheat flour, and oatmeal. Then he pointed to two fleece-filled baskets in the wagon bed.

"I brought ye this wool that's lately been sheared. The boys done the washing. Ye'll do the carding."

He set the baskets on the ground and reached back for two carding combs, curved paddles with bent metal teeth that brushed the tangles from fibers to prepare them for spinning. "Card the fleece into rolags and I'll be back in a week to pick up the bundles. By then, I'll have more fleece. This'll pay for yer keep. Whatever over that ye can do, there'll be a few coins in yer pocket."

Brea shuffled from foot to foot. "'Tis not safe here," she blurted. "Not for a lass like Eveleen, all alone."

Old Will's shoulders tensed. "I've done all I can."

Frowning, he returned to his wagon. Pulling out a knobby walking stick, he said, "Take this, Eveleen. Hold it like a lover when ye sleep, and if ye use it, make it whistle."

✤

For the next several weeks, Richard followed the same routine. Upon returning from his mid-morning ride, he marched up the front steps and handed his coat and scarf to Hogan, who, on this day, startled him.

"Sir Ethan is in the parlor, Mr. Richard, with Miss Anne."

Richard sneered. "Uncle Ethan? Whatever is he doing here?"

Hogan looked sheepish. "Miss Anne informed me of his intended arrival last week. Begging your pardon, but I thought you were aware of his impending visit."

"No. It's quite the surprise."

Richard fumed inside. Who did that wench think she was? It smelled of treachery. "Inform them I will change from my riding hab—no, I believe I'll greet my uncle now."

He strode to the parlor door, then stopped at the sight of Anne and her father-in-law huddled together, whispering on the settee, as yet unaware of his presence. Anne's abrupt giggle assaulted his head like drumsticks. With widened eyes, her mouth jabbered and her hands flew with excessive emotion. Uncle Ethan seemed enthralled. While not exactly smiling, his lips curved up at the ends, which passed for delight in his circles. Oddly, Thomas was nowhere to be found.

Richard entered the room. "Well, Uncle, to what do we owe this unexpected pleasure?" He glared at his cousin's wife.

Startled, the two glanced up, neither with the decency to appear contrite. Uncle Ethan rose.

When Richard held his ground, the older man said, "This is how you greet your uncle when he visits? Surely, I am welcome here. I've missed my dear family so these last three months." He nodded to Anne, who smiled at her father-in-law in a nauseatingly devoted pose.

There was no doubt in Richard's mind of their sordid conspiracy against him, but he could come up with no way to challenge them at this point.

"Father!" Thomas burst through the door, straightening his waistcoat. "If I'd known of your plans, I could have greeted you properly. To what do we owe your much-welcomed company?" He rushed to give his father a quick embrace.

Uncle Ethan appeared confused. "I sent word of my arrival a week ago."

Anne, flustered, looked from one to the other. "I told each of you the good news. You're both so sheep-headed, it's a wonder you remember to feed yourselves." More rat-a-tat giggling.

Thomas frowned. "Anne, I would have remembered." He sighed. "Never mind. It's so wonderful to see you, Father. I'm anxious to show you my—" He looked at Richard. "Our plans."

Richard seethed. Anne had said nothing of this, yet challenging her would be, at best, unchivalrous and, at worst, could reveal himself as overly suspicious.

Perhaps he was too skeptical. Thomas seemed as flummoxed as he was.

Richard scrutinized his kinsmen as the three prattled on about nothing. Anne may have been the ninny she projected, but she was likely more conniving than stupid. Uncle Ethan needed no analysis. He'd made his goal clear at Sir Edward's funeral: eliminate Richard through means foul or fair, with Thomas well positioned as his replacement.

But what of Thomas? He seemed a decent sort. Or were his acting talents simply more refined?

✦

In mid-afternoon, the four sat down to dinner. Looking over the feast, Richard scowled. Clearly, the cook had been informed of his uncle's arrival.

Uncle Ethan spoke too loudly. "It's a shame Lady Nancy cannot join us at this table."

"It is," Richard responded.

"I visited with her in her chambers earlier. Pitiful, really." The older man stuffed a forkful of pheasant into his mouth and spoke while chewing. "So like her mother in her later years." He swallowed. "Do you remember your grandmother, Richard?"

"I have only one memory of her. She was at home, resting on her chaise longue. I remember she smelled of jasmine, and smiled while she petted my head."

"A blessing it's such a pleasant memory." Uncle Ethan wagged his head back and forth. "It couldn't have been long before she was assigned to Mr. Chesser's Asylum. A very sad day when she left home."

Richard grunted. Thomas stared at his plate as though he wished the gravy would swallow him up. Anne studied Richard, eerily over-eager.

Oblivious, Uncle Ethan went on. "As difficult as it was, we all realized it was for the best. The affliction in her brain was worsening, causing talk throughout the earldom. With the dear woman's behavior so erratic, your grandfather's influence in the House of Lords had begun to erode."

"Grandfather couldn't have that, now could he?" All heads turned at Richard's sarcasm, to which he feigned innocence. Eyes wide, he said, "He had responsibilities."

Thomas returned to the examination of his plate while Anne and Uncle Ethan exchanged frowns. They ate in silence for several minutes, but Richard saw that Uncle Ethan's jaw clenched and his nostrils flared.

Squirm, you weasel, Richard thought.

His uncle cleared his throat. "Lady Nancy suffers, no doubt, surrounded by the memories of her beloved husband. I'm told she worsens by the day."

Richard glowered at Anne who, this time, had the courtesy to fidget.

Uncle Ethan's eyes narrowed. "You, like your grandfather, have responsibilities. You are trying to establish your authority, prove yourself, if you will. Are you man enough to do what needs to be done? Are you willing to commit your mother to Mr. Chesser's care or will you allow Duncullen to fall into an ill-reputed bastion of insanity?"

Thomas dropped his fork. "Father!"

The man's crudity stunned Richard. "I hardly think—"

Stone-faced, Uncle Ethan turned to his son. "You, too, have much to prove. Have you curbed the boy's rabbit-livered sentimentality or have you encouraged it?" To Richard, he said, "I am aware you have your own bouts with lunacy. Being taunted by demons, are we? Or was it visitors from the grave?"

Richard reeled with rage, humiliation, betrayal, and fear. His body shook as he leapt from the table, sending plates, bowls, and cups crashing to the floor. He was shouting, yet he knew not what he said. It seemed to be coming from someone else. While others' mouths were moving, he heard nothing but Anne's shrill screams.

Somehow, Hogan was beside him, attempting to take his arm. Richard shoved the old man with uncommon strength, causing him to stumble backward and crash into the wall. Thomas lifted the butler to his feet as Richard staggered past, mentally chanting, Get me out of here! Get me out of here!

Thomas's cry of "Let him go!" was the last Richard heard.

✟

Hogan sat in the chair before his small desk and gingerly fingered the knot on the back of his head. He winced at the touch of a particularly tender spot. Dusk approaching, the butler had snatched these few moments of peace in the midst of one more day of turmoil.

Touching his lips to his cup of tea, he set it down. Too hot. His mind replayed the afternoon's events. This decay of the Lynche family sickened his heart. He was too old and had seen too much.

Unlike the majority of the staff, including Mrs. Bridge, he was born to his profession. His father had been a valet and his mother a lady's maid. They taught him the honor and dignity of service. He was expert at assuming the cloak of invisibility, only stepping from the shadows precisely when needed. He kept his own counsel and was unfailingly loyal to the family. Which sadly, now consisted only of Lady Nancy and Mr. Richard.

Yet, he was a human being, after all, with eyes and ears, and a rational brain with which to process what he witnessed. Far too much of it brought him great sorrow.

He straightened in his chair at a soft rap on the door. "You may enter."

He leapt to his feet too fast at the sight of a timid, disheveled Mr. Richard pushing through. His head spun with dizziness.

"May I come in?"

"By all means, Mr. Richard." Gripping his chair, Hogan scanned the room to see if anything, uncharacteristically, was out of place. "I would gladly have come to you had you called."

"No. After my shocking behavior, it was I who needed to seek you out."

The young man's hair, normally tied back in a neat queue, was tousled, and his clothes were in disarray. Had he run through briars? Most disturbing, though, were the lad's red eyes, his dusty cheeks etched by trails of tears.

"May I sit?" Mr. Richard asked.

This unsettling display of humility flustered Hogan. "Of course, of course."

He stepped aside of his own chair and waved, inviting the young man to use it. Hogan lowered himself onto a stool for his underlings. The butler's conscience harried him as he watched Mr. Richard fiddle. The boy was tortured, but what could he do?

Mr. Richard raised his head to look Hogan in the eye. "Um, have I hurt you?"

"A slight bump is all, sir."

With trembling lip, Mr. Richard said, "It appears I've made a right bloody fool of myself. I was accused of something, then promptly gave evidence of its truth." He studied his wringing hands. "I've gravely hurt myself, the Lynche name, and the Baronetcy of Duncullen." Looking up, he added, "And you. Please accept my sincere apologies for that."

Hogan's ire rose, but not at this tormented boy. He realized the worst. Sir Ethan and his crafty daughter-in-law had evil designs on this house. He could see it, taste it, smell it on them both. "No apology required, Mr. Richard. But if you feel the need to offer one, rest assured, it is graciously accepted."

"Thank you." He sighed and closed his eyes. "I suppose I must apologize to my uncle now, though I am loath to do it."

Apologize to a man who hoped to twist the lad's anguish into a diagnosis of insanity? The butler wondered how he could stand by and watch such deceit. But could he do otherwise? Anything he said to Mr. Richard, once repeated to any of the de Barneforts, would lead to his dismissal—a dismissal that would result in ostracization by every potential employer in the British Isles.

Yet, if he remained silent, how would he rest his head in the home he did nothing to save?

Richard placed his hands on the armrests of the chair and pushed off. "I appreciate your forgiveness."

"Wait," said Hogan, perhaps too abruptly. "Please wait."

Richard sat back down.

"May I speak freely?"

Richard cocked his head to one side, then nodded.

"I have been a servant at Duncullen since before you were born. I take pride in my discretion, but also to my loyalty to your family. Because of that, I feel compelled to speak outside my station, if you will allow."

Richard sighed as his shoulders slumped. "Say your piece."

Hogan struggled to choose his words. He had so much to tell Richard. How his parents, through bad judgment, crossed messages, and misperceptions, had let their youthful dreams slip away. How they'd laid it all on their young son's shoulders, each determined he fulfill their own lost hopes. How it was all too much, especially for a young fellow as sensitive as he.

Instead, he said, "While you are understandably upset by your behavior at today's dinner, sir, you are not to blame."

Richard's brow furrowed as he focused intently on Hogan's next words.

"I risk much by saying this, and I hope I can depend upon your prudence in where you take it." Hogan inhaled deeply.

"You were provoked this evening by your uncle. Using gossip he gleaned from Miss Anne, he made every effort to upset you. Unfortunately, he succeeded."

The relief Hogan saw in the young man's eyes eased the tension in his own body.

Mr. Richard nodded. "Too late that occurred to me."

"While I believe Sir Ethan has rather devious motives, in hopes of furthering his son's career, I do not believe Mr. Thomas has a part in it." He glanced down. "I flatter myself that I'm a rather good judge of character."

Also, Sir Ethan was far less clever and more transparent than he believed.

Mr. Richard wore a hint of a smile. "I can see where you would be." He shrugged his shoulders, once again grim. "And yet, the damage is done. I have unwisely played straight into their hands."

"Perhaps not. You are a mere three months into the mourning of your father's untimely death, your mother is gravely ill, and you are but seventeen years old. Today's outburst may be overlooked if it can be perceived as a singular incident."

The young man's eyes brightened with comprehension. "Uncle Ethan and Anne laid a trap and I stumbled directly into it. But being aware, can I, perhaps, dodge these pitfalls?"

"You can, sir. Reject the bait, so to speak."

"I assure you, I will." His jaw became set. "They will never again see such an emotional display." He seemed to be speaking more to himself than to Hogan. "I will be the picture of calm, rational behavior."

"Very good, sir."

His face once again darkened. "But does it even matter? They can spread any lie they choose, take what they've already seen and exaggerate or distort it."

"Mr. Thomas may speak up for you."

"One cannot count on that. Call his father and wife liars? I wouldn't think so." He bit his fingernail, seeming a thousand miles away. "Unless people saw for themselves."

"I beg your pardon, sir?"

"Never mind, Hogan," he said, rising from his chair. "You have done me a great service today."

Hogan stood also, relief flowing through him like water into a dry well. "Very good, sir."

Mr. Richard walked out of the butler's office only to immediately return. Hogan could already see a renewed strength in the boy's eyes and posture.

"I realize what you've done, placing your position in peril as you have. A slip of the tongue from me and ... well, I promise you that will never happen. You have won my eternal gratitude and I won't let you down." Then he left.

Hogan took back his chair and sipped on his cooling cup of tea, which tasted a little like hope.

Chapter Twenty-six

Weeks plodded into months. Eveleen had to roll onto her hands and knees in the mornings, and pull up on the table to stand. She panted like a tired, old grandmother from the effort.

Sometimes the terror of it all brought on a spell of heavy, jagged breathing, but she knew she was more fortunate than most in her position. Mrs. Bridge had arranged weekly visits from Mrs. Bannon, the midwife, whose kindness and sure manner kept Eveleen from going completely mad.

"It won't be long now, love," the older woman had told her just a day ago. "Before ye know it, ye'll be holding the cherub in yer arms."

The little one's fist—or was it his heel—swept across her bulging stomach. "Yer a strong one," she told him. "Just wait 'til yer father gazes on yer sweet face. He'll gather us both in his arms and whisk us back to the Big House."

Eveleen loved to imagine the adoring faces of Brea, Biddy, and even Lady Nancy as they beheld Richard's beautiful son. This dream kept her going despite staggering loneliness.

She spent most of her daylight hours inside, combing as much fleece as she could handle. The wool Old Will brought was "in the grease," with some lanoline left in the fibers. Not only did that make the woven fabric resistant to water, but Eveleen's hands became as soft as a fine lady's who dallied her day away.

When with Richard, her rough hands had brought her shame. He'd now see the lady she could become.

Inside her cottage, all her fantasies seemed not only possible, but probable. Once outside in sunlight's harsh glare, life's new realities slapped her in the face.

If, with a few coins in her pocket, she ventured to the shops, she withered under the scrutiny of townswomen who shuffled their children out of her way. Men who didn't openly leer at her glowered, or worse, behaved as though she didn't exist at all.

In the squalid outskirts of town, she was a curiosity. It was common knowledge that she'd been cast out of the manor house. Her growing belly left no question of the cause. Yet, the overseer, and sometimes his wife, Mrs. Bridge, visited her weekly. On the servants' fortnightly outings, one or two of the maids would stop in for a chat.

Mrs. Farrell, a busybody from across the road, quickly circulated the story the Bridges concocted and spread through her younger son, Doolin, the groom: A wandering rogue, whom Eveleen refused to name, had ruined the girl and, as was proper, she was dismissed from service. Old Will, however, had vowed to her father, his childhood friend, he would protect her from harm and, in his steadfast way, was keeping that promise.

This quieted all but Winnie Dunn, who, when drunk, took great pleasure in goading the girl.

"What's to become of that Lynche bastard ye carry? One more misborn to litter the countryside" or "Yer babe is no more special than the rest of the Lynche-looking mongrels grubbing for the odd potato or onion."

Three days previous, in the midst of an outburst, the old crone collapsed to the ground, awash with tears. "They ripped me own babe from me belly. Murdered, he was, to save a few miserable farthings of Old William's fortune." Her loud wailing brought all from their cabins. "My poor, pitiful child! Yer mama misses ye still."

The young girl, Moll Conroy, stepped from their shack. "Aw, she's full as a goat, Johnny. Help me haul her inside."

Eveleen glanced toward the entrance to the cabin. There, half hidden behind the doorway, stood Johnny Farrell, her neighbor's older son.

"Johnny?" Mrs. Farrell's face burst in horror. "Me own Johnny Farrell?"

With the determination of a riled she-bear, the woman tramped across the road toward Winnie and Moll's hut. Onlookers pointed and laughed, eager for entertainment.

Mrs. Farrell stopped and broke a long, slender branch from a birch tree. Ripping off leaves, she stomped toward her target.

Old Mr. Downey, the only one with a kind word for Eveleen, cupped his hand to his mouth and called, "Watch out, Johnny, me boy! Yer in for a real rib-roasting." The whole crowd whooped and cheered.

Eveleen caught sight of the humiliated fellow climbing out the back window. As his mother plowed through the door, he crashed over the spring, through the hedgerow, and out of sight.

Moll, propping Winnie from the back, shouted, "Get yer flabby arse out of me house, ye old fool!"

Mrs. Farrell stumbled out, gasping, and pointed her switch at Moll. "Keep yer slatternly hands off me boy, do ye hear? I'll have the constable after ye, ye filthy slut!"

Mr. Downey leaned on his cane and cackled. "Leave the young hemp alone, Madge. Little fun ye allow him in life."

"Yer not among yer foul-mouthed seadogs now, Downey. We're decent folk and I'll not have me boy befouled by that whore."

"Yer boy is twenty-seven years old, madam," he called out, playing to the crowd who guffawed and slapped each other on the back.

Mrs. Farrell scanned the onlookers, stuck out her chin, and said, "He'll get hungry by and by." In a huff, she strode into her house.

The neighbors, standing in groups of twos and threes, slowly broke apart and headed to their homes.

Moll remained crouched over Winnie Dunn, now passed out. "None of ye lowdown belly-guts are going to help me get her inside?"

Some turned to scowl at the frustrated girl, but none came to her assistance. Eveleen sighed and walked over.

"What do ye think ye'll do for me, ye fat cow?" the young harlot asked, tears in her eyes. "Ye can hardly lift yerself."

"Well, I ..." Eveleen glanced around to see Johnny skulking by the side of the house furthest from his mother's view. "Yer ma's gone." She nodded to Moll and Winnie. "'Tis the least ye can do."

As Johnny and Moll struggled to get Winnie inside undetected by the dreadful Mrs. Farrell, Eveleen turned to see Mr. Downey had not gone, but was still leaning on his cane.

"Madge leads him around by the nose," he told her, "but he's not a bad sort."

Eveleen walked closer to the grizzled old man. "Before the ruckus, Winnie was crying out of a murdered child, sired by Lord William Lynche. The gin talking, I suppose."

Mr. Downey's face darkened. "She spoke the truth. She was a bright and bonny girl before Old Man Lynche got hold of her. When he found she was with child, he brought in a butcher to wrench the little one from her womb."

"I don't understand."

He studied her face. "No, I don't suppose ye do. Just be glad yer fella isn't one of them Lynche bastards. Many-a fine lass was destroyed by that bunch." He humphed. "Can't help it, I suppose. In the blood, it seems."

Eveleen swallowed back some bile as her baby leapt and rolled within. Mr. Downey saw the movements beneath her shift and smiled. "Yer in a bad way, missy, but not so bad as them living there." He nodded to Winnie's cabin. "Don't let yerself fall by the wayside like the two of them. 'Tis a mournful life."

⊕

Now, three days later, while whispering and cooing to the babe in her belly, a shrill, high-pitched scream terrified Eveleen, causing her to fling her paddles into the air. Leaping up, she kicked the hand cards away and rushed outside.

Moll Conroy, fists clenched and elbows cocked, hurled another piercing scream into the air.

Scowling, Mrs. Farrell lumbered from her hovel. "Shut yer gob, ye hussy! Yer throbbing the earholes of decent folk."

Moll looked past Eveleen and jabbed her finger toward the house. "Mrs. Farrell, in the name of all that's holy, come quick! Help me."

"What now?" grumbled the old harpy, hands firmly planted on her hips.

Gasping between sobs, Moll called, "Someone's bashed her in the head. She's dead, is what!" She squeezed her own head. "Oh, Lord! She's dead."

Mrs. Farrell's jowls waggled as she shook her head in disgust. "Ye hear that, don't ye?" she called to Eveleen. "'In the name of all that's holy.' What would that doxy know about what's holy?"

She snorted as she trudged past Eveleen. Calling louder for Moll to hear, she repeated her nasty joke. "What would you or Winnie know about anything holy?"

Moll's eyeballs were so wide and round, it seemed they could easily roll from her head. "Covered in blood, she is. Some whoreson beat her, Mrs. Farrell. Beat her to death!"

"Plug yer hole, lass." Mrs. Farrell grabbed Moll by the elbow. "Yer putting on quite the show for an old hag who's more likely dead drunk than dead."

As the two tramped into Winnie Dunn's seedy hovel, Eveleen waited, wringing her hands.

In no time, Mrs. Farrell came back out. "She's dead alright." She returned home and shut the door.

Eveleen waited. Surely, she'd come back with the dressings to prepare Winnie Dunn for burial. But she did not; nor did any other woman.

Moll stepped outside, her face red and puffy. She searched up and down the road until she spotted a young stripling batting rocks with a stick. "Peader, come here."

The lad looked all around before creeping to the edge of Moll's yard. He came no farther.

Moll ran her sleeve past her nose. "I'll give ye a farthing to run for the constable."

The boy frowned, then shook his head.

"Two then. A ha'penny."

The lad cocked his head, then shook it again.

Moll reached into her pocket and flung three coins at him. "Three farthings and a kick in the arse, Peadar. Run off with ye. Tell him Winnie Dunn's been whacked to death."

With a wide grin, Peadar gathered his treasure and raced toward the village center.

Moll turned to Eveleen with pained, weary eyes. "Why would someone kill an old hussy like Winnie, too broken down to harm anyone?"

Except with that razor-like tongue, Eveleen thought. "I'll help ye clean her up, if ye like."

Without warning, Moll's face filled with fury. "Ye'll not touch her. Nor will anyone else 'til the constable has his look. Whoever done this will dangle by the neck in the sheriff's picture frame, by God." She spun on her heel and went back into the house.

Eveleen sat outside her cabin on a wooden bench Jack had carved for her. She carded her wool and watched for the constable—or at the very least, the coroner. But neither came.

The little imp, Peadar, shouted to Moll on his return. "Constable Deegan ain't coming. He says she likely fell down drunk and cracked her head."

"Ye bloody imbecile," Moll called from inside her cabin. "I'm sitting next to the murder weapon right here."

Peadar continued walking as he yelled, "The coroner says to get her fixed up. He'll send Quinn Adams in his wagon as soon as he sobers up."

Moll stuck her head out the door and screamed to a blind and deaf neighborhood. "A fine lot of Christian people ye are! A woman is slain that's lived amongst ye all these years and ..." Her face turned a dangerous shade of scarlet. "Bugger ye all! May ye rot in hell, every one!"

Eveleen gathered her things and went inside. What kind of place was this for her—or a newborn child? A woman murdered and no one cares. She shivered at the idea that the killer still roamed the streets. She got Old Will's walking stick and set it beside her, grateful it was loaded, the end hollowed and filled with lead. It could do serious damage.

Later that day, she glimpsed Mr. Downey hobbling over to Winnie's house. Stepping outside, she opened her mouth to offer help.

Mr. Downey cut her off. "No, lass. The fewer the better. And meaning no harm, but especially not you."

It was two full days later that the souse, Quinn Adams, rolled up in his creaking cart. He stumbled into Moll's hut, and came out with Winnie Dunn's shrouded body, which he dragged into the yard. He laid one end on the cart, then picked up the other and flipped it onto the bed of the wagon. The poor woman had started to reek.

Eveleen stood in her doorway and watched with a kerchief to her nose. She hadn't seen Moll set foot outside since her rant against the neighbors. How had she stood the stench? Quinn Adams snapped his reins and Eveleen watched him roll the woeful, unloved creature away.

Not a quarter hour later, she heard the raucous laughter of Moll and some unknown man. She once again peeked outside to see her young neighbor with Ronan, the cruel flogger, as they staggered down the road, drunk as emperors.

Moll was holding Ronan up, it seemed, but Eveleen thought it could be the other way around.

The brute waved a quart bottle in the air. "So the wife, boozed up, lay down in the sty."

"Aaaah, ha ha ha," Moll roared.

"No, no wait. And when Davy went to show off his prize pig, they all saw the inebree--, inebree--, ah shite, boozy wench, and said, 'Lookit Davy's drunken sow.'"

Moll's eyes were rolling in her head.

"Now ye can laugh."

Ronan spotted Eveleen's head poking out her door. "What the--? Well, looky there. 'Tis the whore from the Big House."

As Eveleen pulled back and latched the door, she heard, "I need me a piece of that."

"Hey!" Moll yelled. "Yer with me, ye mangy cur!"

Eveleen heard footsteps approach and grabbed her club. Her heart was in her throat as the door rattled.

"Lemme in, ye bitch," she heard Ronan say. "I know who ye are."

She stood silently beside the door. God, protect me and me baby, she prayed as she raised the cudgel over her head. She gripped it even harder at the grunts and heavy breathing outside her door.

All at once, the door exploded into splinters of old, dried wood. She closed her eyes and, with all her might, lowered Will's bat. She opened them to see Ronan crumbled to the earthen floor, his head a bloody mess.

Panting, Eveleen's eyes fill with tears. Her head snapped up at the sound of Moll's footsteps. The woman had crept to Eveleen's doorway with little notice, then studied the grisly scene before her.

"Well," she said, slurring, "the bastard had it coming."

✦

Thomas de Barnefort, armed with his bundle of plans, paced the main hall of Duncullen, wrapped in a fidgety combination of worry and excitement.

Overnight, his cousin, Richard, had gone from a dour, sometimes petulant juvenile to a single-minded, self-assured young man. The first weeks following Uncle Edward's untimely demise, Thomas had gently nudged Richard to take an interest in his proposed improvements for the estate, but the poor fellow had lost his powers of concentration. He either put Thomas off or excused himself within minutes.

Thomas feared Sir Ethan's shameful display had pushed the boy over the cliff, but instead, Richard seemed to have awakened from a deep sleep. His new energy and enthusiasm for all aspects of the estate left Thomas, at times, breathless.

Could his father have provoked Richard for the lad's own good? That was a generous thought, but Thomas knew otherwise. He'd worshipped Sir Ethan de Barnefort as a boy, but with maturity came the recognition that his father was an arrogant bully without even the cunning to conceal his self-indulgence.

Thomas's brother, Jonathan, heir to the family's holdings and titles, was the apple of their father's eye. Jonathan strutted like a solitary rooster in a henhouse, and Sir Ethan deferred to him on every count. Thomas was the hapless younger son whose only options for success were the wilds of their Carolina plantations.

Thomas smiled to himself. Therein lay the irony of it all. He wanted to go to the Carolinas.

A student of agricultural innovations, Thomas had well thought out ideas and suggestions he knew were viable—ones dismissed by his father and brother before he could spit out a complete sentence. In Ireland, he would remain forever under Ethan de Barnefort's thumb. In Carolina, he could make his mark on the world.

He sighed. A dream he dared not tell even Annie. She dreaded the idea of moving, fearing the horror stories she'd heard of the treacherous voyage as well as the foreign climate and deadly diseases. Even more, she couldn't bear to leave her family and his own, whom she'd come to love.

A pall fell over his heart. Annie'd been not only his lover and wife, but also his best friend. Unusual, he knew, and a source of mockery from his peers, but now she was merely his wife and occasional lover. He'd lost his best friend.

Petrified of their likely future, she had allied herself with his father against her own husband. The two became fellow conspirators in Sir Ethan's dastardly plan to undermine Richard's sanity, replacing him with themselves. It sickened Thomas.

His affectionate name for his wife now felt bitter on his tongue. It was he who suggested the more formal addresses of Mr. and Mrs. de Barnefort. Though Anne was bewildered at first, she came to embrace it in her drunken lust for the position of Lady of the Manor, unaware of the distance it put between them.

"You're so right, Tommy," she'd said. "We need to project a more dignified demeanor if we're to get the respect we deserve."

He recognized his father's words in Annie's now irritating voice.

"Are you well, Thomas?"

He snapped out of his musings. Richard appeared at the top of the staircase, straightening his waistcoat. He sported a newly-made velvet suit in the softer, less full style now in fashion. Wearing the smaller wig young men preferred and his tricorn hat tucked under his arm, Richard cut a fine figure.

Thomas smiled. "You took me seriously when I said appearances matter."

"You look a bit drawn and pinched, Cousin." Richard descended the stairs. "It anything wrong?"

Thomas squared his shoulders, chastising himself for his dispiriting thoughts. "On a day such as this?' What could be wrong? Today, we lay our awe-inspiring plans before the banker who will be dazzled by our genius."

He slapped Richard on the back at his approach. "And then, we're off to glory!"

Chapter Twenty-seven

Leaning over her crude table, Eveleen shared a cup of tea with Brea in her run-down cottage while the rest of Duncullen's staff enjoyed their Sunday outing.

Brea's eyes were aglow. "People can speak of little else. You knocked that oaf, Ronan, senseless." She giggled. "For two days, they say, he lay abed, nursed by his old ma. Even now, his left eye's yellowed and barely opened. A bandage, he wears, wrapped 'round his wounded head."

Eveleen squirmed. "He meant to ravish me, the drunken fiend."

"No one doubts it. Little chance ye'll have more trouble after the thrashing ye gave that lout. Yer Duncullen's own Jack Slack."

"Who?"

Brea laughed. "He overthrew the boxing champion, John Broughton, a few months back. The one they claimed couldn't be beat."

Eveleen shrugged. "I will say the lewd old men and smutty lads have quit their ogling." It was hard to concentrate. The muscles in her belly were cramping. "Rehearsing," Mrs. Bannon said, for the task they were soon to perform.

"He's become a laughing-stock now that a tiny lass like yerself laid him low. All who groveled before the bully, lad and lass alike, mock him." Brea sipped her tea. "Still behind his back, of course. Ye learn folks' true feelings for a fella when he's taken down a peg, don't ye?"

Eveleen was beholden to Brea for her visits. Fiona sometimes came with her, but Eveleen suspected she came only for the gossip she could carry back to the Big House. Brea likely prattled as well, but she seemed to genuinely care about Eveleen. Strange, after all the ugliness when Maeve was there.

Nevertheless, Eveleen no longer wanted to discuss Ronan. The incident had rattled her to the core. "Ye've said nary a word of the grand ball. I want to hear every bit. 'Tis me own misfortune the excitement starts once I've left." And tell every morsel concerning Richard.

"Until this, I'd seen nothing like it, meself. Before the guests arrived, we worked ourselves into collapse. Miss Anne dashed about barking orders in a frenzy, driving us all mad. Not a thing was done to her liking. Mrs. Bridge told us to do each chore again and again when even she knew 'twas done right from the first."

"Poor Mrs. Bridge. What about Mr. Thomas? Is he a taskmaster as well?" Get to it. How fares Richard?

"Mr. Thomas is quite the reverse. He's calm and kindhearted. I've yet to hear him raise his voice." Brea sighed. "Now Mr. Richard is a story unto himself."

At last. Eveleen perked up while struggling to feign disinterest.

"He's changed so ye'd hardly recognize him. Ye remember how he was, so moody and restless, like his skin didn't fit right."

Eveleen's heart pounded. "I hardly knew him."

Brea laughed. "Who did, besides Old Will and Jack? Well, remember the time he knocked Mr. Hogan on his arse? I told ye all about it."

Eveleen stretched her lips, hopefully into a smile. "I do."

"Well, 'twas right after that he changed. As though he went to sleep a boy and awoke a man." Brea shook her head in wonderment. "Not just how he acts. He looks every bit the lord-in-waiting."

She rose and walked around, imitating Richard's new demeanor. "He holds his head high with that strong chin jutting and his shoulders square, like this. He even looks taller." She sat back down. "His scar gives him a bit of the dash as well. The sad part is what little playfulness he had in his eyes is gone. Samuel and the others say where once he'd share a laugh, now 'tis business and no more."

Eveleen grimaced in sympathy.

Brea leaned in. "Back to the grand ball. I told ye Biddy was grooming me to help as lady's maid. Well, all the week while the gentlemen hunted and rode their horses, the ladies chatted, sewed, or read aloud to one another. All rather dull, if ye ask me. Yet, each time they switched to a different amusement, off we went to change their finery and hair to match. Well, that kept me nimble since three of the younger ones arrived with no maid of their own."

"How did ye do? I'd have been worthless, overrun by the fidgets." Which one caught Richard's eye? Eveleen found herself both eager and fearful to hear more.

"Oh, at the start I was as fretful as ye please, but the young ladies I served were kind. Except one. Miss Hannah Allison was a bit snippy. I got nervous and poked her with pins five times. The fifth time, she slapped me hand and said she'd do it herself." She sighed. "But it was mostly fun. Far better than emptying chamber pots."

They both giggled.

"The best part," Brea went on, "was listening to their chatter. They were going on about Mr. Richard the same way we did when Mr. Alistair arrived. Remember? Now there was a handsome fella. Why did we not see our own young master the same way?"

I did, Eveleen thought.

"The young girls tittered about Mr. Richard's broad shoulders and said his scar gave him a mysterious air." Brea rolled her eyes. "Ha! They didn't ask me, but I could have solved that mystery for them. Gallant, they called him. Masterful on the dance floor. I never seen so much blushing and gesturing with fans."

Brea drained her tea. "Mr. Richard excused himself early, it seems. Still in mourning, he claimed, and I promise ye, every one of them ladies would've loved to be the one to comfort him."

Eveleen's heart ached, knowing it should be her.

✟

Two weeks after the grand ball, Richard received his first letter from Alistair.

_____, 1751

Richard, my dear friend,

We have, at last, arrived in Paris after a grueling journey of over 180 miles, being jounced to bits in our stagecoach, which here they call a carrosse. I rode with five other travelers like myself who are mostly fine fellows. One, Charlie, the scion of an English earl, is the greatest of blusterers and a torment to us all. It is my misfortune that he has chosen me to be his chum during this journey and, as a Wild Irish rustic, deems I should be grateful for the role. Which I am not. My first lesson on this educational enterprise is that one's station in life does not necessarily equate with one's degree of rectitude.

How different is our friendship, Richard! I have confided thoughts and emotions to you that I dare not share with another, as you have with me. You are a brother to me, sharing an affection that, I daresay, will last a lifetime.

Paris is a glorious sight, my friend, with its magnificent churches, gardens, and majestic stone houses. Yet, our bear-leader, Mr. Gerald Stewart, has warned us of the many extravagances that can leave us impoverished in short order. I, as are the other travelers, am staying with a family of some substance where I can learn the language and keep my expenses within reason. Ah, I know what you are thinking. Alas, they have no comely daughter nor even a female servant below the age of forty. What they do offer are some peaceful hours away from Charlie.

As reputed, the wines are exquisite compared to our own. The food, however, leaves much to be desired. We all complain that despite several courses, we find ourselves hungry a short time later. They drown the victuals in sauces to give it more substance, but our bellies know the truth.

On a darker note, a more sordid side of this fair city disturbs me. Only the destitution of the people overpowers the stench of the streets. Just outside the door of my hosts are several beggars, wallowing in filth. The harlots who shamelessly ply their wares seem plagued with disease. The most difficult to bear are the wide-eyed children, pleading for a scrap of food. My companions scoff and kick them aside, but I cannot. I am tortured by the unfairness of my position, gained only by accident of birth.

On our first night here, all the fellows were anxious to test the libertine reputation of the city. The son of Charlie's host took us to a bordello of some repute. I chose a tart with rosy cheeks and full, red lips, neither of which were natural. I will not deny the pleasure she imparted, but her eyes—they were dull and listless, as though something were dead inside. Saddened, I tried to reach out to her, but there was nothing there.

We will soon be visiting le Salon at the Louvre and the grounds of the great palace, Versailles. I shall write you of these glories of France. Thank you, dear friend, for listening to me. There is no one else with whom I can share my deepest thoughts.

As always

Alistair

✟

_____, 1751

Dear Alistair,

It was with great joy that I received your first letter today. The adventure on which you've embarked has evoked a great envy in me. One day, I will take my own continental tour, but for now, I must live vicariously through your exploits, some of which are quite provocative, I must say.

While part of me longs for the experiences you share, I am more confident than ever of my decision to remain at Duncullen. (Despite your former indiscretion, at considerable risk I share my thoughts with you in the confidence you will divulge not one iota to anyone. Like you, I have no one else.)

It has become increasingly clear to me that my esteemed uncle and his dear daughter-in-law, Anne, conspire to rob me of my birthrights. Cousin Thomas seems forthright and, I daresay, is not part of the diabolical plot. Yet his wife and father seem determined to have me, along with my piteous mother, committed to Chesser's Asylum! They have used my grief during this difficult time of bereavement to challenge my sanity in a fiendish effort to transfer my holdings to Thomas and Anne. Likely, my titles as well, if they can wrangle it.

I am determined to show none but the most refined demeanor, though my uncle sorely provokes me. To forestall the malicious rumours they may cultivate, I have opened Duncullen to neighbors of standing and other local personages of import so they, with their own eyes and ears, can determine the accuracy of these tales.

Oh, what a woeful situation it is when your family seeks your demise! My mother sinks ever lower into despair, but I will not succumb to the callous wishes of others and shuffle her off to a madhouse, away from whatever small comfort she derives from our home. With the exception of Cousin Thomas, a meek, artless fellow, I have no comrade in this house.

I must commend your father to you, however, since I see no sign of his collusion with my uncle in this scheme. Thomas and I have made considerable plans to modernize my holdings, including impressive improvements to the grounds themselves. We recently met with your father, as Duncullen's trustee, at Gleadowe & Company, that illustrious bank in Dublin. There, both he and our financier, Sir William Newcomen, approved of our endeavor and the bank has agreed to subsidize these projects. I am very grateful for Sir Nathaniel's confidence in Cousin Thomas de Barnefort, but also in myself.

We are on our way, Alistair. I will overcome the forces that threaten me and become, as you've teasingly dubbed me, "Ireland's premier baronet." Undervalue me at your own peril, my friend. I may go further in life than that.

Stay out of harm's way. I eagerly anticipate your next rousing epistle.

Your homebound chum,
Richard

Chapter Twenty-eight

Holy Mother of God!" Eveleen screamed.

She stumbled from one side of the cabin to the other, gripping her belly. "Oooohh, Lord Above, spare me this agony."

"Yer travail is upon ye, lass. What's done cannot be undone."

Eveleen looked toward the door to find Madge Farrell, a smirk on her face and arms akimbo.

Lord, she silently prayed, why do ye increase me misery with the presence of such a shrew?

Mrs. Farrell stepped inside. "Too late, it is, to be calling for mercy. Ye should've thought of it before ye spread yer legs for that shiftless cur." She looked around. "Where is Mrs. Bannon's lass? Has she gone for her ma?"

Eveleen continued her pacing. "She has. I'm to walk back and forth like this, she told me. I've been stricken with pain all through the night."

"Well, I'll act as yer gossip, but not if ye continue squalling and wailing like some ninny. There's none who'll put up with that nonsense."

Eveleen moaned. She'd worried who'd serve as gossips and help Mrs. Bannon with the birth. While Meara, the midwife's sweet and able daughter, had stayed by her side the last two days, she was but ten years old. Mrs. Bridge had promised to come if she could.

I want my mama! she inwardly cried. Aloud, she said, "I must lie down." After Mrs. Farrell helped her onto her pallet, she added, "Thank you for your kindness."

"A good Christian woman, I am. Even Jesus Christ stooped so low as to aid a sinner. What food and drink have ye for the gossips—and yerself?"

With the next throes of pain, she winced and gritted her teeth. Once they eased, she saw that Mrs. Farrell had found the stash of ale, bread, and eggs she'd bought with her meager savings. "I'm sorry there's no more."

"Not to worry. 'Tisn't the Big House. I've some broth and butter at home. I'll get it."

Eveleen sighed with relief when she heard her neighbor call from outside the door. "I'll be back, Mrs. Bannon. I've a bit I can add to the gathering."

The midwife burst into the cabin wearing an apron over her dress, her valise in hand. "Yer little one is clamoring to be born, then?"

She set her tools aside, knelt beside Eveleen, and pushed down on the top of her belly. She then pressed the bottom until it tightened with another pang. Mrs. Bannon sat back on her haunches and smiled. "The top is empty and fallen. The babe is warning us to prepare."

As the throes eased, Eveleen saw Maura struggle through the door with Mrs. Bannnon's portable birthing chair. The wooden device sat about eight inches from the ground with a back for the mother to lean on and arms to grip as she pushed. A hole was cut in the seat to give Mrs. Bannon access to the womb's entrance.

"Set it over here, closer to the fire," her mother told her. "Ye've done well, Maura. Eveleen's pallet is away from the door's drafts with plenty of room for me and the gossips to get around." Then to Eveleen, "Have ye been walking? That will draw the waters. They've not broken yet, have they?"

Tears rolled down Eveleen's cheeks. "Nothing is happening except I'm being ripped asunder."

Mrs. Bannon petted her head. "Yer doing fine, missy. The Good Lord and Our Blessed Mother Mary will see ye through. Maura, bring me the grease."

The heavy smell of pig fat assaulted Eveleen's nose, and her stomach roiled with queasiness. When the midwife asked if she'd eaten, Eveleen shook her head.

"Maura, bring some bread and a cup of ale. She'll need her strength."

Mrs. Bannon reached under Eveleen's skirts and between her legs to anoint the area with lard. "The womb is opening. 'Tis going to be quicker than I thought. Maura, why did ye wait so long to fetch me?"

The girl held a cup of ale to Eveleen's lips. "The throes seemed too far apart. They've only quickened since the sun rose."

Mrs. Farrell returned. "I've brought Branna Ryan with me. She's willing to help."

"To be sure," the small, chirpy woman said. "I don't know what I'd have done without me neighbors when Peadar came into the world."

"Branna, can ye send yer boy to the Big House for Mrs. Bridge?" Mrs. Bannon asked. "It won't be long and the house-keeper wants to be here."

Branna's eyebrows rose and she scuttled from the door. Mrs. Farrell added butter, broth, and another jug of ale to the table. She took a hunk of bread from Maura's hand, slathered it with butter, and gave it back. Then, she collected some cups and poured ale for everyone, adding a dollop of water to Maura's.

Once Eveleen finished her bread, the women lifted her so she could resume tramping from wall to wall. She had hoped the ale would dull the pain, but she felt no relief.

Branna Ryan returned shortly with more food and drink. With her own cup in hand, she joined the chatter, but it went in one of Eveleen's ears and out the other.

Me ma should be here, Eveleen lamented. The memory of her mother's rough, but gentle hands cupping her cheek brought an ache to her chest unlike any she'd felt before.

A hole, she thought. There's a gaping hole inside me heart, like someone has scooped it out with a spoon.

When she next lay down, the gossips propped her head with a pillow and placed the folded cloth beneath her hips. Branna Ryan stroked her belly downward, guiding the baby to the womb's opening. The throes came even faster and stronger. Remembering Mrs. Farrell's warning to squelch her howls, she growled through clenched teeth and squeezed Maura's hand 'til she feared the child's fingers would pop.

"Arm yerself with patience, lass," urged Mrs. Bannon, "and let nature do the rest."

Eveleen spat, "Nature is a cruel bitch."

Everyone laughed. "That she is," said Mrs. Farrell, and began a long chronicle of the torture her son's birth put her through, which set off other such stories, one after the other.

Eveleen bit her lip bloody to keep from screaming, "Shut yer damnable gobs!"

✤

At Duncullen, Mrs. Bridge gave the curly-headed lad a penny and sent him happily on his way. She then ran to the stable with the news.

"Will," she said, a bit out of breath, "Eveleen's in the midst of her travails. I need to be there."

Her husband smiled. "I know ye do. Me and Jack can fend for ourselves this one night."

"I'd like to take Polly Egan with me. Mrs. Bannon may be struggling all alone, knowing that neighborhood. Could ye send one of the grooms for her?"

"Of course."

Back in the servants' hall, the housekeeper was huddling with Orla and Biddy, whispering orders to be obeyed in her absence, when she spotted Mr. Hogan shuffling toward his room.

"Are ye clear what's to be done?" she asked both women. When they nodded, she took each of their hands. "I am grateful to ye both. Ye know, Eveleen ..."

"We know," said Orla. "Yer all the mother she has now."

Mrs. Bridge pretended she didn't hear the cook mumble under her breath, "And lucky she is to have anyone at all with her wanton behavior."

Mrs. Bridge knocked on the butler's door. "Mr. Hogan, may I have a word?"

"Certainly," he said, rising.

"'Tis Eveleen," she said. "Her time has come and I promised to be there for her. She has—"

"No one," Hogan finished, frowning. "You've mentioned that before. I fear the family might not appreciate her situation in the same way you do."

One part of the family would do best to keep mum, Mrs. Bridge would've liked to say. "I asked to be alerted when the birth was near, so I'll most likely be back by morning. Orla and Biddy will perform me duties." She peered at Mr. Hogan from the corner of her eye. "Must we disturb the family with the news?"

Hogan's grimace turned to a small smile. "Not this time, I suppose."

Noreen Bridge returned to her cabin and gathered a few items they might need, including a pot of stewed mutton. She opened a wooden storage box and pulled out some old linens.

She then removed a white knitted blanket she'd recently finished, inhaled its warm, woolen scent, and held it to her cheek.

Will brought the small wagon around, ready to go, and Mrs. Bridge loaded her supplies. As soon as Polly Egan came huffing up to the cabin, the two set off for the village.

☦

Just past noon, Noreen Bridge heard the commotion as soon as she pulled up to Eveleen's hovel. Polly jumped from the wagon and rushed inside, leaving Mrs. Bridge to haul the supplies.

Spying her young messenger lolling across the street, she called out, "There's another penny in it for ye if ye carry these things to the door." He'd never be allowed inside.

Once in the cabin, Mrs. Bridge found Eveleen perched on the birthing chair with two older women and a child gathered around her. Polly Egan was at the table, pouring herself a cup of ale. The ruddy faces of the other gossips made it clear they'd been savoring the refreshments for quite some time.

Mrs. Bannon was on her stool, waiting for the newborn to make his appearance. "Noreen, yer just in time. The water broke and it's the reddish color we've been hoping for."

"A lad, then." Mrs. Bridge smiled. "What of that, Eveleen?"

The almost-new mother looked haggard. "Somehow I've known it would be a boy the whole time." Eveleen tried to smile, but was in the midst of throes once more. "Aaaagh," she cried. "Mother Mary, make it stop!"

"Yer doing well, Eveleen," cooed the midwife, her hand beneath the girl's skirts. "I feel his head now, so round and smooth, right where it should be. He's doing his part. The travail is yer part. It won't be long now."

Mrs. Bannon reached into her pot of pig's grease and once again anointed the neck of Eveleen's womb to make for a smoother passage. "Noreen, could ye take Eveleen's hands so she'll have someone to squeeze? Polly, hold down her shoulder when the pangs hit. Maura, hold the other shoulder so Mrs. Farrell and Branna Ryan can partake in refreshments. They can use a rest."

Any more refreshing for Madge and Branna, Mrs. Bridge thought, we'll have to wheel them home in a cart! "Let us pray together for the good health of Eveleen and her babe."

They recited a Pater Noster and several Hail Marys as Eveleen's throes came closer and closer together.

"Hold yer breath, Eveleen," Mrs. Bannon was saying. "Push down as though yer going to the stool."

Eveleen wept. "I'm too weak. I can do no more. Make it stop."

"Patience ... patience."

"Oh, Mama!" Eveleen cried out in anguish. "I want my mama. Where are ye? I love ye, Mama!" She sobbed in that breaking, halting way from deep inside. "I want my mama!"

Tears poured from Mrs. Bridge's eyes. "I'm here, Eveleen. I'm not yer ma, but I'm here."

"Oh, Mrs. Bridge, 'tis me ma I want. She should be here."

"I know she should. It won't be long." Such rubbish we tell each other, she thought. Mrs. Bridge found herself furious with the men that surrounded her. The cruel pride of Eveleen's father and immature arrogance of Mr. Richard. Sir Edward filled her with disgust, though rotting in his grave. Even the lost, confused expression Will sometimes wore irked her.

Bastards, every one! But Will's sheepish face planted itself in her mind until she had no choice but to smile at the sweetness of the man, and her rage passed. She was left with no more than 'Tis a cruel, difficult world.

"I've got his head," Mrs. Bannon called out. All the gossips gathered around. "Not much hair."

Mrs. Bridge held her breath.

"The shoulders are out. One more push, Eveleen. One more!"

Eveleen gritted her teeth and heaved until her face was nearly purple.

"I've got him! He's out."

Everyone waited for the most joyous sound on the face of the earth, the baby's first cries. But no cry came.

Mrs. Bannon's face looked stark. "Maura, get the ale. Quick!" She whispered to Mrs. Bridge, "She's not breathing."

When Maura stumbled over with the jug of ale, Mrs. Bannon squirted some into the infant's mouth, waited, then splashed more into the nose and ears. The cabin was deathly quiet.

Mrs. Bridge's heart beat furiously. No, not after all this!

It seemed time stood still until the baby squirmed, then whimpered. Her mewling grew into wails as she became pinker with every breath.

Mrs. Bridge gasped for air as she realized she'd been holding her own breath. More tears sprang from her eyes. Looking around, she found she was not crying alone. Nervous laughter filled the room.

"Show me my son." Eveleen's voice was gravelly.

"My dear, God has blessed ye with a little girl. A sweet and beautiful girl," Mrs. Bannon told her.

"That cannot be. The water was reddish. 'Tis supposed to be a boy." She gaped at Mrs. Bridge with panic-filled eyes. "What will I do now? 'Tis supposed to be his son."

Mrs. Bridge tensed. Ye've come so far, lass, she wanted to scold. 'Tis no time to loosen yer tongue.

She pressed a finger to Eveleen's lips. "Hush now. Yer too tired to talk. 'Tis God's will ye have a lovely lass, darling. She's a blessing, to be sure." Miraculously, no one seemed to notice.

Stupefied, Eveleen stared at something only she could see.

Mrs. Bannon said, "We've work yet to do, Eveleen. There's afterbirth to come. Press down on her belly, Mrs. Farrell."

"Oh, it still hurts!" Eveleen cried.

"Just a little longer," the midwife said. "Maura, put the salt in her hands."

The girl filled each of Eveleen's hands with salt and told her to hold fast.

"Why am I doing this?" Eveleen cried.

"Because that's how it's done," said Mrs. Farrell.

"Cough!" instructed Mrs. Bannon. Eveleen did so, and the midwife said, "Now blow into yer hands. Both of them."

Perhaps from the salt, the afterbirth came quickly. Mrs. Bannon laid the child on her mother's pallet and tied the cord with good double thread. She then took the scissors from Maura and started to snip the cord.

"Don't make it too long," said Polly Egan, "considering she's a wench."

"That's right." Branna Ryan recited the old adage. "If it be a boy, make him good measure, but if it be a wench, tie it short."

"I've cut many-a cord," the midwife said. "I know well the consequences of me actions."

"Ye nearly cut me boy's far too short, poor fella," said Mrs. Ryan. "Luckily for him, me husband stopped ye. Too short, he'd have a short tongue and a short member!"

"Well, the way Peadar rattles on," said Mrs. Farrell, "his tongue's quite long enough. So me guess is, he'll prove quite serviceable to the wenches."

They all laughed. All but Eveleen who stared, in dread, at the tiny, pink girl who would not win Richard's heart.

✟

Over the next several days, Mrs. Bannon and Maura came by to apply ointments and change Eveleen's dressings. Mrs. Farrell and Branna Ryan stopped in daily with eggs, broths, and pan- ade—a milk and bread paste.

"Stay away from the door and keep yer window closed," Mrs. Bannon had instructed. "The cold can work its way into yer womb and cause fierce cramping."

She wiped down the baby before anointing her with fresh butter. "To strengthen her and firm up her skin," she explained. After wrapping the child, she dosed her with a little ale and sugar in a spoon.

Eveleen's body continued to get stronger, but her mind whirled with dread. She'd been sure the birth of their son would stir Richard's curiosity, drawing him to her door like a magnet. Once his eyes fell upon his son and heir, his own flesh and blood, the love she believed he still felt would blaze anew for her and the child. He would then whisk them both to Duncullen, formal- ity be damned.

But she had not given him a son. The child was more like her than Richard, even to the wisps of red hair on her head. Would he be drawn to a wee, powerless lass? Eveleen began to weep.

Where are ye, Richard? How can ye leave me like this? And the most agonizing question, Was it all a lie?

✟

On an early Sunday morning eight days after the birth, Mrs. Bridge appeared at Eveleen's door. Not far behind her came Mrs. Bannon and Maura.

"'Tis a sacred day for our little cherub," said Mrs. Bridge. "The day of her christening. Me and Will are pleased to serve as the child's godparents."

"I'm thankful to ye both," Eveleen said. "And to you, Mrs. Bannon, for presenting me child to Our Lord."

Eveleen would not be attending the sacrament since she had not been churched, a ceremony to bless the new mother forty days after delivery. It was said no woman should step outside her home beforehand. Faeries were wont to kidnap an unchurched mother.

Maura lifted the baby from the crude cradle Jack had made for her. "Yer a beauty."

Mrs. Bannon leaned over and kissed the child on her satiny head. "There's nothing like the smell of a newborn babe."

"Will awaits outside to take us to the chapel in Lurganlea," Mrs. Bridge said. "Have ye chosen a name, lass? Mary, for yer ma, is it?"

With chin held high, Eveleen announced, "Her name is to be Nancy."

"A lovely name," said Mrs. Bannon. "Just like the mistress of Duncullen."

"Is she named for Lady Nancy?" asked Maura.

Eveleen refused to look Mrs. Bridge in the eye. "She is."

"Ye must have greatly admired her, even though she sent ye off," Maura said. Seeing her mother's scowl, she mumbled, "No harm meant."

Mrs. Bridge's stomach twisted. "Are ye sure? Yer ma—"

Eveleen turned to her with a set jaw and determined eyes. "I could not be surer. Her name is Nancy."

In less than four hours, Noreen and Will Bridge returned little Nancy to Eveleen's arms. After offering their best wishes, Mrs. Bannon and her daughter were on their way.

"Is there anything yer needing, then?" Will asked.

Eveleen looked at the floor. "If it's not too much, Old Will, could I have a word with Mrs. Bridge before ye leave?"

Old Will smiled. "I'll leave ye to yer woman-talk."

After he left the cabin, Mrs. Bridge asked, "What's troubling ye?"

"Have ye told him? Does he know his child has arrived?" Her lower lip quivered. "Why hasn't he come?"

Mrs. Bridge sighed. "Eveleen, ye know what was agreed. Mr. Richard will provide this house and we can bring ye food, but he will not set eyes on ye nor hear yer name. We gave our word and we've kept it."

"Surely, he wonders about me. And the babe." Her stare bored into Mrs. Bridge's eyes. "Ye must find a way. I beg ye. Tell him about his little girl, that her name is Nancy. That she is beautiful and sweet and will be needing a father. Can ye do that, Mrs. Bridge? Can ye find a way?"

The older woman's throat closed. She could hardly swallow. "I cannot, Eveleen. He's no longer the young man ye knew. He doesn't even talk to Will like he did." She wiped a tear from Eveleen's cheek. "I gave me word."

The young mother's face crumbled. "What's to become of me? What's to become of little Nan?"

Chapter Twenty-nine

Over the next week, Eveleen was left to fend for herself. Wrapped in a heavy cloak of sadness, she tried to resume her life, carding wool Will had brought in hopes of scraping together a few coins. Yet, she was unable to prevent the tears that constantly sprang to her eyes. Her arms felt too heavy to lift. Planning to work while Nan slept, her baby's wakeful cry would snap her from her melancholy musings only to find she'd accomplished little.

Then, things worsened. The Sunday evening following her baptism, Nan began wailing as though tortured. With legs drawn and fists clenched, she screamed in agony.

Eveleen wiped Nan's bottom and tied on a clean napkin, but the shrieking persisted. She put the child to her breast, but the baby wouldn't latch. She cuddled Nan and rocked her back and forth. She walked her up and down the cabin, but nothing worked. Eveleen could offer no comfort.

She held her squalling baby before her. "What do ye want? What do ye need? I can do no more."

Darkness fell and Sam Farrell, on his way home from the tavern, called out, "Shut the brat up! A man's got to work at the rising of the sun."

Eveleen burst into tears. After several hours of bedlam, the baby quieted and drifted into a fitful sleep. No sooner had Eveleen closed her own eyes, it seemed, the infant awakened for another bout of bawling. Eveleen nursed her, but the baby began to scream again, her little stomach hard as a rock. This went on throughout the night. Shortly before the sun rose, little Nan, at last, drifted into a sound sleep.

Eveleen awoke to see that she, along with her exhausted little girl, had slept well into the morning. She dragged herself from her pallet, relieved to see Nan still dozed. Her head in a fog, she took the soiled diapers to the small stream behind her house. She could hardly walk as her arms and legs felt weighed with fatigue. Eveleen dipped and scrubbed the napkins in the rocky brook, roused somewhat by the cold water.

Before she could finish, Nan began to cry once again. Her heart sank. Quickly wringing the clothes, she slumped into the cabin. After lifting her baby from the cradle, she sat down and put her to her breast. Nan nursed lustily and immediately dropped into a heavy slumber.

Eveleen's eyes stung. It was hard to keep them open, but there sat the basket of washed wool, waiting to be carded into rolags. I need to eat, she thought, remembering Mrs. Bannon's instructions, but she had no appetite. She craved only rest.

Just for a little while, she promised herself as she dropped onto her pallet.

"Ye finally got the little imp quiet."

Eveleen opened her eyes to find Mrs. Farrell peeking in the door.

"I knocked, but ye didn't answer." She entered before Eveleen could invite her and stood over the cradle. "Who would believe such a humble-looking cherub could be so vexing?" She looked to Eveleen. "Me husband is riled. He barely slept a wink. Ye've go to keep her quiet."

Eveleen rose from her pallet. Tears fell once again. "I did all I could, Mrs. Farrell. I got no peace meself." And thanks to her and her blasted husband, she was getting none still.

Her neighbor frowned and placed her hands on her hips. "I'm not here to listen to yer sass. There's folks who don't have the Big House handing them lodging and eats without working themselves to an early grave. We toil for a living and no one around here's likely to put up with a crying infant keeping them up nights. Ye best muzzle the little bastard!"

With that, Nan awoke and began to cry.

"God save us!" the older woman spat and stomped out the door.

Sadly, things got no better. While Nan slept soundly during the day, Eveleen could not. She had napkins to wash, food to prepare, and wool to card. Each evening, the baby repeated her night of torment and anguish. As Nan cried, Eveleen cried with her.

"Me baby is miserable. I'm miserable. I cannot do this."

Mrs. Farrell returned with Branna Ryan. "Yer baby's got the colic," Mrs. Farrell said. "Did ye fan the wee one? That'll bring on the cramping every time."

"I didn't. I've kept her warm, away from the cold, but I've not fanned her."

"Did ye kiss her on the mouth?" she asked next.

"I believe I saw Maura kiss her mouth," said Branna Ryan.

"By the Virgin Mary, her mother's a midwife. Has she no sense whatever?" Mrs. Farrell lifted little Nancy into her arms. "I'm going to walk her around the house. Three times, it takes. But it should've been done before the ailment started, so it's probably too late. These young mothers know nothing about babies. What did yer ma teach ye?"

Eveleen's hands shook and her eyes filled. "None of me sisters nor brother were afflicted like this."

"Bah!" said the woman as she and Nan headed out the door.

Branna Ryan whispered, "Pay her no mind. Her husband hounds her night and day. There's no pleasing the old goat, but Madge keeps trying. And the son, John. A sluggard who runs her ragged without lifting a finger to help."

She quickly hushed as Mrs. Farrell brought a peaceful Nan back into the house. "Madge, what about calamus root? Me own ma said chewing it can stop the colic."

Mrs. Farrell sighed. "Do ye see any teeth on the child, Branna? What Eveleen needs to do is make tea from the white dung of a dog and give her a teaspoon every hour."

"No." Branna Ryan shook her head. "I believe it's chicken droppings yer thinking of."

But nothing helped. They sent for Mrs. Bannon who rubbed the infant's stomach with the oil of sweet almonds and blew tobacco smoke on her belly.

"Are ye eating, lass?" the midwife asked Eveleen. "Yer eyes are dark and yer skin, a pasty white."

"I eat all I can."

"Make sure ye do. Ye need yer strength and baby Nancy does, too." She touched Eveleen's cheek just as her mother had, bringing on another round of tears. "Don't despair. This'll not last forever. I'll leave some oil and this black silk ribbon. Tie it 'round the child's neck. The old folks swear by it."

Weeks went by with little improvement. The baby slept well during the day, but screamed to the high heavens at night. Her neighbors stopped coming altogether. Children threw dirt clods and insults at the house.

Jack Bridge came with foodstuffs and more diapers his mother had sewn. He told her there was, once again, entertaining at Duncullen and his parents couldn't get away. Brea had a new suitor in the village and had only visited once.

"I made this for Nan," he said, holding out a smoothly carved wooden rattle. He shook it over the baby, who squirmed and cooed. "I think she likes it."

Ever-present tears fell from her eyes. "'Tis beautiful," she said and kissed Jack on the cheek.

But that night, during one of Nan's naps, Eveleen lay awake, fighting a pulsing pain in her head.

What am I doing? she wondered. I can't think. I can hardly see straight. I cry night and day. I've no family, no friends. Richard is never coming, she sobbed. Never!

It became clear that no one would miss her if she were gone. Nancy needed her, sure, but she couldn't make her child happy. "I'm a terrible mother," she said aloud. "Me baby hates me."

Eveleen was suffocating. She rose from her pallet and opened the door. Cold air, be damned, she thought. I need to breathe.

Stepping outside, a midnight breeze hit her face like a refreshing splash of water. She gazed up and down the road at her neighbors' houses. What relief they'd feel with her gone.

Footsteps shuffled up the dirt path from the village square. Eveleen noticed Moll stumbling toward her cabin. The hussy saw her standing in the moonlight and stopped short, swaying.

"So, ye finally got that demon brat to shut her clamoring gob. Ye've been chasing away me business, ye rusty-headed bitch! Keep that squalling bastard quiet." With that, she lurched into her cabin and slammed the door.

Eveleen looked to the skies. "What's the use, God?" she called aloud. "Ye gave me a little girl who'll be scorned and despised her whole life. Treated no better than an animal."

Her head pounded and sharp pains gripped her chest. The sleeping child knew nothing of the suffering she was to face in life. Eveleen shook her fist and shouted to God Almighty Himself, "It's not fair! Aahhh! It's not fair!"

From somewhere, a man shouted, "If not the babe, 'tis the mother. Shut yer bloody gob!"

Eveleen returned inside and lay on her pallet. "The whole world would be better off without me," she whispered. "Without Nan." She took several deep breaths, trying to calm herself. She was undone. She saw no life left for her and no future for her child.

She tried to curb her sinful thoughts. Do ye want to end this turmoil only to sentence yerself to the fires of hell? she chided.

Nancy was baptized and pure in the sight of God, but killing, even to save a loved one from suffering, would mean an eternity of torture for herself.

She tossed and turned. "I don't know what to do. God help me, what should I do?"

Nan woke and Eveleen put her to the breast. The baby suckled for a while, but then the high-pitched wails once again assaulted Eveleen's ears. She looked at her baby's pinched face and balled-up fists. She watched Nan's little legs curl in pain. How many times had Eveleen curled on her pallet, calling to God for relief?

She could not stop her little girl from crying, so she let loose and wailed along with her. "I'm sorry, little one. I'm so sorry. Please forgive me."

It was not until the first light of morning, when Nan had finally fallen asleep, that the answer came to Eveleen. It seemed to have dropped, fully formed, into her head. Was this God's answer to her prayers?

They could do it. They could find relief from this horrible world and still be together in heaven. It would be hard, but she had to be strong for both of them.

"Ye'll suffer no more, me sweet child. I'll release ye from this agony. Straight to the arms of Jesus yer little soul will fly."

She would then turn herself over to the constable and confess her crime. On the gallows, she would repent before the priest. He'd grant absolution for her sin, and just before she hanged, her soul would be wiped clean. Once her breath left her body, they'd both be free, together for eternity in paradise.

Little Nan looked so peaceful in her cradle. A calm washed over Eveleen as well. She knew Nan would look like that forever once released from her earthly body. There was no need to wait. She would do it this day.

Eveleen spent the next two hours setting things to rights around the cabin. She found the nicest clothes baby Nancy had, ones Mrs. Bridge had made for her. After carefully dressing her child so she didn't wake, Eveleen set her gently in her crib and petted her head.

"I'm so sorry I brought ye here, but I'm going to fix it. Ye deserve to be happy and yer ma is going to release ye from the pain and the hate and the struggle. Ye'll miss me for a short time, but don't be afraid. I'll be joining ye soon. I love ye, Nancy, with all me heart. Always remember that."

She kissed Nan's sweet head, then lifted a folded swath of cloth and pressed it firmly over the baby's nose and mouth.

✚

Moll woke with a queasy stomach and a head stuffed with wool. The night before had been a doozy. Losing control of herself like that was too dangerous. The sorry lads at the tavern would rob her blind given a peek at a chance. The evening's events came back to her one by one, and she analyzed each for missteps.

She sighed. Mostly laughs. She remembered spewing a mouthful of ale into Tim Kennedy's face when he grabbed her titties. He roundly cursed and threatened her, but the other fellas held him back. A hopeless boozer. She thought no more of it.

The sun was well into the morning sky when Moll struggled off the pallet. A rinse in the cool stream would set her right. She stepped out her door, looked around, and frowned as another memory of the previous evening unfolded. There, alone in the darkness, had stood the shadowy figure of the girl next door. She scowled remembering how unmercifully she'd taunted the lass. The whole village had turned on the girl, and now her.

Moll had called Eveleen "Little Miss Uppish" when she first arrived, coddled by the Bridges as she was. But since she'd become undone by a screaming whelp, it seemed when the neighbors weren't tormenting the girl, they were shunning her. As Moll well knew, they'd turn on you in a snap for all their talk of being Christians.

Taking a deep breath, she sauntered across their yards to Eveleen's cabin door. Inside, a frantic whimpering came, not from the infant, but from the mother. The hairs on Moll's arms stood at attention. Something was amiss.

She pushed the door, which swung open easily. There knelt a bedraggled Eveleen pressing her weight into the cradle.

"No!" shouted Moll. She rushed forward, grabbed Eveleen by the waist, and hurled her across the room, with the folded cloth still clutched in the young mother's hands.

Moll then grabbed the tiny bundle into her arms and squealed at the bluish lips and blood running from one nostril. She plopped onto the bench, sat the baby on her lap, and firmly slapped her back once, then twice more.

The child coughed and gasped before her whimpers rose to wails.

A more beautiful racket there'd never been. Moll clutched the baby and sobbed along with her.

Once her own wails waned, Moll rocked the baby back and forth. "Yer fine now, me sweet. Moll's got ye." She kissed the top of her little round head, then wiped the blood from her nose. "Yer a beautiful girl and no one will hurt ye now."

She could hear Eveleen blubbering in the corner where she'd landed in a heap. Moll's ire rose. "Why don't ye drag yer wretched arse over here and give this poor child a bellyful of mother's milk? If it don't be sour, that is."

Eveleen lifted her tear-streaked face and spit her venomous words. "Why'd ye interfere? Do ye think I'd hurt an innocent babe, me own flesh and blood? Ye blasted fool! I was trying to save her." She flung away the folded cloth. "Save her from people like her worthless father and the rest of the world who want no more than to molest and malign her. The ones who would take her tiny heart and smash it with their cruel fists like a boiled potato. I was saving her from people like you!"

Puzzled, Moll cocked her head. "Ye thought murdering yer little girl would bring her happiness? Did ye stop to think she might want her own say in that? And what of you? Ye'd end up swinging in deadly suspense right before roasting over hellfire on an eternal spit."

While Eveleen's chin jutted in defiance, her eyes showed glimmers of doubt. "I'd confess at the gallows. After me absolution, me and Nan could live together in heavenly bliss."

Moll burst out laughing. "I can't say what God thinks of me, but I know what I think of him. Me guess is he's a wee bit smarter than that." She stood and jiggled the infant in her arms. "Are ye truly repenting if ye connive to be sorry before ye ever commit the act? Do ye think the Almighty, Creator of the bloody Universe is a feeble-minded fool?"

Eveleen's mouth dropped as she sat up and blessed herself. "'Tis blasphemy! Have ye no fear of the Lord?"

"Blasphemy? And killing this lovely creature, then lying yer sorry for it, isn't?" Moll sighed. "Once again, yer righteous Christianity has me glad I've no part in it."

The baby continued to cry. "Come over here," Moll told Eveleen. "Claim the child ye love so much."

The young mother clambered to her feet and stumbled toward Moll. New tears rolled down her cheeks as she took her baby, sat on the other bench, and put her to the breast. The tiny thing sucked hungrily.

"It seems she wants to live," Moll whispered.

Eveleen's lips quivered. "I suppose she does."

Moll grew sad watching the newborn suckle, forcing her to relive things she thought she'd stowed away forever. No older than this girl, she was, when her own little fellow'd been born. There were no kindly Bridges to pick up her pieces, to make sure a roof covered her head and food filled her belly.

"Yer luckier than most."

Eveleen's head snapped up. "Lucky? Me da claims I'm not his daughter. He set me on the road to starve. R—uh, the father is gone and will never marry me. I am scorned and despised by everyone."

"Ye think yer the only one who's lived through woes such as these? I was fifteen with a round belly when me own father threw me out. There was neither Will nor Noreen Bridge to feed me and tuck me in at night." She strained to hold back tears of her own. "I done what I had to do to stay alive and I make no apologies for it." She swallowed. "But 'twasn't enough."

"What do ye mean?"

"How could I entertain me guests with a child in the house? What kind of life is that for a little boy to see his ma--?" She quieted her voice. "I wanted better for him." Her throat tightened and she couldn't speak. She saw that Eveleen's tears had dried and the girl was hanging on her every word.

"What happened to the lad?"

Moll took a deep breath. Her words came out harshly. "I scraped together what money I could. An older woman—Winnie Dunn—gave me the name of a nurse and I took Georgie to her. She promised to care for him and find him a good home if she was able." The tears she'd struggled to control spilled. "He'll be nearly nine years old now. I like to think he's with fine people, maybe learning a trade."

Against her will, the scene that haunted her sleep overwhelmed her. A short time after Moll'd handed Georgie to the sinister witch of a nurse, some children blundered upon the corpses of five infants dumped on the edge of a bog. The constable urged her to have a look, to see if her own son was among them, but she refused. She could go on only if she believed he wasn't murdered and thrown aside like so much rubbish.

Today, he could well be a farm boy or a blacksmith's apprentice. They dangled that old hag of a nurse from the end of a rope, but it was too good for her.

The girl needn't know that.

Moll resolved to shake off her melancholy. "Where's yer ale? We could both use a nip."

Eveleen pointed to a cabinet. "There's not much left after me travails."

Moll poured two cups, gave one to Eveleen's free hand, and gulped some herself. "It don't matter how ye got to this place. It only matters that yer here. What's past cannot be changed." She took another sip. "The secret is to quit caring what they think, that yer an outcast. When they look at ye like dung on their shoe, smile, and go on."

"I don't know how to do that. I'm ... lonely. And scared."

"Ha! Everyone's lonely. 'Tis what keeps me in business. And if the truth were known, most of us is scared. Even the big, burly men."

Eveleen pursed her lips. She put her cup on the table and switched Nan to her other breast.

Moll pulled her chair closer to the two of them. "Yer wishing ye were married. That yer wee one weren't a bastard to be spurned by fine Christian folks."

Eveleen looked at her, confused, so Moll went on. "What if yer ne'er-do-well had done the right thing? Would ye be happy now? Look around. Fat Madge Farrell has plenty to say about proper behavior. Yet, ye should hear the cutting jibes Sam Farrell makes about her at the tavern. And she, working night and day to please the old man enough so he won't slap her silly."

"Me own father was no better."

"And what of the richest of us? Ye worked in the Big House. How does Lady Nancy fare?"

"She's miserable. Sir Edward was a pig."

"I, on the other hand, am free. I may be a whore, but I obey no man. I have me own money to spend as I please. I'm with a man if I choose to be. But if he treats me wrong, he can kiss me fat arse."

A smile finally crept onto Eveleen's face.

"They try to keep us down," Moll went on. "If ye don't want to be cast out, they say, keep yer mouth shut. Do as yer told, even if yer man has the sense of a tree trunk. Keep the fella happy though he makes yer life a cursed misery. Never question, don't disagree." Moll smiled. "Well, the price of escaping all that is to be an outcast. Like me."

Eveleen laughed, lifting Moll's heart. "All the men aren't bad," she said.

"Name a good one, then."

"Will Bridge. He's cared for me when me own father turned me out. He's good to Mrs. Bridge and Jack, too."

"Has he been by yet to be paid for his troubles?"

Eveleen thought for a moment, then her eyes widened. "Of course not! He's a decent man. He cares about people, that's all."

Moll smirked. She couldn't dispute it. "Right. Then Will Bridge is a good one. Of course, his wife rarely lets him out of her sight. If she doesn't come to the village with him, she sends that lackwit of a son." Eveleen opened her mouth, but Moll waved her aside. "Never mind. The ones who really set me bristles up are the priests and ministers, be they Catholic or Protestant."

Eveleen stared with wide eyes as she made the Sign of the Cross with her free hand.

Moll shook her head. "Ah, if ye'd seen what I've seen. How they rail from the pulpit about wanton women and the evils of fornication. Yet who sneaks up to me window in the dead of night?"

Eveleen sat agape. "Not Father Egan! Not a priest."

Moll chuckled. "Knowing how to keep me gob shut is part of the job. If I start blabbing what I know, they'll run me out of every town I set me foot in. Let's just say, at least I'm honest about who I am. It boils me bile to listen to those toad-eating charlatans spouting off like they're God Almighty, judging poor folks trying to get by."

Moll took a deep breath and stood. "Ye've run yerself down so, ye look no better than a corpse. I've got a stewpot on me fire. I'll get it. Ye've got to eat."

As she walked back to her cabin, she saw Madge Farrell glowering at her as she weeded her garden. Moll opened her mouth to call out a crack, but shut it again. We've all got our troubles, she figured.

When she returned, she stopped at the door to watch Eveleen return the child to her cradle.

"A great price has been paid for ye to come into this world," she heard the girl whisper. "Yet the same world will count ye as raff. No matter, me lovely Nan. We'll look them in the eye, you and me. They'll slap us down, and do all they can to hold us there, but I promise ye, we'll crawl back up. Every blessed time."

Chapter Thirty

Richard sprang up in his four-poster bed, blinking his eyes. Blast! He'd been jabbering in his sleep again. He sighed. What had he called out? His dream had seemed urgent. His heart still raced, but try as he might to recall it, the nightmare had already faded from memory.

When he leaned on his elbow to lower himself to the pillow, he heard it. Holding his breath, he turned his ear toward the sound. There it was again. A rustle. Someone was lurking outside his chamber door and he felt quite sure he knew who it was.

Stealthily, he eased off the bedcovers and lowered himself to the wooden floor. He froze, listened, then smiled. There it was again. A crumpling of skirts, no doubt.

Before slinking across the floor, he moaned and murmured to mimic one turning over in his sleep. Weeks ago, he'd stuffed fleece into the keyhole, sure he was spied upon as he dozed, but he avoided its field of vision anyway.

Approaching the hinges of the door, he paused once again, all ears. From the soft breathing he heard on the other side, it was either a child or one stooping over. Apparently, trying to peek through his woolly blockade.

Richard reached across the door, laid his hand on the knob, and with one swift movement, twisted it. He jerked the door open.

A startled Anne de Barnefort tumbled in.

"Are you hurt, Miss Anne?" He commended himself. Always the gentleman.

Admirably, she hopped to her feet, smoothed her dress, and said, "I heard noises, dear cousin. You called out." She reached up and petted his cheek. "I feared you were in some sort of distress." She narrowed her eyes ever so slightly. "Were you?"

He adopted what he hoped was a penetrating stare. "I was asleep. I've been told I sometimes speak out in my slumber. I would be quite distraught to learn, however, I talk so loudly I could be heard as far off as your chambers, madam."

"Were you having another of your horrific nightmares? Perhaps your father visited you in your dreams. I am at your service if you care to tell me about it."

A clever circumlocution, she thinks. "Do you believe it best to be seen so far from your bedchamber this early in the morning skulking, as you are, outside the room of an unmarried gentleman?" He looked down. "Wearing no more than his nightgown? The servants do talk, you know."

"Skulking? Why, I merely—"

"Frankly, Anne, I prefer to have no distasteful rumors circulating Duncullen. I am aware of my father's unsavory reputation and plan to elevate it under my tenure."

He gave a look he hoped resembled pity. "Despite your irreproachable intentions, I think it best you behave in a way more fitting to your station. Any assistance I need will be rendered by Hogan."

"Well ... I only ..." she sputtered.

Richard leaned in. "I think it best for us both if you go on your way."

When she scuttled off, he closed the door and chuckled. Anne's underhanded ways no longer worried him. Both hers and his esteemed uncle's brains could sit together in a china teacup with room for two more like them.

He propped his pillows and climbed back into bed. His counterplan to their charge of lunacy was going well. He'd hosted neighbors and relatives several times now and they seemed to find him charming. He surprised himself with his talent for conversation.

He could have enjoyed popularity earlier if he'd known he needed only speak of silly, useless things wearing a bright, albeit false, smile.

It was exhausting, though. He played the bountiful host as long as he could tolerate it, then excused himself, saying this remark or that watch fob reminded him of his dear father. He inwardly gloated over the other fellows' frustrations since the young girls seemed to love him all the more for it. What a farce! He hadn't decided what he'd do when the reasonable mourning period was over.

Of the girls, especially those with ambitious mothers, he could take his pick. But a more vapid bevy of goldfinches he'd never heard. According to custom, he danced with as many different young ladies as time permitted, and the conversation rarely varied. It seemed they'd all read the same book—if they read it at all. Richard suspected one homely girl did the reading and schooled the others on its contents. He was also sure they practiced their coy smiles before the glass for hours.

One young lady whose name he'd forgotten found his comment genuinely funny and burst forth with a proper peal of laughter. Too loud, unfortunately, for polite company. Heads turned. Her mother and several other old biddies glared at the poor thing as though she'd spit in her food. Her face turned a severe shade of red and she knew not where to look.

"Your mirth warms my heart," Richard whispered in her ear, which caused her to cover her face in even greater shame. He sighed, knowing that delightful laugh would never be heard again.

How different it had been with Eveleen. She'd truly listened, without the wide-eyed vacant stares of those twittering geese. Her questions belied her inherent lack of intelligence, but he'd been too absorbed to realize it. He took a small key from a secret compartment in his desk and opened the cedar box in which, since boyhood, he'd kept his treasures. One drawer held a solitary prize, a snippet of Eveleen's coppery locks.

He'd tied it with a scrap of ivory ribbon he'd snatched from Biddy's sewing basket. Now, gently lifting it from its velvet-lined bed, he relished the silky feel across his palm. Lifting it to his nose, he inhaled the earthy perfume of the only girl he'd ever loved. His heart ached as it pounded in his chest. Richard's throat constricted and his eyes swam with unwanted tears.

Stop! he ordered himself. These thoughts would be his downfall. He knew the danger of letting down his guard even briefly, for his folly stood ready to consume him. He gazed another minute at the curled lock of hair.

You are torturing yourself, he scolded. Cast this into the fire. Now! But he couldn't. Later, he promised himself and tucked it into his pocket.

Richard strode to the window and flung it open, hoping the crisp morning air would clear his head. Already, laborers continued Richard and Thomas's first project—clearing the brush between the Big House and the Multeen River. It was Miss Anne's suggestion and Thomas hoped to appease her.

For Richard, it meant expanding the front lawn of Duncullen, giving it a noble, sweeping landscape. Next, they would develop a deer park fit for royalty, manned with estate workers whose sole responsibility would be to protect the deer from poachers.

On this morning, however, Richard saw only the destruction of the secluded sanctum he'd shared with Eveleen.

It was all an illusion, he lamented. She tricked me into believing she loved me, and only I am to blame for swallowing her machinations out of hand.

A sharp rap on the door followed by the butler's entrance snapped him from his reverie. He quickly wiped the tears from his cheeks. "Good morning, Hogan."

"Good morning, Mr. Richard." He held out a silver tray. "Here is something that might cheer you. Another letter. It appears to be from Mr. Alistair Moore."

Richard retrieved it. "Yes. It's a pleasure to read of his adventures. He has a rather unusual perspective on most things."

Hogan smiled. "I'm quite sure he does, sir. Shall I have your breakfast sent to your chambers?"

"No, I will be down later. I will want to compose an immediate response."

"Very good." With a curt bow, he left.

It was ironic to Richard that, due to Hogan's unfailing loyalty to his father, he once considered the man an adversary. Now, he was the only servant on whose allegiance he could fully depend. Old Will seemed consumed by the wants and needs of Eveleen and, while his deportment was exemplary as always, Richard no longer trusted his old friend's true sentiments. Mrs. Bridge was completely unreliable where her loyalties were concerned.

There was always Jack, without a skeptical bone in his body. Despite his half-brother's bloodlines—that of the feisty Noreen Bridge and the lowbrow Lynche stock they shared—he was the most kind-hearted, gentle soul Richard had ever known.

He sat before his desk and broke the seal on Alistair's new exploits. These letters unexpectedly whetted his appetite for such travel and exploration. One day, when his station in life was well established and he could be received with the stature he deserved, he would go. Perhaps an extended wedding trip if he could find a young lady worthy of sharing it.

He read Alistair's letter with growing concern.

_____, 1751

Dear Richard,

Through nothing short of a miracle, God has, at last, laid peace upon my heart.

In my previous letter, I regaled you with stunning sights of Florence, from the chariot races in the Piazza di Santa Maria to the works of the masters at the Medici Chapels. I have no way of knowing in what order you shall receive my letters, but this missive I am writing from the center of Western Civilization, the august city of Rome.

My supposed chum, Charlie, has grown weary of me, as have several others with whom I travel. I must confess to you, my fine friend, that my letters of late have been deceptively lighthearted. In truth, I had become more and more forlorn in my sojourns over the continent, eating my fill and guzzling fine wines while my fellow man scratches for a morsel to eat. Charlie was quite scornful when I explained my melancholy, saying, "You fool, those drudges are not your fellows. God chose you for a baronet as surely as I was born to be your superior. Let the peons bear their burdens as we bear our own."

Then, Richard, the Lord intervened. Our group was admiring the Sistine Chapel, a cool, cavernous structure containing the most astonishing array of artistic wonder ever created. From the middle of the musty sanctorium, our party migrated to Michelangelo's controversial Last Judgment on the altar wall. The guide's echoing whispers followed by muffled guffaws broke the silence as he pointed out the master's eternal revenge, having painted his critic among the damned wearing the ears of an ass.

I, however, had not moved from beneath the fresco, The Creation of Adam. Sketches and artists' reproductions cannot replicate the power of this image, in particular, the fingertip of the Almighty stretching to give the sacred gift of life to Adam.

How profoundly this struck me! The others left me gawking in an insensible fog (Charlie departed for a sitting with the eminent painter, Giorgio Vasari, whom he had commissioned to depict himself posing nobly amongst the ruins).

With this eternal truth, I awakened anew as though I had spent my life, thus far, asleep: The Divine spark lights us all. From the beggar on the church steps with outstretched palm to the gondolier who propelled us through the canals of Venice to our sovereign, King George himself, the Father's gentle touch has illuminated each one of us.

I was jarred from my reverie by a gentle voice saying, "Clearly, God Himself guided the master's hand." A priest, a Jesuit it turns out, was on a pilgrimage from his home in Salamanca, Spain, to the Holy Land. As I mumbled some barely coherent response, I am afraid I boorishly gawked at his face, for it had what I can only describe as the flush of inner peace. He spoke no English and I so little Spanish—or Latin, for that matter—our communication was labored. I will spare you the tedium and paraphrase our conversation.

He smiled and nodded to the fresco, stating that God is in all things. "All people," I said in agreement. "Everywhere," he went on, explaining that while we were in a sacred place, God touches us wherever we are, in every aspect of our lives. The little man stared directly into my eyes, as though in search of something. I heard, or more accurately, felt a voice within urging me to listen to the priest's next words, for in them was a message for me. The priest poked my chest. "God is touching you right now, in here." Unexpected tears filled my eyes. I was dumbfounded. "Ita vero," I told him.

The priest whispered, "He is calling you to a vocation, is he not?" I told him that was impossible. The man frowned and said, "You seek freedom, but something is holding you back. You have a disordered affection." I had never heard one speak like this, but the truth of it clanged in my head and in my heart. He explained that the founder of his order, Saint Ignatius, taught whatever held one back from growing closer to God was an affection placed too highly in importance.

I tried to smile. "I am not a Roman Catholic and am heir to a baronetcy in Ireland. Those are formidable obstacles, wouldn't you say?" My next words caught in my throat before spilling out. "Yet, I am summoned ... my place is with the poor, Father. What am I to do?"

Father Hugo Torres extended his stay in Rome and, in every spare moment over the past week, has listened to my woes, counseled me, and shown me a possible path to freedom and serenity. Each time we spoke, it was as though another stone block was removed from my heart.

As my confidant, Richard, I will share with you my decision. I am leaving the tour. From here, I will journey to Salamanca where an Irish College exists and, there, I will pursue my vocation. I know what you are thinking: "They will not accept you. You are a Protestant, the enemy. They will perceive you as a spy." Father Torres assures me it was an Irish Jesuit who started the college and the Society of Jesus believes there are many paths to the Almighty. I admit, mine is more unorthodox than most.

I have claimed the last payment from my father with which I will travel to my destiny. I realize he and most of those with whom I grew up will disown me. It is my fondest hope you will not be amongst them. Pray for me, Richard, and be joyful for me as I am finally happy.

Your humble servant in Christ,

Alistair

PS—This may be the last uncensored letter you receive from me. While we have come far from the days of the despised priest hunters, I am told many still fear the gentle clergyman who has set foot on foreign soil.

⚚

Richard reeled from the shock of Alistair's letter. The bloody fool! In a frenzy, he rushed to his desk to form a reply as though he could send his writings through the air rather than the untold weeks or months it may take his epistle to arrive in—of all places—the seminary of Salamanca, Spain. The page was marred with scribbles, blots of ink, and crossed-out words as his sentiments surged onto the paper.

_____, 1751

My Dear Friend,

It is with great distress that I read your letter from Rome. I fear by now you have arrived in Spain and seen for yourself the contempt in which you are held by the banished Irish priesthood. I pray fervently that your father will forgive you the impetuous forfeiture of your birthright and restore it to you without penalty.

We became friends through our shared frustrations with our fathers' refusal to see us as men in our own right, and not merely offshoots of their loins, bowing to their narrow perceptions of what our lives should be. I do not back down from that in any way. Could you not, however, find a less personally destructive way to stand up for yourself?

I clearly see that you have struck your father in his most vulnerable spot. In his day, was there any in all Ireland considered a more voracious priest-catcher than your own grandfather? I remind you, he did this, not for money, but to save us all from their traitorous meddling and reconnoitering, sure to lead to invasion and subjugation by the papist French armies. Is there a man today more dedicated to the Established Church than your own father? Ah, the irony is delicious. Although the consequences for you, my friend, are lethal. For not only do you renounce your church, but as you must be aware, some will deem your actions treasonous. While embracing the pope, you deny our king.

You have a soft heart, which can be commendable, but the facts speak for themselves. It is clear you and I are of a superior species and with that comes a greater obligation. Our intelligence, our craving for the customs of a civilized life, even our very bearing proclaims the veracity of our supremacy. Remember

Luke 12:48: "For unto whomsoever much is given, of him much shall be required." You have a duty to your country, true, but also to your station.

You may find me too bold, but I must enlighten you of a distressing possibility. This priest who, seeming so kind, has shrouded you in his web, has taken cruel advantage of you in a moment of spiritual weakness. He may very well be manipulating you through the dark arts of sorcery. Finally out of its spell, I can admit I fell victim to similar cunning based on nothing more than Satan's own ploys.

The Irish are crafty, my friend. One may display sincere trust and deep affection for them, but what is returned? A knife in the back. They are clearly prone to lies, deceits, and a lack of morals that must cause Our Lord and Savior to weep in despair. As quickly as they will steal a pig, they will snatch your heart and mangle it to a grisly pulp. They are savages, Alistair, and unless they agree to civilize themselves as Englishmen, there is no hope.

You are one of the finest of our species. Do not allow these undeserving wretches to drag you into the mire in which they gleefully wallow.

I am, dear friend, affectionately yours,

Richard

Snatching the parchment from his desk, he paced his room, reading over his words. He could not bear to see Alistair sink so low.

"I fear my words are too weak; they may be unable to sway him."

An uneasy sensation swept his neck, as though someone's hand had brushed it. The hairs on his arms rose. That now all-too-familiar laughter rushed through his ears. He heard the words, "Of course they're weak. Just as you are weak."

"God damn you, Father!"

He looked at the paper quivering in his hands. Crushing it, he cast it into the fire, and watched it char and crackle to ash.

"Damn you, too, Alistair. Figure it out for yourself."

Chapter Thirty-one

Alistair's letter was little more than dust as Richard whirled from one side of his chamber to the next, seeking some way to behold the source of his father's voice.

Why are you still here? he silently wondered.

"Where else would I be?" The voice wafted through his mind. "I live in death where I lived in life." Howling laughter reverberated through Richard's head.

He was puzzled. I can reach him through my thoughts.

"Such as they are," came the voice. "It's all rather fascinating to examine the profundity of an arrogant buffoon. Your pomposity is boundless."

Richard grabbed his hair in his fists as though he could rip his father from his head.

What is the meaning of this? I killed you! You feed worms in a moldy grave.

"A great cosmic joke, is it not? Indeed, you destroyed my body, but my spirit will lurk here. Perhaps ... forever."

His father's chuckle was a crawling, prickling irritation ravaging his brain.

"Whatever can you do about it? You, like a woman, were very adept with poison. What next? Don an apron and whack my noggin with an iron pot?"

Get the bloody hell out, you piece of shit. Return to the cesspool you clambered out of.

"Oh, come now. I live here because you need me. You are utterly hopeless without my fatherly counsel." A cool gust poured over Richard's face. "Until later then," swirled through his ears before the room returned to a more orderly air.

Richard dropped to the floor, panting. He squeezed his head as though he could expel his father through sheer physical force.

I've taken his life. What else can I do? I am powerless.

He stewed over his father's mockery, grinding his teeth in anguish. The bastard could ultimately win. Determined to avoid the tears that threatened, he jammed the knuckle of his thumb into his mouth and bit. One more blow to his manhood would cripple him.

His father's words echoed in his ears. "I live in death where I lived in life." He sat up. His eyes widened.

Oh my God. I know where he is. It's the study!

A chill shot through his body. He no more wanted to face his father's refuge than to submit to the surgeon's leeches. The door itself vibrated with the man's essence. He noticed Cousin Thomas entered only to collect the documents he required, then cleared out. Nevertheless, Richard knew.

I have to face him.

He gathered his nerve, rose, and stole to the second story. As he made his way down the corridor, an electrical current buzzed throughout his body.

The door to the study was a massive hand-carved monstrosity, personally designed by his grandfather, William Lynche. The old man believed this and the entryway to the house should reflect the elevated stature of the occupant.

Richard smirked. He overrated himself.

The pilasters replicated fluted Ionic columns entwined with ornate carvings of leafy vines and rosettes, topped by a substantial pediment that surrounded the image of a garish, snarling wolf.

Breathing heavily, Richard inched his hand toward one of the flat wooden panels. When his fingertips brushed it, he flinched. The door pulsated with a force that shook his confidence to its core.

His heart raced. I've been too rash. I must think this through.

He walked away, then stopped. He could sense it.

He's daring me. He believes me a coward and I am.

Turning back, his hand trembled as he reached for the door once again, forcing himself to lay his palm on the glossy surface. He held it there. Every nerve in his body twitched as he slid his hand toward the brass knob, then folded it over its scalloped edges. He turned the knob to the right and pushed, swinging the massive door open.

Stepping inside, he closed it behind him. He scanned the study, noting the surfaces were free of dust. The servants had kept up the room, yet the air remained stale.

Like a compass needle to the north, Richard's eyes fixed upon Sir Edward's large desk, the old man's pride and joy, where he wagged his wee cock over his dominion as though he were a fat, stupid emperor in a fairy tale.

Did you hear that? Richard shouted in his mind.

"Fat, perhaps. But stupid?" the voice answered.

He's here.

Richard exhaled, more relieved this time than frightened by his father's presence. He glared at the offending piece of furniture, his fury building.

From behind his desk, his father had harassed him—repeatedly—to the point of abject humiliation.

Aloud, he yelled, "You stood before it and ripped open my fucking face!"

A sigh breathed through the room.

Richard's face and neck burned. He grew louder.

"Atop this desk, you committed your lewd perversions, bringing disgrace upon my mother and this house."

He began to pant with rage. "The worst—the most despicable bloody offense was against Eveleen Scully."

He swept his pointed finger before him. "You knew I loved her. You knew it, you son of a burnt-arsed whore!"

"I apologized for that," came the voice.

"You died for that!"

Richard tore behind the desk and wrenched open the top drawer. He rummaged until he found his father's dagger, the one he'd been forbidden to touch. A young Sir Edward had bought it from an English salt who was nearly home from India. His father loved to impress his guests by slicing open letters with a ridiculous flourish. Richard weighed the jade horsehead hilt in his hand, then ran his finger over its nine-inch blade. It remained razor sharp.

Perfect.

He swept away the inkstand, quill, papers, and trinkets from the surface and climbed atop. On his knees, he clutched the dagger with both fists, and gouged the tooled leather surface. The room turned colder, but Richard barely noticed.

"I K-I-L-L-E-D Y-O-U," he etched in three-inch letters. "S-T-A-Y D-E-A-D." The blade ripped through the leather and into the wood beneath.

A wailing moan arose from the floor and reverberated against the walls.

Richard leapt from the desk and, out of breath, gazed at his handiwork with satisfaction. Then, it hit him.

"I've carved out my own confession! You tricked me, you son of a bitch."

His head grew light. Mocking cries from inside and outside his mind threatened to undo him.

Desperate, he searched the room for a way to break apart his damning message and tear the desk to bits. A pair of cast iron feet held up the unlit firewood in the hearth. He dragged one from under its neat pile, sending the logs rolling across the floor.

Someone will hear!

In his panic, he lifted the andiron easily, holding it by the foot. Stretching before him, the decorative front was about twenty inches of solid metal topped with an ornamental finial.

Richard stood before the desk, raised the andiron over his head, and plunged the tool into it, again and again. He ripped through the leather top and tore the carved words into as little pieces as he was able, prying them from the surface until a large hole remained.

Panting, he ran to the window, opened it, and slung the pieces, one by one, into the yard below. A lad who worked in the stables leapt aside to avoid the debris that rained upon him.

"You there!" Richard called out. "Rory, is it? Bring me an axe. Right away!"

Wide-eyed, the boy nodded and ran off.

Richard turned to see the door ajar. His alarm rose. Who had opened it?

Within seconds, Hogan plunged into the room with that scrawny maid, Elly, directly behind him.

Hogan's mouth was agape. "Mr. Richard—oh my Lord, Mr. Richard, sir, what are you doing?"

Richard lifted the andiron and placed another gash into the desk.

Hogan seemed near tears. He waved his arms, then stumbled forward as Richard sent the andiron crashing again. "Stop! I beg you. This piece is the finest on your entire estate. It was crafted by a student of the great Antoine Gaudreau, furniture maker for King Louis XV." He scrambled to pick up fragments of the former desk. "Oh, that it may be repaired!"

"What in the name of ...?" Thomas had appeared and was surveying the room in disbelief.

At that moment, little Rory squeezed by the butler with the requested axe.

Hogan pressed his fingers to his temples. "Lord, have mercy."

Richard dropped the andiron and took the axe from the boy before sending him on his way. Only one presence could make this any more of a circus, he thought.

As though he'd summoned her, Anne's rattling voice began beating a drummer's tattoo on his forehead.

"Oh!" the woman cried as she slipped in behind her husband. She clapped her hands onto both cheeks. "Poor, poor Richard! Not again. You're such a tortured, pathetic soul." She lowered her hands and clasped them before her in some posture of pity. "My heart bleeds for you. It truly does."

"Let your heart bleed for itself, Cousin." Richard hefted the axe. "If you're so bent on soothing torment, perhaps you should start with your own husband."

Anne de Barnefort's face dropped as though struck. "Richard Lynche, how dare you—"

"Silence, Anne," Thomas said.

Her eyebrows shot up. "Tommy?"

"As so often happens, my dear wife, you know nothing of what you speak. Richard is exorcising his demons. Not the childish boggles you so love to deride. The ones his father heaped upon him, one atop the other, his whole life long. The ones that threaten to crush him."

He looked to Richard. "And they will crush you unless they're annihilated." Lifting the andiron, he said, "You have my total support."

Tears spilled down Anne's cheeks as she wrung her hands. "Tommy, put that down. You can't mean this. You're ruining everything."

Anne screamed as Thomas slammed the andiron into the nearest corner of the desk with such force, the entire side collapsed to the floor. He and Richard looked at each other and burst into laughter.

"I should have done the same ten years ago." Thomas turned to a pasty Anne. "I am going to the Carolinas to run our plantations, to become my own man in the colonies. It is your duty to come with me. But if you don't, I will go alone. At this moment, I care not which you choose. I'm helping my dear cousin clear out the past and prepare for the future—his and mine."

Thomas ignored his weeping wife as she fled the room. He held up his hand, prompting Richard to wait. "First, I'd best gather the remaining documents."

While Thomas sorted through the desk, Richard tore books from the shelves, hunting trophies from the walls, even the drapes from the windows, tossing them into the yard below.

Hogan stood, blinking. He inhaled deeply. "Mr. Richard, if it's a clean sweep you want, the staff will clear the room in a much more orderly manner."

Richard flung a candlestick out the window. "I assure you, that would never give me the pleasure I get from heaving his belongings myself. You may have the laborers chop it all up and form a pile away from the house. A large bonfire is in order."

He picked up a small table and shoved it through the opening. "Summon Mrs. Bridge, if you will."

Moments later, the housekeeper came as commanded and stared at the debris. Hands folded, she awaited orders.

"We are emptying this room," Richard told her. "I want it scrubbed from top to bottom by daybreak, no matter how much of the staff it takes. All else can wait."

Richard watched the housekeeper's mask crack into a hint of a smile, with lines crinkling at her eyes.

"You may depend upon it, sir."

Once the paperwork was removed from the desk, Richard and Thomas picked up their tools and resumed breaking apart what Richard considered the primary symbol of his father's power. He looked at his accomplice. "Have we the money to put this back together?"

Thomas smiled. "I believe we can provide suitable quarters for promising men of influence such as ourselves. A worthy investment by any standard."

Richard went to the window to throw out a leg of the nearly demolished desk. He glanced down to see Old Will holding a fragment of the surface. His heart stopped when he saw scratched upon it the corner of a K, half of an I, and both Ls.

With furrowed brow, Will turned his face upward. They locked eyes. Richard read the wordless questions on the overseer's face and lifted one side of his mouth in a smirk.

None of those ignoramuses can read.

⊕

Richard's thoughts bounced from one place to the next as he finished a cold plate in the dining room. A glimpse out the window informed him that dusk had fallen. He wiped his mouth with the tablecloth as Hogan entered the room. Richard noted his still-wan complexion.

"The refuse pile is ready to be lit, sir."

"Thank you, Hogan."

Richard stepped outside and neared the heap--the shattered trappings of his father's tyranny.

He somehow felt taller and more broad-shouldered. It surprised him to see Thomas, hands clasped behind his back, already standing amongst the stable hands and laborers.

All chatter stopped at Richard's approach. Some of the drudges stared in bewilderment while others looked down or away, one or two studying their grimy fingernails. In the near-darkness, he spotted Old Will Bridge, who interrogated him with his eyes. The audacity! He'd been far too lenient with him. His jaw tightened at the affront.

"Light it!" he commanded.

Using flint and a fire starter, Will lit the torches held by two hirelings. Each of them stepped up to the rubbish and brushed their flames over the books and papers. Once ablaze, they enkindled the small pieces of wood, which in turn ignited the larger pieces.

The sun's fading light sank into the western mountains, its soft orange glow illuminating the clouds.

All watched in silence as Richard's purging fire grew, its white-hot intensity lighting up the firmament. His heart swelled with its power as twinkling sparks flittered into the darkness and smoke billowed through the night air.

Thomas broke into his thoughts. "Fire is a fearsome thing, yet it has a mesmerizing beauty."

"Yes," answered Richard. "As alluring as it is purifying."

"I feel my own yoke burns with yours. You have inspired me, Cousin."

Richard watched the firelight flutter on Thomas's face. "When will you go?"

"Don't worry. I won't renege on my obligation to you and Duncullen. This is the best preparation I could get for my new colonial life."

"That means three more years of your father's conniving manipulations."

Thomas chuckled. "That's the strange part. In helping you smash your own chains, mine fell away, too. Somehow, his hold on me has dissipated." He turned to Richard. "Besides, he still has my brother to manipulate. Though Jonathan will prove more of a challenge than I've been."

He took a deep breath. "I've changed, Richard, in a fundamental way. I can never go back to my former self. Nor do I want to."

Richard smiled. Without Thomas's cooperation, Uncle Ethan's schemes dissolved into the ether. He turned toward the Big House.

At Lady Nancy's chamber window, a candle held by Biddy illuminated his mother's silhouette. He was puzzled to see her there since she left her bed so seldom now. By the slant of her head, she seemed to be looking straight at him, studying him as he studied her. His body straightened and he lifted his chin.

This is me, Mother. For better or worse.

Abruptly, she turned away and Biddy let the draperies fall. Richard's eyes filled with tears for a time gone by that would never return. He was truly alone now.

He thought of Alistair Moore who had recklessly thrown away their potentially lifelong friendship. The fool had spit on everything Richard stood for, from the social structure ordained by God Almighty to the cultivated ideals of England to the very order of the universe!

Alistair had proved himself a traitor. He would likely realize the error of his ways, but his betrayal was too heinous and Richard doubted he would ever forgive him.

Since the disappearance of the sun, the air took on a biting chill that sent a shiver down his back, while his face basked in the fire's warmth. He heard the crackles and pops of his father's red deer trophy as the flames reduced it to cinders.

He mentally called out to him. See that, old man? Your pride and joy is turning to soot, hopefully just like you!

Richard stood stock still. He heard no voice, felt no whirring gusts of air.

He stuck his hand in his right pocket to find Eveleen's silky lock he had placed there—could it have been just this morning? It felt like days ago. Pulling it out, he cupped it to obstruct prying eyes. When he glanced down, however, he saw only an ordinary clump of hair tied with an unraveling scrap of ribbon.

He walked to the edge of the fire and let the tuft slip from his hand onto some smoldering embers. The hair frizzled and curled into a tiny charred mass, indistinguishable from the ashy remains of his father's dross. Richard felt curiously cleansed.

When the peak of the fire had passed, Thomas tapped Richard on the shoulder. "Are you ready?"

"You go on. I'd like to watch a little longer."

Thomas nodded and went inside. The flames continued to dwindle, and onlookers drifted away one by one.

Old Will came up to Richard. "'Tis getting late, Mr. Richard. Roddy and Kevin will watch the fire through the night. They'll make sure yer wishes are carried out. All will be dust by morning."

"I know. Go off to bed, Will. Your new day will start early. For myself, I find comfort in the fire's warm glow. I need to savor this moment."

Richard did not miss the sadness in his old friend's eyes. "As ye wish, sir," Will said, and lumbered off to his cabin.

The two fellows stood on the opposite side of the fire, heads together, whispering. One held up a pipe. "Do ye mind, sir?"

The young master shook his head, and Roddy or Kevin lit up. Richard squared his shoulders and inhaled. He needed one final test, just to be sure.

Father! he called out in his head. Do you see what's left of your legacy? Ashes and soot, soon to be blown into nonexistence.

He awaited the laughter, the whish of air he associated with his dead father's presence.

Nothing.

Father, you cocky bastard! Where are you? Make your presence known.

No swirl of air passed his ears. No obnoxious, booming voice resonated within. Richard lifted his chin, straining to listen.

Sir Edward, the Buck Fitch! Sir Edward, the Sniveling Prick!

He looked around.

Edward Lynche, I demand you reveal yourself or know you are a coward.

He waited. Silence.

Richard smiled.

Good.

Acknowledgments

Thank you, first, to Rev. David Turner, for asking me the question, "What have you always wanted to do, but haven't?" My answer, writing stories, set me off on this wild and exciting ride.

I also appreciate Rev. Elizabeth Wilder for her encouragement and enthusiasm, as well as the rest of the Barnwell Writers Group. I thank the talented authors of the Blue Diamonds, an online group for young adult writers, whose successes have been inspirational.

I have great love for the South Carolina Writers Workshop, especially the Aiken Chapter, which has encouraged me to move to adult literature and go places with my writing I could not have imagined. A special thank-you to the Assassins' Guild, without whom I'd still be working on this story.

My family has always believed in me. The love and support I get from each of you is unconditional—an amazing gift. Thank you Emily, Sara, and Hannah. You've watched me work my dream from the beginning. Where would I be without you?

To my husband: You have tolerated my ups and downs, my highs and lows, and never wavered in your support and belief in me. You are the best thing in my life. Thank you for it all.

About the Author

Aroon, M. B. Gibson's debut novel, has been awarded the Carrie McCray Literary Award for Novel First Chapter and was a finalist in the Pacific Northwest Writers Association Literary Contest for Historical Fiction. Her first chapter, printed in the anthology, *The Petigru Review*, was nominated for a Pushcart Prize.

She is currently writing the sequel to *Aroon*, which occurs fifteen years later and explores the battle between landowners and the secret agrarian society determined to avenge their oppression.

Gibson dedicated over three decades to teaching adolescents everything from literature to mathematics to conflict resolution. She passionately believes in the value and dignity of every human being, which she's carried from her classroom to the pages of her books.

After raising three headstrong daughters, she lives the quiet life with her husband in rural South Carolina.

Find M.B. Gibson at

Website: mbgibsonbooks.com
Facebook: facebook.com/mbgibsonbooks/
Twitter: @mbgibson345